Last Fling
in Venice

To Michael

Marlene Hill

ALSO BY MARLENE HILL:
Alone with Michaelangelo:
A Woman Follows Her Dreams to Italy

it was. A vaporetto had bumped the floating bus stop nearby and the vibrations were passing through the forest of ancient trees that supported the original foundations beneath them—and all the rest of Venice as well. Except for a glow from the light near the stop, the night sky was velvety black. Mmm, vibrations from their love-making had swept through her, too. She wanted him. Why did he have to be unavailable? Was she setting herself up for heartache? She eased off his warm body and curled onto her side scootching her back against him. He was snoring lightly. She felt as relaxed as her old rag doll. As she began drifting into sleep, a warm arm wrapped across her shoulder to place a hand around her breast. Mmm yes, he was indeed throwing her off balance, but with a contented grin on her face, she slipped back to sleep. Like Scarlett, she'd worry about all the rest another day.

Later still, a hardened rod poked her. She reached behind to feel it.

"Watch it, woman. You might be invaded again."

"I can only hope," she said and turned around to face him.

They played with each other's tongues, nuzzled noses and nibbled lips. He took one of her breasts as far into his mouth as he could and suckled. Hard. A shiver ran through her and when his hand reached down to discover she was wet again, he slid himself in as they lay on their sides. This time they went for long, leisurely movements fitting their bodies to each other until the angle of his cock stretched her eager folds and tantalized that hidden nubbin again. She couldn't wait any longer and tried to roll on top. He slid onto his back and she rode him until they trembled together.

"Could this be what heaven is like?" he said.

"Exactly," she said.

They lay there sated. Content.

* * *

After a while, she asked, "Henokiens?"

"Uh oh, you're not sleepy."

"Are you?" she asked. "If so, I'll be as quiet as——"

"Nah, rejuvenated, though, and hungry. Before the Henokien story, which isn't all that exciting, let's see what's in the fridge. I asked Maria Grazia to put something there today."

"Maria Grazia?"

"She cleans and sometimes prepares eats for me. She's been coming for all of us as long as I can remember."

"I think I might eat something too but first more water." She got up and started gathering her clothes from the floor. He turned on a small lamp behind his head. It sat on a shelf that formed a continuous headboard across the large bed. An identical lamp sat on the other side—her side. Holes had been bored through the back of the shelf for each lamp cord. Clever, she thought. This bed was made for reading!

"Let me find something for you to wear instead of having to get dressed."

"That'd be nice, but I better hang my things up now or tomorrow they'll look as if someone had torn them off me and tossed them into the far corners."

"Wouldn't want that," he said and stood up. She watched him move to his closet. Now there was a picture of male beauty. His back muscles flexed smoothly, his haunches were powerful and his walk was that of a dancer, a very male dancer.

"You move like a dancer, Marc. What kind of workout makes you look like that?"

"Why thank you, Wench. I'm glad you approve. I swim some, lift a few weights and practice Pa Kua, a Chinese system that uses spiraling, coiling and spinning. How do *you* stay so delectable?"

"You know how to make me feel desirable, don't you?

"Babe, that's easy."

"In California, I swam most everyday but the chlorine finally got to me. I power walked and did some yoga. Here, I've only been walking."

"Maybe I can help with the swimming part. Several years ago, some of us younger members of glass-making families decided to create a place to work out close to our *fabbricas*. Together, we invested in a derelict old factory and produced a *palestra* with a pool."

"*Palestra?* Gymnasium?"

He nodded. "As long as one is a member or friend..." and he pointed both forefingers at her, "one can swim there. The best part, though, is we brought in salt water a couple years ago. It's fantastic. Want to give it a try? Did you bring a suit with you?"

She nodded. "Always. But tell me more about this... Ba Gua?"

"That's the way to pronounce it but the spelling is Pa Kua. There's a place in Mestre where I work out. Of course in Southern Cal you can find every kind of martial art in the universe, but Pa Kua suits me. I tower over most people here, but in martial arts, size isn't important. Once they get used to me, I can get a decent workout."

"That must be why you seem to move fast and smoothly." She shivered.

"Oh yeah, clothes." He handed her a thick sweatshirt and for himself, his lordly robe. See if this will help and I'll find some knee socks for you. The combination ought to cover you," he said snorting to himself.

The dark-blue sweatshirt was lined with a fleecy stuff and felt wonderful. He helped her roll up the sleeves. It reached her knees and the grey socks reached above them. He led her to the full-length mirror in his closet and let her see herself.

She whooped, "Weird but warm. You shouldn't have made fun of me when I suggested packing an overnight."

"I was afraid you'd say no. Hoped by the end of the day, I could persuade you."

"And you did, " she said as she dived inside his robe to hug his naked body before he had time to tie the belt. She laughed as she saw them in the mirror. "You look far too elegant for my outfit."

"Mmm," he said. "Where were we? Oh yeah, food."

In front of the gas fireplace, they ate cold roast chicken and fruit salad and drank more water. In a few minutes, they were toasty. "My cousins teased me about this instant fire saying it was decadent, but now they're making plans to install one for themselves."

"It feels good," she said. "The Henokiens?"

"You're a persistent wench. Let's move into the big chair and be even cozier," and he pulled her onto his lap. "That's better."

She squirmed into a comfortable position and said, "All the facts, Signore."

"Okay. While working in the office mess, I came across a letter of inquiry from the Henokiens Association. It's a world-wide organization of family-owned companies. It focuses on the family as a kind of alternative to the multinationals."

She nodded to indicate it was a good idea.

"I knew you'd like the idea, except I didn't know you at the time." He went on to say a company had to have been in business for at least 200 years, and the family must be owner or majority share holder with at least one managing member. The crucial requirement for membership, though, was good financial health. Whoever stuck that letter away must have thought Barovier Fabbrica wasn't eligible.

"While I was delving into whether or not we had embezzlement, I looked into this too. I wanted to know what the advantages might be. Henokiens don't exchange services, only ideas. Some are even competitors with each other. It's not a brotherhood like the old Guilds of Northern Europe or the Schools of Venice—you know, like the School of San Rocco where I followed you up the stairs," and he gave her a light kiss. "There are forty-two members in the Henokians: fifteen are Italian, twelve French, and the rest scattered around the world," he said nuzzling her neck.

"And the advantage?"

" For us, the main advantage was to offer strength and aid to each other against hostile takeovers."

"Did you have trouble convincing the rest of your family?"

"Not much. They were intrigued with the idea of being included in this prestigious group."

"The name sounds German," she said.

"Nope, it's a made-up name. Have you heard of Enoch?"

"Yes, but I have no idea where he stands in all the begats."

"Enoch was Cain's son and 365 years old when he rose to heaven without having died."

"A good example of longevity," she said. "Speaking of names, I've always wondered if your dad changed his name to Barove in America because it's easier to pronounce. And maybe he didn't want Americans to think he was French. To me, Barovier sounds French, and many Americans are prejudiced against the French."

"I never thought of that, Sprout. You do come up with interesting theories."

"Stick with me buddy, I've got lots more like that up my sleeve."

"Don't know about your sleeve, but this is worth serious investigation," he said as he lifted the loose sweatshirt and stuck his head underneath.

"Exploration might get you everywhere," she said holding the neck of the shirt open to peer at him nuzzling a breast. "I'm impressed with your ability to persuade your company to do what you think is best."

"Mm–Hmm," he murmured from beneath her sweatshirt with a mouthful of nipple. "And what's best for you, right now," he said coming out from under, "is to catch up on your sleep. I have an idea of how to affect that." He stood up with her still on his lap and dumped her onto his bed.

I could get used to this. He's not free, but… I'm not in a hurry.

CHAPTER THIRTY-FOUR

"Hey, sleepy head, I've brought you hot coffee," Marc said coming into the room. "We're due at the fabbrica in thirty minutes. Giovanni will show us the Goto before he gets his team back on the big commission started yesterday."

She sat up and stretched her arms over her head. "What did you put in me last night?" she said with a wide grin. "I slept better than I have for years."

"Here's your coffee and stop talking dirty, we don't have time."

"Good coffee too."

"Hungry?"

"Later. How long have you been up?"

"Not long. I slept well too," he said and leaned down to kiss her cheek. "Drink up while I make a couple-three calls before we leave."

* * *

"Right on time. You look a helleva lot better than yesterday when I found you scared out of your wits."

"Not scared any more, thanks to you."

As they walked to the fabbrica, Marlowe said, " I can hardly wait to hold the Goto."

Marc led her to a small room where Giovanni was sitting at a table talking to Luca. They stood up to greet her.

"Buon Giorno, Marlowe," Giovanni said picking up a box from behind him. *"Ecco è il tuo Goto,* here's your Goto." She took the box and placed it carefully on the table.

"May I hold it?" she asked.

"*Certo*, it's very strong." She noticed that he and Marc looked at each other with another secret communication. She was getting used to their telepathic exchanges. Carefully, she lifted the red goblet out of the box. It was more beautiful than she remembered. Reverently, she held it to the light shining down from the modest crystal chandelier above their table. Placing one hand over the open mouth of the goblet, she grasped the bottom of the Goto with the other and turned it upside down and back two times trying to see what was inside the stem.

"Giovanni, yesterday I thought I saw something gold inside the stem but then decided my eyes had played tricks on me. But there *are* golden flecks in there. How'd you do that? Did you blow the stem too?"

"I did blow the stem, but what is a fleck?"

"Um," she hesitated looking at Marc, but he didn't help her. "*Granelli?*" she ventured.

"Si, si, *granelli d'oro,* grains of gold. Yes, it does have flecks of gold."

"Thank you for letting me watch you create it and allowing me to handle it," she said putting it back in the box.

"But Marlowe, it's yours, I made it for you. According to Marc, you're not only beautiful on the outside but full of golden surprises inside."

She fell onto the chair overwhelmed. "What? I understood you to say 'Here's your Goto' but assumed it was a figure of speech. Giovanni, are you sure?"

He laughed and nodded.

"I'm honored, Giovanni, no... I'm blessed," and she jumped up to give him a hug and tears started to fill her eyes. "Thank you. Thank you." He responded with a gentle hug. She felt grateful to be allowed into this family, at least part of it. Marc squeezed her shoulder.

"When you get ready to go home," Giovanni said, "we'll talk about how to package it. It might be best if we mail it to you. For now, I'm assuming you want to take it to your place."

"I do, but if someone should break in... No, I better leave it with Marc, for a while."

"Fine with me. That way you can visit it from time to time," he said grinning. The brothers laughed. "And now, we need to leave and let them get back to work."

"*Vediamo*, see you later," she said and carefully picked up her precious Goto.

"Giovanni and Luca said, "*Vediamo*," as Marc and Marlowe left.

"I never expected this," she said as they walked outside. Then she looked up at him, "You knew all along didn't you?"

"Yep. It was fun to watch the whole process, Marlee. You're a trip."

"Are all your family members this generous with their time and love?"

"Pretty much."

"I envy you, Marc. When you sort things out with Elise, your life will be perfect."

"Oh yes, Sprout," he said pulling her so close she could hardly walk. "How about something to eat after we drop off your Goto?"

"Lovely, but don't say drop in the same sentence with *my* Goto. Then I'll head home, I'm sure you have work to do."

"I do but can't call the West Coast until later. It's eleven here, middle of the night there. Say, we talked once of visiting Santa Maria e Donato. If you can hold off eating a little longer, we could visit Donato before it closes and then find lunch."

"Are you sure?"

"I am. I want to see it with you."

"I'd like that," she said.

* * *

"I feel foolish," he said, "for having this wealth of beauty right under my nose all these years. That Madonna in the apse is magnificent. Elegant and simple. The Mother of God and gold. Of course gold is *de rigueur* in Venice."

"And no brooding figure with a white beard or a sad-faced Jesus hovering over her. She doesn't need them."

Marc sniggered. She knew he was laughing at her blatant feminism but liked that he'd enjoyed seeing this glorious church with her. Neither of them was religious but they weren't immune to beauty.

"Enough? Hungry?"

"That's two questions," she said with a mock frown.

"Shall I rephrase that?" he said mimicking her as he led her to a small café on the other side of the bridge just across a canal from the church.

"Mmm, good," she said as she held a bite of crusty bread in her mouth while adding a swallow of wine before chewing.

"What, no dunking?" Marc asked.

"I would, but don't want to embarrass you."

"In here?"

"Most of all in here," she said. "Don't want to look like I think I'm slumming. You probably know some of these fellows."

"You're right, I do," and he looked around at the noisy men enjoying lunch in this workers' eatery. It was simple fare and everything was delicious.

"This tomato sauce and the salad greens must be straight from a nearby garden. Reminds me I want to get myself out to that veggie island, what's the name again?" she asked.

"Sant'Erasmo," Marc said.

"Yes, that's it, Sant'Erasmo. The next clear day, I'm taking Number Thirteen out there."

"Maybe I can take you. Not long ago I helped one of the farmers get materials for his greenhouse; he's a great old guy and would be delighted to meet the likes of you."

At the vaporetto stop, she thanked him again and he pulled her in for a small public kiss. Affection demonstrated in public meant a lot to Marlowe. Ty would never show any—at least not with her. In the beginning, it was a macho thing with school buddies; later she suspected he didn't want to appear married. Ah, but that was another life.

CHAPTER THIRTY-FIVE

Saturday morning, Marlowe was filled with renewed energy. The two days on Murano with Marc had been intense and fabulous. She'd had no idea he was so close to his Murano family; his cousins were like brothers. And that incredible apartment. She'd choose him for her personal decorator any time. Damn, she'd choose him for every aspect of her life if she had that choice. He'd hinted he needed more time with her before she returned to the States. For what reason? More fun and sex? Surely other women clamored for his attentions. But he wasn't interested in other women now. And how did she know that? Yet, she did. There was a deep-seated honesty about him—not because he told her he didn't lie—she'd felt it back in L.A. Could they keep in touch after she returned to the States? Would they? Probably not.

With her latch bolt in place, she'd slept better than she had for two weeks. Now she felt like venturing into the city again before going to a Casino with Rich in the evening. With that thought, she sensed a grey cloud hanging over her head. It reminded her of the little guy in her dad's favorite comic strip, *Lil' Abner*. A dirty cloud hung over Joe Btfsplk's head moments before something dreadful happened. Was little Joe telling her she shouldn't go with Rich tonight?

* * *

Marlowe was weary when she got back from tramping through the city and plopped down with a strong cup of coffee in hand when the phone rang. She picked it up but before she could speak, Rich growled, "You don't waste much time."

"What?"

"In less than two months, you seduced me, now Barovier. How many more?"

She could call herself a slut but she'd be damned if he would. She slammed the receiver down. The phone rang immediately.

"I'm sorry, Marlowe. Uncalled for. May I come over and talk face to face?"

She couldn't speak. Why did she pick up again? Finally she said, "No! Don't come and don't call me again."

It rang again. This time she didn't pick up. She sat stunned. He'd saved her from making a fool of herself by going out with him again. Tired as she was, she gathered her things and left. She had to breathe and move. As she stopped on the little bridge where "her" canal flowed into the Grand Canal, she noticed a wiry man coming from the Zattere. He stopped at her door. He wore a dapper black Borsello or was it a Fedora? She saw a scruffy chin beard. He must be the one. When he saw her turn toward him, he scurried around a corner into one of the calles leading toward the back of the Salute. He was gone by the time she got to that corner. She hurried back to call the police. After a long wait on hold, she told her story. They recognized her name and said someone was on the way.

Within ten minutes, a man and woman appeared. He was in his fifties and his young partner, though slender, had a solid stance about her. Marlowe supposed a woman in the Italian police force would have a lot to prove. Marlowe described as best she could what happened and mentioned his Borsello. It was a little after four when they left. Marc's offer to move into his place was looking better and better. She locked the door, put the bolt in place and stayed in for the night. The juggling game had blown up in her face, but she was glad. Rich had shown his true colors.

CHAPTER THIRTY-SIX

Marlowe spent most all of Sunday wandering and thinking. By late afternoon, she was weary both physically and spiritually and looked forward to a cup of coffee with a few Grancereale cookies made by the Nabisco of Italy. They were crunchy oatmeal with a butterscotch flavor and one of the first things she always purchased on arrival. Her phone rang and a sense of dread came over her. Rich again?

"Hey Marlee, I caught you at home."

With a happy sigh of relief, she answered, "Marc, what's up?"

"Not much. You're not close enough."

"Oops," she laughed.

"Want to swim tomorrow afternoon?"

"Where and when?"

"I'll take that as a yes. How about 1:30? I have conference calls lined up all morning, could you come here? We can go to the palestra for a swim, maybe sit in the hot tub afterward."

"I'd love to."

By the way, any sign of the creep?"

"I think so," and she told him how quickly the police had come.

"Sprout, you're becoming a well-known figure about town."

"I'd rather remain incognito."

"Your cover's been blown. Besides you couldn't be unnoticed."

"That's nonsense. All I have to do is mind my own business and—"

She heard his rumble as he said, "You haven't done very well at that lately."

"Guess not."

"One thirty tomorrow. *Va bene?*"

"*Va bene.*"

The cream had gone bad, and she grabbed her backpack and headed for Billa's Supermercato at the far end of the Zattere. She might have to stand in line a long time for one carton of cream since they had no express line, but Marc's call had energized her. She felt light again. She picked up a bottle of wine along with a couple of other items. On the walk back, she considered how differently Rich had behaved when he heard about Marc compared to how Marc had handled the gossip about Rich. Well, no matter, she was finished with Rich and felt relieved. But as she crossed her bridge, she wondered if her apartment would be empty? The uncertainty was getting to her, and she wanted that dead-bolt Marc talked about. As she neared her door, she pulled the wine bottle out of the bag ready to swing it down on the jerk's head never expecting anyone to be there. But as soon as she opened the door, she *knew* someone was.

* * *

She yelled out and rushed up the stairs to see the Borsello man opening the sofa bed. He looked up, growled something and exploded toward the stairs shoving her against the wall at the top of the steps. She smelled his over-powering minty after shave as she lost her balance and began to fall. But while flailing to keep her balance, she swung the bottle wildly in his direction. It hit him, probably on the leg and he yelped in pain but kept going out the door. She dropped the bottle as she fell and half bounced, half rolled to the bottom landing on some of the broken glass. Her upper arm felt a sharp bite of pain, but she ignored it trying to follow him. All she could think was she *had* to follow him. But when the door slammed behind him, all her resolve slipped away. She slumped against the bottom step and began to sob, and couldn't seem to stop.

When she was all cried out and breathless, she noticed her arm was bleeding and making quite a mess. Maybe she ought to call 911. No, no, that's not right, what was the number? She really wanted Marc, but his number was on the list on the phone table, and that was at the top of the stairs—a long way up. By the time she struggled to her feet, her arm was throbbing. Then 113 came to mind. Yes, she'd try that. Or 112? One of those. Her health insurance wouldn't work here, but surely, they wouldn't turn her away. She'd have to pay cash. At least her money belt was still on. One more step and she'd reach the phone. She was beginning to shake. All her energy and her courage were gone. Courage? No, stupidity! How foolish she'd been. God she was tired. Towels in the kitchen. Only a few steps to the towels, but the phone was closer. The couch was half open and she collapsed on the edge of it then forced herself to rouse up and reach for the phone. It rang in her hand.

"Hello," she panted.

"Sprout, running another marathon?"

"Marc. Oh Marc, he got in and—"

"Is he there now?"

"No."

"Are you okay?"

"I'm bleeding a little."

"Stay quiet, don't move. I'm on my way. Right around the corner. Hold tight. Don't move. Marlowe?... Marlowe?"

"What?"

CHAPTER THIRTY-SEVEN

Marc ran. His long strides quickly covered the distance from the bar near La Fenice to the Academy Bridge. He'd been meeting with the new construction manager for the burned-out opera house. He maneuvered around people sauntering up the bridge. He looked at his watch. Five minutes since he'd called her; he'd be there in two more—faster than the medics could get there, but maybe he should have called them anyway. He'd know soon. As he ran, he began worrying about her door. If she'd locked that latch bolt, he'd have a devil of a time getting in. If so, he'd call the firemen and they'd bring medics, too. They'd be the quickest because the fireboats were near her place. Jeezus! Why hadn't he installed his own dead-bolt until he could get another? When he got there, he reached toward her door hoping... hoping...

Thank God, it opened. "Marlee," he shouted and saw broken glass and blood everywhere.

She was lying on the partially-opened sofa; her eyes fluttered open. She held her hand out and said, "You're here," and closed her eyes again.

"Wake up, Sprout, wake up, you'll be fine."

"I know," she smiled trying to sit up.

"Don't move yet. Lie back." He ripped her sweater sleeve where it had been torn, and found the source of the blood. Not an artery, good. But it was a deep slice in the upper arm. So where did all the blood come from? He sniffed and then decided he was probably smelling more wine than blood. "It's not too bad, love, but you'll need stitches. I'm calling the medics."

"No! I'm fine. Call the police. I want them to catch him this time. He might be limping, I hit him with the bottle. Tell them to look for man in a black Borsello—and limping. He might need the hospital more than me."

Marc chuckled and went to her bathroom for towels and band-aids. He also brought her a glass of water. He got her to take a swallow or two and then called the police. She began to tell him her story.

"Don't talk. Just rest."

"Could you get my robe? I look as if I've been in a brawl."

"Sounds like you're feeling better," he said, "but drink up, you probably need water," and he pushed the glass toward her again. "I'll rustle up hot tea for you. Where's your sugar?"

"Don't have any. Honey's somewhere, though," and she started to get up.

"Stay down, I'll find it."

* * *

When the police arrived, Marc had Marlowe in her robe sipping hot, sweet tea and sitting at the tiny, ornate table that was her dining area. He directed them in, told them her story and showed the sofa bed the man had begun to open. A Commissario Gallina came and already knew something about the situation. Marc told him Marlowe thought the man had been trying to get in because he'd left something behind. He nodded and they began to search the couch. When they tried to pull it all the way, something blocked the mechanism. One of the police men started to reach for it and Marlowe yelled, "*Aspetta!* Wait!"

They all looked at her with mouths open.

"Commissario, maybe that's what the man was after."

Before Marc could translate, the Commissario answered in English. "Signora, I think you see too many crime stories," and smiled.

"But what would it hurt to use gloves or a cloth?" she asked.

"Va bene," he said pulling out a handkerchief. Then pulled a small, silver box from the mechanism and laid it aside. "We'll take it, and, for you, Signora, we'll make the finger prints." Then to Marc he spoke in rapid Italian saying they'd need to finger print the apartment too."

When Marlowe recognized the words for finger prints, *le impronte digitali,* she said it wouldn't do any good because the man had worn strange green gloves. The Commissario sighed and asked her to come to the Questura the next day to make a formal statement.

While waiting for the technicians, Marc said, "Okay. You're coming to my place tonight... *after* we get your arm stitched up."

"I won't argue. I'm ready. But I need some things."

The Commissario overheard and agreed she could go to her bedroom and bath for a few things before they left. After she reported to the Questura, he said her apartment would probably be hers again.

* * *

On the vaporetto going toward the hospital, Marc said, " Marlee, I can't believe you charged at him. What were you thinking?"

"I wasn't," she said hanging her head." I was foolish. I'd worked myself into a nice bit of rage, and when I came in and found him there, I exploded. But I think he *was* scared," and she couldn't keep a grin off her face.

Marc shook his head.

CHAPTER THIRTY-EIGHT

Monday morning, Marlowe wandered in to find Marc's papers strewn over his dining table with laptop and cell phone lying beside them. "Am I interrupting something?" she asked.

"Nothing too important for a hug," he said coming around the table with his arms open wide. She slid into his embrace. "I have to go to Frankfurt tomorrow for a couple of days, and I won't come back without that dead-bolt lock."

"I'll admit I'd appreciate that," she said and lifted her crimson goblet up to the kitchen window. "The grains of gold look as if they're moving inside the stem again. I know it's a trick of light, but incredibly beautiful." She was still overwhelmed by the whole experience. *Whatever comes later, I'm in heaven now.*

Marc watched her face glow as she handled the Goto with cautious care. "It's almost as beautiful as you are," he said coming behind to put his arms around her. "But not nearly as precious," he whispered kissing the nape of her neck.

"You're full of it but keep it coming," she laughed turning to face him.

He took the goblet and set it on the table. "Come here. Tell me how you're feeling." He pulled her to the couch.

"Fine. Truly fine and you have work to do. Our plan was for me to arrive for swimming about 1:30 this afternoon, so—"

"You still plan on swimming?"

"Yes and salt water will be good for this scratch on my arm."

"It's a bit more than a scratch."

"The doctor thought it'd be fine. I'll leave you in peace. I haven't explored nearly enough in Murano."

"Do I have to work? I'd rather feel you up," he said.

"Ever heard of delayed gratification?"

"Yes, and it's not much fun."

*　*　*

Later, when Marlowe pushed Marc's intercom, he said, "Whatever you've got, I want all of it," and buzzed her in. He stood at the top of the stairs with open arms. "Your timing is perfect. I'm finished and ready for our swim. But, are you sure?"

"Positive," she said. "I'll take it easy."

"The doc did say it required only a few stitches," he said, "and most were internal. We'll take an extra bandage from those he gave us."

"Let's do it," she said, and they left for the gym.

Marc was in the water when she came out of the dressing room. Ordinarily, she would have dived in but to protect her arm, she slipped in over the side and lazed over to where he was treading water.

"This feels heavenly," she said.

"It does, doesn't it. No rough chemical feel to the water. Want to race?" he said.

"No."

He laughed and pushed off. She swam slowly. No way did she feel in competition with Marc whose one stroke took him three times the length of hers. Always would. Later they sat on the edge of the pool. A few others were there, five or six men and three women. She was glad for the women; she felt less conspicuous.

"Marlee, you look fantastic in that sleek, black suit."

"Thanks."

"But I can't say the purple bruises on your arm and thigh add to your ensemble," he said.

She laughed, "I hadn't noticed them until this morning. They'll go away."

"I like the peek-a-boo hole in the top of your suit," he said peering down at her chest.

"See anything you like?"

"I might but it's not much of an opening. Maybe I need to explore more fully elsewhere."

"Are you obsessed with my breasts?"

"At this moment? Yes. Other times, other tempting parts," he said, and his large grey eyes held hers. The first thing I obsessed about was your ass climbing those narrow stairs at our temporary office on Wilshire."

"I do remember *feeling* your eyes."

"Ready to follow me to my lair where I can feel other things?"

"Almost. I'd like to try for one or two more laps, *va bene?*"

"*Certo, certo.* As many as you want, I see someone I want to talk to."

Later, when she came out, he introduced her to a couple friends from school days. They both had that look she associated with men from the Dalmatian Coast, stocky and blond with light eyes. One had beautiful topaz-green eyes.

"Could I see the rest of the facility?" she asked as they started to leave.

"Sure, but there's not much to see beyond the pool and the weight room."

He led her to the upper floor and opened a door to a large room with a hardwood floor.

"Do you have concerts or dances here?"

"Seldom. A band comes in occasionally. Our next project is to add a small kitchen for special occasions."

"Nice."

"How'd you like the place?" he asked as they left the building.

"The water was heavenly, and the colored tiles around the edges and on the bottom are gorgeous. People seemed friendly and accepting."

"Why not?"

"I'm an interloper. Only here because of you. I have the feeling, though, that if I came without you, they'd still treat me well."

"Want to come swim when I'm out of town?"

"Would that be possible without upsetting anyone?"

"Done. I'll get a card that vouches for you. Hungry?"

"Only starved."

"There's a little café around the corner, let's see what Lorena has today." They'd talked of going all the way to Cannaregio where Marlowe wanted to treat Marc to Antica Mola, but this sounded easier since he was getting ready for Frankfurt tomorrow. Lorena's felt crowded and they were the only customers. No tables, only a counter and six stools, but the narrow counter was topped with beautiful dark marble or some kind of granite. The round woman coming from the kitchen made a big fuss over Marc. After a while she turned to Marlowe—a typical female reaction to males in Italy. Marlowe remembered female teachers in language classes who ignored female students in the same way. Lorena's cheeks were smooth and looked like a young farm girl's, but she couldn't be under fifty, maybe sixty. Her hair was snowy and cut short into pixie-like wisps. For today she'd made gnocchi with a thick cheese sauce. That was it. With the gnocchi, they had red wine served in juice glasses.

"These are the best gnocchi ever—better than Corte Sconta's," she whispered.

"Glad she didn't add crab today, you don't go much for fish do you?"

"I might have eaten that in a pinch," she said with her mouth full. Then embarrassed, she slapped her hand over it. After she swallowed she asked, "Why are you going to Frankfurt?"

"I need to see a client from whom I buy some products and to whom I provide others directly from the States. How about those whoms?" he said.

"Impressive."

"And I'll bring back a strong lock for your door."

"If that guy comes back, he better watch out. I have another bottle waiting for him."

"You do look dangerous, but maybe it's because there's a

smudge of cheese sauce right here," and he used a paper napkin to wipe her chin.

"Sometimes I'm such a pig."

"I noticed," and his eyes crinkled along with his smile.

When they got to his apartment, Marc began pulling her to his bedroom. "Are you feeling all relaxed after a swim and lunch?" he asked.

"Mm-hmm," she replied. "You?"

"Oh yeah," he said bending down for a greedy kiss. Soon she was turning into liquid fire. How does he do this to her, she wondered? Like magic her clothes were off.

* * *

Later, as they lay together breathing heavily, she said, "Marc."

"Hmm?"

"I'm such an easy slut with you."

He gave out a soft, self-satisfied chortle.

"Seriously, you're like magic with me."

"We're magic together. I knew we would be," he said.

"Mm-hmm. You feel good inside of me."

"Oh yes I do," he sighed. "And I love that trick."

"What trick?"

"That trick you do when I'm in there."

"I don't know 'a trick.'"

He raised up and looked at her narrowing his eyes, "Yeah, you do."

"I do?"

"No complaint, mind you, it's terrific," and he flopped back onto the bed.

"Grazie, Signore."

"*Il piacere è stato tutto mio,* the pleasure was all mine," and his arms tightened around her, careful of her bandaged arm. They dozed but she must have slept because it was dark when she woke up and Marc was in the other room moving about. She should go. She'd be in his way. She sat up, threw the covers back and stretched feeling absolutely marvelous. Well exercised, well fed and definitely well fucked.

Now there's a sight," Marc said as he poked his head into the room.

"I must have slept," she said. "I should get out of your way."

"Hold it right there, I need to kiss one or maybe both of those," he said and sat on her side of the bed leaning over to lift a breast to his mouth.

"You shouldn't start in again, that can only mean——"

"Just one taste." And at that moment, she knew she was the luckiest woman alive to be adored by this magnificent man.

"Marc?" she asked.

"Hmm?" he said playing with a nipple.

"I've noticed that strong men like you, don't strut around and play macho. Tell me what it's like to have such power? To know you can handle yourself in most any physical situation?"

"I never thought about it," he said leaning back to look at her. "I've been oversized as long as I can remember."

She looked at him waiting.

"Okay. At first I was embarrassed."

"Then?"

"When I saw I could handle most situations, the times I didn't know what to do, I realized I could do nothing. Since I was big, it seemed no one thought I was a coward. What's going on? Penis envy?"

"Why is it always penis envy? It's muscle envy. I wouldn't know what to do with a penis."

"Ho! That's the biggest fable I've heard in awhile."

"No, no. I love a cock when it comes with a loving man like you. It's that sometimes…oh never mind. I need to get dressed and out of here."

"I think you're more nervous about that jerk than you care to admit. Maybe you're not so tough. Huh?"

"Sure, I know that. But—"

"Wait a minute. You're not thinking of going back there *now!* Not until we get a lock to keep him out even when you're away. You need to stay right here until I get back."

"I *need* to?"

"I mean… I think you'd be safer here."

"I couldn't do that."

"Why not?"

"I have a date with Carla tomorrow."

"You can meet her from here. First thing tomorrow morning, we'll get whatever you need from your place for a couple more days, and I'll arrange that swim pass. My plane doesn't leave until eleven. I'd feel a helluva lot better knowing you're here safe. Anything you want to do, you can do from here. You can use my landline. Call your Aunt Belle or anyone else. How about it?"

"That's asking an awful lot," she said.

"Not at all. Peace of mind is worth everything."

"Let me get dressed and think about it, okay?"

"Sure."

As soon as she was alone she visualized how it might be. She could see Carla, no problem. Then she imagined walking in to find that man again and shivered. Her hand went automatically to her sore arm. She had to admit it made sense to stay here. But, she reasoned the police had probably marked it off with some kind of tape while they did their thing, and the creep would have watched. Surely he'd guess they'd found his box. She convinced herself she wouldn't cower because of that jerk. She wanted to be in her own place, and that was that. When she walked into the dining room, Marc was coming with a cup of coffee.

"Marvelous service," she said taking the cup but merely looked into it.

"Well?" he said.

She hesitated and said, "It sounds good to stay here, Marc, and I thank you for your offer. But I'm not letting that rat scare me out of my place."

His face flushed. "No Marlowe! I can't let you do that. It's a stupid thing to do," and he clapped his hands on her shoulders spinning her to face him. The coffee spilled and the heavy mug fell to the floor. He ignored it, and said, "Are you crazy? He could come back." He gripped her shoulders. "Look at me," he said. "Next time he'll do more than give you a shove. Don't you know that?" Then he saw the look on her face realizing he'd gone too far. She was frightened. Of him!

"Oh Marlee, I'm sorry," he said pulling her head onto his chest rocking her back and forth moving her to the sofa to sit on his lap. She didn't resist but kept her head buried.

"I couldn't bear it if anything happened to you. Did I hurt your arm?"

"Only a touch."

"I'm so sorry." He wanted to kiss her arm; kiss her everywhere but instinctively knew it was *not* the time. "It scares me sometimes, the chances you're willing to take."

But she continued her argument saying the Borsello guy would know better than to come back after the police had been there. She raised her chin and said it would be the safest time for her to be there then saw something like disgust or maybe distaste move across Marc's face. This was a time when she could read *his* mind. It was clear he was certain she was being stubborn and foolhardy. Then something shifted—his head twitched —and he heaved a sigh.

"It seemed a good idea, love. At least do me this favor, take a key to my place. If you feel nervous for any reason, come here till I get back. Promise?

"Promise," and she kissed him.

CHAPTER THIRTY-NINE

On the way to the airport, Marc grabbed his cell phone. "Giuseppe?" he said. "Are you and Vittorio still interested in pick-up work until your construction jobs come through?... "Good. I'd like to hire you for a couple days and nights. Here's what I want you to do."

After Marc left, Marlowe went straight to the Questura. She was thrilled to be inside the police station where Donna Leon's Commissario Brunetti had an office. It was as drab as Leon had described. Its walls were a worn-out beige and hallways were dimly lit. Certainly, the floors didn't sport beautiful terrazzo floors found in palazzos she'd been in for concerts about town.

Commissario Gallina's assistant told her the apartment would be ready as soon as their team cleaned it explaining it was a city policy that whenever a tourist had this kind of problem, a crew was sent to make it right. Marlowe was amazed. But after thinking it over, she understood but felt saddened that Venice had to depend that much on tourists for their survival. She wondered what the proud Venetians of its heyday would have thought about such a situation. No doubt they had assumed their prosperity would last forever.

After giving her statement, she dropped by her apartment to put on her walking boots. Walking aimlessly was the best antidote for what ailed her. The clean-up crew was gone. As she started to leave, Carla called to change their luncheon date. They settled on Friday. Marlowe was glad realizing she needed quiet time. As she stood at the top of the steps ready to leave, she finally focused on what had happened to her and *saw* every frightening detail of the night before. She felt a cold shiver run across her shoulders and berated herself for being reckless with her life. She *must* be crazy. Had she survived the loss of her first son to adoption, and little Petey to a mysterious fever, then gone through a horrendous auto wreck and now... now with the possibility of the best relationship she might ever have... was she going to throw it all away on a cheap criminal?

With renewed energy, she headed straight back to Marc's apartment. As she turned into the calle leading toward the vaporetto stop, she passed a fellow smoking in a doorway. He had topaz-green eyes like one of Marc's friends had at the pool. For a moment, she almost said "Ciao," but he'd already turned the other way. She hurried on thinking Venice was probably full of green-eyed men from Dalmatia.

* * *

Recognizing his landline number, Marc said, "Marlee, what a surprise to hear your voice."

"Marc, you were absolutely right. I'm back in your apartment."

"Super news! Listen, I'm about to go into my appointment; I'll call you later this evening, but thanks for letting me know. You've made my day."

"Good," she said, "and good luck with your client."

"Client to be, but your news is all I need to pull it off. Ciao, mio amore."

After a dip in the pool, Marlowe decided she wanted to talk to a close friend. She called Ellen in L.A. No answer. Same with Angie and Aunt Belle. She sighed knowing Carla wasn't available either. She flopped onto Marc's couch with one of his books. Then the phone rang.

"Lovey, what's going on with those two hounds sniffing around your sassy tail?"

"Auntie Belle, so glad you called back. Things have gotten complicated. Maybe you can set me straight." She explained why she was staying in Marc's place altering the story to say it was because a lock on her door needed fixing. It was true, wasn't it? What could Belle do from New York but worry? After listening to the rest of Marlowe's tale, Belle said, "I'd say you have what every woman wants, two gorgeous lovers who can't get enough of you."

"Only one now. I doubt if Rich will want me anymore; I know I don't want him."

"Want to make a bet he won't want you? You certainly are a chip off the old block," and she let loose with an uproarious cackle. "What is it with 'some' of us Osborne women?"

Marlowe laughed with her. "Maybe we give as good as we get, huh?"

"You're got a point there, Sugar, maybe that's it."

"But I'm going around feeling horny all the time. What do I do about that?"

"Girl, you're coming into your lust. It's about time."

"I'm certainly having the best sex I've ever had, but—"

"You want my advice?"

"You know I do."

"Grab every bit you can get while you're running hot."

"What if I'm so hot I scare him away?"

Aunt Belle crowed a long time and almost choked. After she caught her breath, she said, "I've never seen a man—a real man—run because a woman's too hot."

"You ought to know." Marlowe laughed.

"This Marc, your Viking, sounds better and better. He seems to be made of good stuff. But you do have a legitimate concern about whether his tune will change when he's finally free."

"Auntie Belle, he makes a lot of comments that sound as if he wants something long term. I admit I want it too. I find such joy with him. Such freedom to let go and be me."

"I can tell, Sugar. But what about this other lovely? For now the poor man's suffering from jealousy, but he'll come around."

"He is gorgeous and loving much of the time, but... he's got problems that he can't or won't try to resolve."

"Yesss. Those dark moods and that religious business with his mother," Marlowe heard Belle clucking her tongue. "You have to ask yourself if he'd ever be free of them or her."

"I have. I feel sorry for him, but frankly I don't want to deal with him after he called me a whore. Making love with Rich was an adventure. I'd never had it as good… until Marc came along. Oh my, that man sends me soaring."

"Yep, you're in lust. I'm thrilled for you… but I don't want you hurt. Sugar, you've got the rest of November and all of December to figure them out."

"Not all, they'll both be back in the States for a couple of weeks in December."

"But that's perfect. You went to Venice to sort yourself out didn't you? Now what better time to sort those two as well?"

"You're right! It *is* good they'll be gone isn't it?"

But…Marlowe?

"Yes?" she said and began to feel nervous. Belle seldom called her Marlowe. She knew whatever was coming had to be serious.

"There is something you need to think about."

Marlowe was quiet.

"Marc shared his past with you, didn't he?"

"Yesss. And…?"

Belle was silent.

"I must do the same, right?" Marlowe said.

"You got it, Lovey. Take it from me, if you want something lasting, you know what you have to do. Then, give me a jingle."

"Thanks for calling, Auntie Belle, how do you always manage to lift me up?"

"Magic, my girl, magic. Love you."

"Love you too."

CHAPTER FORTY

Wednesday morning, the fog lay low, and the sounds of the city were muffled. It was like being blindfolded as she made her way to the pool for her morning swim. Later that afternoon after picking up a few things from the deli nearby, Marlowe unlocked the door to Marc's apartment wishing he were back. She'd been thinking about how she might reward him for all the goodness and caring he'd shown her in and out of bed. It might be fun to blindfold him and tease him into focusing on himself for a change. As she entered the living room, she stopped in her tracks. She wasn't alone. Oh God, now what? Then he called to her from his bedroom.

"Whoee," she yelled, "you're home a day early." She walked in to see him stretched out on the bed totally naked with a bottle of Dom Perignon in an ice bucket beside him.

"I'm celebrating. Care to join me?"

"What's the occasion?" she said dropping her back pack at the doorway.

"I closed a big deal with the Hochteif Company in Frankfurt this morning."

"Which do I taste first?" she said pulling her sweater and turtle-neck off in one single motion, all the while watching his cock begin to rise.

"Take your pick, but didn't I tell you once it's not polite to stare?"

She stumbled toward the bed wriggling out of her slacks, fell to her knees beside the bed and guided his penis straight into her mouth. He gasped.

She let go a moment and looked up, "Should I have stared at something else?"

He laughed and leaned over pulling her onto the bed. She straddled him and went back to his cock taking tiny sips on its very tip. He sucked in his breath and reached up to unfasten her bra and began molding her breasts trying to pull her down.

"Wait, I'll be back in a jif." She dived into his big closet and came back with one of her silk scarves draped around her neck. "Now," she said and straddled him again.

"What's with the scarf? Should I be afraid?"

"M... a... y... b...e.... I've been thinking of how you always take charge—not that I mind when only good things happen—but this time, it's going to be different."

His eyes widened and his cock trembled. She gave him no time to argue and wrapped her scarf around his eyes tying it on the side of his head so the knot wouldn't bother the back of his head because she planned to take her time. She wanted to taste him and make it all about him. Her tongue flicked out to lick along his shaft and around its smooth mushroom head continuing to gently lick the place where the cap divided on the underside. His breath exploded out of his lungs. *Ah, I found a sweet spot.* She sipped and nipped gently at the seam all the way to the root. Again running her finger tips along the soft skin there and stroked his tightening sac. She could tell he was holding his breath, and she drew out the anticipation letting her tongue tease and torment. She liked his peppery tang as his fingers tightened in her hair and his hips began a slow thrust forward.

She was getting into it but left that area—temporarily—and moved up to spread her hands out on his chest and feel those fabulous pec muscles. They were hard, everything about his big, beautiful body was firm and hard. Her fingers feathered across his chest stopping on one nipple, then the other. He sucked in a breath and by feel reached for her panties, but she batted his hands away and placed them beside his head palms up. He didn't move.

She danced her fingers lightly across his palms; he trembled and she began to suck each finger slowly first one hand then the other. When she looked back, she saw his cock swell and rise again. She moved to it and hovered above as it jerked straight into her mouth. She burbled low in her throat and pressed her lips around him to begin a slow descent. He grew more and more excited.

"Babe, your mouth is hot, fiery hot," he gasped and tried to lift her onto his cock.

"Not yet. Marc, let me pleasure *you*—indulge yourself for a change."

She loved seeing him this way and relished her power. She moved back to his nipples and sipped one flicking her tongue across it as she reached for his shaft with one hand. It was a long reach; there was so much of him to love. Had he ever been caressed like this before, she wondered? His cock quivered. His breath began to come in short bursts.

"Marlee, climb on," he said trying again to lift her.

She was tempted but pushed his hands away and moved them back toward his head. "Let me have my way, this time, Marc. Please... let me."

He obeyed. Again she tripped her fingers across his chest following the path of sandy hair that began around each nipple and moved on to the center of his chest like two rivulets. They joined that exciting river that flowed straight toward his pubes. Her hands followed that river of thickening hair to where it flourished into the bronze bush around his cock. Her fingers circled the root and played with the busy curls but teased again by leaving his pulsing erection to journey down his long, powerful thighs. She kissed and laved with her tongue and lips ever so slowly moving to his muscular calves and on to his toes where she massaged each one. He sighed and moaned with pleasure. Beginning to move back toward his stiff cock, she saw that it stood at an unbelievable angle aiming for the ceiling. Every vein stood out; it was trembling as if it might burst. Again she fought the urge to climb on determined to make it all about him. A glistening drop of moisture was on the tip now hard as an iron rod yet it felt soft as velvet. She gathered him into her mouth and stayed motionless to let him savor it. Then she closed her lips as far as possible down his shaft and created a suction while she slid her mouth up and down tickling with her tongue with every stroke. She was able to take him deeper into her throat than she'd thought possible. His enjoyment increased hers.

"Like liquid fire," he panted.

It was impossible to take all of him. She moistened her hands and began to slide them downward from the place where her lips stopped moving them down to the root then back up to meet her mouth. Soon she found a rhythm with her hand and mouth moving almost as one going from the root to the tip and back to caress the entire length even spending time on his balls which felt as hard as baseballs. He seemed unable to stop thrusting into her throat, and somehow she managed to open for him without gagging. She sensed he was about to explode. She used the same words he sometimes used with her, "Easy does it. Easy, love."

But rather than easy, she began to suck faster, harder. The end of his cock expanded in width and filled her mouth even more. Then she felt a vibration begin.

"Babe, I'm close, so close, climb on." But she sucked harder. A surge started somewhere from his toes and moved through his body roaring with such force that she could feel the tremors. He held his hands on his head as if it would explode and tore off the scarf. She imagined hot, raw pleasure rushing through his entire body. He came with an overpowering intensity; she almost choked as his life force spurted and continued to gush. She swallowed some and grabbed the towel from the champagne bottle for the rest.

It was climax to behold—a fountain of delight.

"Son of a bitch, Marlee, you damned near killed me!"

She leaned back with a glow on her face pleased with herself.

"Give me a few minutes, Babe, then we'll see who nearly kills whom."

"As a former English major, I'm always impressed with your whoms, Signore, almost as much as with other parts of you."

He grabbed her and held her against him where she might like to stay for a hundred years. Much later, after they'd both recovered from more leisurely lovemaking and with her head in the hollow of his shoulder, he said, "I set the scene but never expected such spectacular results."

"*Il piacere è stato tutto mio,* the pleasure was all mine," repeating his exact words from another time.

"Your Italian is improving by leaps and bounds. Maybe we've discovered a new method for teaching language," he said with a grin that came from his eyes and spread across his face.

"Tell me all about your Hochtief deal," she said.

He explained every detail from the beginning of the effort almost ten months ago when acting as a representative for the huge Morrow Company of Salem, Oregon, he approached Hochtief, another huge company, headquartered in Essen. The original office had been in Frankfurt where Marc had met the old founder and offered turn-key packages of huge cranes and earth-moving equipment all to be distributed and serviced by Morrow. The Morrow company hadn't yet reached Europe with this kind of proposal, but because of the weak dollar, the whole project had become attractive to Europeans. It was a coup for Marc and he hoped to expand to other European companies.

"Again, congratulations. It's a grand stepping stone to your next big sale."

"Hope so. Are you hungry?" he asked.

"Ravenous. Didn't you mention that your Nonna had put a special spinach tart in your freezer?"

"Spinach, leek, cheese and rice tart," he corrected. "My favorite, and I took it from the freezer before you came back."

"Sounds great," she said. "And I won't need an appetizer."

"You're an imp," he said grabbing her ass. "If I can maneuver up, I'll put it in the oven."

"Take your well-deserved rest. I can do it."

"I'll take you up on your offer, but don't ever let me hear you say you wouldn't know what to do with a penis."

"*Allora*, it did seem primed for some kind of festa," she said.

"And what a *festa* that was," he said laughing.

What fun it was to provoke that deep, jubilant laugh. She wanted to be his jester for the rest of her life.

"Marlee," he said taking her hands in his, "I've never felt... so cherished."

"But you are," she said and noticed a blush spread up from his neck into his face.

"It *was* spectacular. Mm - Mmm Good," and he hummed the Campbell's Soup jingle. The spinach tart was good too, and if she ever met his Nonna, she might even ask for the recipe.

* * *

The next morning, they left for her apartment carrying the dead-bolt lock made by the same company that had made the original lock in her door. She admired her Goto again, but Marc suggested it stay with him until they were sure about the lock. While he drilled, pounded and cursed removing the present lock and installing the new one which needed the strike plate slot enlarged, she made coffee and sandwiches. She knew it'd work beautifully, but it seemed that men need to curse and grunt and make out it's a disaster until the final bolt's in place. Later, when asked, they always say it was nothing.

"Done," he said. "Now you have a solid deadbolt which Parduzzi should have installed in the first place since your door opens directly onto the fondamenta."

"It looks perfect. No one would know you changed it. Come have a snack."

As they ate, Marc said, "I can't decide whether to remove the latch bolt mechanism or not. It's almost overkill."

"Why don't I ask Parduzzi what he wants?"

"Good idea. Here's the receipt and a set of keys for him. Maybe he'll reimburse us. If he balks, I'll go see him," Marc said.

"What do you plan to charge for your labor?"

"Nothing, that was for you," and he leaned across the table and planted a kiss on her forehead.

"I'll emphasize that. Maybe I can make him feel guilty for doing nothing."

"Give it a try. He might go for it, then again I've seen him switch moods. Strange guy."

What a relief to have that lock in place. I admit, it *was* weighing on me," she said.

"Me too. I'll clean this mess and be off. I faxed the order from the hotel in Frankfurt, but want to make sure it's in the works."

"Leave it, you've done enough. And congrats again about Hochtief."

She stood on the second step and took his face in her hands and said, "Marc, I appreciate everything you do for me, but most of all I appreciate knowing you."

"Marlee, you'll never know what you do for me," and pulled her into another embrace. "Now, about sailing on Saturday."

"Say when."

"I'll get back to you. One more hug and I'm off."

CHAPTER FORTY-ONE

"Venice is gossipy, isn't it," Marlowe said to Carla as they settled at a table in Remigio's. After ordering lunch, Marlowe brought Carla up to date telling her that Rich had called her a whore.

"Whore?" Carla asked.

"*Puttana*," Marlowe said.

"Oh Marlowe, that's horrible. You must have felt terrible."

"Yes, but it showed me how he thinks. So differently from Marc. When he learned about Rich, he didn't attack me! He upped his attention."

"*Oddio*, your life is complicated."

"To make matters worse, there's been a strange man trying to get in my apartment with a key. Last Sunday night, he succeeded." She told her but made light of her injury since she felt foolish about her part in it.

"Then Marc was upset with me because, I wouldn't stay at his place while he was gone to Germany."

"I'm sorry, but I agree with him. It was foolish to go back without a better lock."

Marlowe nodded. "I know. When I realized how stupid that was, I did go back. Now I have an excellent lock."

"I'm glad you came to your senses about that," Carla said with a frown. "Did Rich know about this man trying to get in?"

"No, but I think he sensed something and wanted to stay with me a couple of times. Both times," Marlowe raised her hands in exasperation, "I was expecting Marc early the next morning."

"Marlowe, you're living in a French Farce!"

"You're right," Marlowe said and whooped. Carla laughed too. The waiter and other patrons looked shocked, but settled down when nothing more happened. After their pastas were served, Marlowe told Carla about Marc's marital situation with his wife and her blackmail scheme and emphasized that no one, except Giovanni, knew those details.

"I will not tell a soul," Carla said, "besides, I don't know any of the people involved except Rich. Does he know?"

"I doubt it. But Carla, it helps that you know Rich."

"I wouldn't have thought he'd act like that. I'm sorry... sorry for him too," she said.

"I did care for him," Marlowe said, "but I'll not go back. Besides, I'm falling too hard for Marc. My Aunt Belle keeps reminding me they've made no commitments and I should enjoy both. She thinks Rich will try to come back, but..." Marlowe took a sip of wine and shook her head. "Ah well, they may both walk away and then, poof," she shrugged her shoulders up to her ears in the eternal Italian gesture of resignation, "problem solved."

"I doubt that."

"Enough of my drama. What about you?"

"In the spring, my dance group will bring in a Turkish dancer as our feature teacher, and we're busy planning Turkish dinners with dance demonstrations to raise funds for the event."

"Have you thought about creating calendars to sell? They're all over Venice and since they're inexpensive and easy to carry away, tourists buy tons of them."

"What kind of calendars?"

"Maybe like the ones with good-looking gondoliers—one for each month?" Marlowe asked. "They cost less than—"

"Yesss, but do you mean we should show ourselves as belly-dancers?"

Marlowe nodded and leaned forward. "They could be tasteful and sexy. Tourists would delight in bringing home pictures of

Italian belly-dancers—something different from the usual art, architecture or Carnival stuff."

"Your fellow Americans would buy anything vulgar," Carla said.

Marlowe squirmed at that phrase even if she did tend to agree. "Carla, I can't believe you're stereotyping all Americans that way. What about the vulgar French and German tourists?"

Carla sat up stiffly and said, "I'm absolutely sure Kismet members wouldn't want to degrade the art of belly-dancing or themselves that way," and for a moment Marlowe saw Carla as a righteous prig.

"Why degrade?" Marlowe said uninterested in the rest of the food on her plate.

"Belly dancers already have a bad reputation," Carla said. "Making vulgar calendars would—"

"Forget it. Just an idea."

"Oddio. I didn't mean to insult *you*."

Marlowe shook her head indicating she was done with the subject. "How are the rehearsals going?" she asked.

"Fine," Carla said putting down her fork too.

"Will you have a performance within the next month. Before I must leave, I mean?"

"Maybe a Christmas show with music from the Middle East—after all it's where Jesus was born. You'd come?" she asked brightening.

"Since I'm one of those vulgar Americans, I'd love to come!" but she smiled.

"Marlowe, I didn't mean you."

"I know," Marlowe said taking her hand and squeezing it.

"We're still working on a program. It will probably be early in December."

"That'd be great. I could meet Franco."

"I'll let you know when I know." They settled up and went out the door.

"I almost forgot," Marlowe said. "I'm going sailing with Marc tomorrow and have nothing suitable. Where could I find some inexpensive deck shoes and pants this time of year?"

"You could try Standa," Carla said wrinkling her nose.

"Yes," Marlowe said making a face too about the K-Mart-style department store.

"*Aspetta*, wait," Carla said, "there is a little shop before you get to Standa. Do you know that shop with all the heads on the floor with hats on them?"

Marlowe nodded.

"After you pass the head place, in the far corner of Campo Santi Apostoli, there's a boutique with some nice things."

"Thanks, I'll try it. What a lucky day it was when I met you."

"The feeling is 'mootual,'" Carla said.

"You love the movie "Young Frankenstein" too? Marlowe asked as they hugged goodbye.

After the boutique, Marlowe went on to Standa because she wanted a white Tee shirt or two. If the sun was out, her black Tee would draw rays like a magnifying glass.

* * *

What a relief to walk into her place feeling secure. Shopping was not a favorite thing, and she was ready for a quiet glass of wine with her feet up. The phone jangled her from a doze. She noticed she was still holding her wine. "Pronto," she said.

"Ciao, Marlee, did you have a good day today?"

"Ciao, Marc, I did and have a nice check for you written by Signor Parduzzi," she was pleased to hear his voice and proud of herself regarding the landlord.

"Tell me."

"It was easier than I thought," she said putting her wine glass down. "First of all I told him you'd installed the deadbolt. He knew you and said you were a good man. Said I was very fortunate to have such a good man looking after me. Of course I knew all that."

"Did you tell him how I really look after you?"

"Didn't think he'd want to know."

"Oh yeah? He's a Venetian. He's dying of curiosity. So, how did you convince him?"

"You did. I mentioned that you were sure he'd want to take care of the cost."

"Sprout, you're hired for my next tough negotiation."

"Then I had lunch with Carla Minato. Do you know her?"

"Don't think I've had the pleasure."

"A wonderful young woman, in her mid thirties, close to your age," she said.

"Too young for me."

"She's happily married anyway and different from a lot of Italian women. No stilettos, no heavy makeup, no gold spilling from ears, wrists or fingers. I don't mean to be critical about the Italian beauties—"

"Of course not, I don't hear an iota of judgment in your voice," he said.

"Not only do you read my face, my voice, too?"

"And other things. "I'm glad you've found a woman friend. Where'd you eat?"

"Remigio's. Do you know it?"

"A fine little trattoria," he said. "Are we still on for sailing tomorrow?"

"*Si, si, non vedo l'ora!*"

"I can't wait either. That's an idiom you've learned along the way. You'll soon have the language down pat."

Oh yes. That was the first idiom Giancarlo had taught all those years ago.

"I found a hat in our boathouse for you," he said, "it has ties in case the wind gets up."

"Perfect, please bring it."

"And Marlee, you will bring a few things to stay over this time?" he asked sounding almost tentative.

"You *had* mentioned it." She was surprised he still had doubts whether she'd want to stay with him. "Is nine early enough?" she said.

"Could you make it eight?"

"Eight it will be."

CHAPTER FORTY-TWO

What fun to josh with Marc, she thought as she pulled eggs and cheese from the fridge for a light supper. Then someone knocked at the door. She didn't want visitors and quietly slipped down the stairs and gently pulled the curtain aside a fraction of an inch. It was Rich with a bouquet of bright lime-green flowers. Darn. Okay. It's time to end it.

"Rich," she said opening the door.

"May I come in?"

"Yes," she said and stood aside. "How beautiful. For me?"

"*Per te, Signora,*" he said bowing. "Please, please accept my apologies for being a lout."

"Thank you."

"The little florist near San Vidale called them *il ragno del crisantemo,* literally the spider of the chrysantheum."

"Spider lilies, yes. They're exquisite," she said.

"I only hope you can forgive me for what I said."

"Forgive? Does that mean forget too? I might forgive you, Rich, but I'll never forget that you called me a whore."

"I didn't call you that!"

"Didn't you?" she said carrying the flowers up the steps.

"I didn't mean it that way. I'm sorry," he said following her.

She turned to him and said, "I believe you're sorry, but you can't take words back."

"I was… I was… I am jealous."

She was quiet.

"I have no right, I know."

"No, you don't," she said as she lay the flowers across the flat trough and turned the water to a bare drip. *The first worthwhile use for this stupid sink.* She crouched down to find a vase. "We're not going steady," she said over her shoulder. "I'm not even wearing your class ring."

He was silent for a long time.

"I've just opened a wonderful red wine a friend brought me a while back," showing him the bottle he'd brought her long ago. *Was it only six weeks?*

"May I offer you a glass?"

"No thanks."

"I have some sparkling water, how about that?"

"Sure."

She went back to get a glass and he came behind her putting his arms around her trapping hers. Why does he show up on an evening before I'm scheduled to see Marc first thing in the morning? *Maybe that's an important message for me.*

Rich, you're moving too fast."

"I didn't move too fast that first night here."

"A lot has happened since then."

"Like Barovier?" he asked.

"What's happened between us has nothing to do with Marc."

"I think it does."

"I knew Marc before I met you."

"You knew him before?" he said letting go of her.

"We knew each other in Los Angeles."

"Were you lovers?"

"No. I was involved with someone else."

"You know he's married don't you?"

"You don't have the full story, Rich."

"Yeah sure, the wife who doesn't understand him."

She ignored that. "Rich, you don't understand me either," and she poured her wine. He walked away and sat down with his head in his hands. She followed handing him his water.

"Why don't you tell me what I should know," he said.

"What do you want from me, Rich?"

"I want to be with you. I've known that since Carla first introduced us. I thought you were interested in me."

"I was. But what started out to be light hearted... feels heavy and dark."

"I know," he said. "Guess I need my head examined," and he sighed.

This would be the time for her to kiss his skinned knee and make it all better. "Don't know about that," she said, "but too often I find myself in the wrong and have no clue."

"It's not you, Marlowe. I need to clear old tapes and other things back home."

"When will you leave for the States?"

"Sunday, the 24th" he said. "What are you doing this weekend?"

"I have plans for early tomorrow morning and Sunday, but a Mozart concert is coming from Salzburg to Santo Stefano's next Wednesday." *What the hell am I doing?*

The acoustics are good there. Okay, sounds good," he said.

She walked to the door with him. He took her in his arms and gave her a sweet kiss, but she stiffened and backed away, "Thanks again for the flowers, Rich. They're lovely."

"Not as lovely as you are," he said looking into her eyes and turned to leave. "Wait," he said, "what time's the concert?"

"Seven thirty, I think. How about I call you?"

He nodded and left. She closed the door and turned the dead bolt feeling lousy. It was as if a burden was hovering around her shoulders. If he knew my whole story, would he keep trying? More to the point, would Marc? But, as Aunt Belle always says, "now is now," and by damn, tomorrow I'm going sailing. In the Adriatic Sea!

CHAPTER FORTY-THREE

Marlowe was right on time as she pushed the intercom button at Marc's apartment.

"Ahoy, who goes there?" he called and then appeared at the top of the stairs.

"A lowly swabbie," Marlowe said looking up.

"Free to come aboard, matey."

Always a rascal making light of life, and she loved it.

"You found some deck shoes," and he swept her into his arms. Yes, another fun day had arrived. When he put her down, she saw a small frown and had an idea why.

"Where can I unload some things for later?" she asked as she grabbed her zaino.

"Come on in the bedroom, there's space in a drawer and hangars in the closet. For a second, I thought you hadn't brought anything."

"I know."

"Bitch," he said with a bear hug that turned into a long, deep kiss. "Maybe we should sail another day."

"I'm the deckhand not allowed to make decisions."

"The burden of duty," he said wiping his brow. "But we're scheduled to meet Giovanni and Sandra in ten minutes, so if you're ready, we'll head out."

"I'm glad they're coming with us," she said as they went down the steps.

"We'll take the inboard from here to where our sloop is anchored," he said. "The only channel in the lagoon deep enough for keels is the one for cruise ships and tankers and we'll be going the other way."

By 9:30 they were underway on a Jensen twenty-five foot sloop named *La Ninfa*. Giovanni and Marc handled it as if they'd been born on it. Marlowe loved watching them together. She couldn't hear their banter, but it was enough to see their affection for each other. A lump formed in her throat; she swallowed hard to tamp it down. Marc may have been an only child and adopted at that, but he'd been embraced by a warm family of cousins with aunts and uncles who had filled in for his parents when they were away. She envied him.

After passing the little mainland city of Chioggia, they went on south hugging the coastline heavily forested with cypress, laurel, and pines until they came to the immense Po Delta where smaller versions of the coastal trees grew in its rich, black soil. Their craft had been gliding through the green Adriatic, but when the muddy Po swept out of the trees, Marlowe was thrilled to see geography swirling before her eyes. Soon, the sky darkened and all of a sudden it was chilly. They came about and started back toward Chioggia where Giovanni kept his promise to Sandra and they all ate *sarde in saor* in her favorite restaurant.

Sandra had felt ill on the first part of the trip until she took extra sea-sick pills. On their last leg in, Marlowe said, "Sandra, I'm so glad you recovered. It would have been a disaster if you couldn't have your sardines." With their heads together, they giggled. It felt as if they had the beginning of a girlish bond. If Marlowe could stay, she might have Italian girl friends after all. Of course, it was true she'd never have met Sandra if it hadn't been for Marc, but she was pleased anyway.

By the time they'd docked and said good night to Giovanni and Sandra, Marlowe was pooped and Marc put his big hands on her butt boosting her up each step to his apartment.

"You're one tired kitten," he said.

"Aren't you?"

"Not too bad. How about I run a big tub of hot water for you?"

"Sounds heavenly."

"In fact, let's use the jacuzzi," he said. "It's big enough for two."

"Mm-hmm, " she said dragging herself toward the bed where she sprawled on top of it.

He chuckled as he turned on the water and put things away. "Hey Sprout, time to get up and take a bath. I'd say it'd help you sleep but that doesn't seem to be a problem."

As she inched carefully into the deep tub full of steaming water, Marc appeared and she was treated to another long look at him from head to cock—her gaze never made it to his toes. "What a luxurious remedy," she said as he slid into the tub facing her.

"You like all these hot bubbles, huh?"

"Sure, but I wasn't referring to the jacuzzi," and reached under the water. "Now where's my boy toy?"

"You little bitch, you've come alive again. You better watch it or a man toy will get you."

With that he pulled her toward him. She slipped all the way under the water coming up smack into his chest laughing and sputtering. They played awhile and made their way to his big bed where languid lovemaking took the place of silliness until they fell asleep entwined. She woke briefly in the night to find herself on her side with Marc spooned around her with one hand holding a breast.

Later, as morning light slipped into the room, he whispered, "Are you awake?"

"I am now."

"Your toy's awake too."

She reached behind and brushed his penis marveling how he swelled right into her hand. That amazing growth was like an aphrodisiac. He played with her nipple and nuzzled the back of her neck. As his hand slid down her belly to insert his long fingers inside, she moaned and felt a surge of moisture. Yes, she thought, we both love the thrill of arousing the other.

"You've got a regular little geyser there," his voice was hoarse and breathy, and it wasn't long before she was burning for completion.

"Easy, Sweet, easy, take your time," he whispered. When he thrust his tongue in her ear as if making love there too, she sucked in a breath and wave after wave of pleasure spread over her until the tips of her toes zinged. At the same time, his hot, thick cock moved inside her stroking slowly until, on a ragged groan, he plunged in and she felt his own quivering waves of pleasure.

"Good morning, love."

"Morning," she said turning to face him. He wrapped his arms around her and they lay looking into each other's eyes.

"Your man toy has a nice way to start the day," she said. "Can I keep him for a while?"

"Only for forty years," he rumbled and she lay her head against his chest to feel each deep tone resonate within his breast.

Then he looked at her and laughed. "I think you stuck your head in an electric outlet."

She reached up to touch her frizzy hair and ran into the bathroom.

"Jacuzzi hair," she yelled, "All your fault," and turned on the shower. When she came out, he was gone. She grabbed her much maligned robe, found her slippers and went looking.

"Marc?" He was sitting at the table with coffee and a newspaper.

"There she is—unplugged. Want some coffee?"

CHAPTER FORTY-FOUR

"The fog's burning away. How about Sant'Erasmo today?"

"Really? On the Lagoon two days in a row? But first what's in that white paper bag?"

"Brioches. I picked some up when I got the paper. Have one."

"Hmm, they're still warm."

"Not as warm as you, when you produce that hot geyser. It turns me on like crazy. How do you do that?"

"You do it. You're the one who primes the pump." she said kissing the back of his neck.

"Spoken like a farm girl."

"Hardly. But my favorite Grandpa was a gentleman farmer, and my cousins and I learned to pump the handle first if we wanted to bring water up. That's what you do with me."

"You may be right." He reached out an arm to pull her close enough to stick his nose into her robe for a nuzzle.

"Marc?"

"Yeah."

"You know what I found the best yesterday?"

"Seeing the Po?" he said still looking at his paper.

"I *was* thrilled to see the Mighty Po. Like seeing the Mighty Columbia back home. The whole day was super, and I think I made a connection with Sandra, but what touched my heart was watching you and Giovanni together. You're like brothers and best friends all wrapped into one. I felt happy for you…jealous too."

"I am lucky aren't I?"

She nodded feeling squishy inside and thought of another adopted child who might not have faired as well. His arm drew her closer somehow knowing she felt squishy even though he hadn't a clue why.

* * *

Marc guided the launch past barren mud flats. Standing in the shallow water near one of the islets were two snowy white egrets. Beautiful and desolate. How'd those first people brave it, she wondered? The launch slipped behind a larger flat, and the water was a deep, dark green with not a single ripple. *It's another world out here.*

Soon Marc throttled down and eased to a landing stage with a faded sign that announced they'd arrived at Punta Vela on Sant'Erasmo. Beyond the dock, she saw a vast, expanse of green but not a rooftop in sight. Not a cloud either. It seemed far away from the whole world. He climbed out of the boat to tie it to a heavy metal ring embedded into the rather high dock, and she was about to struggle up and out herself when he lifted her onto the dock.

"Thanks," she said.

"I know you could do it yourself, but—"

"I don't mind being helped, not one bit. Now what? Walk around and see what's growing?"

"We could, but there's this old fellow, Bruno Zanella. People out here stick to themselves even more than most northern Italians do, but we've become friends of a sort."

"I read somewhere they're inbred on Sant'Erasmo," she said, "and when I looked in the phone book, I found lots of identical names."

"Yeah, that's what they say. Some folks call them *i matti*, the crazy ones. I kind of doubt there are more crazies here than anywhere. Eccentric maybe, but... here he comes now. I offered to bring him some supplies. He wants to add on to his smoking shed."

"Ciao Bruno," Marc said walking toward the sturdy white-haired man coming along the dirt road.

"*Ciao gigante,*" he said reaching out his hand. Marc slipped into a dialect with him that sounded more guttural than the Venetian dialect she'd been hearing. Marlowe wondered if she could ever switch into Italian with that ease, let alone a dialect? Marc motioned her to come be introduced. The old man spoke Italian carefully to her and she spoke back even more carefully. Marc explained they were going to unload some materials he'd brought, and they lifted out a few heavy poles and what looked like shingles. She followed them to Bruno's small house hidden behind trees she hadn't noticed from the dock. A rough-hewn table sat in front of the cottage. Red geraniums in terra-cotta pots were lined up on both sides of the steps leading to his door. The men carried the materials to the side of the building. Marc indicated she could wait there.

She sat with her back to his house and leaned against the table looking toward the water remembering Aunt Belle's advice as to what she should do. When they came back, Bruno brought out a jug of red wine and some cups. He poured and they all sipped.

"Mmm, *buono,*" she said smiling. It was dark, almost black with a fruity element to it.

"Bruno poured more in her cup."

She accepted. She held her fingers to indicate only a little and looked into his deep-set golden-brown eyes. He smiled looking directly into hers. He'd also brought a chunk of cheese and something that looked like small pieces of dried meat. Marc explained it was smoked eel and she must take a little bite. She did. In spite of not liking smoked things, she had to admit it was tasty.

"I'd like to help him with his project; it might take thirty or forty minutes. Do you want to come or stay here in the shade?"

"Shade."

As they walked behind the cottage, Marlowe called, "Marc? I might walk down to the water. I won't go far."

"Fine. Take care."

"Don't hurry," she called to him.

She sat awhile under a leafy tree bending over the table. It was time. She'd fallen hard for this big man. Technically, he wasn't free. Technically, she shouldn't be wanting him. He was an alpha male through and through, but in him, it was sexy. And he was a good man through and through. Aways fun. Fun's important. Aunt Belle had instilled that in her, probably to counteract her parents' somber outlook on life. But each day spent with him was harder to continue living her lie. Aunt Belle was right. If she wanted more from Marc—like a real partnership—she should not have secrets from him.

She'd left her hat in the boat and needed to pee. Maybe she'd find a place down the road from the dock. She hadn't wanted to ask Bruno for fear he wouldn't have indoor plumbing and be embarrassed. She'd figure something out; that was the least of her problems. After hoisting herself out of the boat and back onto the dock, she set out on a road into the field area in search of toilet facilities. Even at this time of year, everything looked lush, the soil must be extraordinary and the farmers used every possible centimeter for produce. Maybe she could buy some nice tomatoes and onions while here. She recognized that she was avoiding the problem at hand.

Her little Tomaso would be... twenty-seven. Twenty-seven! He might have children of his own. She might be a grandmother. And her Mandy has a brother somewhere and doesn't even know of him. Tears began to blur her vision; she could barely see where she was going. She hadn't allowed herself to think this way for years. Why now? Why on *this* visit to Venice? Marc, of course. He'd shared with her but she'd held back her own secret and the deceit was tearing at her. Aunt Belle's words, always in her head, reminded her that no matter what, life was for the taking. She knew this at one level, but her secret continued to punish her at another.

She found a tissue in her pocket to wipe her eyes and blow her nose and looked around. Nothing but growing things. And not a comforting cloud in the sky. Waves of heat billowed up from the soil. She'd go a little farther and then turn back. Back to Marc. He'd understand the pregnancy and her teacher's treachery. What he could never accept was the adoption. She dreaded to see his face when she told him she'd given her baby away. He'd been given away. How could he ever understand?

They'd all wanted it kept quiet. Aunt Belle, the Sisters, Father Tomaso and most of all Giancarlo Corombo. Now? She would fight to put him behind bars no matter what the others wanted or who found out. But then? She'd thought it was her fault. She and Belle agonized for days over what to do. At first, Marlowe had fantasized that her mom and dad would welcome the baby with open arms. But dreams, that's all they were, mere dreams. Even then, she'd sensed they'd found raising one girl child too much to deal with. They wouldn't want a rambunctious baby boy in their house in their later years. And illegitimate at that!

Belle had assured Marlowe she and the child could live with her if her folks threw her out. In the end, Marlowe made the decision herself. Even at sixteen, she wasn't a fool and knew she could never do right by him even with Belle's help.

But how had she ever given him up? Knowing he'd never meet his mother? Knowing she'd never see him again? How?... Fear. It was fear. Fear she'd ruin his life. When the time came, though, when she held him that one and only time, she'd felt an overwhelming love. Marlowe stumbled on a clod of hard dirt. She rubbed her eyes and blew her nose again on the bedraggled tissue. With no shade in sight and no sign of facilities either, the dry, dusty road seemed to go on forever. Keeping that damned secret had gone on forever too. She'd been trying to find the right time to tell Marc. There was no right time. She coughed at the dust her feet were kicking up and the hot sun pushed down on her back like a heavy weight.

Could she tell him? No, she couldn't. He'd never trust her again. The only thing was to walk away. He wouldn't turn it on her as Ty had when she'd finally told him, but Marc would never forget the lie she'd kept after he shared his past. Once she was back in the States their connection, would shrink and shrivel away.

Shrink and shrivel, yes. Whew, it was hot and she was desperate to pee. She couldn't wait longer and squatted behind some laurel bushes to relieve herself. When she came back to the road she turned toward the dock, thinking, thinking. The heat rose from the ground and pounded down from above. What a mess. If she walked away never to see Marc again? Never feel his arms around her? Or hear his rumbly laugh? A whole new flood of tears burst through. She loved Marc as she'd never loved anyone. No matter what happened with Elise, she wanted him. But what about this lie? After he shared his secret, he'd feel betrayed. He'd be angry. Worse, disgusted. Her mind was caught in the same circles.

Should she leave and never tell him? He might feel hurt and rejected for a while, but plenty of women would want to comfort him. He doesn't deserve rejection after their closeness. What to do? What should her next step be? She looked down the dry road; somehow it looked different. She was thirsty. Her face and head felt hot and waves of heat were like dizzy, jagged lines in front of her eyes. She dropped beneath the shade of a small tree and wept as she had never done before. She wept twenty-seven years worth of tears.

When she couldn't cry anymore, she sat up and took a deep breath. What to do? She'd kept it buried. She'd pushed it all down and learned to move on. Then Marc appeared. He'd become more important to her than anyone else. Except Mandy. Should she do nothing? Tell no one? Leave it alone as she and Belle had decided years ago? But now Belle was saying something else. Since he'd shared what he considered his shameful past, Belle implied there could be no true relationship with Marc if Marlowe kept her own hidden. Belle was right. She also knew Belle would be as crazy about Marc as Marlowe was. What to do? What to do?

CHAPTER FORTY-FIVE

"Marlee! Marlee!" She heard Marc calling.

"I'm here, Marc." She must have dozed. She stood up and staggered onto the road, and then swayed feeling dizzy. He saw her and ran toward her.

"What are you doing so far from the dock?"

"I must have come too far looking for a bathroom."

"You're flushed. Your face is swollen. Has someone hurt you?"

"Yes. No. No one hurt me. I'm fine. Really, I'm fine." But her head was pounding and jagged sparks kept bouncing in front of her eyes.

"I don't think so. Water, you need water. There's got to be a pump nearby."

Come here in the shade of this tree while I find a pump. She tried to pull herself together but things were going dark She slumped against a little tree.

"Found it," he said and came back to walk her behind a clump of bushes to a pump. "Let's cool you off. Guess I need to prime *this* pump, too, huh?"

"Signore, you know how to do that," she said trying to switch into a jocular mood but ended up losing more tears. He got the water going, and with one arm he continued to pump and with the other, splashed her face. "Lean down, Marlee, splash on more water. You're overheated. Go ahead and drink, it's safe. But only a few sips to start."

"I bet Signor Zanella thinks I'm crazy," she said wiping her chin with her arm.

"No, but he's worried about you. Wait a sec." He stepped into the rutted road. "Bruno," he yelled and waved shouting something in dialect.

The old guy drove up in a small pickup. Marc lifted her into it and climbed in beside her. She was embarrassed but thought Bruno would chalk it up to a foolish, foreign woman. *"Mi dispiace, Signor Zanella, Mi dispiace,"* she apologized.

When he responded with, *"No problema Signora,"* she almost laughed. Hadn't expected that saying would have reached Sant'Erasmo.

Back at Bruno's cottage, Marc led her to the bench under the leaning tree, and Bruno brought cold white wine and a jug of cool water. He insisted she drink a little wine. It was so icy it hurt the back of her throat, but it was dry and delicious. She began to relax. Marc urged more water. As she sipped, they talked softly in dialect allowing her to gain some composure.

"Did you ever find *una toletta?*" Marc asked.

"A bush."

"How large?" he asked.

"None of your business."

"Good to hear your sass. You're coming back, Sprout. Listen, Signore Zanella has offered you his bathroom to freshen up. I'll show you." He led her into the cottage. The interior was spotless with cool tile floors the color of the terra-cotta pots. Wide, old-fashioned wooden-slat blinds drawn against the heat of the day were at the windows. She wanted to lie down on those smooth tiles and stay forever. Marc pointed to the bathroom. It was a fine bathroom; she felt embarrassed to have thought he wouldn't have one. When she came out, they were shaking hands and Marc held two large plastic bags of veggies: tomatoes, arugula and green onions. Bruno walked with them to the boat. She wanted to thank him for his hospitality but all she could think to say was, *"Grazie tante per il tuo gentilezza, Signore."* At least she could thank him for his kindness. He seemed to feel that was enough and bowed and held her hand to his lips. Tears came to her eyes as she looked at him thanking him once again. My God, where were all these tears coming from?

Marc helped her into the boat, handed her the bags of veggies, then stepped down himself. Bruno untied the line and waved goodbye. As they pulled away, Marc said, "Are you up to eating something? You should, you know."

"Wandering the fields works up an appetite," she said again trying to be light.

"Good. We'll go to a small trattoria in Treporti in the northern part of the Lagoon. It's peaceful and seems a thousand miles away from anywhere."

"Did you and Bruno get his shed built?"

"I helped him plant the heaviest posts. We got them solidly in place, and he can do the rest at his leisure. He liked you, you know."

"I can't see why. He probably thinks I'm a fat lot of trouble."

"No. I've never seen him that gentle with anyone. He took the trouble to speak in Italiano which he seldom does. After all these years, buyers and sellers in the Venetian markets understand each other's varying dialects."

"Does he have family?"

"His wife died some time ago. I never knew her. A son works in Mestre. From time to time, his daughter comes from Asolo. Like many, they want nothing to do with farming."

"He seems lonely," she said. "Is there a dog? I thought I heard one."

"A marvelous Spaniel who hunts with Bruno. He's usually at his side. Maybe he put him up thinking you'd feel nervous around him. He's grown but acts like a pup and might have knocked you over."

"You told him you were bringing me?"

"Yeah, I called him, thinking he needed a warning that a pretty woman was coming for a visit. Next time we go, we'll ask him to let Orion show *his* pretty face. I bet you'd take to him."

Next time? There'd never be a next time.

Marc looked at her—sensed something—but said nothing and revved the engine. They sped across the water and landed at Punta Sabbioni in no time.

* * *

"Are the people who run this Trattoria Zanella related to Bruno?"

"Not that I know of... maybe. There's one table left in the back, let's grab it."

"What's good here?"

"Everything. But I know exactly what you'd like, trust me?"

"Of course, " she said but thought how untrustworthy she'd been.

"What's wrong, Sprout? I've seen that same shadow move across your face lately."

"Maybe you see shadows where there are none."

"Nah. You're usually sunny; the slightest frown is noticeable. I read you, you know."

"That may be, Marc, but you don't know everything about me."

"I'm working on it," he said reaching to cover her hand.

The waiter approached with a carafe of red wine and a basket of bread. Marc began giving his order and added mineral water as well.

"Drink up, Marlee. You're dehydrated again. Guess we'll need to strap a flagon of water on your back from now on."

She tried a weak smile and lifted her wine glass saying, "To you, Marc, my Viking savior."

"And to you, my darling wench."

"Did Bruno make that crisp white wine?"

"Yeah, the red too. It's a lot like this."

"I wish these simple reds would make it to the States," she said. "I've never had a bad table wine in Italy, sometimes a little bitey, but never bad."

"I know. There's a lot to staying on this side of the Atlantic."

"You're thinking a lot about that, aren't you?"

"Yeah, I am," he said. "And after your comments about the comfort I get from my family here, I've been making the proverbial list of pros and cons."

She nodded knowing exactly what he meant.

"Except for Katy, there's not much in the States for me. Even if I did locate back there, I wouldn't see my parents much more than I do now. A lot depends on her."

"Yes."

"A penny, Marlee?"

"I was thinking of Mandy. Now that she's finding her goals in life, maybe my going to Portland isn't wise. She probably won't stay. I can't chase after her every time she moves. I won't. She'd hate that, I would have in her shoes."

"But your relationship with your parents was different from yours with her."

"I hope so."

A plate of steaming *pasta al pomodoro* with a sprig of dark green *basilico* lying on top was set before her. She leaned over it and sniffed the freshness of the tomatoes and almost swooned from the heady scent of the basil.

Sant'Erasmo tomatoes?"

"*Certo,*" Marc said grinning. "Ever since you coveted my tomato sauce at Corte Sconta, I've been planning to bring you here."

"Mmmm, *deliziosa*. Wanna bite?"

"All yours, I'm having *linguine ai frutti di mare*. Never get enough fresh seafood, and here it comes now. Mmmm, *deliziose*. Wanna bite?" he said.

"All yours," she mimicked.

He urged more water on her. She was feeling better by the

minute. But that always happened around Marc. She dipped her head down so he wouldn't see the sadness move over her again knowing she had to give him up. Finally, she leaned back unable to eat another bite.

"More?"

She waved her hands palms out. "*Sono gonfia.*"

Marc was taking a sip of wine and sputtered.

"What?" she asked.

"You probably want to say *mi sono riempita di pasta*, I filled myself with pasta, or to be even more genteel you could say *sono sazia*, I'm thoroughly satisfied, you know, sated."

"So what did I say?" she asked grinning for the first time that afternoon. "I love your laugh even at my expense."

"You said you were blown up, as if you were bloated or filled with gas."

"Oops."

"Where did you pick up *gonfia*? You'd be understood, but it's slangy, I wouldn't expect you to know it."

"So sue me," and she lifted her chin.

"I'm thinking of doing other things, milady," he said raising his hand to catch the waiter.

The trip back was heavenly in spite of the fact it would be her last with him. The sun was almost gone, a few clouds had moved in and a golden glow lay on the water. Images of the city emerged against a peachy, Titian sky. The familiar silhouettes looked different every time depending on where the sun rode or from what angle a boat approached. Or on one's inner viewpoint. This evening a melancholy aura hovered over it all. After living here, only briefly, she knew there'd be no way to live fully anywhere else, especially anywhere without Marc Barovier. As they climbed the steps to his apartment, she planned to gather her things and walk out of his life. He'd be fine after a while. There'd always be a woman ready to move into his arms. His arms! And at the top step, tears streamed down her face again. Damn.

He dropped everything and pulled her to his large chair dragging her onto his lap. "Now, talk to me. You're not moving until you tell me what's going on."

CHAPTER FORTY-SIX

Marlowe kept her head down. "Marc, I have to say goodbye. My past is…If you knew, you'd hate the sight of me."

"How could anything in your past—"

"Believe me," she interrupted. "It's best. I'll get my things and leave." She started to get up, but he held her down and drew her closer.

"Let me put it this way," she said forcing herself to look up. "I'm being totally selfish here. If you knew the truth, it would crush *me* to see the look in your eyes."

"How about I get a chance to decide?"

They were quiet. He kept his arms around her and began massaging her neck and shoulders. She sighed, closed her eyes and as always with him, knew she might as well spit it out. Then he'd gladly let her walk away. He'd wish her well and that would be that. She began again with the story of Aunt Belle taking her under her wing when Marlowe was twelve and introducing her to *Auntie Mame*'s philosophy.

"It took, too," he said kissing the side of her neck.

Marlowe looked away as she told of roaming all over Venice in 1974.

"Ahhh so," he said, "now I get it. You seemed familiar with certain things I wouldn't expect you to know if your first time here was in the 90s."

"That's what's tearing me apart," and she turned to face him. "I've been living a lie with you. I've lived that same lie with everyone except Aunt Belle and it never mattered before. You shared your past expecting I might not believe you." She looked down. Her hands gripped themselves in her lap. "I haven't done that with you. I'm a… a coward, and—"

"Coward? Not you. But why did you keep your time here in '74 a big dark secret?" he said with a growly voice.

"Because it is, I…" she took a long breath and let it out slowly. "I…"

Marc turned her face toward him again and touched the tip of her nose with such a loving touch, she feared she'd break down all over again.

"You what?"

She blurted, "I got pregnant. I had a baby boy just before my sixteenth birthday. Aunt Belle helped me through it and we've never told anyone."

"The father?"

When she got to the part about how Giancarlo had understood how she'd been ignored by her dad, Marc's face turned raw and red with fury.

"He manipulated you into his bed using your need for your father's attention."

"But I was flattered. He was sympathetic and I flirted."

"You were a child. A little girl. Not much older than Katy. What's his last name? Where'd he go?"

"What good would it do now?"

"He needs to be locked up with criminals who hate child molesters."

"But we all wanted it kept quiet.

"That doesn't let him off. What's his last name?"

"I haven't spoken his name aloud since…"

"Marlee," he said slowly, lowering his voice.

"Corombo. Giancarlo Corombo. He probably skulked back to Genoa, at least that's where he said he was from."

"Oh, love," he said resting his chin on her head.

She sank back into his embrace wishing she could stay.

"Then what happened?"

"He wanted to send me to someone in Trieste for an abortion."

"Send you? Not go with you?"

"Oh no. He was scared of losing his job and afraid his wife would find out."

"*He* was scared. You were fifteen! God almighty, what a feeble excuse for a human being."

"Aunt Belle arrived and took over. I didn't want an abortion but couldn't go back to my parents with an Italian man's baby. My folks—Dad for sure—would have called him a dirty little Dago. And it was all my fault."

"*Your* fault. You do see whose fault it was… Don't you?"

"Oh yes. I see now. As it was, Aunt Belle and Padre Tomaso and the Sisters worked it out so no one would know. They didn't want the convent's name sullied. Now? I'd chase him down and not worry about the name of the convent or what people would think." She took a deep breath and he massaged her shoulders. "They were all kind. No lectures, no punishment, but they insisted that Giancarlo leave Venice."

"I bet he got out of town as fast as he could. You can also bet he's still preying on innocents."

She nodded and began to cry quietly. "Innocent?" she blubbered. "Until I had Mandy, I'd never felt innocent. But as I watched her grow, I realized how trusting I'd been."

"So," Marc said, "the Sisters found a good Catholic home for your son, right?"

"What?" She turned to look at his face. "How'd you know?"

"But what else?"

"But… to have you of all people find out I gave up my baby for adoption."

He sighed. "Marlee, I've always suspected my birth mother went through something like that. There's a lot of scum out there."

"But—"

"Hush. Did you get to see your baby?"

"Once. He was perfect. I memorized everything about him," she swallowed a big lump. "I can still see him. He weighed 2,860 grams and was 48.6 centimeters long."

"Hmm, that'd be about six and a half pounds, and um...19 inches long, right?"

"All I know is how he felt in my arms."

"Oh love," and he pulled her against him even closer.

"Marc, he'd be twenty-seven. He might have children of his own. I could be a grandmother," and she sniffled again.

"I don't know any grannies like you," he said kissing her tears.

"And Mandy has a brother somewhere. She knows nothing about him," she cried again.

"So, let me get this straight. You thought I'd never want to have anything to do with you because you had a child out of wedlock?"

"No, no. I knew you'd understand that. But I let my baby go," she whimpered. "And you were adopted and always wondered why and who and—"

"Marlee, you've got it all wrong. When I look at you, I see someone who was manipulated by a bastard. Someone who managed to move on and create a decent life."

"Really?"

"Really," he said lifting her chin and forcing her to look at him, "I see someone I love."

Marlowe heaved a sigh and put her face into his chest and wept again, this time with relief. His shirt was soon wet with her tears but he held her and waited. When she couldn't weep anymore, he said, "It's time to tuck you in. You're worn out."

"But, I should go home. You've got things to do tomorrow."

"I do. And you are not going to be alone tonight," he said.

"But it's perfectly safe there, thanks to you."

"Yes. And you'll stay here tonight. You'll soak a bit, have a sip of brandy and sleep. Knowing you, you'll be right as rain in the morning."

CHAPTER FORTY-SEVEN

Marlowe was up making coffee and slicing bread when Marc walked into the kitchen.

"What's this?" he said snuggling the back of her neck. "You're up before me?"

"After ten hours of sleep?"

"You do look better, Marlee."

"I feel lighter. Confession's good they say. But," she turned to look him in the eye with a small crease in her forehead, "what about you? Now that you've slept on it, what about you?" She slumped at the table. Her face was marred with lines of anxiety.

"Well, I have two questions," he said pouring two cups of coffee and handing one to her.

Her heart began to race. Trying to stay calm, she took a small swallow.

"First, why didn't you ever tell anyone? I understand not telling your parents, although you must have found that difficult. Surely, you knew they loved you."

"During those months of waiting, I dreamed they'd be thrilled to have a grandchild. But in the light of day, I knew they were dreams."

"You didn't give them a chance, though, did you?"

"No," and looked back down at her coffee.

"I'm sorry, that wasn't fair."

"You're right, though," she said still staring into her coffee. "After having Mandy and… Petey, and knowing I'd forgive them anything, I did wonder if I'd been fair to my parents."

"And your husband Ty? Not even him?"

"Not at first. Shortly before Mandy's birth, I did tell him. A big mistake," and she slowly shook her head back and forth. "He was angry. Right away, he blamed me and threw it back at me more than once. I admitted it was wrong to not tell him up front, but we'd met right after it all happened and the whole idea of 'keeping the secret' was too strong. After a while, I guess I was afraid he'd say it had been my fault and—"

"And you were right."

"He let it go finally, but after that, I didn't share much that was real."

Marc sat down opposite her. "Why not tell close friends?"

"Aunt Belle knew I'd have friends I'd want to tell, but she said the fewer who knew would be best because I wouldn't have to remember who knew and who didn't. Years later, I figured the old story wouldn't have changed how friends felt about me. If it did, well… " she shrugged.

"Not even your best friends Ellen or Angie or the one in Florence?"

"Lucia? No. No one. After the disaster with Ty, I guess I closed down even more."

"And the man you were involved with when we first met? Paul?"

She shook her head.

"Why am I different?"

She looked straight into his beautiful grey eyes. The dark rim around each iris seemed bigger and darker. "You don't know?"

"Tell me," he said holding her gaze.

"Your pain of being adopted—"

"You could have kept that from me forever."

"No! I couldn't."

"Why? Marlee. Why?" and he reached for her hands.

"Because," she let out a breath she hadn't been aware she was holding. "I've never felt so loved and accepted. It was crucial that I be honest because..." tears began to slide down her face.

"Say it Marlee," Marc said still holding both her hands across the table. "You know how much I love *you.*"

"Because... because I love you more than I ever thought I could love any one. Because," she whispered, "I love everything about you. Your rumbly laugh, the way you tuck your smile into the left corner of your mouth when you watch me do something gauche, the way you accept me, the way you make love to me and—"

With that he moved toward her and pulled her into his arms, "Babe," he sighed with his lips on her neck. "That's the right answer," he whispered. "The words I've been wanting to hear for a long, long time."

He picked her up and started toward his bedroom. Make note, she thought chuckling to herself. Don't gain weight, this is too much fun.

"What are you snickering about?"

"It's a dark secret."

"No more secrets, right?"

"But it's trivial!"

"Let me decide."

"I was telling myself not to gain weight because this is too much fun."

"It is fun, isn't it?" he said nuzzling her neck and spinning in one circle after another all the way to the bedroom.

He stood her beside the bed and slowly removed both their robes—his lordly one and her "pilfered" one—and laid her down as if she were spun crystal. He crouched over her settling his mouth on hers like a tentative, first-time lover. Marc's gentleness was rare. She put her arms up to his chest wanting to hold on forever. Moving her hands down his arms, she tried to squeeze his biceps but couldn't close her hands around the hard muscles. So solid. So strong. She felt boneless as she melted into his chest feeling a security never felt in anyone. He began caressing her anew beginning with her eyelids and moving on inch by tender inch.

"Marc," she breathed, "It's like——"

"I know. You're a new woman, my love. And I'm the lucky man to be with you."

The tips of her nipples were sensitive against his hot, hard chest, and she felt every feathery wisp of hairs curling down the center of his belly. He was sleek, and oh so male. The amber scent of his body intoxicated her. When his tongue came back to invade her mouth and make love to it, she opened eagerly. And when he entered her, she was ready. They moved slowly, voluptuously, in perfect harmony. She wanted this luxury to go on forever.

CHAPTER FORTY-EIGHT

On Wednesday afternoon, Marlowe returned to her apartment about four. She held a cup of tea and a book then remembered Rich and Mozart tonight. Damn. She hadn't called him about the time and didn't want to, but it had to be done.

"Pronto."

"Pronto yourself," Rich replied. "Are we still on for Mozart tonight?"

She sighed. "Ciao Rich. I've been out searching for cranberries," and she told him that her friend, Lucia, was coming the next day to celebrate Thanksgiving a week early because a childhood friend from New York would be in Florence for the real holiday.

"Did you find any?"

"At an exorbitant price at that specialty store near the Rialto," and she gave a half-hearted laugh. "On the way home, I noticed that concert time is indeed 7:30. Since it's free, we ought to get there at 6:30."

"Sounds fine to me. We can eat afterward."

"Have you been working a lot?" she asked.

"Mostly organizing for business while in the States. I leave on Sunday. I've also been working on my daughter, Jeri's, flights. She's coming back with me for a while."

"And your son?"

"He's waffling. Fourteen and doesn't want to leave his friends and his workouts; he's a long distance runner and dedicated."

"Like you and tennis."

"Yes. And I'm dedicated to working something out—or in—with you," he said chuckling.

She was quiet. Too much had happened in the short time since she'd stupidly suggested the concert. Marc knew her secret. He'd declared his love and she'd admitted hers, she ought to call this thing off... but how? An uncomfortable silence lay between them. "I'll see you soon."

"Yes," he said. "Bye for now."

He must intuit how things are with me. Belle seems to think I don't owe Marc anything, but I do! I could never face him... or myself, if I continued on with Rich.

* * *

Mozart did it right," she said as they walked out of the church. "Not too many long solos like most oratorios. That contralto was magnificent, though."

"Does pizza sound good to you?" he asked.

"Sure. Do you have a place in mind?"

"Serenissima over in Cannaregio. Do you know it?" he asked.

"I do if it's on Nuova Strada"

"That's the one."

"I remember a delicious pizza late one rainy night when I'd been lost in heavy fog on the way back from a program some-where in that area. Serenissima's colored lights through the mist had looked like a magical lighthouse."

Let's do it," he said taking her hand. "It's not far, I know a shortcut."

When they walked into the café, the aroma of warm garlicky oil struck her with a tremendous force knocking her all the way back to another chilly night when the bastard Corombo had brought her here as a young innocent.

"Let's go on through to the booths in the rear," Rich said.

Leaving the front window tables they passed the working counter where the immense jar of oil with garlic cloves floating on top was still there. Years ago, the cook had demonstrated to her how the jar needed to be turned upside down and rotated to make certain the garlic permeated every drop. She was sure he'd wanted to show off his bulging muscles to a wide-eyed teen.

"*Vino rosso?* " Rich asked.

"Yes, please." I'm hooked on Italian red wine.

Marlowe chose the Pizza *Aglio e Olio*, garlic and oil, and Rich ordered Pizza *Salsiccia*.

"Sausage is more to my liking here," he said. "In the States, who knows what's in a sausage pizza?"

"I know," she said. "I'm told, though, that Portland has excellent Italian restaurants."

"When will you go back?"

"Around the first of January. Mandy's off to Greece for the holidays with Ty and his wife, and I keep hoping she'll stop here on her way home. I'm glad, though, that Ty wants to spend time with her. Hope he doesn't decide to go off somewhere and leave Mandy with his wife." In a gesture of disgust, she back-handed the air as if pushing something away. "That's mean of me, isn't it?" She was babbling remembering how she'd babbled when Rich first came to her apartment. Maybe she hadn't felt as comfortable with him as she'd once thought.

"Going on past experience?" he asked.

"Probably, but I'm trying to break that habit and give him the benefit of the doubt."

"That's what I hope you'll do for me, Marlowe," he said holding her gaze.

Uh-oh. She dare not dive into those espresso eyes even though he *had* been the first to fulfill her sexually. After leaving Ty, she'd tried to come alive, and, finally, with Paul she'd given up on herself as a passionate person. Instead, she'd grabbed onto the occasional orgasm that came her way as a lucky accident. Lord, at forty-three, she'd been such a sexual novice. How blind she'd been until Marc walked in. With him, she woke up as a sexual being and they'd become good friends as well. No. She would not jeopardize what they had.

"Marlowe?" Rich asked.

"What?" she said wondering how long she'd been out of it.

The pizzas arrived. She had a short reprieve giving her a chance to regroup.

"This is as good as I remember," she said concentrating on the thin, crusty pizza with shavings of Parmigiano Reggiano melting into the bubbling garlicky oil.

"Be careful you don't burn your lips," he said.

She said nothing.

"They're sweet lips," he said.

She smiled a little.

"No sassy comeback about what those lips could do?" he asked.

The waiter stopped by to re-fill Marlowe's glass.

"You seem uneasy," he said softly.

"Ah Rich," she said leaning back taking a gulp of wine. *How to do this?* "I did care for you but... I can't see you any more," and she swallowed back a lump in her throat wishing she could do this some other way.

"He's not even free," Rich said his eyes flashing. Then he sat up straighter obviously struggling to control himself.

She sipped more wine and said, "It seems you aren't either."

"I'm working on it, Marlowe."

Lord, it was uncomfortable to have someone love you more than you love them. At least he seemed to *think* he loved her. What a mess.

"Pardon?" he asked.

"I must have been thinking aloud," she said.

"Yeah, it is a mess," he said.

They each poked at their pizzas.

"When will your friend go back to Florence?"

"Sunday morning."

"Same time I leave for the States.... can I call you while I'm gone?"

She hesitated.

"Please," he said.

"I'll probably move out of my apartment at the end of November because Parduzzi expects that Doctor Carocci for December."

"Where will you be?"

Marlowe told him she'd move into Marc's place because he was going to the States for a while. And if all that did happen, she'd be looking for another place for the rest of December because Marc's daughter might come back with him for the holidays. *Why am I justifying myself?*

"I see."

She didn't say anything leaving a long silence.

"You must know his number?"

"I know his cell but he'll take that with him. I don't know his landline.

"If you do have to move, you could call my cousin, Silvia, and give her the number."

"Yesss," she said. His cousin had barely been civil to Marlowe. Then she thought of Carla. "You could get it from Carla. I'd rather not bother your cousin."

"Good. And Marlowe, I don't want to lose touch with you after you go back to Portland."

"Sure," she said looking down at her withering pizza.

"Sorry for ruining your meal."

"Yours too," she said.

Their vaporetto ride back was cold misery even though the night air was balmy. Lights from the palazzos shining on the water must have been beautiful, but she didn't notice. At her door, he didn't press himself in as usual, but they did embrace in a kind of forlorn way. Then he tipped her head back and gave her a fierce kiss pressing her tightly against him.

"I'm not giving you up yet," he said and strode away not looking back.

But, she had given *him* up.

CHAPTER FORTY-NINE

During Lucia's visit, they went to a couple places she wanted to see again. The water sparkled under a cloudless sky on their trip into the Lagoon. Both women enjoyed the little museum about Venice's ancient memories on Torcello Island. Later they spent at least an hour wandering inside the church where Tintoretto was buried. Lucia had never been that far into Cannaregio. Marlowe led her straight to her favorite Tintoretto painting, *Presentation in the Temple*. It spread up and across one entire side wall of a huge chapel next to the main altar and focused on little Maria climbing up a long flight of golden stairs—alone. It was similar but very different in feel from Titian's version in the Accademia. Lucia admired Tintoretto's work almost as much as Marlowe did. The area around Tintoretto's church was familiar to Marlowe having wandered its calles daily as a teenager. But she wasn't ready to tell that story. She might never tell anyone else. It was like a scar healed over. Now that she felt free of it, did she want to pick at it with this person and that? She wasn't sure.

On their way home, they carried a warm roast chicken from a deli as a stand-in for turkey because Marlowe had no oven, but when they got off the water bus at Santa Maria della Salute, they heard organ music coming from the church's open door. They couldn't resist going inside. On wrought-iron tables set up between two of the eight massive pillars supporting the dome in the center of the church, at least a hundred candles were glowing in anticipation of the festival tomorrow. It was to commemorate the ending of a horrible plague in the 1630s. While Lucia moved through the church, Marlowe couldn't keep her eyes from that mass of individual flames. Each held meaning to whoever had lit the taper, but for her, each one represented a lie she'd told to cover her past. They drew her toward their light, and, as if seared by their heat, she felt cleansed. A sense of deliverance washed through her. Lucia joined her chatting about the pull of Venice and how she hated to miss the festivities the next day but had to leave early because her friend was expected in the afternoon.

"Too many good things at once, right?" Marlowe said coming out of her reverie.

Early Sunday morning at the train station, when Marlowe waved goodbye, she speculated how it might feel to wave Lucia off from a permanent home here in Venice. With Marc? What a beautiful dream, she thought. Back in her apartment, she collapsed in splendid silence but not for long; she'd promised herself to attend the Festa set to begin at eleven.

* * *

It was late in the afternoon and the sky was already darkening. The Festa was over. People passing her place from the food fair outside the church dropped trash beside and into her canal. Marlowe wondered how they could foul their beautiful city that way. The phone rang, and she was surprised to hear Commissario Gallina asking to come by with pictures of suspects. After she agreed, he became more and more casual even calling her Marlowe. That seemed odd for an Italian policeman. On a Sunday night? She felt foolish for having said yes, and strangely uneasy. She picked up the phone again.

"Marc, I hope I'm not disturbing you. Are you free for a minute?"

"Of course, love. What is it?"

"Remember Commissario Gallina? He called a moment ago. When I recognized his voice, he said he was flattered. Without thinking, I agreed to have him drop by to show me some suspect pictures. Then he turned oily and even called me Marlowe."

"Is your friend, still there?"

"She left this morning. He's coming in about an hour. I feel foolish, after all, he is a policeman, but it seems off for him to—"

"I'm on my way. I'll be dropping in unexpectedly."

"Marc, you're a love."

"You're *my* love."

* * *

After Gallina had gone, Marc and Marlowe looked at each other, broke out laughing, and fell into each other's arms.

"Marlee, you were right. Don't ever mistrust your instincts about such things."

"Because his English was good, I guess I slipped into a flip manner which he took for flirting. I need to be careful about that."

"No, you should not have to change one bit for arrogant bastards like him. And you're right to question any policeman wanting to be on a first-name basis, especially in Italia."

"I'd like to have that creep caught, but a marvelous person installed a marvelous lock system, and frankly my dear, I don't give a damn," she said.

He chuckled. "Have you had your evening meal?"

"Does a fried, sugary fritella from the Festa count?" she asked.

"Probably not. Nonna sent me some home-made lasagna this afternoon; I was about to turn on the oven when you called. Interested?"

"I wouldn't turn down your grandma's special lasagna. Can I bring anything?"

"Nah. She sent salad too. We could have a nice red by the fire, eat Nonna's dish and who knows what might happen after that? You could bring a few things in your handy-dandy zaino that the Venetian harpies cluck about."

As they left her apartment, Marlowe asked, "Do you suppose the Commissario heard those cluckings and decided to cash in on the foreign strumpet?"

"I'm sure of it."

"None of those pictures looked anything like the creep I saw," she said. "I bet they were all from old, dead files."

"Probably. You've been out all day haven't you?" he said.

"Pretty much. After Lucia left, I went to the Festa."

"Oh yeah. I forgot about that. How was it?"

"Have you been to Salute's festa before?"

"No. I've been to a couple summer ones for Redentore, the other plague church."

"I bet they'd be more fun, with picnics in boats and fireworks over the water. The Redentore was built about fifty years before Salute wasn't it?" she asked.

"You know Venetian history far better than I do. All I know is that tens of thousands died in those two plagues."

She told him about the big tv screens set up on the massive pillars giving the majestic sanctuary a sports-event look and about the colorful costumes of various religious orders who made their grand entrance followed by the Patriarch of Venice. "The best part, though," she said, "was when a couple children lost their balloons, and they floated over the heads of the crowd."

"It sounds more fun than spiritual," he said as they got off at his stop. As soon as they were inside, Marc suggested they soak in the jacuzzi while the lasagna cooked.

"Only if you don't give me jacuzzi hair again."

His eyes crinkled and his mouth almost smirked.

As they eased themselves into the hot water, she asked, "Don't harpies screech?"

"Have no idea—cluck or screech—they're all busybodies. Don't fret about them."

"Why do you think the commissario wore a fancy dress uniform?"

"That's easy. He wanted to dazzle you. It's a fact that *all* women are drawn to men in uniforms."

"It was pretty," she said, "but those fancy buttons didn't quite hide his paunch."

"You want to bet there was no full-dress meeting he'd come from?" he asked and turned on the hot water spigot again.

Marlowe slid lower into the soothing water and sighed in contentment. After a while, she asked, "What have you been up to lately?"

"Some work and last weekend, ski patrol."

"Ski patrol? Where? Are you on a regular team?"

"I'll show you counselor. I'll answer all in one sentence. Cortina d'Ampezzo is a large resort and there are many of us, and we're called in rotation."

"Is it like a rescue team or general patrolling?"

"Both. It's general unless there's a problem, then whoever's there goes in to help. If it's an overall disaster everyone is called."

"How long have you been doing this?"

"Giovanni and I started skiing in our teens. We signed up because we got perks that way. He continued after I went back to the States for high school; when I returned, I started in again."

"Do you have to take some kind of medical training?"

"Of course. They require basic paramedic training for typical ski injuries. When you get a job here, I'll take you with me next time."

She ignored his remark about an unlikely job but said, "I might take you up on that, oh ye of many talents."

As they soaked in the hot, bubbly water, he said things were looking good that Katy might come back with him.

"That's great, Marc."

"Speaking of talents, would you be willing to show her some of the art in Venice?"

"Would I ever. What's she interested in?"

"She mentioned something about Veronese."

"She probably read the famous story of how he got himself out of trouble with religious authorities by changing the name of his *Last Supper* to *Supper at the House of Levy*. Whether it's true or not, it's a fascinating story and a fabulous painting. In the Accademia."

"And something about the Palazzo del Bovolo," he added.

"Oh yes. That would interest her. It *is* fun to come upon that bizarre place all of a sudden."

"Would you believe, I've never been there? I might come along."

"I bet she'd be thrilled if you would."

"Hmm. Sprout, you know what would thrill me right now?"

"I have a hunch."

He reached for her feet but she snatched them away and stood up to get out. He stood up too putting his arms around her. Their wet bodies slid together and his penis was growing even as he lifted her out of the tub. She loved to be the cause of that growth. She didn't have powerful muscles, but there were certain other powers in being female. They grabbed towels and began drying each other off and one thing led to another.

* * *

Later he said, "It's a good thing I had sense to not put the lasagna in the oven yet."

"Premeditated, huh?"

"I like to think of it as careful planning."

As they sipped wine by the fire waiting for their supper, Marc said, "Why don't you move in while I'm here to help you? My cousins would be more than willing to move things for you later but… it'd be nice to have you around before I have to face certain people back there—like my ex and ex to be."

"I am tempted, but I keep thinking Parduzzi will call any day and say I've got the apartment for December, then I wouldn't have to move at all. Your apartment is gorgeous; it has an oven and a real sink, but I do like waking up in the heart of the city."

"Think about it, will you?"

"I will," and she snuggled into the hollow of his shoulder. "This *is* pretty nice," she said. *Even nicer with no more secrets.* The next morning in the pool, she began to rationalize: from Marc's place, it's only a few minutes to the city; the pool is wonderful; his apartment is divine; and on and on. But after Marc was off to his Pa Kua workout, she locked up and headed home. On the way, she gloried in the snow-white gulls flying randomly with dark clouds roiling above them as a dramatic backdrop, but when she saw cups left in the sink from the Gallina tea party and remembered how that bastard had seen her as fair game, she felt disgusted. Damn him, and damn the gossips. For her to be a known hussy, as her Mom would say, was so out of character. As a child, she'd learned to keep a low profile so her mother wouldn't get upset over each little thing. But now? She almost liked being a "celebrity," even a wanton one and she chuckled as she twirled herself across the small room.

CHAPTER FIFTY

With a cup of steaming tea in hand, Marlowe sat warm and dry after coming in out of the pelting rain. She'd managed to get thoroughly soaked while trying to race the rising waters. In her over-sized Tee and robe with feet encased in thick wool socks, she re-played her adventure at Piazza di San Marco. The wind had been blowing, rain was pouring down and water lapped at the edge of the quay. The lagoon was grey with white caps riding in faster and faster. The magical forces of nature held her as she watched water fill the Piazza. She'd stayed too long, she knew it but couldn't tear herself away. It had been mesmerizing. She should have gone out of her way toward the Rialto and higher ground to catch a vaporetto. Venetians would've known she couldn't follow the path she'd chosen to get home and expect to keep her feet dry.

Now, inside her cozy cave, it was quiet and she wondered if it was still raining. She padded down the steps and poked her head out, and there stood Marc about to knock.

"Marc, come in. You're soaked!"

"I know you want a warning but—"

"Forget that. Come sit beside my wimpy heater." He huddled into himself and shivered.

"Are you okay?"

"Didn't dress right," he said through chattering teeth. "I came here for succor. How'd you know I was out there?"

"I didn't. I was curious to see if it was still pouring."

"Did you find out?"

"What? Oh, very funny. What I found was a wet Viking."

"You're convinced I'm of Nordic descent, aren't you?"

"I'll hush about that. Where would you prefer your ancestors come from?"

"Now that's an interesting question. And Marlee, I'm not bothered by your speculation, not at all. In fact, I'll take *all* the attention you give me."

"Yes, I've noticed. But first, let's get you out of these soppy things," and she started to pull at his shirt and unfasten his pants. "You could help," she said laughing.

"I could, but it's nice to be pampered."

"Go stand under a hot shower; I'll make more tea." She pulled out the largest towel she could find and lay it across her fancy towel heater in her fancy bathroom and found the same wool blanket she'd wrapped him in once before.

"That's better," he said when he stepped out of the bathroom with the towel around him. She handed him the blanket and led him to the sofa where she wrapped each foot in a small warmed towel.

He opened his hands to the heavens, "Bring on the storm."

"Oh my love, better now?" She handed him a mug of steaming tea.

"Much, now that I'm your love," he said putting his tea on the table and opening his blanket to pull her in.

"You feel good, Sprout. Can I stay with you tonight?"

She leaned back, "Is this all a trick? Shall I take these away?" she said standing up and pretending to pull his covers.

"No trick, no trick," he said. "Can I? Can I?" and waggled his praying hands.

"Only if you behave yourself, otherwise, I'll turn you out into the dark and stormy—"

"I'll do anything you want," he said bobbing his eyebrows.

"Promise?"

"Promise," he said. And in that moment, he realized he would.

"Good."

"Well?" he said.

"I'm thinking, I'm thinking. Are you hungry?"

"Is this a trick question?"

She stared at him.

"Yes. I'm hungry… for you."

"Correct answer! You can stay if you devour me from head to toe."

"When do we begin?" he said following her to the bedroom.

"Now." She'd already pulled the covers back while he was showering and stood in front of him beside the bed.

"You are such a trollop," he said pulling her close then whispered, "I've been wanting to use that word for ages."

Time didn't touch them that afternoon. Slowly, he untied the belt on her robe letting it drop and drew the night shirt over her head. With one hand on each side of her head, he kissed her gently inching his tongue inside. *I want this to be a magic time for her.* But as he ran his hands down her neck and cupped her breasts, he knew he needed all the self control he could muster to pull it off

"Do you know that your nipples are different shapes?"

She was quiet.

"Your left aureola is round and your right one is almond shaped. Nice to have variety for feasting," he said as he leaned down to nibble first one then the other, humming as he went. "They even taste different."

"Marc, you're outrageous."

Gently his large hands slid over her rib cage and down to her waist encircling it. Then he moved on to her round butt and pulled her against his growing hardness. He could tell she was already cooking, and he hadn't begun to dine yet. Her immediate response to him brought his own blood to a boil. Could he do this without losing it? He eased her onto the bed and climbed astride.

"And now for the first course," he said in a voice that was hoarse and raspy. After a while, he said, "Tasty."

"Maybe you could skip the entrée and use your special dessert tool," she said breathing hard as she reached down to take his full erection in her hand. He moved her hand away.

"No ma'am. An order's been signed and awaits fulfillment.

"But what if I change the requirements?"

"Too late. You'll have to suffer through to the end," he growled playfully.

She was aflame, but he calmly placed one hand on her mound and held it there saying, "Easy does it, Marlee."

Later while he feasted on her breasts, he began to move his fingers inside and found her hot, wet and ready.

"Dessert now?" she begged.

"Entrée first."

He kissed and licked, nipped and sipped down her belly tonguing the ugly scar. Then leaning back and using both hands, he eased her thighs apart and buried his face into the folds of her open sex thrusting his tongue inside. She arched and trembled and pushed against him. He held her still and lifted his head to whisper, "Easy, Marlee, I'm not going away. Let it happen, I'll catch you."

He dropped back and continued to lick, almost like a cat licking up cream, and savored her spicy taste and scent reminding him of cloves and oranges again. He pushed his tongue into her very core of sensation. And finally he sensed her trust. Her head fell back on the bed and the orgasm overtook her. At first, it lifted her almost off the bed. When she came down, he felt her spasms continue to move through her body. He watched with fascination. When she opened her eyes, he said in a choked voice, "Look at you. You're beautiful."

"I'm not, but when you say it that way, I *feel* beautiful." She sighed. "That was the best entrée ever. Don't forget the recipe."

His soft laugh was full of masculine confidence; he felt appreciated. "Did you save anything for dessert?" he asked and began touching the outer lips of her vagina with the tip of his penis. With the pad of his thumb, he feather-stroked around her clit again while his cock began sliding in and out through her slippery folds. When he suckled her nipple, he felt a luxurious tremor move through his groin in response to her reaction. She was ready to soar again almost sending him over the edge. And then... he *was* going over. He groaned, "Oh Babe, I'm going to fuck you now." As he exploded into her, she went with him, and he collapsed on top of her.

After a few moments, she grunted, "Marc."

He moved to the side and they lay there silently coming down together.

"Sorry if I crushed you," he whispered.

"Your weight held me together, and felt good until I couldn't breathe."

He put his arm around her pulling her into the hollow of his shoulder. Not saying anything, he wrapped his other arm around her. He savored the closeness and knew she did too.

"We're good together, aren't we?" he said.

"Mm-hmm," she breathed.

After a time, "Have you thought any more about moving in with me before I leave?"

"A little."

"We could have more meals like this one," he said nuzzling her neck.

"That would be an intensely rich diet."

"Can't handle it huh?" he said.

"I didn't say that!"

"Maybe I should say I can't handle it."

"How *do* you hold off so long?"

"Trade secret."

"I've never been so pleasured. Never. How many times did I say yes?"

"I lost count but was pretty damned sure you meant it."

For a while, they lay in a suspended stupor, then she asked, "Why do you say you can't handle it?"

"I think what I meant is that after loving like this, I can't handle letting you go." He began his argument again. "Besides you're planning to move in when I'm gone anyway, why not a few days before?"

"Why not, indeed."

"Good." He expelled a large sigh and held her.

"Marc?"

"Hmm?"

"I'm hungry."

"For what?" he asked raising up to look at her.

She laughed.

While Marc created a large, fluffy *frittata* including eggs, cheese and whatever else he found in her fridge, Marlowe organized things to move. Much later, she woke to find him curled around her with one hand cradling a breast. This was becoming a habit—a nice one.

CHAPTER FIFTY-ONE

"Marlowe, we can settle up later," Paolo Parduzzi said the following morning, "there's another storm coming and I'm closing the office. But if you're moving to Signor Barovier's, are you still interested in the apartment for December?"

"Yes, I am."

He nodded but seemed puzzled. Since she couldn't explain to Marc why she wanted her own place for December, she wouldn't try with Parduzzi.

By two p.m., Marc and Marlowe had moved her things out. Even the red begonias were loaded into his launch. Dark clouds flew across the sky when they arrived at his apartment, and the air was heavy with the smell of ozone. They hurried to unload everything inside the stairwell before heavy drops started to fall. She adored being with Marc, but as they carried her stuff into his place, she felt anxious not knowing why. From his large bedroom window, they watched the lightning and heavy rain as if they were at the helm of a solid ship. Storms seemed to stir their passions and they spent another night of lovemaking.

The next evening over pizza in a shop near the apartment, they lifted a glass to Thanksgiving. She said she was thankful they'd met again. He reached across the small table and lifted both her hands in his. His silver eyes glistened.

"Do you know how much I treasure you?"

"I'm getting the idea," she whispered feeling adored.

"Let's continue our Thanksgiving celebration by going to bed early," he said. "I plan to give you a Thanksgiving Fuck and need to be up early for conference calls."

"I've never had a Thanksgiving Fuck before. How will it be different?" she asked on the walk back to his place.

"You'll see."

When they walked into the apartment, Marc grabbed the ringing phone. When he hung up, he said, "We're invited to Donatella's New Year's Eve party. Remember Donatella?"

"Of course." She recalled the elegant woman walking to their table at Cipriani's, of the storm and the boat and…

"Will you go with me?"

"Sounds interesting."

"I know. You have nothing to wear."

"Ordinarily, I wouldn't mind, but at Donatella's?"

"If you had a smashing outfit?"

"Yes, but I'm sure she wouldn't mind if you went stag. Hostesses appreciate having extra good-looking men at their parties."

"We're going then," and he picked up the phone and dialed. After a rapid-fire discussion with Donatella, he hung up and turned to Marlowe. "Here's what's going to happen. After my calls tomorrow, we're going to Milano to find you a dress."

"Milan? I don't know where to shop in Milan. And if I get a dress, I'll have to buy shoes and pantyhose and who knows what else?"

"Don't worry. It'll be fun," he said.

"Fun? Shopping? I haven't shopped for party things for years. I've forgotten how."

"It'll come back. Milan's about 350 kilometers. Shall we go by train or car?" he asked.

"Miles?"

"About 215," he said.

"Let's go by car. I have my international license. Unless you take one of those fierce Italian speedways, I could help drive."

"They're all fierce, but I need to keep my hand in for being in the States. Maybe I can arrange a business call as well."

"Now," she said, "about this Thanksgiving Fuck."

"Insatiable!"

"Curious, just curious."

Marc had a bottle of oil with rosemary leaves floating in it and began to massage her, but she grabbed it and slathered oil all over him too. They slid on and over each other laughing and playing until he announced they were well basted and ready for the oven.

Later, he asked, "Can you sleep without changing the bedding?"

"Sure. My body can soak up a ton of oil and cry for more."

"Sprout, your body seems to cry for more of lots of things," he said pulling her closer.

"Like your arms around me?"

"Mm-Hmm."

"Marc, let's pretend it's Thanksgiving other times too?"

And, of course, he rumbled and hugged tighter.

* * *

"I feel spoiled in Venice," Marlowe said as they sped toward Milan. "Already I want to be back."

"It does that doesn't it? We're going to find you a frisky dress for your Venetian debut."

"Frisky?"

"Yes. I know conservative black is smart for traveling, but I'd like to see you in something that reflects the real you."

"Maybe the real me *is* conservative."

"I know better. It's not the same as when your ex wanted you to dress provocatively. That was all about him. This… hmm, I suppose it's a little about me wanting to show you off, but I'd be proud to take you in your usual dark togs." He turned to her and laid his hand on her thigh, "You do know that, don't you?"

She visualized going in her black slacks, then said, "Yes, Marc, I do."

They drove on. "I don't want to show up in drab duds," she said. "Parties are for flamboyance."

He nodded energetically.

* * *

With gorgeous clothes in the windows and beautiful people strutting the sidewalks, the street reminded Marlowe of Rodeo Drive in Beverly Hills. The first dress she tried was a black chiffon with no sleeves, a deep V neckline and layer after layer of ruffles ending in a short, kicky skirt. It was a definite possible. She liked herself in it and was ready to take it and be done. Marc liked it too but wasn't ready to stop looking. Next came a strapless red satin also with a tiered skirt. Short and cute, but she'd never liked strapless. With not much cleavage, she'd have to wear a serious push-up bra and be miserable the whole time. They also had a black dress with a split panel down the side of the long skirt. It had a graceful cross-over bust line with ruching. In spite of the full length, it was slinky and revealed a lot of skin. She could see Marc getting interested in that one. What man wouldn't?

"Let's get a coffee and confab," he said.

She'd never enjoyed shopping this much before. He was actually interested in the process.

"Babe, that last slinky dress makes my mouth water, but it wasn't exactly frisky. The red one was nice, but right now, I'd go for the first one, the black frothy one. When you move, those frilly things in the skirt are positively frisky."

She agreed with his choice and explained why she didn't want the strapless.

"Marlee, don't know if you've noticed how much I enjoy your… cleavage," he said and bent to kiss the top of her head. "But surely we can find something more comfortable."

"Surely," she said grinning like a ninny. "Marc, here's an elegant-looking bar."

They ordered coffees and grabbed the last black-marble-covered table standing on curlicue wrought-iron legs. The gleaming mirror behind the bar had old-fashioned beveled edges that sparkled.

Marc said, "There's another shop in the famous Galleria that

Donatella told me about."

"She gave you advice?"

"I almost asked her to come along but thought better of it," and a wicked smirk spread across his face.

"That was a wise decision," she said.

"I know. Still, Marlee, she could be a good friend for you."

"I'll take your word for it, Marc. I will."

After their coffees, they window shopped through the halls of the Galleria, and suddenly, he struck himself on the side of his head. "It's not *in* the Galleria, it's on a street near by. Spiga something, Via della Spiga and... now I remember, the shop is Dolce e Gabbana."

"Dolce e Gabbana! Oh no, Marc. Even I know that's where celebrities like Madonna shop. I can't afford that."

"We can look. We can look," and he hurried her along. As they approached a street called Via Monte Napoleone, he said, "Hold on. We're close. Let's pretend we're celebrities slumming in our ordinary duds."

"Why not?" she said, remembering doing just that with a former gay boss who'd taken her for a Christmas lunch on Rodeo Drive where she'd tried on a full-length mink coat and he pretended to be her hubby.

Soon she was in a Dolce e Gabbana dressing room trying on some incredible dresses at incredible prices. Marc had taken a seat in a cushy over-stuffed chair and showed signs of thoroughly enjoying himself. The clerks flitted around him with coffee and fancy cookies, no doubt assuming he'd be paying their high prices.

Marlowe paraded out for him and he nodded or shook his head at each one. She walked over to him and whispered, "You're playing with fire, Mister." He rumbled and the sales women tittered. Then she tried the one that had caught her eye when they'd first stepped inside. By now she'd bought a pair of pantyhose, no heels yet but with the hose covering her stark-white skin, she could stand on tip toe and get an idea. The clerk handed her a pair of pumps to wear with the zingy dress made of a silky, shimmery fabric cut on the bias so that the short skirt would swing and flip when she breathed let alone walked. Marc would go for that. It had a black background covered with small red lozenges running across the fabric in diagonals and it appeared to be a shimmery pink. From the back, it looked like a halter dress, but it's neckline was U-shaped with a band of black studs that might have been glittery pieces of onyx considering the price tag. From the bottom of that U-neck band, a peek-a-boo slit went down the front almost to her navel. The assistant said she shouldn't wear a bra and suggested sticky bra pieces that fit over each breast. Marlowe decided to try it without anything first and discovered two bands of sticky tape on each side of the slit to hold it in place. Ah, that's how starlets manage those slit-to-the groin gowns.

When she stepped out in this one, Marc put down his coffee cup and held up both fists with thumbs up. The older saleswoman was no dummy and held out a pair of shoes saying, "While you have the dress on, you might want to try *these*." Marlowe sat on an ottoman across from Marc and put them on. In elegant simplicity, they were high-heeled sandals with a sling-heel, but the thin strap truly supported the back of the heel. A small flat bow lay across the toe area. They seemed to be made of black satin, but smooth leather lay beneath the satiny cloth and they felt almost comfortable. She liked what she saw in the mirror and *loved* the look of approval in his eyes. She said she'd think about them and sashayed back to the dressing room. Was the dress frisky? Yes. Pricey? Indeed at 495 Euros. She hadn't dared look at the price of the shoes.

She put the dress back on the hanger and as she was reaching up to the hook, Marc took it from her and hung it out of the way. She squeaked. He put his hand over her mouth. In a low Bogart growl he said, "Quiet moll, if you know what's good for you."

She started to laugh and turned around to face him. "What are you doing in here?" she hissed. "Did they see you come in?"

"Nope. Came to tell you I've bought the dress and they gave me a discount. You needn't try on any more."

This man was a better shopper than I'll ever be. "I can't let you," she started to argue, but he was standing very close and pushing her pantyhose down. Then she heard his zipper. In that small booth with the three-quarter-length door opening to the changing-area hallway, the zipper sounded wildly erotic. The clerk asked through the slatted door if she needed any help with the next one? Either she wasn't aware of the purchase or thought Marlowe might want a second dress. There she was naked except for pantyhose around her ankles and Marc, though fully clothed, had his cock standing out in the open and was playing with her breasts. Then he began pushing against her.

The clerk called out, "Is it too small? I can get a larger one?"

Marlowe hesitated then hoarsely replied, "No thanks, I think this will do."

"Bitch," he hissed cupping her bottom in his hands and lifted her. "Wrap your legs around me," he ordered as he dragged the panties from her ankles.

"In here?" she whispered.

"I want inside you—now!"

She shivered with excitement and did what he said, first one leg and then the other.

"Hold on, I won't let you fall."

She grabbed his shoulders and hung on.

His fingers stroked her as his erection pushed against her. She gushed; he felt it and in one smooth thrust buried himself inside of her. She wrapped her arms around his head and held fast while he rocked against her, pressing high and hard. The angle was awkward yet somehow worked because with each thrust, he brushed that most erogenous place of all. And when she realized she was about to have an orgasm in a Dolce e Gabbana dressing room, she started to laugh but he covered her mouth with his. One more thrust and it was all over.

"Signora? *Il suo marito* purchased the dress for you. If you want to hand it to me, I can wrap it for you."

Catching her breath Marlowe said, "*Un momento.*" Marc handed Marlowe the dress and stepped into the corner away from the door. "I'll take the shoes, too," she said thrusting everything under the door into the clerk's eager hands.

After the clerk walked away, he slipped out. Marlowe collapsed on a small stool and waited for her heart to settle. Using tissues sitting on a tiny table, she put herself together the best she could. When she emerged, the manager was waiting and told her what a fine choice they'd made and how sweet her husband was.

Sweet? Marlowe just smiled.

Here he comes now from the men's room," the woman said.

Marlowe went into the ladies and left him to deal with the clerks who were still bustling around him. She argued with herself that she had to buy the shoes because they were perfect with the dress. She'd not make a scene now but planned to settle with him later for the shoes, at least, knowing he'd put up a fight about the dress. Marlowe reasoned that she hadn't splurged on clothes for ages, and even her mother would have agreed about the shoes because she'd worn heels until she was seventy-nine.

Marc was outside on the sidewalk holding both parcels. They moved away without speaking. Once out of sight and hearing, they erupted into laughter.

"Do you think she knew?" Marlowe asked.

"Maybe. Maybe not. But she got the sale."

"If she would have looked down, she'd have seen your big feet."

"My big feet? You were making noises, and what was that business, "I *think* it will do?" he said in a simpering falsetto voice.

"Gotcha, right?"

He nodded and said, "Was it good for you?"

"I *think* so."

At that, he bent over with laughter and they hurried down the street. "Let's find something to eat," he said. "I'm starved."

CHAPTER FIFTY-TWO

At his apartment, Marlowe said, "You must be worn out; I dozed while you were with your prospects."

"Not too bad, but I'm going for a soak. Want to join me?"

"Great idea. But is it okay to use the closet in the second bedroom for my things?"

"Sure. Want your new dress to have plenty of room?"

"Sort of." She didn't want to mention her feelings of not having a separate space. It seemed petty since she'd be here only a short time. As she slid into the tub facing him, Marc said, "I'm going to miss this while back in the States."

"You could have one there, too," she said thinking he meant the jacuzzi.

"Sure, but more and more, I don't want to live there."

"I can understand that. Already I dread having to leave this enchanting city. Being gone today seemed too long."

"Are you still thinking about living here?"

"All the time."

"What's keeping you?"

"Money. I need to work. What could I do here? Jobs are scarce for Italians let alone someone like me."

"You might teach law at the American base outside of Vicenza."

"What are you talking about? It'd have to be basic stuff since I've had no experience."

"I remember a Business Law class in undergraduate school that was taught by someone who'd never practiced. We learned about contracts and such."

"What an exciting idea. I think I *could* do that."

"Would you move to Venice if you could find a position at Vicenza?"

"Would I ever!"

"I know someone out there. I'll ask him about it. And you *would* consider it?"

"Of course! Donna Leon used to teach English at that base. After her fabulous success with crime novels, she probably doesn't anymore. Have you read any of her books?"

"One or two, but I'm not much for mysteries. I like ancient Roman history better."

He turned on the hot-water tap.

"That feels good," she said sliding deeper. "I agree about ancient history. Used to hate assignments in current-affairs class. Events go too fast; there's no time to digest what they mean."

"Like this afternoon," he said.

"This afternoon?"

"I'm thinking our quickie in Milano went by too fast. For me, it was pure, flaming lust. I couldn't take more of your dressing and undressing and sashaying out to show me your wares."

"My wares? Whose idea was the shopping thing?"

He ignored that and said, "I'm thinking about slow, leisurely lovemaking. You?"

"Allora, Signore, mi piace a fare l'amore lentamente, molto lentamente."

"Your Italian is improving by leaps and bounds. I wouldn't change a word you said. Slowly, very slowly, is definitely best."

He stood up and pulled her with him. They stood together warm and slippery with suds from the bubble stuff Marc had added. Who would have thought a giant-sized man would like bubble stuff? He grabbed towels and they went to his bed that still held the aroma of rosemary. Later as they lay curled together on their sides, he said, "I enjoyed shopping with you. You looked good in all of them, and that red strapless was intriguing."

"It would be intriguing if a boob popped out at the party."

As if making a good catch, he grabbed a breast and said, "I'd have to come to its rescue. Your cleavage tantalizes me and feels good. Mmm."

"It's always better lying on my side like this when the girls are all scrunched together."

"The girls?" he chortled. "Well, these girls are perfect sideways or upright."

"Glad you approve."

"Marlee, I approve of everything about you, and I'll miss you a lot more than the jacuzzi. You know I leave on Sunday."

"I know," she said dreading the day. "How long?"

"Plan is until the fifteenth. I'm still hoping to bring Katy back for the holidays."

She scooted her butt backward closer to him. "In the meantime this is nice," she said.

"Mm-Hmm," he said drifting.

CHAPTER FIFTY-THREE

Marc was still curled around her when his phone rang at five the next morning. Marlowe could tell by the sound of his voice something was wrong. It went flat as soon as he recognized who was speaking.

"When?" he said. "What's the prognosis?... I see. My plane leaves tomorrow morning. Do I have time or should I try to get out today?"

Was it about Katy? No, Marlowe had heard him talk once with her mother, and his voice hadn't been this cold. His Mom and Dad in San Diego? Definitely not. Must be Elise.

When he hung up, she hugged him.

"It's Andy, my father-in-law. He's had a massive stroke. In a coma."

"What did—"

"They don't know, but I want to see him before he goes. I'm going to try to leave today."

She left him to it and went to start measuring coffee, but in a few minutes he said, "I'm on standby but chances are I'll be leaving on my regular nine o'clock to Paris tomorrow."

"Then direct to L.A.?"

"Yeah," but he was distracted.

Marlowe went to the fridge and looked for something to eat. "You hungry?"

"Not much, but I'll go for some pastries," he said.

"No, I'll go. You've got lots on your mind." She dressed quickly and started toward the door. As she turned the doorknob, he was there with his arms around her. She'd never get used to this giant who moved so fast and quietly.

"Babe, I'm scared."

"Yes."

"I've been waiting to be free for so long, but it's macabre. I do like the man."

"Do you need to feel guilty for a situation she set up?"

"I shouldn't, but she's part of why I'm scared. What new scheme will she come up with?"

"What's the worst that could happen?"

"Turning Katy against me."

"How?"

"You don't know her."

Marlowe pulled him to the couch and got him to sit facing her. "Let's think," and she took his hands. "What kind of relationship do you have with Katy?"

"Good, I think. She seems to tell me anything on her mind."

"You're lucky, she's not a teenager yet," she said with a low chuckle. "But Marc, she's almost twelve. Do you need to keep this ancient lie from her any longer?"

He looked at her, his eyes wide. "She's still a little girl. She wouldn't understand."

"Of course she would. Maybe I wouldn't at her age back in a small town in Nebraska, but Katy lives in a different world."

"Oh, God. I hoped she'd never know what her mother accused me of."

"Wouldn't you rather tell her yourself?"

"Of course."

She was sticking her nose in but forged on, "I think it would strengthen your relationship with Katy."

"If Katy knew and still loved me—"

"Why wouldn't she love you? In the first place, you didn't do it. Would Julie lie again after all these years?"

"I don't think so, but I'd hate to turn Katy against her mother."

"And you have to take the blame *again* to protect Julie?"

"Whew, counselor, who says you couldn't hold your own in court?"

"I do and don't change the subject. If Katy knew, what hold would Elise have over you?"

"My God. You're right."

She cleared her throat and said, "You may call me Marlee in private."

He laughed and picked her up dancing around the room. Then he set her down at the door and gave her butt a soft smack.

"Go while I think this out."

Marc was packing and excited when she returned. This time she made the coffee.

"I've been on the phone again and have a flight out of Pisa this afternoon. I called Katy and told her I want to come by as soon as I land and take her for supper. She's excited and has a surprise for me."

"Wonderful," Marlowe said, but her heart sank knowing she'd lose him one day sooner.

"Elise thinks I'll be arriving in the wee hours. After I see Katy, I can grab a few winks and go to the hospital early Monday morning."

"A perfect plan. It'll take a huge load from your shoulders."

"The load's already gone. Wish I'd met you sooner."

"You did."

"Yeah, but I was too entangled in her web."

"Timing is all, isn't it?" she said.

"It is."

"What time's your flight?"

"Three this afternoon, straight to New York."

"How are you getting to Pisa?"

"Giovanni will drive me. Come along and keep him company on the way back."

"Would you rather spend the time alone with him?"

"No. I want your comfort all the way."

* * *

"We're going to sit in the back and neck," Marc announced.
Giovanni laughed aloud.

Marc turned to nuzzle Marlowe's neck and said, "I'll call you
and let you know how things are going."

"Please do. And here's the plan. I won't—"

"Oh ho. Now you're making my plans?"

"Wait. See what you think," she said. "I won't take your calls;
I'll let the answering machine do that. As soon as I hear *your* voice,
I'll pick up. That way when you come back, your other messages
will be there for you."

"But you'll listen when you've been out won't you?"

"Sure."

"When I get back, we're going to get you a cell phone so I can
reach you at all hours."

"But I'll be leaving for the States in early January; I won't need
a cell phone here."

"What if you get work?"

"Maybe then." She went through the same story about cell
phones that she'd done with Rich, but with Marc, she knew she'd
relent because she'd want every single call from him. In the meantime, she needed to focus on plans for Portland, and look for an
apartment here for the rest of December. With Katy coming—
surely that was her big news—they'd need alone time without
some strange woman in his home.

"Marlee… Marlee, are you there?"

She nodded.

"I want you to take notes on our route to Pisa then you can
guide Giovanni home. Agree, Giovanni?"

"*Va bene*," Giovanni said. "Give me the Lagoon any day over
this mess."

Marc was in high spirits. She was happy for him, but already feeling lonesome. Two whole weeks. When she'd said she'd miss Rich, he'd withdrawn and become surly. Would Marc react the same?

"I feel lonesome for you already, Marc. Two weeks is a long time."

He hugged her tighter and said, "I know."

She sighed with contentment.

* * *

"Wish me luck with Katy," he said holding her closely as they stood beside the car.

"She loves you."

"Hope so." He turned to give Giovanni a hug too.

"One more kiss, Sprout, and I'm off."

CHAPTER FIFTY-FOUR

"Allora, you're Sprout," Giovanni said as they drove away.

"Among other names. What does he call you?"

"Too embarrassing to say," he chuckled. "What highway are we looking for?"

After giving directions, she asked, "You know why Marc left a day early don't you?"

"Si, si. He wants to tell Katy the dark secret he's been hiding too long."

"Today I talked him into it. Hope it doesn't backfire on him."

"It won't. She adores him," he said.

"What's not to adore?"

He nodded. "Speaking of adoring. He's never talked as much about a woman as he does you. I'm glad for him… for both of you."

"I think I fell for him when we met in L.A."

"Why didn't you two connect then?"

"He was married and I was involved with someone else."

"He's married now."

"Yes," she said, her voice cracking as she dropped her gaze to the dashboard.

"Sorry. But you do know it's a… a sham marriage. Didn't he tell you that in L.A.?"

"No. The attraction between us was there, but he didn't press. I like to think, though, I wouldn't have dated him since we worked together."

"Always a good rule. They say, anyway," and he sniggered under his breath.

"I smell a story."

"Sandra was an employee at the fabbrica when we met."

"It worked out for you two."

"We're lucky."

"Tell me more."

"When I saw her, I knew she was for me."

"That's exciting. She *is* beautiful and fun too. I'd certainly choose her for a friend. Did you ask her out right there in the fabbrica?"

"No. I didn't want to embarrass myself in case she turned me down. I even followed her home a couple of times before I asked her for a coffee. Later, she told me I'd make a terrible detective."

"And your families? Were they happy with the two of you?"

"Mine was; if I was happy, they were happy. Hers wasn't sure they wanted her to marry a glass blower."

"I bet they're glad now."

"Maybe. I think they still wish she would have married someone with money or at least, someone who'd make a lot. There's not much in glass making these days. Murano's monopoly is long gone."

"But anyone who knows anything still looks to Murano for the best."

He shook his head. "Other places around the world make exquisite pieces."

"I bet they don't make anything as exquisite as my Goto."

"Where are we?" he asked.

"We're on A-11 heading toward Firenze. After Prato we need to watch for A-1 heading north. It could also say E-35."

"Too much information."

She snorted softly. "There's a sign for Prato," she said. "We're close to the turn off."

"Before we get back on A-11, how about we stop?" he said. "Use the toilet and get a bite to eat."

They had coffee and a panino in a roadside establishment

probably similar to places along freeways in every country of the world.

"Have you thought about what you'd do if you couldn't make glass anymore, Giovanni?"

"Oddio. You ask hard questions just like Marc said."

"He said that?"

"Si. That's one of the things he admires; you dive in even when it's difficult."

"Hmm," she said and decided maybe that was a compliment.

"Shall we get back on the road?" he said.

"Sure. But—"

"I know, you won't let me off the trap," he said.

"Hook," she said.

"Hook?"

"I won't let you off the hook."

"Marlowe, I haven't thought much about finding another profession. But first, tell me again what we're looking for."

"A-1 toward Bologna."

They rode in comfortable silence. She dreaded being alone in Marc's place. She hadn't felt that way for... maybe never. Once he's free, though. *Stop futuring!* Damn she wanted him but dared not hope. This would be a good time to do serious studying for the Oregon Bar.

Giovanni broke into her thoughts, "I'd probably teach glass blowing here or maybe in the States like Gianni Tosi does. Sandra wouldn't mind moving to the States for a while."

"That's a great idea. Do you know Tosi personally?"

"Si, si. We worked together some. He's a loner, but we've had some laughs together over drinks. You know, the male bonding thing.

This man was more enlightened than she'd ever expected.

"I think Tosi would help me find something or point me in the right direction. And Dale Chihuly's always been helpful to people in the business. Yes, that *is* a possibility."

They drove on into the darkening sky toward Venice.

"Marlowe, thanks for that question. I need to think about that. Our company will probably be one of the last to go thanks to Marc's re-organization a few years ago, but it's getting tougher to support all of us."

"But, Giovanni, if you left, you'd be taking away more than another salary, two with Sandra. Your expertise is invaluable."

"Maybe. But fewer and fewer people buy quality stuff. Most tourists come out to look and then buy trinkets along Lista di Spagna."

"But you have centuries of skills built into your muscles and veins. Your very DNA!"

"So?"

She realized she didn't have an answer and put her hand on his arm for a moment.

"There's a sign for Bologna. We're getting closer. Can hardly wait," he said.

"Me too. I hate being away from Venice for a few hours, it must be worse for you."

"Sometimes I think I want out. But when I'm away, I want to be back. Venice is like a girlfriend who drives you crazy, but the kind of girl you couldn't leave if you tried!" He chuckled. "Won't be long now, Sprout."

She looked at him.

"Sorry, that's Marc's pet name for you. I won't do it again, but it does fit."

"That's okay, it just made me miss him all over again."

"He'll come back to you."

They drove on through the night. The darkness was intense.

"Giovanni?"

"Si?"

"Why do you say Sprout fits me?"

"*Allora*, first you're small compared to *il gigante*."

"Well, yes."

"In Italiano, sprout is *una gemma*. Una gemma is a bud on a plant. According to Marc, your thoughts and actions pop out like buds in springtime. And una gemma is also a jewel."

She remembered Padre Tomaso calling her *una piccola gemma*.

"I don't know whether to be flattered or embarrassed."

"Embarrassed?"

"That Marc has told you so much about me."

"We've shared everything since we were kids."

"Everything?" she asked almost croaking.

"Not everything," he laughed. "Marc doesn't kiss and tell. Maybe I shouldn't tell you, but he's crazy for you. But you already know that don't you?"

Did she? Had he felt "safe" declaring his love knowing he couldn't commit? Certainly she'd been reluctant to admit her own love. It had seemed safer to cling to the idea of their affair being a simple fling before she had to face real life. Ellen would say she was buying insurance again. The truth was she wanted him insurance or not. "Yes," she said, "I do know."

"At last, a sign for Padova; I know my way home."

CHAPTER FIFTY-FIVE

Sunday morning Marlowe missed her big Viking; the crackling energy was gone. She arranged and re-arranged the bar-review papers. She used Marc's computer to complete the application form for the Bar-Review Course she'd take next June. Progress was being made and she felt enthused, until she went to refill her cup and saw his still there on the counter. Then all ambition dissipated. She'd never felt lonely for someone before; it was usually a relief when Ty had gone on a trip. She knew she was procrastinating but needed to get out.

After wandering mindlessly, she stopped to watch a lonely gondolier silhouetted against the sky. Ah, the gondoliers with their strange sideways lurch. Nothing quite like that motion. She'd miss that sight. She'd miss everything here. She always did when she was away, but now, it'd be Marc she'd miss the most. She remembered the day she'd learned about *forcolas,* oarlocks for gondolas. She was fifteen and the heady scent of freshly cut wood drew her into a forcola shop. One of the men working with sandpaper looked up and waved her in. Of course he would, she was a cute young thing and a possible conquest. She had watched as he polished the finished piece made of dark walnut worthy of being in a museum. He took a break to step out for a smoke and motioned her to follow. He explained, speaking slowly in Italian, how every gondolier uses a custom-made forcola to fit his own style. He told of the different sites on which the oar could pivot for various maneuvers: one to start off, one to turn right, to go left, to slow and one to reverse.

"But how do they know when they're on the correct location?" she'd asked in her careful Italian.

He had smiled and said something about practice makes perfect and slowly rubbed his hand along her arm back and forth until he managed to brush against her breast. She had jerked back and left feeling embarrassed. But she'd learned two things: the idiom for practice makes perfect and, even more important for a young girl, to be careful around helpful men. She might have been safer, though, with that stranger than with the teacher who took advantage of her more than once. No. She sighed. That's done with. But her eyes filled anyway because it never could be done with. The not knowing of what happened to her son.

Memories dogged her all day long. By late afternoon, she couldn't put it off any longer, it was time for her ritual visit. There'd be tea and dry cookies at the convent, but she needed more than that before facing the Sisters or even Padre Tomaso—if he happened to be there. She hadn't seen him in twenty-seven years and remembered how often he'd sat with her during those months before giving birth to *her* Tomaso.

She turned onto Fondamenta dei Mori and there was the bar with only one window open to the walkway. The same large man with florid cheeks still leaned on the ledge watching everyone pass by. He didn't remember her. She'd changed; he hadn't. She ordered a prosciuto, mozzarella panino and an espresso and carried them to a bench beside the canal. The sandwich was probably delicious but it held no taste for her. She forced some of it down anyway and went for another coffee. After the second cup, she felt better. She stood facing the direction toward the convent wondering for the millionth time if finding Tomaso would be disastrous for him—or her. She turned away deciding to close that door forever.

Back at Marc's place, she tried to study but felt antsy. Maybe another swim would help. As she entered the palestra, she couldn't believe her ears. The haunting strains of Koritza, her favorite Albanian dance, came from above. She ran up the stairs, and in that big room was a group of Balkan dancers. She asked to join them, and for a while, she got off the world.

* * *

Early Monday morning, the answering machine squawked, "Sprout, are you there?"

"I'm here," she said rousing to catch the phone.

"Did I wake you?"

"Sort of. How did it go with Katy and how's Andy?"

"Which one first?"

"Katy."

"You were right. She listened and watched with those big eyes. She was almost scared, I think. She put her fork down and didn't say a word. I've never seen her that immobile."

"Then?"

"She wondered why her mommy had done that. I said I wasn't sure but thought she'd been very angry with me."

"And?"

"Did we have a fight?" she asked.

"I told her sometimes we argued about not having enough money. The next thing she said was strange. She asked if Phil, her mother's husband, told Mommy to do that. I said I had no idea but didn't think so. She nodded and looked solemn, even sad. Was she trying to find an excuse for Julie?"

"Could be. Maybe you can ask her sometime."

"Maybe. Oh Marlee, I was scared she would be afraid of me, I couldn't keep tears out of my eyes. That moment seemed to last forever. Then she jumped up, came around the table, crawled on my lap and gave me a huge hug and kissed me again and again all over my face like I do her sometimes. She said I'd never hurt her. And... she loved me."

"I'm thrilled for you. A ton has been lifted off your back."

"Ten tons," he said with a catch in his voice. "Then she told me *her* surprise. She'll be coming to Venice with me."

"I know you're happy about that too," Marlowe said.

"I swooped her outside the restaurant—it wasn't even rain-ing—and danced around on the sidewalk with her in my arms and feet flying. She squealed the whole way."

"I bet she loved that."

"She did but pretended to be offended. She said I should put her down that she was too old for such silliness."

"Uh oh. I hope you told her you know some grown women who relish that kind of thing."

"I went along with her. Maybe you can tell her that grown women can be silly too."

"I won't have to. She'll see me do something to embarrass her 'grown-up' sensibilities."

"Hope so."

"Andy?"

"I'm at the hospital waiting to see him. I'm not worried about Elise any more, and too keyed up to sleep. How are you doing?"

"I'm lonesome. When you're not here, your apartment is emp-ty... void... barren!"

"Good," he said. "I'm glad you miss me. What'd you do to-day?"

"I hope it's acceptable that I spread all my papers into Katy's room."

"Of course."

"I'll move them when she comes, but I did get them organized for studying. By the time I did that, I noticed your coffee cup and crumbled. I'd already had my swim, so I went over to Venice. I made a big decision yesterday. I was heading for my ritual visit to the Convent but first I was hungry—"

"It figures," he laughed.

She laughed too. "Then, in a flash, I knew I wasn't going back."

"Maybe it's best."

"Yes."

"Gotta go, here comes the nurse. I'll call you later. Love you."

"Love you, too," she said.

Ah yes, she did love him but still feared she was heading for a long, hard fall. What would he want when he's finally free? She squared her shoulders. If it came to that, she'd face it as she had other disasters, one step at a time. But... those glowing moments with Marc had been worth it.

After coffee and toast, she worked herself up to reviewing Tort law, but the phone rang.

"Buon Giorno, Signora Osborne. I used my detective skills to track you down," the Commissario sniggered, obviously proud of his American idiom.

She ignored it and remained silent. They'd caught a man trying to open her door again and he wanted her to confirm if he was the one she'd seen. In his unctuous way, he asked for directions to Marc's place to show her pictures. Marlowe produced a Lady-of-the-Manor voice and said she would be delighted to drop into the Questura immediately. And the troublesome Torts were put aside.

* * *

After seeing Gallina, Marlowe hurried to Remigio's to meet Carla. They were seated immediately at a nice window table.

"They recognize us now," Carla said.

"I can use a nice red after slimy Gallina. But I do believe they've caught the guy."

"Was the doctor from Rome involved?"

"Gallina was careful about that, but I'm thinking Parduzzi won't rent to him anymore and I probably didn't have to move after all."

"You're staying with Marc though; that can't be all bad."

"Not too bad," she said swiping the back of her hand across a suffering brow, "except he's in the States, and damn, I miss him. You know that, for me, being alone is nothing new, but loneliness is."

"Sounds like you've got it bad," she said and put her hand on

Marlowe's. Carla hesitated a moment and then said, "But Marlowe, he *has* been married twice, hasn't he?"

Marlowe nodded and took a swallow of wine. "Yes he has, but..." How to explain to her or anyone how sure she was that Marc was right for her in spite of his past.

"He called today and Katy's coming back with him for the holidays. He's thrilled."

"What do you think?"

"Thrilled too and hope I have a place before they come. He'll want me to stay but—"

"You think it'd be better for her?"

"Don't you?"

"She might like the idea that her *babbo* has someone nice."

"I doubt it."

Carla tilted her head and pursed her lips.

"Carla, remember when you were eleven? Now imagine you hadn't had your daddy all to yourself for ages. Would you want to share him?"

"No! Of course not," and she laughed.

After their waiter served the pasta, Carla said Rich had called to get Marlowe's number, and Marlowe lamented how sweetly their romance had started before turning so sour. "If Marc weren't on the scene, I might have tried harder to accommodate Rich's baggage. Marc's not free of problems with his spiteful wife and his daughter far away, but none of that carries over to affect us."

She nodded with a sad smile on her delicate face.

"Enough!" Marlowe said. Tell me what's going on with you."

"We're performing Friday night. Could you come and stay over with us?"

"You stinker, letting me go on and on. Of course, I'll come. Can you suggest a train?"

"I have it written here for you," she said handing Marlowe a slip of paper.

"Now, that's what I call confidence."

* * *

Late Tuesday afternoon, while waiting to call Marc, Marlowe stacked her study papers and went for a glass of wine. She was determined to move out even though she knew Marc would mount a strong argument. Yes, she was playing it safe, but if Andy died, Marc might realize he couldn't handle commitment after all. As Carla had reminded her, he'd been married twice. He might not be ready to take another leap. Still, she didn't want him to feel rejected either.

"Hello."

"Good morning, Signor Barovier."

"Marlee, good to hear your voice. What have you been up to?"

"Nothing without you. Katy still love you? Andy?"

He chuckled. "Katy still loves me and according to Julie she's packing and re-packing for her big trip."

"What a thrill to finally have her to yourself here in Venice."

"I want to have her with you, too, Marlee."

"Marc, if I had a daddy like you, I'd want you *all* to myself."

"But I want her to know you and love you as I do."

Uh-oh. She should tell him she's making room for Katy.

"Have you been swimming?" he asked.

Saved, she thought. "Yes, every day. It's a great place. People treat me as if I belong."

"You do."

"Sunday night I felt lonesome and went for a second swim, but when I got there, I heard familiar music. I ran up the stairs and people were dancing one of my favorite Balkan dances."

"Did you join them?"

"I did. Haven't danced for too long what with night school and all, but it felt good."

"Balkan? Like Greek and Albanian?" he asked.

"Yes, and Macedonian, Bulgarian, Romanian and other countries in that fascinating area. The music captivates me. It's almost exotic. No partners needed; all line and circle dancing. Most steps are simple, but the odd rhythms always absorb me. They took my mind off missing you... for a while."

"Do you need special shoes?"

"No, but it helps. Protects the floors. A swimsuit and dancing slippers always travel with me. They're soft and don't take much room."

"You're full of surprises."

"No more than you with ski patrols and Pa Kua and who knows what else? It's fun to be surprised, don't you think?"

"Yeah. Which reminds me, how is it you know about Thom Price, the American who has his own *squero*?"

"I came across his name when I was trying to find out about the life of a gondolier. I emailed him and asked if he'd be willing to teach someone like me."

"Did he answer you?"

"Mm-Hmm. He said he taught anyone who was serious about learning. At the time, I was, but then Mother got sick and my law classes were coming to a close. Nothing came of it."

"Another surprise," he said. "Maybe when you get that job at the base, you can try gondola making on the side."

She laughed. "Or maybe I should settle on gorgeous forcolas."

"There's got to be a story there," he said.

"An old one. I'll tell you sometime. But has Andy come out of the coma yet?"

"In and out. I happened to be there once when he opened his eyes. He reached for my hand and held on tight. I was moved."

"I bet."

"Sprout, what else?"

"I'm going to Pordenone on Friday to see Carla's group perform and meet Franco. I'll stay with them and come home Saturday afternoon. I hope you two meet before I go back."

He groaned, "Hate those words, but don't give up on that job. Chuck, the friend I mentioned, has agreed to help me with the teaching position."

"Marc, that's intriguing but with no actual experience, it's probably pie-in-the-sky."

"*Vedremo,* we'll see. Jeez, Babe, I miss you."

"Oh, almost forgot. Commissario Gallina called here. He must have gotten your number from Parduzzi. He wanted to oil his way over here with pictures of a guy they caught in the act. Somehow he knew you were gone."

"And?"

In a sickly sweet voice, she mimicked how she'd told Gallina about being on her way into Venice that very moment and would stop by his office. "The dirty old man had to accept that."

"Was it the guy?"

"I'd say so. He didn't have that god-awful chin-whisker thing, but I'm pretty sure."

"Did Gallina come onto you?"

"Didn't get a chance. I managed to keep a police woman engaged in conversation with us; I think she knew all about him. How's Southern Cal treating you?"

"It was fun for a few days. But now? Too much sun. Too much everything."

"Miss Venice?"

"Always."

"Me too even for a few hours. Giovanni's relief to be back was palpable."

"I know," Marc said. "Wish *you* were palpable right now."

"Me too. Your bed is sooooo empty without you."

"I'll call soon," he said. "Buona Notte." He waited a beat and whispered… "Buttons."

"Buona Notte," she whispered back.

God, he'd gotten her hot with a few words—always did, always would. What if she *could* work and stay on in Venice? Had she been applying for the Bar Review as some kind of magical thinking like "If I apply *there,* I'll get the job *here?*" It was a long time before Marlowe fell asleep, too many ideas and worries raced through her mind lying alone in Marc's big bed.

CHAPTER FIFTY-SIX

"So you won't be staying at Barovier's when he gets back?" Rich asked.

"No. His daughter's coming."

"My daughter Jeri's coming back with me too. Maybe we can all go to dinner together?"

"How long will she stay?"

Marlowe needed to stop asking Rich questions. Needed to stay out of his life in all ways.

"Sorry, Marlowe, gotta go. I miss you and look forward to seeing you when I get back."

That wasn't too bad. Maybe he's not going to push much after all. Was her ego bruised? No. It's better this way.

* * *

"*Come stai, mia piccola gemma?* How are you my little sprout?"

"Marc, that's exactly what Padre Tomaso called me years ago."

"I'm ready to be with you again," he said. "Wish I weren't staying here this long, but—"

"Me too," Marlowe interrupted.

"Good! Glad you miss me. I've been sorting through stuff stored with my parents and also wrapping up things like bank accounts. The best part, though, is good times with Katy. Thanks to you, we're easier with each other. I'm thinking it's because that secret is gone."

"Could be. Kids are sensitive to what's going on with their parents."

"Hope she didn't think something was wrong with her."

"At some level, maybe she did, but you're setting it right now, that's the important thing. What about Andy and Elise?"

"I spend time with Andy. Seldom see her. She made it clear, though, it was up to me to file for divorce as soon as he dies."

What a cold bitch, Marlowe thought. "Maybe she's tired of the old saga."

"I hope. Still swimming?"

"Every morning. My routine is swim, shower and study. I'm understanding better some aspects of Tort law that I hadn't quite absorbed before."

"Hate to sign off, but the nurse is signaling. I'll call tomorrow."

"I'll be waiting. Take care of yourself."

"You too, love. Sweet dreams—of me I hope."

"For sure."

After her morning routine, she had visited three apartments. Should she have told him? She knew the answer to that.

* * *

Late Saturday afternoon, Marc called, "You're back."

"Walked in from Pordenone five minutes ago. It's a lovely old city on the Noncello River. Been there?"

"No."

"It was an important river port long before Venetians took over in the fifteenth century and enlarged it to transport their goods to the rest of the mainland. Later when the railroads came, the river business died out. And—"

"Whoa, am I getting a history lesson here?"

"Sorry," she laughed. "Anyway, Carla and Franco were marvelous hosts. He's quiet and doesn't speak a lot of English but a real mensch—like you."

"The important thing is did you see belly-dancers?"

"You get right to it don't you? They danced in a ballroom of an old castle in Udine near Pordenone. All the women moved beautifully, but Carla and one of her associates, Alessia, were exceptional. She explained the dance form. It's sensual, but much more than swaying hips and shaking bellies, it requires hours of practice and a tremendous amount of skill to get the different belly muscles to move separately. Fascinating."

"When can I see your muscles move? Did she teach you how? Can you show me?"

"That's three questions. And mister? I can show you lots of stuff, but not that."

"I love it when you talk dirty even over the phone."

"And I love it when *you* make me feel clever and sexy."

"With you, that's easy. By the way, when's the next performance?" he asked.

"Not for several months. The trouble is my time is running out."

"Hush about that. If I get you an interview at the base, you will go won't you?"

"Of course, but—"

"No buts until you look behind the door, right?"

"You're right. But I must tell you something. I didn't remark on it while there because I don't know her husband well. I had asked Carla about the painter Pordenone because I finally went inside that little church you showed me near the Rialto. Remember?"

"Yes, Missy, I remember."

"Missee," she yelped. "Never mind… for now," and she lowered her voice trying to sound menacing. "They took me into the church where his famous fresco of San Rocco is, and Marc, it's pornographic."

"Honestly? Not your special take on it?"

"Another remark ignored… for now," she said in a stern tone.

"Uh-oh, I'm in trouble," but he couldn't keep from chuckling.

"So there's San Rocco standing with one leg propped onto a pedestal with his legging unwrapped to show the wound in his thigh. That's his symbol of martyrdom you know. He's pointing to it with a long, tapered finger. Behind him, an emaciated Sant'Erasmo leans against a wall dressed in a loin cloth. Ol' San Rocco has this *huge* cod-piece in the shape of a triangle of cloth with the point of the triangle hanging way down between his open legs. It's not exactly a codpiece like the Elizabethan codpieces we've all seen, but—"

Marc was beginning a soft rumble.

"And... and..." she lowered her voice, "There's a small horizontal slit in the codpiece with a string tied in a bow. Very instructive. I'm guessing it was a handy opening for when he needed to pee, don't you think?"

Marc was laughing harder but said, "I suppose. Only *you* would notice that."

"No way. It's right there in everyone's face at eye level."

Marc was sputtering.

"The explanation card states that Pordenone claimed this painting was a self-portrait dressed as San Rocco. So I'm thinking he was proud of his huge cock and wanted everyone to know about it, OR he wished he had a big one."

Then came the deep rumbling, and she wished she could lay her head against his chest.

"Wait, wait. There's more. When I looked again at Sant'Erasmo, I noticed he had one hand on his head as if holding it down. Does that have anything to do with why he was a saint?"

"Lord, I don't know," Marc said still chortling.

"Well, his other hand was inside his own loincloth. I think he was playing with himself because he was turned on by Rocco's apparatus."

Marc exploded with laughter and when he finally caught his breath, he said, "You have a dirty mind, Marlee. You *do* know that's one of the many things I appreciate about you."

"You've mentioned that before. Enough on Ol' Pordenone, what's going on with you?"

"We don't have large codpieces here, but I've spent good times with Mom and Dad and finished going through lots of stuff."

"Will you bring it with you?"

"Most of it's already at Goodwill. Don't know why I kept it."

"I understand about that. Is Katy still coming?"

He laughed. "I'm trying to convince her she doesn't need two suitcases for two weeks."

"Everyone has to learn that the hard way. And Andy?"

"Not long for our world. His old drive and toughness is draining away. It's sad to see."

"Has he been able to talk to you at all?"

"Barely. But whenever I go into his room, he seems to try to pull strength from me."

"You're so vital and have plenty to share. Wish I could absorb some this very minute."

"There you go, talking dirty again."

She laughed.

"I'll be in touch again soon, *really* in touch," he said. "*Sogni d'oro.*"

"Golden dreams to you too, love."

* * *

Sunday afternoon when Marlowe came in, Marc's voice on the recording sounded strange. She called right back even though it'd be early there.

"Hello."

"Marc, what's wrong?"

"Andy died a few hours ago. How'd you know?"

"Your voice. Tell me about it."

"I was with him. Ironically, I'd been partying with buddies from his company. It was late but I'd decided to drop in on him before I went home."

"Was he conscious?"

"I think he recognized me. I sat and talked to him about this and that. Told him about Katy and you, too. Then he sort of coughed and his monitors went crazy. An older nurse came in, looked at him, and shook her head. She said I'd just heard the death rattle. I'll be free, but, Marlee, I hate that it has to be this way."

"But, didn't Andy set it up?"

"I guess you're right. Elise came marching in within minutes. You know what she said?"

"Do I want to?"

"She glared at me and said, 'Keeping vigil, eh? You can file now, but get your own lawyer, can't use mine.'"

"Whew."

"Yeah. And here I was prepared to put my arms around her for comfort."

"I don't know what to say."

"Neither do I, but it helps to hear your warm voice."

"When's the funeral?"

"Doesn't matter. I won't go. Paid my respects while he was alive. It'll be a huge affair with his long-suffering bimbo widow and grieving daughter. Ought to be a grand show."

"You'll be back next Sunday?"

"Yep. Katy and I. It'll be good to leave that part of my life behind."

She was quiet.

"Sprout, what'd you do today?" and he yawned.

"I woke you didn't I?" she said.

"Sort of. I think I'll go back to sleep and dream of you."

"Only good ones."

"One major problem, I can't spoon your round butt and play with your buttons."

"*Fra poco, mio caro gigante, fra poco.*" Soon, my dear giant, soon.

"I can hardly wait," he said.

"Ditto," she said and he laughed aloud. His laugh was magical to her.

She sat watching the fireplace with a glass of wine in her hand and re-counted the days until he'd be back. Where would she be living then?

CHAPTER FIFTY-SEVEN

Marlowe was making toast when Paulo Parduzzi called to offer her old apartment for the rest of December at less than a third of the price she'd been paying. She told him she was on her way to look at another one and then she'd stop by. As she dipped her toast in olive oil and took a bite, she wondered if she was foolish to move out. Why not enjoy Marc as long as she could?

By the time she got to Parduzzi's office, however, she was ready to accept his offer. First, she knew the apartment, and he'd been a decent landlord. The other place was one of those absentee arrangements where she'd have to depend on an agency when—not if—something went wrong. She'd done that before and swore never again. It did have a view of a rio, a decent sink and even an oven, but the place was ugly beyond belief and filthy. It was an easy decision, that is, if she wanted to move out of Marc's.

* * *

"Paulo, do you think your Doctor Carocci was involved with the man who broke into the apartment?"

"He's not my Doctor Carocci, Marlowe. He only rented my place a couple times, but," he shook his head, "it does seem too risky to rent to him."

"*Allora*," she said, "it seems like a good arrangement for both of us."

He was pleased and added that he hadn't closed out the landline phone system for which she'd already paid an extra fee. That was another benefit for her.

"But with Signor Barovier in the States," she said, "I'm not sure how I'll transport my things back to your apartment."

"No problem, I have a friend with a boat. We can help you."

She knew Marc's cousins would help, but this seemed cleaner. They settled on Thursday, the twelfth—three days away. She'd made a good decision, and Katy would have him to herself which was important. Marc might feel rejected, but... he might feel relieved. For all his talk, not once had he mentioned any plans for "us" when he's free. Only hints and always when in lust. This way, if he decides to run, they'd both have an easier out.

* * *

"You're moving out? Angie shrieked so loud she didn't need a phone all the way from Portland.

"Yes."

"How does Marc feel about that?"

"I'll tell him next time we talk," and Marlowe explained her thinking.

"From this vantage point, I can't imagine Marc as the rejecting kind. Just because he hasn't proposed, doesn't mean he doesn't want to live with you. Hey, do you need marriage?"

Marlowe was silent.

"Marlohhh?" Angie said dragging out her name.

"Angie, I think I do. It's not the same as moving in with someone in the States. I don't have a job. Other than his family, I have only one friend and she lives an hour away. What if it doesn't work out? Where would I be then?"

"Well yeah, I see your point. But he sounds like such a dream."

"He is."

"Why dump him?"

"I'm not! But I need to have my feet on solid ground."

"What about this other guy?"

"Oh darn, don't remind me. Next week when he comes back I have to be ruthless. I already told him it's over, but he doesn't act like he heard me. I dread it. Any good advice?"

"Don't you want him waiting in the wings if Marc fades?"

"No way. Can't play that game. I'm too connected to Marc."

"When do you think you'll be coming back?" Angie said.

"I'll stay through December, maybe even into January because I told Marc I'd look into that job possibility. Who'd interview in December? And if Marc doesn't dump me, I could probably move back with him in January, which isn't all that bad. I love every minute with him."

"That's a lot of moving."

"Nah, only a couple of small suitcases plus a few things I've accumulated. Most of my stuff's in your basement. Are you eager to get rid of it?"

"Goose, I never see it. Don't worry about that. If you do stay on, though, you'll have to come back and decide what to take and what to leave."

"I know," Marlowe groaned, "but can't focus on that now. And, your love life?"

After they signed off, Marlowe knew she had to tell Marc of her decision as soon as he called. But he didn't and she chickened out about calling him.

* * *

Tuesday morning Marc called sounding excited, "Marlee, are you there? I've got news."

"I'm here. I'm here. What's up?"

"Nothing and I miss you so much it hurts… literally."

"Oh Marc, I miss you too.

"One hundred and twenty hours."

"I know."

"You counting too?" he asked.

"Of course."

"Listen up. Drum roll. You have an appointment on Tuesday afternoon the 17th."

"Of December?" she yelled. "A week from today?"

"Yes, of course."

"Really? Truly? I thought government shut down for December."

"Not this time."

"How'd you manage that? What kind of position is it? How shall I prepare?"

"Which first?"

"I did it again didn't I? Take your pick."

"A good friend from Pepperdine days has a high-ranking position over there. We see each other often, in fact he's on my ski-patrol team. He says they do need someone to teach a basic course in law as part of the undergraduate business curriculum."

Marlowe had been thinking about the idea ever since Marc mentioned the possibility. Her first thought had been to worry about maintaining control in a class of young cadets, mostly male, but she thought again. In their military situation, they might be ultra disciplined—at least on the base.

"I think I could handle that. It might be fun. You answered all three questions, unless you have more information."

"I don't, but we'll meet Chuck for lunch the day before. His work isn't in that field but he wants to meet you and will probably have more information then."

"Marc, thank you, thank you! You're always doing wonderful things for me—and *to* me I might add."

"Those are the most fun."

"You have great connections. I'm excited but shouldn't get my hopes up."

"Why not? It's time you quit buying insurance, don't you think? Besides who wouldn't want to hire you?"

"Could you be somewhat biased?"

"Maybe a little. Hell, Marlee, I'm totally biased when it comes to you, you know that."

"Do I?"

"You do."

"Then, I'll hope to get paid in Euros instead of dollars."

"Whoa, that's a tough one but maybe Chuck can pull that off too. If not, I bet there'll be compensation for any dollar-euro difference."

"Enough about me. What have you been doing in your Southern California Paradise?"

"Tennis, surfing, sailing, the usual things we *all* do *all* the time here in La La Land."

"Sounds tough."

"And you?"

"Swimming, dancing, studying. I'd been concentrating on Tort Law but I'll go back to contracts with a different eye. Wish I had my notes with me. When would classes begin?"

"Don't know. You can ask when we meet on Tuesday. Hey, why not call him yourself? He'll take your call, he knows all about you."

"Uh oh."

"Oh yeah, he knows which position you like best and that one nipple is round and the other's almond shaped and—"

She chuckled low in her throat.

"Hold on I'll give you his number."

While she waited for him to find the number, her mind was racing. Could she teach law? Yes, and she'd work her ass off to do it well. Many things to think about. Go back to Portland, find her notes, clear out Angie's place and—"

"I'll give you his full name, rank, and extension. Here it is, have a pen?" he asked.

"Thanks, Marc. It *would* help to have an idea of when I need to be ready."

"Speaking of being ready, hope you're ready for me."

"Thor, I'm always ready for you and your mighty lightning bolt."

"Talk like that makes my mouth water."

I should tell him now. Shouldn't put it off. But he's done something wonderful for me, yet again. How can I deflate it all? Tomorrow's time enough.

"You're quiet. Lots to think about, huh?"

"Maybe I can live in Venice after all. Ever since we met in San Rocco's, you've been doing wonderful things for me. How can I ever re-pay you?"

"That's no problem, love. I've learned a thing or two about business agreements, and the best are when both parties get what they want. Isn't that the basic definition of a contract?"

"Yes, it is."

"We'll trade our goods back and forth and back and forth."

"We will indeed. Maybe I'll use that concept in class."

"Jeez, one hundred and twenty more hours. Don't know if I can make it."

"Me either. Take good care of yourself, Marc."

"And you too, Sprout. Gotta go."

"Will you call tomorrow?"

"Yes, about this time."

"Tomorrow's Wednesday. I'll be going to folk dancing from seven to nine. Can you make it before or after?"

"No problem."

"I plan to keep coming out here to dance even after I'm back in Parduzzi's apartment."

"What are you talking about?"

She swallowed. She cringed at the sour taste but couldn't back down now and told him of Parduzzi's offer even mentioning she'd been looking elsewhere too.

"Wait a minute. Why are you leaving me?"

"I'm not leaving *you*, Marc." She could hear her voice rising. "Our plan from the start was for me to stay here until I could find something else."

"Yes, but—"

"Marc, it's best for you and Katy. She needs to have you all to herself and not have a strange woman competing with her."

"You're not strange. I've told her about you. Don't move, Marlee."

"I... I need to, Marc."

"You need to get away from me?"

"Please don't see it like that."

"I thought we were getting along great."

"We were, we are. I've thought a lot about this."

"I see."

"I can tell by your voice you don't. Think about Katy."

"Katy and I are fine and she's eager to meet you. I don't detect an ounce of fear over you. What are *you* afraid of, Marlee?"

"Me? Afraid?"

"Are you afraid things might not work out? You'd have no safety net?"

She was quiet.

"No safety net?" he repeated.

"Maybe something like that, I... need to know I'm on my own, not depending on you for everything."

"This job offer—"

"If."

"Yes if, but if not that one, I'll find something else to keep you in Venice."

"Marc, you've been so good and generous with everything, especially your time. It'd be too easy for me to slip into letting you take... total care of me."

He laughed but it was not his warm, comfortable rumble; it sounded harsh, even bitter. "Is that what you think I'm doing? Trying to control you?"

"No. Not you. Never you, Marc."

"You don't want to be with me that much? What have I missed here?"

"Oh my love. I *never* tire of being with you, and I miss you so much... it's complicated. We need to talk, but you need to know I'll be moving day after tomorrow."

"So, when were you going to tell me?"

"I was going to call last night but I chickened out. Then I planned to tell you first thing tonight, but your exciting news turned the tables. I'm a wimp, Marc. A loathsome wimp."

"Don't play that card, Marlee. I don't buy it."

"It's not a card. I feel lousy for not telling you as soon as Parduzzi called."

"When was that?"

"Yesterday."

He was quiet. Damn, now she'd blown it.

"Can you put him off and not move until I come back? At least I could help you move if you still feel the need."

"He offered to help me with a friend who has a boat."

"So it's all set just like that. Were you going wait to tell me after I arrived?"

"Of course not. Truly, truly I planned to tell you tonight but I couldn't puncture your wonderful balloon."

"Christ! This was not done for a glory balloon. It was for *you*. Can't you believe that?"

"I want to. It's... not something I've ever experienced before."

"Well, get used to it," and he sounded disgusted. They were silent. "I have to go, Marlee."

"Okaaay," she said with a sinking feeling.

"Ciao."

"Marc? We'll talk tomorrow?"

"I guess."

After hanging up, she stomped around wailing what have I done? What have I done? If she hadn't blurted it out like an after thought. If only she'd called him last night. If only she'd told him up front tonight. If she hadn't said that stupid thing implying he was trying to control her. What a mess she'd made all because she was afraid he'd change his mind and drop her. He was right, she did want a safety net. Would she lose him? Damn, she punched her pillow for the tenth time before finally slipping into a restless sleep.

CHAPTER FIFTY-EIGHT

The whole next day, Marlowe wondered and worried whether Marc would call. He didn't. She busied herself trying to study. She turned on the tv. She paced. By ten thirty p.m., long after she could expect his call, she went out. She moved quietly through the darkness all around the Barovier factory and living quarters and even farther afield. The quiet of a Venetian night wrapped everything in a soft cocoon, but underlying that softness was always the sound of water lapping somewhere. Venetian waters were never totally silent, always moving no matter how gently, always their sibilant sounds slipping past boats and barges tied to the sides of canals. She heard the quiet dipping of an oar from a gondolier making his last trip. Finally she felt chilled and tired enough to go back to her lonely bed hoping to fall asleep.

The next morning while swimming laps, she got an idea that made her feel more hopeful about the situation. She'd surprise Marc and Katy at the airport and maybe that would somehow show her love for him. Giovanni would know Marc's arrival time. But the urge to apologize again drove her crazy. After another lap, she decided to call Marc at four; it'd be seven in the morning in L.A. Maybe she could catch him before he was up and out.

When she left the building, she almost ran into one of Marc's friends, the one with the topaz eyes. They each apologized and went on their way. Where had she seen him recently? She remembered Marc introducing him one day at the pool; something about him niggled at her as she went on back to Marc's place.

Around three p.m., Marlowe was packing for her move when Giovanni rang the doorbell.

"Come on up, Giovanni," she said through the intercom.

"Ciao, Marlowe," he said as he reached the top step.

"I'm glad you're here. I have a favor to ask."

"*Certo*. What is it?"

"Do you know what time Marc and Katy will arrive?"

"I'm going to pick them up. Want to ride along?"

"That'd be perfect. I'd like to surprise him. We're... we're on the outs right now."

"Why is that, Marlowe?"

She told him and said, "Giovanni, I think he's angry with me."

He grinned, "He's gotten spoiled having you right here for him."

"But I've enjoyed being here. My leaving has nothing to do with not wanting to be with him, but I'm afraid he thinks so."

"Then why are you leaving?"

"See, you don't get it either," she said feeling frustrated then realized they were still standing at the door. Marlowe stepped back and gestured for him to enter. "Sorry for being inhospitable," she said. "Please come on in. Would like a coffee or tea... a beer?"

He shook his head.

"At least have a seat," she said. He took the chair and she sat on the couch.

"I think Katy should have her daddy to herself not a strange woman to compete with."

"Mm-hmm there's something to that. But what else?"

"Does there have to be anything else?"

"*Credo di si*. Yes, I believe so," Giovanni said looking directly into her eyes.

She sighed and hung her head. "You're right, there is something else. If... if things don't work out with us, where do I go? What do I do? Back in the States, if he decided to dump me, I'd have a job and a life and close friends. Here I have no job and few friends. Giovanni, I'm an outsider." She could hear the anxiety building in her voice.

Giovanni moved to the couch, sat facing her and took her hands. "It's none of my business, Marlowe, but I can not see Marc 'dumping' you. He's had bad luck with women before and you're the best one for him. And he knows it."

"He's certainly the best for me. But—"

"*Allora*," he said getting up. "You have to do what you have to do. In the meantime, I came here for something different."

"Oh, Giovanni, I'm sorry. I didn't give you a chance. What can I do for *you*?"

"I feel like a…what do you call someone who gives you something then wants it back?"

"An Indian Giver. But that's a terrible insult to American Indians, because most believed that nothing is ever owned."

"Yes, Indian Giver. Could I borrow the Goto? It was an experiment when I made it, and I want to show it to a colleague about a technical problem we're working on."

"Of course. I'll get it for you."

When she handed it to him in the box, he said, "Thanks, Marlowe, I better be off, but don't worry about Marc. You'd have to do a lot worse things than move back to your old apartment. When will you move?"

"Tomorrow."

"Do you want help?"

"Thanks, but Signor Parduzzi offered. I think he's nervous about getting no rent for the rest of the month."

"Probably," he said. "We'll talk about what time to leave for the airport on Sunday."

"Wait, let me give you my phone number," she said. He pulled out his cell.

"If I get that job, I'll have to break down and carry one of those."

"I hope you get it, Marlowe. Then maybe you could stop being an outsider."

She smiled but knew she'd have to be here forty years before that happened. "It'd be good if you'd keep the Goto for a while," she said.

"I'd like to keep it about a week."

"Perfect. Thanks for everything, Giovanni."

"It's nothing. *Abbi cura di te,* Marlowe."

"And you too, Giovanni. *Grazie.*"

Abbi cura di te, she repeated to herself. How sweet to tell her to take care of herself. No wonder Marc loves him so. God, she wanted to stay in Venice. She wanted to be a part of his family. Of everything to do with Marc. Had she ruined it all? After sharing her darkest secret, it was stupid to keep anything else from him. Why did she do that? *Stupida, stupida.*

* * *

"Hello," Marc said in a sleepy voice.

Good, she'd caught him in bed. Then she heard a woman's voice. He had someone with him! Old fears and terrible embarrassment crashed in on her. She hung up feeling frozen in place. Maybe it was best she moved. It was only four, but she poured a big slug of wine anyway and felt such deep despair. Then the phone rang.

"Marlee, are you there? Did you call me? Marlee? Pick up."

She reached for the phone but it went dead.

She walked into Marc's bedroom and looked at the domes and towers of Venice. She wanted to stay... stay with Marc. She took a deep breath, arched her back, and decided to fight for him. She turned toward the phone, but it rang again.

"Marlowe? I know you're there, what's going on? Pick up please."

"Yes, it was me. I wanted to catch you before you were out and—"

"You heard a woman's voice, right?"

She hesitated.

"And you hung up?"

"Yesss."

"You want to know who that was?"

She held her breath. It was all happening to her again!

"You heard my travel alarm with a sexy woman's voice. It was a gag gift from some of the guys at the palestra. The thing is, it works."

"I see."

"No, you don't. Just because I was upset with you, doesn't mean I'd go out and bring a woman in. Who do you think I am?"

"I think you're the most wonderful man I've ever known, that's who. It's... me."

"Sounds like it."

"Can we work on that when you get back?"

"You're still moving out on me, right?"

"It's not like that."

"Just something you have to do?"

She was quiet. He was quiet.

"Did you get hold of Chuck?"

"I did. He sounds like a man in charge. He didn't know the start of classes but said he'd get back to me. He called back within fifteen minutes. Imagine! The start date is March fourth, so if I get the job—"

"You'll get it," he interrupted.

"Maybe. I'll have time to go back to Portland and get rid of things and find my old notes. They might give me an idea of how to proceed although I've got *some* thoughts about it. Marc, I'm so excited about this chance, and once again, it's all your doing."

"It's my pleasure, Marlee. I'd like to do things for you for a long, long time."

She sighed feeling thrilled and full of hope again. "Do...you forgive me?"

"Nothing to forgive. You have to do what you do. Guess I'll have to wait until you feel safer with me."

"Oh lord, Marc, it's my demons. I owe you so much, you should start making a list."

"Marlee, you owe me nothing. But maybe I could make a list anyway," and she heard some of the old joshing slip back into his voice.

"Giovanni came by to borrow the Goto this afternoon. What a dear person. But, of course, you know that already."

"Yeah, he's a prince."

But Marlowe knew Marc was her prince. "What's on your agenda? Surfing? Tennis?" she asked, trying for more lightness.

"Not that lucky. I have another meeting with my divorce attorney and need to see Andy's personal lawyer who called me. I have no idea what that's about. Maybe another hoop Elise wants me to jump through."

"Surely not if it was Andy's personal lawyer."

"I'll find out soon enough."

"*Abbi cura di te,* that's what Giovanni said when he left. That phrase sounds sweeter in Italian."

"It does. And you'll be dancing tonight until nine, eh?"

"Yes, they dance in the evenings because most people work. If I start work, evenings would be best for me too."

"*When* you start work. And I bet you'll be involved in a lot of other things."

"IF, always the big if. But if I do get to stay, I plan to save time to keep on wandering and indulging in Venice."

"Would you save time for me?"

"Marc, you're my first priority."

"Am I?"

"You are, you are."

"Well, I'm not the one moving out."

"Please don't give up on me," she said.

"I'm running late."

"Of course," she sighed.

"*Abbi cura di te, dolcezza.*"

"*E tu, dolcezza,*" she responded.

He hung up. Ah yes, he *was* sweetness. What patience that man has with me. Maybe things will be okay after all.

CHAPTER FIFTY-NINE

"Ciao, big boy, time to get up," Marlowe said attempting a sexy Mae-West voice.

"That's the voice I want to hear every morning the rest of my life," he said.

Did he, she wondered? "Tell me your story," she asked.

"You first."

She groaned. "I won't live that down anytime soon, will I? I'm back in my old apartment, and after your elegant place, it looks tacky."

"Are you happier?"

"No."

"Marlee, we'll talk more about that when I get back. My story is I'm almost free."

"How can that be? Doesn't it take at least a year after filing?"

"Ordinarily, but without Andy knowing, we both signed separation papers two years ago. The thing is Elise never told me they'd been filed at the same time. All I need do is get the Decree of Dissolution pushed through. I'm holding my breath in case she drops one more shoe."

"She won't. I'll put the champagne on ice."

"No need for champagne. Neither of us likes it much, but maybe you can think of another way to celebrate, huh?"

"Ah, let me *count* the ways," she said.

"Shivers are running."

"And well they should for what I have planned for you," she said laughing.

"Less than seventy-two hours and I'll be back and we'll see who's planning what for whom."

"Yum, love your 'whom.' Can hardly wait for you to use it on me."

"You little tease, talking dirty when I'm already suffering. Want another piece of news? Remember Andy's private lawyer?"

"What happened?" she said as she picked up her cup from the coffee table.

"Andy left a hand-written letter and bequest. It's a nice sum. It'll be for Katy's future.

"I'd say he recognized your natural integrity from the start."

"Don't know about that, but I'm touched by his letter. You can read it. Makes me think this was for my sticking power, and now I'm wondering if he knew all along."

"Maybe you were the son he always wanted. Obviously, he respected you. Take pride in that, Marc."

"Thanks, Sprout, I think I will."

"I'm curious about the legal aspects. Was this bequest outside of the trust Andy had for his wife and daughter?"

"Yes, with an expressed provision to prevent anyone from foiling his intentions."

"I remember something like that; it might be interesting to mention to my students."

"Hey, glad they're your students now."

"Sometimes," she said.

"I moved today too. Closed out the place I've kept and will stay with Mom and Dad. They have plenty of space for a few things, and I do emphasize *few*."

"How do your folks feel about you staying in Europe?"

"Fine. They're Europeans after all."

"They sound so accepting, I'm eager to meet them." But Marlowe wondered if they'd accept her. Even though Marc and Marlowe had known each other briefly five years ago, they'd only been together a couple months.

"They're curious about you. And, of course, Mom worries since I haven't made the best choices in women—until now."

Marlowe didn't miss those two words. "How much do they know?" she asked.

"Let's see. I told them I've been seeing a wicked wench from the States who hit Venice running, vamped her way through most of the eligible men in town, even a police man, and probably her landlord, too, before settling on me... temporarily."

She yelped. "Marc, is that how you see me?"

"You did start with Tron. Where does he stand with you these days?"

"First off, I was properly introduced to him by Carla; basically he's a good person, but things between us hadn't been good before he left for the States—about a week before you. Wait a sec! Didn't think you gave a rip about whether I saw him or not."

"Hmm."

"Anyway, because of you, I can't see him anymore. We hadn't been close for about a month anyway and I tried—"

"Being close. Is that another word for sex?"

"Yes," she admitted feeling embarrassed.

"It's not like you to be coy, Marlee. But go on, what did you try?"

"Before he left, I told him I couldn't see him anymore but he didn't want to hear that."

"I wouldn't give up either," Marc said.

"He knows about us and the last time he called from the States, I was in your apartment. Our conversation was impersonal. I've been tempted to let it go at that, but I know the only way is to make a clean break. Guess I'll have to be ruthless."

"Sprout, I appreciate your frankness. And by the way, I did and *do* give a huge rip whether you see him or anyone else."

"Good."

"Good? You want me in pain?"

"No... I want you."

"Marlee, my love."

* * *

Marlowe and Carla were shown to a window table the moment they walked into Remigio's.

"What's happening in Pordenone?"

"Very little. Compared to you, Franco and I live quiet lives.

"I came here for quiet times and thanks to *you*, things got complicated."

"You're blaming me, I see," she grinned.

Marlowe shook her head, "No, it's been a fine ride."

"You talk as if it's over."

"Not with Marc I hope."

"Rich?"

Marlowe shook her head as the waiter brought their wine and bread and took their orders.

They sipped wine in silence. "Don't feel glum, Marlowe. Marc won't drop you."

"To tell the truth, if we do live together, I'm not sure I want us to be in his place."

"The family thing?" Carla asked.

"Not at all. They do know how to respect each other's privacy. More a space thing. I need a room of my own. A desk, a computer and space for books and files. Never had that with Ty even when I went back to school. *He* had a home office, but my little desk was crammed into our bedroom although I was the one who also took care of bills and records. Guess a separate room has become a symbol to me."

"Like Virginia Woolf?"

"You've read *A Room of One's Own*?"

Carla nodded. "When I was in England. And my Kismet partners have read it too. By the way, you'll be pleased to know they understood Woolf's essay better than I—the part about women needing money. They're crazy about your idea of a calendar with us belly dancing."

"Really?"

"I feel embarrassed for criticizing your idea so quickly. We don't have time to organize it for the spring show, but we're already planning for next time."

"I'll be your first customer," Marlowe said, "put me down for at least ten!"

As they were finishing up, Marlowe asked Carla where she could find a business suit and shoes. "The same places," Carla said. "No wait, there is a shop in Mestre just across the causeway. You can take a bus directly from Piazzale Roma, " and she wrote down the name and how to find the boutique from the second bus stop in Mestre.

"To my rescue again," Marlowe said raising her glass to Carla. The waiter came over thinking they wanted more. They both shook their heads. As they walked out, Marlowe couldn't resist asking Carla about San Rocco's codpiece.

"You noticed?" Carla giggled.

"*Certo, Signora, certo. Non sono cieco,*" Marlowe said chuckling too.

"You're not blind, that's for sure. One more question. What will you tell Riccardo?"

Marlowe sighed. "The simple truth. My heart is with Marc. I do hope Rich can shed his demons and find someone. He deserves a good woman in his life."

"He does," Carla said nodding.

"Carla, maybe you can find someone for him."

"No. Not again!" and she shook her head waving her hands back and forth palms out as they walked. "Here we are. I won't be at the Marciana much longer, I do have the job and—"

"Carla, that's terrific." Marlowe pulled her into a huge hug rocking her into a little circle dance, mimicking Marc's sweeping circles. God she missed that man.

"It's only a matter of crossing the t's and—"

"Dotting the i's," Marlowe interrupted. "I'm happy for you, but I'll miss our lunches."

"Not for a while."

"*Buona Fortuna,* Carla. Let me know the minute all the t's are crossed."

* * *

"Forty-eight hours and I'll be on my way home," Marc said.

"I can't wait to have you back."

"I'm ready, Sprout. What have you been doing today?"

"After lunch with Carla, I went looking for an interview suit."

"Any luck?"

"Not here but she told me of a shop in Mestre. Tomorrow I'll see what I can find. With all those snappy uniforms at the base, I want to appear professional, at least for the interview."

"New outfit or not, Marlee, as I remember, you interview well," Marc said.

"Thanks, but I wish I knew how to answer questions about teaching. Let's change the subject, I'm getting nervous. Tell me about Katy. I bet she's excited."

"She seems subdued."

"Probably the jitters," Marlowe said.

"She hasn't met her cousins, actually second cousins."

"Haven't any been to the States?"

"Not her age. She knows Giovanni, but he's more like a brother to me and has become her *zio*, uncle. I've shown pictures and talked about the younger cousins, but it's probably a scary experience."

"But you'll be right there with her every step of the way."

"I'd hoped you'd be with us."

"I will be most of the time. By the way, I can meet Chuck myself if you don't want to leave her alone that first day back."

"Won't be necessary. The family will take her under their wing, and also when I slip away for 'quality time' with you. Do I have an invitation to your place after lunch with Chuck?"

"Absolutely. The red carpet's ready to be unrolled as we speak.

I'll be in a red satin gown made for the occasion and have sent out for a fatted calf and—"

"Don't bother with the carpet or calf and certainly not the gown. Wench, that pilfered Heathman robe with nothing underneath sounds—"

"It's not pilfered."

He laughed softly. "Okay, okay, but my mouth waters thinking about pulling that sash."

"Me too."

"Gotta go. Katy's calling. She's learning fast to tell me what to wear, where to go and what to eat. *Abbi cura di te.*"

"*E tu anche, mio adorato.*"

"Am I?" he asked.

"Did I say something wrong?"

"Am I your beloved?" he asked.

"Oh yes. You are," she whispered.

* * *

She found a crisp black suit with a pencil slim skirt that came to mid-knee with a short jacket for her short body. She couldn't believe her luck when the clerk brought out a white silk blouse with a small lapel that seemed made for the jacket. She also bought more panty hose and found a pair of sheer black ones for the frisky dress Marc had bought. The panty part had a skimpy opaque area with lacy scallops running from the crotch to the top of her hip bone. Sexy but it did cover the essentials should the kicky skirt flip up while dancing. If there would be dancing, she wanted to be ready knowing Marc would be a marvelous dancer. She also found a pair of black leather pumps with small heels for the suit. Except for parties, no more *tacchi alti* for her; she would not wear high heels again.

CHAPTER SIXTY

The look on Marc's face when he saw Marlowe at the airport told her what she wanted to know. His eyes widened and filled with liquid silver—his unique look of molten desire. Marlowe was ecstatic. He drew her to him with one arm while his other rested on Katy's shoulder. What a little beauty she was with olive skin, shiny dark hair cut in a smooth bob and bangs that feathered her forehead. Her mother's coloring, but she had her father's silvery-grey eyes that took on a blue glow from her electric-blue sweater. Her matching coat was wrapped around the handle of her carry-on bag, also a brilliant blue. In her blue phase no doubt.

"Marlowe, this is my favorite daughter, Katy."

"Daddy, you're silly," but she giggled in delight.

"Katy, I'm so glad you came to Venice," Marlowe said bending to give her a small hug.

"Ciao, Marlowe," she said and hugged back.

Marlowe was relieved Katy hadn't pulled away. Then Giovanni swooped in to pick her up and turn around in a little circle dance.

"Oof, girl, you've gotten big. How did that happen?"

"Zio Giovanni, you're as silly as Daddy."

Giovanni took her hand speaking Italian as they walked ahead, and Marc pulled Marlowe into an alcove. He held her as if he'd never let her go; his kiss was possessive, demanding and tender all at once. It sucked the air from her lungs, and she wished it could last forever.

"Marlee," he said, "in my arms again. Right where you belong."

"Hey you two, none of that," Giovanni said and turned toward Katy standing beside her blue bag. "You were right, Katy. They were smooching in the corner."

"You're darned right," Marc said. "I told Katy I was starved for a Marlowe hug."

"You're blushing, Marlowe," Giovanni laughed. "Serves you right for dragging Marc behind the posts."

And so it went. A joyful homecoming. Marlowe wouldn't have missed it for anything. Giovanni announced they were all expected at *i nonni's* place for a buffet dinner with as many family members as could make it.

"Giovanni, I can catch a vaporetto—"

"*Everyone* is expected, and that includes you Marlowe. Nonno Angelo and Nonna Chiara have been scolding Marc for not bringing you by and made it clear he must share you today."

"But it's Katy's day."

"Don't worry, she'll get plenty of attention. You'll see. Here's our launch."

* * *

When they entered his grandparents' home—already filled with other family members—Marc beamed. It was clear having his daughter by his side made him feel complete.

Angelo and Chiara were beautiful. He was brawny with steady emerald eyes that pierced straight to her core. She'd never be able to side step a query from him. His hair was thick and wavy. That marvelous salt and pepper so many Italian men have. What a handsome man and when he opened his arms, Marlowe found herself flowing into his embrace.

"*Tu adori il nostro Marco?* Do you adore our Marc?" he whispered in a growl.

"*Si, si. Lui è adorato completamente,* yes, yes, he is adored completely."

He howled with laughter and grabbed her in a squeeze that lifted her off her feet and turned in a circle. These Barovier men had a habit of picking up their women and doing a jig, and Marlowe loved it all. Those around him wanted to know what that was all about, but he wagged his index finger at them and said, "*Il nostro segreto,* our secret."

When she had said Marc was adored completely, it must have had a naughty connotation. Whatever it was, it tickled Angelo.

Sandra and other wives were arranging platters of antipasti and hunks of bread on a large table. Jugs of wine sat on a sideboard. Sandra took her by the hand and led her into a room that reminded Marlowe of her Aunt Ruby's farm kitchen in Nebraska. How far away it seemed right now. She met Chiara, who was stirring a cauldron of tomato sauce that smelled so good Marlowe wanted to dive in. Chiara was what Marlowe had always thought an Italian matron would be but much taller. She had at least three maybe four inches on Marlowe. Her hair was as white as sugar and piled on top of her head into a kind of knot like a soft crown. Her cheeks were smooth and rosy from the steam, although Marlowe guessed that was her usual skin tone. She ruled her kitchen but was soft spoken about it with her daughters, daughters-in-laws and granddaughters. Marlowe couldn't keep them all straight but felt comfortable with that.

Chiara also opened her arms to Marlowe; she felt embraced by the whole family. She knew it wasn't about her, still, it felt good. Chiara spoke excellent English. Like Carla, she'd spent time in England as a young girl. Marlowe wondered why her year in Venice hadn't stood her as well with the Italian language and rationalized that it was because most Europeans were exposed to more than one language from the beginning—if only a dialect.

"It's about time I met you. Some of Marco's women have been unkind. Maybe he worried I'd be critical of his next one. With a beautiful man like Marco, there are always women.

Marlowe nodded.

"I hear good things about you from Giovanni and Sandra. Let me look at you." She held Marlowe apart and took her time appraising her with grey-blue eyes, not unlike Marc's when he wore blue, although she was covered by a pale lavender smock.

She took Marlowe's hand and turned her around. "You are a little one." Was she thinking scrawny? She felt like a prospective hen for the stew pot.

"Marco is large in stature and also in spirit; he can be overwhelming."

Marlowe nodded and smiled. "But, Signora," and she put her hands on Chiara's forearms, "at times he can also be a small boy. You know?"

"Yes," Chiara smiled. "You understand that?"

Marlowe nodded.

"Good," she said and pulled her in for another hug.

"And now it's time to eat. *Mangia, mangia,*" she said and clapped her hands. First, the children were settled with their own antipasti, juice and soft drinks at a long picnic-style table set in a glassed-in area near the kitchen. She saw some of the girls acing each other out in order to sit next to Katy and felt happy for her. Then the feast began.

Marc appeared at her elbow. "This will go on for a few hours. Pace yourself, Sprout."

"Thanks for the tip, Marc, but I'd be happy just with Nonna's tomato sauce."

Later she was able to be of use to the women in clearing away, stacking and scraping dishes. It was fun to mix in with them, and she picked up new phrases here and there amidst their comfortable chatter. At coffee time, Sandra showed her a cupboard where the cups and saucers were kept. The kids had disappeared, gone to Mestre to a movie someone said; only one movie house was left in Venice. Time for Marlowe to slip away. She went to find Marc knowing he'd balk but was determined to not keep him from Katy on her first night here. She caught his eye and signaled that she wanted to talk to him in the kids' eating area.

"I know what this is about," he said when he walked in, "and I want to cut it off at the pass. You're going to stay with me. Katy has her own room on the other side of the apartment."

"Marc, no." She pulled his hands from her shoulders and kissed the palms. "Another time. But not her first night with you in your place. *We* have to be the grownups here."

"I don't like being grownup," he said and at that moment he did remind her of a little boy as his lower lip almost pooched into a pout.

She laughed.

"What's so funny? You don't understand how hard it's been on me away from you."

"Don't I? You're not the only one who's horny around here."

"It's harder for me."

She broke out in a guffaw and said, "I should hope." Some of the family turned to see what was going on. When they saw her laughing, they went back to their conversations.

"If you insist," he said. "But I'll take you back in the launch."

"Nice try, Thor. Tempting too, but you need to be here with all the other parents when she and her cousins return. There's a perfectly good vaporetto down the street. Walk there with me?"

"You drive a hard bargain. I've been counting the hours—"

"So have I, my love. So have I. Can you arrange a fun evening for Katy tomorrow night?"

"Taken care of."

"Good. Let me say my thank yous and get my jacket."

* * *

They kissed over and over waiting at the vaporetto stop until Marc saw the boat approach. "Now, down to business," Marc said. "Tomorrow we're going to meet Chuck at Corte Sconta, he was very specific about where we'd have lunch."

"He's no dummy, it's got zabaglione." He laughed and swirled her in a half circle.

"What time shall I be there?" she asked.

"I'll come for you at twelve-thirty, and we'll meet him at one."

"I can easily meet you there."

"NO."

"Okay, okay," and she put up her hands in surrender. "I'll be ready for you."

"Jeez, I can hardly wait for *that*," he said as the vaporetto nudged the pontile.

"Me too." She stood on tiptoe to grab his collar and pull him down for one more kiss. "Marc, I'm glad to have you back. Before you walked back into my life, I loved being in Venice alone, but now I don't like alone! It's all your doing."

"Good." With another hug, he said, "I'll be a grownup for twenty-four hours—or less."

CHAPTER SIXTY-ONE

"Chuck is formidable isn't he," Marlowe said as they left the restaurant.

"How do you mean?"

"Well, there's a mystique about a military man, of course. And then his size—almost as big as you."

Marc smiled. "Lots of men are as big as me."

"He's attractive in a stern, assertive way with dark hair, straight black brows and trim mustache. At first, those icy, sapphire eyes seemed scary. Made me think of a wolf, but then he smiled revealing that big dimple and seemed less intimidating, more—"

"Charming?" Marc said. "I'll tell him you said he should show his dimple more often so women will fall at his feet."

"Don't you dare. Besides, I'm sure he has no trouble with women."

Marc was quiet. He knew for a fact that Chuck had plenty of women, but it was interesting to hear a new point of view about his good friend.

"He was pleasant," Marlowe went on, "a bit patronizing, but I expected that. Chuck's in a power position to help me and knows it."

"You really see him that way?"

She nodded. "But if you respect him, he's got to be a good man. I suspect that unless I mess up royally, I'll get the job whether I deserve it or not."

"If so, who cares? People get jobs because of who they know all the time."

"It's never happened for me; it feels odd. But if they offer it, I'll take it," she said raising a fist in the air as they walked onto the pontile. "It'll be a dream come true to live in Venice. The thing is, he's got to be sure I won't embarrass him; already he has serious doubts."

"How's that?"

"When I came back from the ladies room, I heard him say 'Where in the hell did you find her?' Don't be surprised if I get a call tomorrow morning saying the position's filled."

"What? Oh, he did say something like that. Guess you didn't hear him say 'I want one just like her.'"

"Honest?"

Marc nodded. "I've known Chuck for years. There's no doubt he was impressed with you regarding the position, and I *know* he's envious of me for having you in my life."

"Still, he's got to feel absolutely secure about me, since you're his friend."

"He's probably had people working on that before today," Marc said tousling her hair.

"I guess I want it too much. What if—"

"No what ifs. Here's your vaporetto, go home and stop worrying. I'll come to you as soon as Katy and I do our tourist thing at Burano. I promised we'd go there on the first sunny day, and this is it. She's not one to put things off."

"No doubt she read about the rainbow houses over there. For sure, their colors dazzle the eyes in the sunshine."

"But the hours keep adding up before we can be alone together. I'm dying for you."

She reached up to touch his lips with her fingers. "I'll be ready."

He groaned.

* * *

As Marlowe hung her suit and smoothed the blouse for tomorrow's afternoon interview, the phone rang.

"Pronto."

"Pronto yourself," Rich said.

"You're back?"

"I'm at the airport with Jeri, my daughter. Wonder if I could stop by this evening."

"That won't be possible and tomorrow night's busy too, but...I could see you on Wednesday for coffee or lunch. I'd like to meet Jeri, but we do need to talk."

"I see."

She ignored that leaden remark. "Tomorrow I'll be tied up all day and into the evening. I'll be interviewing for a job to teach basic law at the post in Vicenza."

"That's amazing, Marlowe. How did it happen?"

"Marc knew someone over there and—"

"Barovier again, eh?"

She didn't respond.

"Would you call me about a place that suits you on Wednesday?" he said.

"I'll do that."

"Ciao, Marlowe."

He was getting the picture. If she never called him back, she could probably let it drop, but no, it would hang over both their heads. Damn. She thought she'd taken care of it at that pizza place. She dreaded that final lunch. But now, something else was on her mind, and she began humming as she turned on the shower.

CHAPTER SIXTY-TWO

Marlowe watched the clock as she waited for Marc. Finally she heard the knock on her door. *"Chi è?"* she called.

"I'm looking for two perfect, brown buttons."

"Do you have a legal instrument for an effective search?" she said easing the door a crack.

"Very effective and my instrument needs validating... now," Marc said as he kicked the door shut and scooped her into his arms in one decisive motion. He strode up the steps and set her on her feet throwing his coat in the direction of the couch all the while never taking his eyes from her. "Too much on as usual," he said inching away the sash of her robe. It too landed somewhere near the couch.

She stood basking in his adoration.

"Oh Babe." He feathered his large hands over her face and then on to the swell of her breasts. Gentle in his caresses, as always.

No matter how many times they made love, she was seduced by him anew and filled with a flaming hunger every single time. As soon as she was near him and his magnificent body, she trembled with excitement and wanted him. Would it always be this way? He held her breasts, savoring their weight in his palms, and began to sip and suckle one and then the other.

"Marlee," he growled softly. One palm cradled the back of her head while the other pressed her against him. She could feel his erection growing and also a throbbing between her own legs. The roughness in his mustache moved across her lips, and the velvety-rough texture of his tongue slipped inside like melted chocolate. She drew it in whimpering with arousal. He groaned, "It's been too long. Too long."

"I knowww." She began to unbutton his soft flannel shirt. "You, Signore, are the one with too many clothes." She pushed the shirt back and pulled at the sleeves as he fumbled to unfasten his belt. But then he lifted her breasts to his lips again and began suckling them. She felt intoxicated.

"Why are we standing here?" he asked leading her to her bedroom.

In anticipation, she'd already removed the heavy spread on her bed. He stripped off the rest of his clothes as if they burned his skin. She lay on her back waiting. My God, look at him all powerful, all male and all ready. She felt wetness gather as she watched. Crouching over her he leaned down to claim her mouth with a masculine hunger that threatened to drown her—no not drown, swallow her whole. His mustache raked her lips tantalizing her nerve endings and when he thrust his tongue inside, it was like penetrating her vagina. She almost came right then. Then he slid a hand leisurely along her inner thigh sending more electric sensations to her very center.

* * *

Her skin felt soft, like hot silk. He wasn't sure how long he could hold off tonight, but he needed her to want him more than ever. He still feared she'd slip away from him in an effort to establish some kind of independence or even try to prove herself back in the States! He lowered his mouth to her breast taking in as much as he could and began to suckle in earnest. When he looked up, he saw her eyes widen with pleasure. God he loved how responsive she was to him. Switching his attention to her other breast, his palm continued to stroke up her leg moving ever closer to the heat of her triangle. He licked and nuzzled her nipple scraping it lightly with his teeth. She shuddered sending tremors through his body. He felt his blood surging in his cock to almost bursting. His gaze held her eyes as he slipped his finger into the hot wetness of her silken sheath. She arched her back and her inner muscles clamped down on his finger as she pushed for release. He felt the first ripple of pleasure spread through her belly and down her thighs.

Her orgasm inflamed him, and he gritted teeth in an effort to keep himself from coming apart. Their separation and his fears of losing her before he got back were still in his mind. He had to put his stamp on her so she'd never want another man again. Damn, he'd never felt this possessive of a woman and needed to be careful about that with her. He strained to slow everything down wanting this to last.

"Marlee, I'll never get enough of you," he said and slowly kissed his way back to her swollen mouth savoring her sweetness.

"The more we make love, the hotter we are together," she whispered.

He couldn't speak, his heart was hammering too much. He covered her mouth with another kiss and lay his hand over her dark triangle to feel her heat and moisture. "I love that little black patch. I want to taste you. Now."

He left her lips to kiss and nip his way down the side of her neck moving to her breasts where he lingered only briefly then on to her small belly button where he swirled his tongue around inside and waited for her to shiver and shimmy. When she did, he chuckled to himself, but unrelenting, he nipped her round, sexy little belly and hated scar before continuing his downward journey. His hands nudged her thighs apart then he moved in to feast on her dark Vee.

"Marc," she gasped. He picked up momentum and licked and suckled and tasted her spicy nectar. He pressed his mouth inward and thrust his tongue into her core. She arched her back, and he was surprised to feel another orgasm rip through her. A terrible lust overtook him. He suckled her like a starving man. When his tongue found her clit, he stroked it over and over until it was swollen and pulsing. She cried out. "Marc," she pleaded, "take me." She sounded desperate. Her head thrashed back and forth and her hands fisted into his hair. "Now!" But he was determined to make her want him more than ever. To want *only* him. He held her thighs wider and drove his tongue deep, seeking that special taste again. By now, he knew where and how to touch her. She arched her body into him nearly as insane with arousal as he was. He knew what he was doing, and for the first time, realized this is how he wanted her—wild and wanton. Again he inserted two long fingers inside Marlowe's silky layers. She was like a flower in full bloom, and when her muscles squeezed and clamped down on his fingers, he couldn't wait for those satiny petals to clamp his cock. He raised onto his knees and dragged her toward him, then lifted her hips and buried himself in her sheath—hot and slick and ready for him. Her scent was in his nostrils driving him on, as he plunged in deeper and deeper.

* * *

She felt every stroke of his burning shaft—marble hard—as it filled and stretched her carrying that white hot fire inward. She loved that Marc always made sure she was ready for him, and that he made her feel beautiful and feminine. She'd never thought she'd want or enjoy rough sex, but with their lust for each other taking over, she recognized a suppressed urge coming forward to go further in sex than she'd ever gone. And now she was taking this wild ride with him, wanting him to hammer into her again and again. She tossed her head and bucked her hips pushing to meet his madness and bring him to *his* finish, wanting to carry him away the same way he was carrying her... over the edge. His heavy shaft stroked over her inflamed swollen bud again and again.

He eased into a tantalizing slow-motion glide sending her every cell into orbit. The exquisite pleasure of their two separate bodies melding into one seemed to lift her from reality. But involuntarily, her muscles brought her back to earth. They clamped around his thick cock in an erotic vise. And her orgasm tore through her body surging through her stomach and into her breasts, down her thighs and into her toes as wave after wave hit her. The bliss was beyond her wildest dreams.

* * *

Her wild response was more than he'd expected and ignited the latent lust he'd tamped down for years—maybe forever. He should have waited until her last spasms subsided, but it was too late; a raging tide swept him to one last convulsive thrust. And jet after jet of hot semen poured into her touching off another small eruption deep inside her. Her inner muscles contracted around him in an ancient, automatic rhythm—the trick she denied even knowing. Connected deeply enough to feel her release on the most intimate level, he felt complete for the first time. At last he fell on her. It had been more pleasure than he'd ever known.

His heavy body was like a comforting blanket that wrapped Marlowe in a safe place and kept her from breaking into a thousand pieces. She wanted him to stay forever.

"Can you breathe, Sprout?" he asked but didn't wait for an answer and rolled off pulling her into the hollow of his shoulder in one tender motion. They lay panting. Both hearts pounded as both quietly processed what had happened.

"A wild ride," she gasped. "Welcome back, Thor." He grunted and sighed as he spooned around her cupping a breast in one hand before disappearing into the first deep sleep he'd had for an age. She breathed a self-satisfied sigh knowing she was exactly where she wanted to be. She too drifted, but it wasn't long before she felt him begin to harden again.

He whispered, "I've been longing to hold you like this. Planned we'd do this first, but I couldn't wait. I needed you too much. Need you again."

"Need you too," she whispered.

"I want to make love to you slowly, Marlee. To make it last and last, but you turn me on so much I may erupt before I can begin again."

"We have all night don't we?"

"God, I hope so."

She felt his cock swell and press against her. She smiled to herself pleased to be the cause of that incredible growth. She was sore but could hardly wait to have him inside again. Then he kissed her neck and tongued her ear. She was startled to note how closely connected her ear was to her cunt. Before Marc, she'd never known about her ear/cunt connection and felt a self-satisfied grin spread across her face. With Marc, every part of her seemed connected to that one place. He turned her to face him and began to kiss and sip every inch from her neck to one breast then the other. She felt herself melting again and arched up to reach for his cock, but he moved away not letting her near it. He continued to caress her, lapping at her navel and nipping at her belly all the way to the top of her entrance again. Then he began to lick and suck all around her clit until she felt herself dissolve into his mouth.

"You're wet for me again."

"Yes," she whispered. "Yes, I am." And his penis was hard and heavy again. In the dim light she saw how thick and long it was. "You're so big."

"I was inside you an hour ago."

"But I didn't see how big you were then."

He laughed, "Then look away."

"But I like to look at you."

"Oh Marlee. How did I ever find you?" Then he began a slow descent. "We'll take it nice and slow this time." She could hardly wait to be filled again. As he eased inside, he moved his thumb pad over her clitoral area and with each deepening nudge of his cock, he feathered that little nub.

"Yes, yes. Fuck me." But instead, he slowly pulled out.

"Marc!"

"Did I hurt you?"

"No. Come back." He moved inside again with more force carrying him further, deeper until her outer lips were drawn back to expose her clit. She felt stretched to her limit but wanted more. Leaning forward to take a nipple into his mouth, he sucked hard continuing to fill her inch by inch.

"Take all of me, Marlee, all of me," he pleaded. His head was buzzing and his cock was about to burst out of his skin. "I'm going to fuck you, Babe, I'm going to... fuck... you... now."

At that moment, her body went rigid. Her inner muscles clamped down on his shaft burning and squeezing like nothing he'd ever felt. In slow motion, a total fusion of their sensual energies brought them both over the edge, no ladies first this time. He was sure he'd never experienced such an outpouring before as he rode wave after wave of electric ripples that radiated in all directions throughout his body. At last, he emptied liquid fire into her and cried, "Marlee, milk me. Milk me dry!"

* * *

Later when their breathing had calmed down, he turned her on her side and curled behind her again. "Spoons," she murmured.

"Hmm?" he asked. "Yes, spoons. Every night in California, I fantasized this," he said cupping her breast in his hand. "Kept thinking about this moment all the way across the Atlantic." She sighed and snuggled back against him.

"Marlee, this is what I want forever."

She was quiet.

"Do you understand what I'm saying?"

"I think so, love."

They slept. The luminous numbers on her bedside clock showed 6:00 a.m. and they made lazy love once more and dozed until the alarm went off at eight. She wanted to catch a train for Vicenza at ten. Chuck had given her explicit directions but she wasn't taking any chances and allowed extra time to find the correct bus from Vicenza to the base for her two o'clock.

CHAPTER SIXTY-THREE

On the 5:15 back to Venice, Marlowe was elated. Here was a time when she wished she had a cell phone. The interview had felt so positive; she could hardly wait to tell Marc all about it. There was the waiting, of course, to learn if she got the job and… another waiting for Marc to propose. He'd been proposing in one way or another already. Why did she need those explicit words? But she did. The train wheels clicked louder and louder. As the carriage swayed and bumped, it felt as if the wheels had become square and were about to fall off the tracks. What was wrong? Was the train coming apart? Abruptly, the wheels felt round again and the train slid softly into the Padua station.

Was Marc waiting for that final decree? How would he feel when it came through? She sat up straight and took a large breath. One thing she knew, she'd stay in his arms as long as he wanted her, and after last night, she had no doubt he wanted her. But if he couldn't face another commitment, with this job—she forced herself to *not* cross her fingers—she could find her own apartment and still have one dream, life in Venice.

The minute the train screeched to a halt in Venice, she rushed to the vaporetto stop for home. It had seemed promising, still it *was* a government operation. She remembered how a State job she'd wanted had slipped away. After all the interviews were over, she'd learned someone else already had it in her pocket. But, to fulfill certain regulations, they had put the rest of the applicants through the process. She had a hunch it was her turn this time. To hell with buying insurance! To hell with magical thinking! Let it all happen. Let it happen with Marc, too.

* * *

"Congratulations, Sprout, when will it be official?"

"In about two weeks. I don't have it yet but..."

"You will. In the meantime, how about joining Katy and me at the ol' swimming hole? I want to hear all the details in person."

"Sounds wonderful. When?"

"Now, silly. Oops, I sound like Katy. And pack a few overnight things."

"Are you sure?"

"Positive. Katy says it's silly you aren't staying here. Who am I to argue with my wise daughter? Bring your dancing shoes, too. She wants to try folk dancing tomorrow night."

"Whew. Eleven years old. I'll be there as soon as I change my clothes."

As she stuffed things into her backpack, she remembered Rich and the lunch tomorrow. Damn. She'd think about that later and jammed the card with his and all her other phone numbers into her money belt. A cell phone was sounding more and more useful every minute.

She could hardly wait to be with Marc. Thank you Aunt Belle! She'd call her soon. She grabbed the door and found Rich there with his hand raised to knock.

"Ciao, Rich. I'm on my way out." It wasn't fair that he was such a gorgeous man. He wore a beige coat with a dark-brown scarf about his neck. His thick, dark hair had grown longer and curled over his collar in a sexy line. And those espresso eyes looked at her with... a deep longing.

"Yes, I see that. Do you have a minute for me?"

"Of course," and she turned with the key in hand. "Come on in. Coffee? "

"No. This won't take long."

She tossed her stuffed backpack on the couch along with her coat and turned to take his.

"I'll leave it on, Marlowe."

"Okaaay."

"You're off to spend the night with Barovier," he said. It was not a question.

"My swimsuit's in here. We're going swimming with his daughter, Katy, in a pool some of the glass makers built. They renovated an old factory into a gym and put in a pool and—"

"Relax, Marlowe. I've known about that pool for years."

"Sorry."

"It's okay." He inhaled slowly. "Let me take the pressure off. I've seen which way things were going. I resisted but... I know I lost you some time ago."

She couldn't look at him. He put his hand under her chin and lifted her face. "I'm sorry, Rich," she said as tears welled up.

"I know you are. Me too. You gave me a wake up call, though. I saw a therapist when I was home."

"That sounds good."

"It's a start. Wish I'd done it before I met you."

She couldn't speak. A few weeks ago, she might have wished that. But now?

"How'd the interview go today?" he asked.

"I have high hopes."

"That's wonderful. When will you know for sure?"

"Not for at least two weeks."

"If you stay in Venice, we'll probably see each other from time to time."

She nodded.

"I hope we can be easy with each other."

"Yes Rich... we can. Of course we can."

"Glad I caught you. You won't have to worry about calling me for a sad little lunch."

When he said that a few tears slipped out. "Thanks for coming by."

He nodded and went out the door. She noticed the shopping cart in the corner, but now was not the time. After he was well out of sight, she left for Murano. She felt both sorrow and tremendous relief and wanted Marc to know what a mensch Riccardo Tron was.

* * *

Katy was a little fish and while she played in the water, Marc and Marlowe sat on the edge of the pool and she told him of Rich's visit.

"Marc, I was not cool. I babbled. He told me to relax, that he'd seen how things were going and wanted to let me know he knew it was over."

Marc nodded.

"He thanked me, though, for the wake-up call. When he was home, he saw a therapist."

"A therapist? What'd you do to the poor man?"

She reached down and splashed water on him. "You dope, I didn't do anything to him. But sometimes out of the blue he'd withdraw or get defensive and make me wrong. I told him I would not walk on eggs ever again."

Marc was quiet.

"When he said, 'You won't have to worry about calling me for a sad little lunch,' I almost lost it."

"That must have been difficult for him, but... I'm not sorry he lost you."

They were quiet letting their feet dangle in the water. "Marc, I have a bone to pick with you."

"What about?" he asked turning her to face him.

"You had someone follow me the day you went to Frankfurt, didn't you?"

"How'd you find out?" She told him about seeing one of his friends near her apartment but it took her awhile to tumble to who he was and why he'd been standing there. "He wasn't much good at surveillance," she said with a little chuckle.

"I was frantic about your decision and almost cancelled my flight but figured you'd be more angry if I stayed, so I called a couple friends. I didn't know what else to do. I couldn't let you get hurt again. They—"

"Two?" she said.

He nodded. "They may not have been good at undercover work, but I know they would have kept you safe." Then Marc snorted, "Maybe their ineptness kept the creep away!"

"At first I was disgusted that you didn't trust me."

"Had nothing to do with trusting *you*, Marlee."

"I know. I was stupidly stubborn, and I'm grateful you cared enough to worry."

He pulled her close to him.

Then Katy came over giggling and shook water on them changing their mood. They went for pizza and then home. Even Katy admitted she was tired. When she said, '*Buona notte* have a good sleep together,' Marlowe looked at him. He shrugged, held his palms up with a big, foolish grin on his face. As they got in bed, Marc asked her to tell him more about her day in Vicenza.

"What's next?" he asked.

"The waiting game, but I think I've got it."

"Terrific. We need to celebrate."

"And something tells me you have an idea of how to do that."

CHAPTER SIXTY-FOUR

Wednesday morning, Marlowe invited Marc to join Katy and her at the Accademia."

"Can't," Marc said, "but call me when you're finished. I might take you two beautiful ladies for lunch."

"That's an idea, right Katy?" Marlowe said grinning.

"Righteo," she said. "But this time, not pizza, Daddy. Something special, okay?" She was wearing navy-blue slacks and her electric-blue sweater and jacket to match.

"Si, si, Signorina," he said making a bow sweeping his hand almost to the floor.

Later as Marlowe and Katy settled in the back of a vaporetto, Katy asked, "Will there be like any paintings by Michelangelo or da Vinci in the Accademia?"

"None. They're all Venetian and far too many for one day. Here's what I suggest we do; see what you think. For sure we'll see your Veronese, and I want to show you Titian's *Presentation in the Temple* because that exact same scene was also done by Tintoretto. But Tintoretto's Presentation is in a church way across town. We'll have to go there another day then you can decide which one you like the best."

"Which one do you like best, Marlowe?"

"I'd rather not say until you decide. They're both magnificent. So, I'll nudge you along so we won't be pooped before we get to the ones we came for. Does that suit you?"

"Mm-hmm," Katy said distracted by the ride in the vaporetto. "Sitting back here is cool," she said as they glided along the Grand

Canal toward the Accademia. "It's perfect because we can like see both sides."

"I agree," Marlowe said smiling to herself.

* * *

Katy stood awhile in front of the Bellini *Sacred Conversation* brought here from Marlowe's beloved church of San Giobbe. Art authorities worried about its safety in the old Cannaregio church where Marlowe had hung out after she'd learned she was pregnant all those years ago. While Katy looked at other paintings in the room, Marlowe remembered the hours she'd spent struggling with her decision as she sat in front of a sweet manger scene painted by Girolamo Savoldo. Shepherds leaned in through windows of a rustic hut smiling at the infant kicking one of his legs in the air. At fifteen, she'd been entranced with that fat little leg kicking in what seemed like pure joy. Later when she'd had Petey, she'd thought of that painting. Now she smiled knowing Savoldo had painted an infant of almost six months rather than a newborn. Six months! She caught her breath. She had visualized Petey's plump legs kicking the air—maybe even before he was born. He'd been exuberantly alive and then... he was gone.

No! She would not do this to herself and turned to find Katy.

Katy was ready to move on and Marlowe followed her unable to speak for the thickening in her throat. Finally, they came to Veronese's *Feast at the House of Levi*. It covered the longest wall of a huge room.

"Katy, what do you think?"

"Awesome. It's huge, and the colors are so bright they almost wiggle, don't they?" she said. When she was ready they pushed on. The Titian painting covered another entire wall in the former Albergo Room.

"Why in the world do they call this room Albergo? It's not a hotel." Katy said in a smart-alecky way. But Marlowe had to admit to herself, every time she heard Katy speak Italian, it *was* excellent. She envied her. Marc had taught her well, but she wondered how Katy got along with kids her own age. Did she lord such things over them?

Patiently, Marlowe said, "My understanding is that the Albergo Room was rented to a brotherhood like a hotel room maybe. Originally it was a Board Room, you know, like a meeting place." Marlowe said. Then she explained briefly that *The Presentation of the Virgin* was designed for this very wall and Titian had to make it fit around a door already cut through.

"See how cleverly he painted a door beneath that huge stairway?"

Katy nodded with a sage demeanor.

"But, Katy, later that other door over there was cut right into his painting. Titian was still living at the time. I've always wondered if he was consulted before the damage was done or if they told him later, 'By the by, Signor Vecellio,'" Marlowe said striking a stagey pose and a fakey bow, 'we cut a door through your masterpiece.'"

"You're funny, Marlowe. Who's Vecellio?"

"His full name was Tiziano Vecellio, the English world calls him Titian."

Katy was quiet and looked for a long time then turned and said, "I'm done."

"Museum walking is exhausting isn't it? Would you like some hot chocolate or tea? I'm dying for coffee, myself."

"I'm dying for a cappuccino. Would that be all right?" she asked.

"Fine with me unless we'd be breaking a rule from home."

"Not really. After all, I'm on vacation."

"You are!" Marlowe said grinning and took her arm. "Let's find the museum bar. It overlooks the Grand Canal. I've always had fantasies of living in one of these palaces and looking down on the pitiful peons below."

"Let's pretend," Katy said.

When they got to the bar, Marlowe placed their order while Katy went to the large windows.

"Venice is so quiet," Katy said as she came back to their table as their cappuccinos arrived.

"It is. Imagine how much quieter it was in the 1300s when this building was built. No motors of any kind; all water traffic was operated by muscle power."

"Do you want to live here?"

"*Magari*, I've wanted to live here for ages. If I get this job, my dream will come true."

"Couldn't you like marry Daddy?"

Marlowe laughed. "It's not that easy, Katy. For one thing, we haven't talked about marriage—"

"But I thought you were going to get married as soon as his divorce came through."

"Hmm. We haven't known each other long."

"Daddy said you'd known each other for five years."

"I worked for him for a short time. We didn't date back then, but we certainly care a lot for each other now." *I need to get out of this.* "Much as I want to live in Venice, I'd go bonkers without some kind of work."

"Shall I call Daddy and see if he can like meet us now?"

Katy's short attention span let Marlowe off that hook. "Sure, let's look for a pay phone."

"No need, he got me this cell to use while I'm here."

"That's handy." Marlowe said.

When they got to Campo Manin, Marc was draping himself over the stone lion at Manin's feet and made a big show of looking at his watch. Katy ran up to him telling about riding in the back of the vaporetto and about a shell game they'd watched on the big bridge. He swooped her up and gave her a big hug and kiss. Then turned to Marlowe and put his arm around her pulling her close for a quick kiss. She felt swooped too. Oh yes she *wanted* this man.

"Well, my dear," he said to Katy, "did you happen to see any art this morning?"

"Daddy, you're silly."

"So where's this special staircase?" Marc asked.

Hidden away in the labyrinth of Venice, *Contarini del Bovolo* was a stairway made for amazement. The tall, red-brick cylinder with stone steps curving round and round inside reminded her of silos in Nebraska. On one side, the "silo" was attached to an awkward brick extension jutting straight out of the rear of Palazzo Contarini. Acting as his own architect, Signor Contarini's result was a wacky piece, but she'd always thought he might have been an interesting person to know. Marc and Katy went inside and started up the steps. Marlowe waited below, ready to take their pictures whenever they poked their heads out at each curve. She heard Katy's giggle and Marc's deep chuckle as they went around and around the stairway.

As they walked out and came toward her, Katy said, "You should have come, Marlowe. It was great. Can we eat now?"

"Whew, you're a demanding imp aren't you," he said giving her a hug.

"Am I, Daddy? I'm sorry."

"Just kidding, punkin', just kidding. Marlowe, lead us out of here."

"Katy can. There's only one way in and one way out."

* * *

When they entered Corte Sconta, Marlowe was glad the garden area was closed for the season; she and Marc had their first date there. Had it been only two months? Marc and Katy put their heads together over the menu. He urged the waiter to make her portions small. She understood his request and frowned but said nothing.

"Don't worry Katy, he orders small portions for me, too. He knows my eyes are bigger than my stomach."

"Mine too," she said grinning. Marlowe wasn't hungry. After rich meals recently, a glass of red and a hunk of good bread would have been fine but she ordered a small appetizer and their delectable spinach dish. A simple sauté in butter with a hint of cayenne and, of course, lemons.

During their meal, Marc quizzed Katy more about the Accademia. She was enthusiastic and talked knowledgeably about what they'd seen. She mentioned the Titian painting with the little Virgin Mary going up the steps and said Marlowe was going to show her another one almost like it by Tintoretto. Marlowe felt good that Katy seemed genuinely interested.

"Where is the Tintoretto?" Marc asked.

"In Madonna dell'Orto."

"One of your old haunts, huh?"

She nodded hoping he wouldn't elaborate. He didn't and Katy didn't pick up on it.

"Dessert time," Marc said and handed each of them the dessert menu brought by the attentive waiter.

"Chocolate torte," Katy said raising her fist.

"Zabaglione," Marlowe said raising hers.

Marc broke out in one of his laughs. "I'm going to pass because I have a hunch I might get a morsel from each of you."

"Don't count on it," Katy said giggling.

She had to admit later she needed help from ol' Dad, and he tasted one or two of the eight beautiful cookies accompanying Marlowe's winy custard.

It was almost dark when they got back to Marc's place.

"Can we build a fire, Daddy?"

"If you help me carry wood up from the storage area."

"Okay, but first I'll put on my old jeans," she said tearing up the stairs.

"Whew, being near that much energy's exhausting," Marc said obviously proud of Katy.

"It is, isn't it, but she's a jewel Marc."

"You think so?"

"I enjoy her a lot. And I'm going to sit and watch the two of you build a perfect fire. *Grazie tante per un pranzo favoloso,* thanks for a fabulous lunch."

"*Prego, Signora, prego.* We should probably go somewhere else, but they do it up so well don't they?" he said.

She nodded. "How is that you don't have a gas fireplace here in the living room?"

"It would have required a major re-do of the building to bring gas lines into this area. We've got the best of two worlds, don't you think?"

She nodded thinking that for her, he was the best of *all* worlds. While Marc and Katy were changing, Marlowe lay back against the sofa feeling at peace. She'd been on edge most of the two weeks Marc had been gone. Worried about his reaction to her moving out; about how to deal with Rich; and then the job interview. But now, she had let it all go. Later she woke to the crackling of the fire and was covered with a blanket.

"How'd you guys carry in wood and build the fire without waking me?"

"Beats me," Marc said. "Are you feeling all right?"

"I'm not sure. I'm chilled and my head doesn't feel good."

"I'll make you a cup of tea," Katy said hopping up to look in the kitchen cupboards. "Daddee?"

Marc chuckled and went to get a box of tea bags then left her to it.

"Could it be something you ate at Sconta's?" Marc asked.

"Seems unlikely. My stomach's fine. It's probably nothing serious, but I don't feel like dancing tonight. Could you take her?" Marlowe asked.

"Sure. Don't worry about it. They dance on Sunday nights don't they?" Marc asked.

"That's okay, Marlowe," Katy chirped. "I'm happy to stay here. What's on tv?"

Marlowe felt some better with the tea but soon slipped off to bed and left them to watch an Italian extravaganza together. Katy was going to see a lot more boobs and bottoms than she'd seen on American television, and Marlowe wondered what she'd make of that as she settled under the covers. Later Marc slipped in beside her and gently turned her so he could spoon around her. She nestled against his warmth and went back to sleep.

CHAPTER SIXTY-FIVE

Next morning, on the way to the neighborhood bakery, Marlowe felt great. She wondered if her body had thought something was wrong when she'd finally let go of her anxieties. That's no way to live, going around feeling that tension is normal! As Marlowe walked into the apartment, Katy said, "Hi Marlowe, how are you?"

"Fine. I think that cup of tea you served me did it. And you?"

"I didn't wake up like all night; guess my jet lag is over, huh?"

"Probably."

"Is Daddy awake yet?"

"Don't think so. I brought us some goodies. Want some?"

"Let me see."

She picked out two pastries covered with gooey frosting. "May I have some coffee too?"

"Fine with me. Are you allowed coffee at home?"

"I don't like drink it every day, but sometimes on the weekends. I love it."

"Me too. I fell in love with coffee when I was about four. My mom let me sip her coffee with real cream in it, and it was love at first slurp."

Katy giggled. "Don't you like the frosting ones?" she asked.

"My favorite morning pastry is a plain croissant but in Italy they either put a sticky coating on them or add a sweet filling. I like these crusty *palmiers* but can't remember what the Italians call them."

"They're *gli ventagli*," Katy said.

"Yes, that's right. You have a wonderful command of Italian and your accent is perfect. You're lucky to speak two languages."

"Three actually." That uppity voice again. "Daddy knows German and taught me some and next year I'm going to take Spanish."

"Amazing. He must spend lots of time speaking those languages with you. I'm thinking your daddy loves you a whole lot. Do you *feel* his love?"

She was quiet for a moment and then said "Oh yes, I really do," but she looked at Marlowe with a question.

"You're a lucky girl to feel it. With my dad, I knew it in my head, but for some reason, I never felt his love deep inside. In fact, I never *felt* love until I met your dad."

"What about your husband?"

"Ty?"

"Why did you marry him if you didn't feel love?"

Marlowe hesitated but knew she needed to be honest and not put her off.

"I know. You'll explain like when I grow up."

Marlowe broke out laughing. "That's exactly what Aunt Edna used to say. I hated that."

Katy giggled.

After a few moments, Marlowe continued, "I was young when we married, and now looking back, I'm thinking I was in love with the *idea* instead of him. Maybe since I'd never felt love from my daddy, I didn't know any better."

"Why did you divorce him?"

"That's harder to explain, Katy. We had a pretty good marriage for a while but... he betrayed me."

"Like he slept with other women?"

Marlowe swallowed. "He did. When I found out, we went to a counselor, but in the end, I realized Ty could never be intimate with me. And for once in my life, I wanted to try for real intimacy."

"But you must have been like intimate. You have a daughter," she said.

Marlowe got up and poured the last of the coffee.

"But Katy, you can have sex without emotional intimacy. You

see, I wanted him to tell me about his inner thoughts and be interested in mine."

"Like good friends?"

"Exactly. I wanted someone who would be my best friend as well as…"

"Lover?" she supplied.

Marlowe nodded.

"I hope you are good friends with Daddy because he sure loves you."

"Me too, Katy, me too."

They sat quietly drinking coffee then heard noises coming from Marc's room.

"Speaking of the devil, I think the big man is up. Did you leave any pastries for him?"

"You're funny. I only ate like two."

Marlowe went to the sink and rinsed the pot to make more coffee.

"Where could I buy some gifts that don't cost much?" Katy asked.

"In the markets around the Rialto Bridge or over in Cannaregio on Strada Nuova."

"Would you have time to take me there?"

"Absolutely."

"Today?"

"Sure."

"And what are my two favorite women up to this morning? Can't believe I slept so late."

"Fresh coffee?" Marlowe asked.

"Sounds great. What's in that white box?"

"Nothing. You're too late, Daddy. We ate 'em all."

"Rascal," he said grabbing her up in a huge bear hug twirling her around the room a la Barovier.

"I'm kidding, I'm kidding," she squealed.

"That's good, or you'd be in deep doo doo."

"Marlowe's going to take me shopping. Want to come?"

"Are you feeling well enough, Marlee?"

"I'm fine. Whatever was wrong has disappeared. How about you? Do you feel good?"

"You bet," and he grabbed her into his arms for an embrace and a kiss on her neck.

"So… Daddy, are you coming with us?"

"Sorry punkin' I do have a living to make, but I can start out with you. I have two sites to visit over in Venice." He looked at his watch and said, "First, though, I've got to reach Gdansk and then Frankfurt. How soon do you two need to leave? It's nine thirty."

"No hurry, Daddy. Whenever you're ready."

Domesticity with Marc was becoming addictive. But while Marlowe was packing, Marc came into the bedroom. Before he could protest, she took his hand and pulled him to the small couch in the corner. "I need to be at my place for a couple of days."

"Sure. But if Katy spends the night with cousins, could I drop in on you."

"Of course. Call and let me know when and I'll be there."

"As soon as you get that job, the first thing I'm doing is buy you a cell phone. Um, maybe the second thing."

They both laughed.

"Wish you'd stay here, but…" He put up his hands and said, "I know. You need to be in your own place."

"You're a greedy dude. You want someone in your bed every night."

"Damned straight. You." And he gave her a gentle hug. "By the way, thank you for being so honest with Katy."

"What do you mean?"

"I sort of eavesdropped this morning. I'd started into the living room but when I heard you ask if she could feel my love, I stopped in my tracks."

"She does for sure."

"I know," he said with a catch in his throat. "And you answered her other questions straight too. I admire you for that. But, wish you could feel 'my love' right now."

"Ah yes, me too."

* * *

After leaving Katy at Marc's, Marlowe hopped a boat home; the connections were good and she was there in twenty minutes. She made a cup of coffee and called Belle to tell her about the job interview and how Rich had let her off the hook.

"Marlowe," Belle lowered her voice.

"Yes, Auntie Belle," she said feeling thirteen again and set her cup down.

"Are you so infatuated with Venice you don't *see* this Viking clearly?"

"That's a good question. I am ga-ga over Venice. But Auntie Belle, I am *very* sure about Marc. If you knew him half as well as I do, you'd understand why."

"It's your decision."

"I know it is, and I'm willing to take that chance."

"Hey Sugar, you've got a party coming up. Wish I could see you in your frisky dress. You'll 'lay 'em in the aisles' as your daddy used to say."

Later, Marlowe realized she hadn't told Aunt Belle about her decision to not go back to the convent. She'd also forgotten to ask her opinion about letting go of the whole secrecy thing. It seemed that secrets had been a burden all her life. Maybe keeping that dark one for so long had made her secretive in everything. Even before she spent that year in Venice, Marlowe had led a hidden life around her mother. Seldom shared anything with her, always marveled at other girls who did—who could. Even now, her behavior about moving out had probably planted a seed of distrust in his mind. God, she did not want that seed to grow. If she wanted a real partnership, she had to be honest with him about every damned thing.

CHAPTER SIXTY-SIX

"It was a lazy Sunday for Marc and Marlowe. Katy was with her cousins until time for folk dancing. You're coming with Katy and me tomorrow noon to meet my parents, aren't you?" Marc asked.

"Maybe I should wear my new suit. I can run back for it."

"Not necessary," he said. "Too bad you moved back to that damnable place."

"It is rather cloying isn't it."

"You can move in here again any time, you know."

Marlowe nodded. "I keep hoping Mandy might stop here on her way back to Portland. She let slip in her last e-mail something about too much time with Shirley."

"Shirley?"

"Ty's wife. It seems he's left them twice to interview hot grad-student prospects for his projects. She expected to be spending more time with her dad than with Shirley."

"Wonder how Shirley feels about that?"

"Who knows?" Marlowe said shrugging.

"Or cares?" he asked.

"Or cares."

"You could start moving your stuff gradually, though," he persisted putting his arms around her.

"Does your family go all out with presents?" she asked.

"No, thank God. Christmas day is a time to be together and—"

"I know, feast. I'm looking forward to it and want to ask Sandra what I could bring."

"Why not take advantage of being a guest. Next year you'll have a better idea. Hey, next year," he said, "that has a nice ring to it."

"It sure does. I wish I knew for sure. A good interview doesn't quite make it."

He tightened his arms around her. "It'll happen with this job or another. I'll keep after Chuck until he creates one for you!"

* * *

"Marlee?" Marc asked as they lay together in his bed Sunday night.

"Hmm?"

"That folk dancing was interesting tonight, but it doesn't draw me much."

"Not a big deal, but Katy loved having you dance beside her. You caught on fast, though, and could be a line leader in no time. But don't worry. We have different interests. I'd never take up skiing again although I might go for the après ski," and she faced him trying to bob her eyebrows.

He snorted.

"Have you noticed that couples who give up their own interests end up kinda dull?"

"Yeah, come to think of it. We still have things to learn don't we?"

"And where's the fun if we know everything?" she asked.

"Which reminds me, I need to go on a voyage of discovery right now," and he lifted the big Tee she'd borrowed to plunge his face into her belly.

"Two can play this game," she said peeking inside his pajama bottoms. He just rumbled.

* * *

The next day at the airport, Marlowe met Maria and Tony Barovier and they seemed pleasant toward her but were exhausted and disappeared into their apartment to rest before the family dinner. Marlowe went back to her place for a few things. If Mandy wasn't coming, she might as well move back with him. Might as well get as much of him as she could before she'd have to leave— *might* have to leave, she amended, trying to stay positive about it all. When she returned to Marc's, no one was there. She dropped everything on his bed, turned on the water and eased into the steaming tub but didn't activate the jets and soon drifted off. She woke to hear voices in the living room.

"But Tony, she doesn't hold a candle to Beth. And what kind of name is Marlowe? That's a man's name."

"Now, now Maria."

She sank lower in the water.

"Don't now, now me. What does he see in her? She's all he talked about when he was home; I expected some raving beauty. She's nothing, and he thinks she's a lawyer. She's tricking him. Probably a gold digger like the others," her voice wailed.

"Elise Midas was hardly a gold digger, Maria."

She ignored him, "Even Katy's infatuated. Thinks she's some sort of art expert."

"Maria, there's nothing you can do. He's a grown man and obviously crazy about her."

"Well, we'll see about that."

Marlowe heard someone walking into the bedroom and held her breath. "It's obvious she's moving in. Her clothes are in his closet and look at this flimsy underwear—reds, blacks and even a gaudy blue like Katy's coat!"

Yipes, his mother was rifling through her bag.

She heard Marc holler, "Hello? Who's here?"

"Hello Marc dear." They walked out of the bedroom and Marlowe eased back up shivering, but dared not add hot water.

"Have you seen Katy? Marlowe?"

"Katy's with Nonna. I have no idea where *she* is but her things are lying on your bed."

"I see. What's going on? Is something wrong with your apartment? I thought Maria Grazia had gotten it ready for—"

"It's fine dear. You know how jetlag is, you think you're sleepy but then you can't. We came in to see our old place. It's certainly not the same," she laughed brightly. "It's beautiful, Marc, and so *you*," she said pointing to him with a graceful arch of her jeweled hand. But, I imagine that woman will make all kinds of changes."

"That woman, Mom, is Marlowe and very special to me."

Silence.

"Make yourself at home, folks, I'll be out soon." Marc came into the bathroom and stopped when he saw Marlowe in the tub. She put her finger to her lips. He went back to shut the door and returned closing the bathroom door, too.

"Why the shushing?" he whispered.

"I was in the tub when they came in. Before I could let them know I was here, your mother was talking about me and then I couldn't."

"Why not?"

She shook her head.

"Marlee, what'd she say?"

"Mainly I'm not good enough for you."

"She never let on in San Diego when I told them about you."

"Guess I don't live up to her expectations. She worries I'm a gold digger."

"For God's sake, she'll never let go," he said rubbing his face as if he were washing it.

"Mothers have a hard time with that, more so with sons. By the way, who's Beth?"

"Oh no. Mom still thinks she's the woman I should be with. I'll explain later. Hold on, let me get rid of them."

He was back in minutes. "Coast is clear. Are you cold?" he asked and grabbed a large towel on the warming rack. "I'm sorry about this, Sprout. Guess I'll be changing the lock on my apartment. She's never snooped before… or has she?"

"Don't worry about it. I can't please everyone; certainly not a doting mother. Long as I please you," Marlowe said stepping out of the jacuzzi as he wrapped her in the warm towel.

"You do, Babe, you do. Whenever you're ready, we'll go to i nonni's place."

He looked at his watch and back at her and began to strip. "As long as you're undressed and squeaky clean, I think I'll sample some antipasto a-la-Marlee before dinner. Let me take a quick shower which is what I'd planned when I walked in on them. Sound good?"

"More than good. But is the door locked?"

"You bet it is, and the dead bolt's thrown."

* * *

Things went smoothly through the holidays. Marlowe and Maria politely avoided each other. On Christmas day, moments before they left for yet another feast, Marlowe got a call from Mandy.

"Mom, do you still want me to stop in Venice on the way home?"

"You're coming after all? Wonderful. How long can you stay?"

"Guess that answers my question," she said teasing. "Not long. I'll arrive on Friday, the 27th but have to leave on Monday, the 30th. Can you meet me?"

"Of course, give me the particulars."

"Sure, wait a sec. Did I tell you I got a T. A. position?"

"T. A.?"

"Teaching Assistant."

"Of course. You know how lousy I am at the alphabet soups. That's great news; I'm so proud of you. Wish you could stay longer, but we'll make the most of it. I want you to meet Marc, and on Saturday there's a special concert."

"I'm eager to meet him, Mom, but will we have time alone?"

"Of course, that's why I'm hanging on to my apartment. He's after me to move in with him but… It's a long story. We'll catch up."

"I can hardly wait. Okay, here's the itinerary."

* * *

Marc's extended family gathered at his grandparents' huge apartment. All was fun for Marlowe except for Marc's mother. His dad was gracious and Marlowe thought he might even like her but seemed careful to not show it. Friday, as planned, Marc and Marlowe met Mandy's plane, went for a quick lunch, then Mandy and Marlowe left for her place. Mandy had been seeing sights up to her eyeballs and didn't want any more. Marlowe was disappointed she couldn't show her more of Venice, but Mandy did enjoy relaxing on the Zattere with a cappuccino. Marlowe told her some about her life, but mainly she was starved to hear about Mandy's. They strolled in the area talking and talking.

Mandy loved being in Portland and wondered when Marlowe was coming back. This was Marlowe's opportunity to tell Mandy of the possible job in Vicenza and explained about studying law part-time without knowing whether she'd go through with it or not and how one thing had led to another.

"Mom, I'm blown away. Congratulations! Vicenza, huh? Home of Palladio, right? How far away is it? Would you live there?"

"No way. It's Venice I adore. I'd commute by train, about thirty to forty minutes, and only three days a week. *If* I get the job."

"That's fantastic, Mom. Your dream come true."

"Maybe," she said holding her hands up with fingers crossed as well as her eyes.

"Stop that your eyes might get stuck."

"Whoever told you that?"

"You did," Mandy said laughing aloud. "It's fun to laugh with you, Mom. I have to admit traveling with Dad and Shirley wasn't a tub of laughs."

"Ah Mandy." She hugged her. "If I do stay here, promise you'll come for a longer visit?"

"I promise Mom. For sure."

CHAPTER SIXTY-SEVEN

On Saturday, Marc and his parents, Katy, Mandy and Marlowe had plans to attend the last chamber concert for which Marc would be in charge. He and his dad had worked on it together. With Tony's approval, someone else had been found to shepherd the group for at least another year. Marlowe and Mandy were waiting at Marlowe's apartment for the others to arrive. They'd all go to the Orientale Ristorante, a favorite of Maria and Tony's. It wasn't far from the concert hall. When Marlowe opened her door to invite them in, another woman was with them. Maria fluttered in to introduce Bethany Bekins.

Ah yes, Bekins, Marlowe thought. Certainly no worries about *her* being a gold digger. Beth was dressed in a dark-blue, form-fitting dress covered with glittering sequins. She was tall, fashionably slim with perfectly coiffed blond hair. No frizzy hair in the moist air of Venice for her, Marlowe thought. Another blond. Marlowe remembered having seen Elise once in L.A. who had also been tall with sleek, blond hair. Had Marc been seeing Beth lately? All along? Was her imagination running away from her?

"Beth has been a friend of our family for just ages, hasn't she, Marc?" Maria said.

Marc nodded and looked more miserable than she'd ever seen him. He tried to catch Marlowe's eye but she didn't let it happen. She rather enjoyed the self-assured giant's predicament. It's his mom. Let him deal with her.

They did their "pleased to meet yous" and Marlowe offered Prosecco before leaving for the restaurant.

"Oh no dear," Maria trilled, "we should be on our way. What a charming little *pied à terre* you have here." She wore black and three gold chains, each larger than the next, lay on her ample bosom. They reflected light as she moved because of their Byzantine style—four strands woven in a complex pattern. Her elegant silk dress with its chiffon skirt swirled around her. Her dangling earrings sparkled like diamonds—probably were diamonds, Marlowe thought. Maria made a graceful turn in the tiny living room and said, "How ever did you find something so... so rococo?" Not expecting an answer, Maria began moving toward the door. "Shall we be off? We'll catch a vaporetto at Accademia and hop off at San Stae. It's a short walk from there. Beth and I can't walk too far in these impossible shoes can we darling?" she said turning to Beth.

Beth agreed and Marlowe flexed her toes in her comfortable walking shoes as she looked at the other two women's high heels and pointy toes. "I do hope Orientale is as good as I remember," Maria said and gaily herded them out the door almost pushing Beth into Marc as Marlowe locked up. Beth took Marc's arm as she stumbled and Mandy and Marlowe took up the rear. Katy bounced back and forth and finally took Marc's other hand. When Maria noticed, she called to her, "Katy, darling, come walk between Nonna and Nonno. We don't get to see you much anymore."

"Talk about maneuvering," Marlowe whispered to Mandy and they laughed to themselves.

"Poor Marc," Mandy said.

"Let's see how it all plays out. He's a big boy."

"He is that," Mandy chuckled.

The smells in the restaurant were wonderful, but Marlowe did not feel hungry; maybe a simple salad. Nervous? Didn't think she should be, but still she felt wary. What *was* the history between Marc and Beth? No one spoke to Mandy, although Tony made a feeble attempt until Maria began to assign seats. Marc was told to sit as far away from Marlowe as possible, and Marlowe assumed he'd acquiesce. But without a word, he ambled over to pull out a chair for her, bent down to kiss her nose, held another for Mandy and sat between them with an arm across the back of each of their chairs. Katy was happily ensconced beside her grandfather. Maria looked stunned but was soon ordering antipasti and wine for everyone. Suddenly Marlowe was starving.

Marc leaned over and whispered, "I knew nothing, Marlee, until Mom and Dad showed up with her."

"You've been a total gentleman until this moment. But Thor, you'll need your magic hammer now because you're in deep doo doo *con la tua mamma.*"

"No, she's in deep doo doo with me," he frowned and then let go to rumble softly.

He turned to Mandy and explained that this was one of the oldest, finest restaurants in Venice run by the Scarpa family. "They specialize in fish, this is Venice after all. Do you like fish or are you like your mom?"

"Actually, I love fish. What do you recommend, Marc?"

"Have you ever eaten grilled eel?"

"No, but since I've been eating raw octopus in Greece, something grilled, even if it does slither for a living, might be good."

Marc tipped his head back and laughed. "You're a chip off your mother's block, Mandy."

Mandy grinned, and for Marlowe the evening was off to a fine start.

* * *

At the concert, Marc and his dad excused themselves after the others were seated. The young artists played with verve, and the first violinist used her shiny mane of dark hair as if it were an adjunct to her energetic bow. The first half of the concert was Vivaldi and more Vivaldi, and they wore costumes from the 1700s. The *Doge* entered first and sat behind and above the players. He was in an elegant red and gold costume with special head gear supposedly from an ancient Byzantine design. The man playing Doge stayed in his role of grand poo bah throughout.

Contrary to what Marlowe had observed at other concerts in Italy, Maria did not sit as silent as a statue and annoyed Marlowe with her constant whispering in Beth's ear. Probably plotting another attack on Marc. She almost felt sorry for Beth, but no doubt Beth was willing to give it a try. He *was* a delectable prize. After the intermission, Marc sat beside Marlowe where he'd left his coat. His dad joined Maria. Dancers appeared in the second half also in period costumes. It was a marvelous show.

Everyone seemed in a good mood and Tony was glowing. It was the first time Marlowe had seen him animated. Then the manipulating began again, but when Maria began ushering them all back toward San Stae vaporetto stop, Marc stopped and said, "Mother, I'm going to walk Marlowe and Mandy home. It's such a nice night we want to stretch our legs."

He gave his mother a kiss and a hug. Goodbyes were said all around, then Katy broke away taking Marc's hand saying she needed to stretch her legs too. When Marlowe sneaked a quick look back, she saw Maria standing with her mouth open. For once she was speechless.

Mandy asked Katy what she liked best about Venice and soon the two of them had moved ahead of Marlowe and Marc. Marlowe silently enjoyed Mandy's clever maneuver.

"Sorry about that whole thing. I had no idea how determined Mom was to hook me up with Beth. We dated in high school and once or twice before I met Julie. Not since then. I'm not sure she's even interested in me, but Mom can be persuasive."

"Don't worry about it. By the way, you arranged an excellent concert, and your dad looked happy."

"Didn't he though. That's his real love. Too bad he doesn't still play."

"But he does. He told me he recently joined a small string group in La Jolla."

"I'll be damned, that stinker never told me. I'll find out more tomorrow. Speaking of which, tomorrow I want to show Mandy around the fabbrica. You haven't seen all of it either. Want to come?"

"Of course. Let's ask her, I'm sure she'd be interested."

It was settled for the three of them since Katy was tied up with her new cousin buddies.

"I think Katy's fallen for Venice," Marlowe said.

"You think so?"

"Being with her favorite daddy might have something to do with it."

They said goodnight, and Mandy and Marlowe went into her "charming little rococo *pied à terre.*"

"Anything to eat or drink?" Marlowe asked.

'No way. I'm stuffed. It was good though wasn't it?"

"Very." Marlowe told her about an experience she'd had a few years ago at the Orientale with one nasty waiter and one nice one.

"That place offers you a surprise every time you go."

Marlowe laughed and said, "I think Marc was flummoxed by his mom's behavior. She must worry about me as a terrible influence." Then she mentioned being trapped in the hot tub. "If nothing else, that and her actions tonight will send him right into my arms."

"Ha. From what I see, he's already there. I'm happy for you Mom. He's a good one."

"Yes, he is," and Marlowe heard her voice grow soft.

Mandy breathed a huge sigh, "Tomorrow's my last day of vacation and then that grinding trip home only to prep for my T.A. job."

"Are you nervous?"

"Not too much but want to make sure I'll qualify for next year's posting. Are you nervous about teaching law?"

"God yes. I've never practiced law or had any teaching instruction. Any ideas?"

"I do. Remember what you told me when I was scared about giving school reports."

"Since I've imparted much sage advice, tell me again, Mandy Dandy," and she gave her a big hug.

"You told me to keep in mind that I knew more about my subject than anyone else there."

"Mmm. That is good advice," she said hugging Mandy tighter. "I love you so much, my little Mandy girl."

"Love you too, Mom."

CHAPTER SIXTY-EIGHT

It was December 30th and the girls were gone.

"I'll miss the little Twig," Marc said, "but it's great to just be us."

"I agree," and Marlowe began fumbling with his belt buckle.

"Something tells me I'm about to be molested."

"You are indeed. First, though, make sure the deadbolt's thrown on your door."

"Don't worry. I changed the lock yesterday, and your keys are next to your Goto."

"What will your mom say?"

"She will not say a word. I had a talk with Dad. He admitted she went through your zaino and picked up 'lacy under things.' I'm afraid he hadn't realized how over-bearing she'd become. When I asked him if he was playing in a string group, he admitted he was but didn't want Mom to know. She has no right to squelch him from doing what he loves."

"I'm glad you had that talk. Do you think it'll help him stand up to her?"

"Hope so. I plan to give him booster talks by phone every so often."

"She might like having a more forceful man."

"You may be right. Hmm. Maybe I should take a stand with you."

"Too late, Buster, because I'm pulling *your* feet out from under you." She leaned down to lift his legs hoping to topple him backward on the bed, but it was like trying to bend two marble pillars. They ended there anyway, which was her goal.

Later, she murmured, "Love in the afternoon's my favorite thing."

"It's certainly one good time for it," he said and then they didn't speak.

Every time Marc filled her, she was thrilled beyond belief. He's the only one for me, she thought. Then his slow movements gathered force inside her and as she drew close to climaxing, he gentled both of them away from the precipice where they seemed to hang suspended for an eternity of anticipation—a delicious eternity. His eyes were molten silver, and she saw adoration melded with fierce desire. "Yes," she sighed. "Ah yes." Together, they moved slowly and she slipped into a realm of elemental pleasure. She rode the crest with him. It carried both of them until they slammed into a tidal wave of emotions that seemed to merge them into a new level of connection. It felt like a place of pure trust. A place where she wanted to stay forever.

* * *

Over their coffee Tuesday morning, the day of the New Year's Eve party, Marc said, "The reason I want you to come here before the party instead of getting ready at your place is that Chuck's date lives in Murano and they want to go with us. I told him to stop by, is that okay?"

"Sure, after what he's doing for me, I'd meet him anywhere."

"Don't forget to bring all your regalia for the party and something for a sleep over too."

"This trip will pretty much empty my old apartment. Then, mister, you'll have me underfoot. Are you sure you want that?"

"Marlee," he said, obviously trying for a stern look.

"No one's scheduled to come in after the first of January, and Parduzzi said we'd settle up when he gets back from the mountains. He's heading out after the party. It seems I'll know a few people there after all."

"He's been a good landlord," Marc said, "but who could treat you badly?"

"You're full of it. But I love every bit of your blarney. How long *were* the Vikings in Ireland anyway?"

* * *

When she returned with her stuff, Marc said, "I know you need space of your own, Sprout, why not start by unpacking in the extra bedroom?"

"Does that mean I don't get to sleep in your big bed anymore?"

"No way. I said you can keep your *stuff* in there not your boobs and butt and delicious black patch."

"Marc! Is that all I am to you, body parts?"

He gave her another fake stern look which only made her feel more adored. The first thing she saw when she went into Katy's room was that one bed was missing.

She charged right back out. "Marc, there's only one bed in there."

"Is that so? Hmm. If you should move in with me, you'll need a place for a desk and computer won't you?"

She ran to him and hopped on his lap wrapping her arms around his neck. He gave out an "oof," but it was a self-satisfied sound

"Marc, you do understand, don't you?" and she began to kiss him over and over on his cheeks, and neck and lifted his sweatshirt to start on his chest.

"I do know a little something about you."

"How lucky for me," she said nuzzling his neck.

* * *

It was New Year's Eve.

"Be still my heart," Marc said placing his hand on his pale-green ruffled tux shirt. "We made the right choice in that dress.

You are absolutely smashing. Maybe we ought to forget the party and stay here. Then I can explore that peek-a-boo slit in your dress."

"Not after we worked so hard to get it."

"Seems to me it all slipped in easily—I mean slipped on."

"There was that," she grinned. "But I'm feeling a little uneasy about how it will hold together. If only I had the perfect posture my gym teacher nagged about."

"You'll be fine. What do you have underneath that frisky skirt?" he said as he lifted it.

"I'm covered."

"Barely. How am I going to keep my mind on anything but you tonight?"

"Well, big man," she said putting a hand on a cocked hip, "you shouldn't have peeked."

"Clothes do make the woman. Another you is emerging."

He helped her into her long, wool coat and they started out, but at the top of the stairs, she removed her spikes and put on real shoes.

* * *

Donatella was lovely in a teal-blue low-cut gown showing off her beautiful breasts. She welcomed Marlowe graciously and accepted the large bouquet of yellow tulips Marc had brought, claiming they were her favorite. At first Marc stayed near Marlowe introducing her to people he knew. Marlowe refused any bubbly and sipped judiciously at the red wine. This was his town and his friends and she didn't want to embarrass him—or herself—as she had at Sandra and Giovanni's. Then they spied them. Sandra looked young and free in a kelly-green dress with a short, swirly skirt. They chatted awhile and then two couples they knew appeared.

Marc and Marlowe had lost Chuck and his date on arrival while she was changing shoes, but later as they walked toward him, Marlowe saw him assessing her with military scrutiny and what seemed an unmistakable lust in his eyes. For a second she felt uncomfortable but remembered tonight she was a party girl. And besides, she wouldn't be working anywhere near him. They hadn't spoken of the interview on the way to the party, but when his date walked away for a moment, she expressed thanks to him again for his help. He asked how it had gone, and she said she thought well. He nodded saying that's what he'd heard too.

The party was everything she'd ever expected of a gala in Venice. Donatella and Cesare had joined forces with other movers and shakers, and they were in Palazzo Loredan, the fifteenth-century Gothic building that had once been the seat of the Ambassadors of the Republic. Chandeliers sparkled, wine flowed, food was delicious and a small combo played. Marc knew many people and was working the room for his business, hoping to make more connections that would pay in Euros. She watched him charm everyone and was thrilled to be with him. In his custom-made Brioni tux, he looked as if he'd stepped out of G.Q. She was eager to eat him up.

"Green ruffles become you, Signor Barovier," she said when he walked back to her. "You're the most glamorous man here. Everyone's eyeing you and not only the women."

He rumbled and took her by the hand to enter the dance floor. Most of the music was swing or from the 70s and 80s. They'd never danced together, and she wondered if she could keep up because she *knew* he'd be a winner on the dance floor. He was, and easy to follow. When they played a twist, she worried she'd twist right out of the sticky strips, but they held. They played a jitterbug or two and a slow number and Marc held her as close to him as possible. He was attentive, and she appreciated that since she knew so few and her Italian was weak. Giovanni danced with her, and Marc and Sandra danced. A couple of other men asked her to dance including Chuck, but mostly she and Marc were together. If I stay here and if we stay together, I will insist that he start speaking to me in Italian. But only part of the time because bantering in English is a powerful aphrodisiac.

"Babe, you're the belle of the ball," Marc whispered in her ear.

"Only because I'm with you."

"We're good together aren't we?"

"Mm-hmm."

As they walked off the dance floor back to where people were standing around the table drinking and eating, she heard a familiar voice from long ago say, "*La mia piccola gemma!*"

For one brief instant, she was tempted to pretend she didn't know the old priest from twenty-seven years ago, but then rushed over to throw her arms around him. "Padre Tomaso! *Come sta?* How are you?" He hugged back and then held her away from him. You've grown up, but I'd know those pretty legs anywhere."

"Padre," she squeaked.

"Well, my dear, I may have been a priest, but I wasn't blind."

"Marc, this is Padre Tomaso, who I've told you about. Padre, Marc Barovier."

"A glass blower, eh?"

"No, Padre, but my family is. *Piacere,*" he said and held out his hand.

"Come both of you, sit and tell me your stories."

"First, Padre, you said you'd *been* a priest. What does that mean?"

"It's a long, long story, and you, my dear, had something to do with it. You must come visit me. I still do some ministry at Orto," and he made hand quotes in the air when he said ministry. "I'm there next Monday. Can you come?"

"Of course. Morning or afternoon?"

"Afternoon. I sleep late these days," he said grinning.

"I'll be there."

"Please come. I might have some news for you."

"For sure?"

"Might," he said holding up his forefinger.

He wanted to know where she'd been living, what she'd been doing in Venice and asked Marc about himself. Question after question. It came back to her how he'd never left anything untouched. It was good to see him; she didn't care what anyone else thought... or knew. Maybe she *was* letting go after all these years.

The band started playing "Light My Fire" by the Doors. Padre saw her perk up when she heard it. Go on, you want to dance. We'll talk Monday." She couldn't resist. She gave him a kiss on the cheek and took Marc's hand leading him to the dance floor. It was the long version of the famous tune, but they stayed with it. What fun it was to dance with him.

"Am I decent?"

"Yes, unfortunately, and I can hardly wait to take a closer look under your tarty skirt."

"You've got a one-track mind. And I love it."

As they walked off the floor, Rich stood there with a beautiful woman on his arm. They couldn't avoid him. "So," he said and his voice sounded rough. Marlowe's heart was in her throat and she wondered what would come next. But Rich seemed to shift gears and introductions were handled with ease. When his date turned to talk to someone, he complimented her saying he'd never seen her in a dress before. Marc laughed and said he never had either.

"*Congratulazioni*, Barovier."

Marc didn't ask what for but said, "*Grazie*, Tron."

Every so often during the evening, Marlowe wandered over to a window to look down on the Grand Canal. She still couldn't believe she was standing at a palace window under glittering candles and sparkling Venetian glass.

"Pinching yourself?"

"Does it show?"

"To me it does," Marc said. "Hey, they're pouring champagne for the countdown."

"Is it midnight already?"

"Yes, love, and I want a kiss to welcome in the new year. Hell

I want a kiss anyway," he said gruffly as he bent her back in a dramatic gesture.

"Here, here," Chuck said coming toward them. "It's not time yet."

"With her, Chuck, it's always time."

"I see that. Everyone wants what you two have."

Then the band struck the first notes of Auld Lang Syne.

"They play that here, too?" she asked.

"Yep. Let's grab a glass and toast two thousand three."

Later when they went for their coats, Marc said, "Chuck and Gloria aren't going back to Murano with us."

"Then let's walk to Salute for the vaporetto instead of Accademia," she said.

"Sure. Where's your real shoes?"

She reached in the large pockets of his long overcoat and pulled a shoe wrapped in plastic from each one. He laughed. As they walked, she wondered about Donatella inviting Rich.

"She always did like to stir the pot," Marc said.

"It seemed cruel at first," she said, "but, in truth, it was good for all of us to get the first time over with. Bet Donatella was disappointed there were no fireworks."

"Probably, but with this gossipy city, it *is* better to have things out in the open. At least for us, don't you think?"

"Yes. But I sensed Rich's pain when he first saw us together and was glad I hadn't been the one to break it off."

"But you were, weren't you?" he asked with a small frown creasing his forehead.

"I guess, but since he took that final step before I did, in a way he saved face."

"Maybe. Nah, I have a hunch he's too honest with himself for that," Marc said.

"I wouldn't blame him if he'd let his cousin, Silvia, believe it was all his idea. The one time I met her at his apartment, she did not like me. She lived in the larger apartment above his, and I have a shopping cart he loaned me from her supply closet. I'll wait a few more days to return it, then he'll have time to tell her in his own way."

"Good of you, but Marlee, he's a big boy."

"Hope he figures out how to let go of that baggage he lugs around."

"We all have baggage."

"We do, but I forget mine when I'm with you," and she pulled him to a small bridge pointing to the moon floating in the chilly sky and then down to its reflection at their feet.

"I'm about to forget mine too," he said.

"I know," and she squeezed his arm. They walked on.

"Padre Tomaso said he had news about my son."

"I heard."

"I almost wish he hadn't because—"

"Will you go?"

"Yes. I must go see him before I leave—unless that job comes through."

"Look, Sprout, if it doesn't come through, I won't let up on Chuck. Although the way he gaped at you tonight, I wouldn't want you to land a position near him."

She was quiet thinking the same thing. "I'd have to resign if he... No, no, he's not stupid. Nothing would happen."

"You noticed his hungry look too, huh?"

She nodded. "Probably had too much to drink."

"Not him."

They walked on past small, quiet canals and over bridges. In the distance, a few fireworks went off from time to time.

"If Padre does have information, you'll help me decide what to do won't you?" she asked.

"I'll listen while you debate with yourself and be there to help after you've made the decision."

"Shirker."

"But I do intend to find out what that predator Corombo is up to these days."

She didn't say anything not wanting to mar this beautiful evening. They held hands and didn't talk much. Each time they came to a small bridge, they paused to look at the moon's reflection on the rio beneath. After crossing Rio San Vio, she pulled Marc into the tiny campo to stand at the edge of the Grand Canal where the moon's reflection rippled across the wide ribbon of flowing water. On the other side were the tall bell tower and domes of old San Marco beside the frothy fluff of the Doge's Palace. He stood behind her with his arms around her; together they inhaled it all.

"Babe, this is the best part of the whole evening. I want this to last for another forty years."

She sighed and snuggled next to him.

"Do you know what I'm saying?"

"I think so."

"Do you want the same thing?"

"I do."

"I had a call from my lawyer."

She held her breath.

He turned her to face him, took a deep breath and said, "Marlee, will you marry me?"

Easing her own breath out, she said, "Ah Marc, my love, I will."

They stood together holding and holding. "On one condition," she whispered.

"Uh-oh."

"That I get that gondola ride."

His rumble echoed in the night air as he swooped her into a turn around the tiny campo.

"You shall have it, Sprout, but for now we're going home." Their vaporetto was approaching and they had to run for it.

Last Fling
in Venice

MARLENE HILL

Cover art by Kelly Kievit

ISBN: 978-1478-262190
Published by:
Marlene Hill Taevs Marketing
Milwaukie, Oregon

PRINTED IN THE UNITED STATES OF AMERICA

BOOK DESIGN BY RAQOON DESIGN

Heaps of thanks to my magnificent Tuesday-critique partners D'Norgia Price, Linda Smith, and Jennifer Fulford.

To Mary Alice Moore my Monday-lunch critiquer.

To Catherine Wilson, a goddess of patience, who held my hand through design decisions.

To Kelly Kievit, my fantastic artist, who created the cover.

To Dustin Keys, who was always there to pull me out of techie doldrums.

And special thanks to Elena di Mattia of Pordenone, Italy for monitoring my Italian!

For George

We got it right, love.

CHAPTER ONE

"I'd know that ass anywhere."

I'll be damned It *is* Marc Barove. I will not turn around.

"Yep, hasn't changed… much."

Marlowe stopped—for a split second—on the first flight up to the Grand Sala.

"Thought that'd get you," he whispered behind her.

It was intermission of the Vivaldi concert, and people were moving up the huge staircase to see Tintoretto's paintings that covered the walls and ceiling of the most incredible room she'd ever been in. And she wanted to see them again.

"What are you doing in Venice?" Marlowe said turning to confront him. He almost knocked her off her feet but quickly steadied her, chuckling in that rumbling way she remembered from five years before in L.A. He put his big hands around her waist to swing her to the side of the stairway letting others pass. Some things never change. Still maneuvering. *And you're letting him.* "So now you're an impresario for Vivaldi?" she asked.

"Hey, that's good. For tonight, I am a kind of impresario."

"I see. I suppose you're making promises to gullible women in the music business now."

"Oh Marlowe, you've never forgiven me have you? You do know I thought I could keep those promises made at Johnson's… don't you?"

She didn't respond.

"Look, we'll talk later," he said taking her arm and walking her up the stairs. "Where are you staying?"

"I'm on Rio delle Fornace," she said. "Got here today. The apartment is fakey, trying too hard to look like rich old Venice."

"Parduzzi your landlord?"

"Yes. Do you know him?"

"He's a wheeler dealer. I helped him with some of the remodeling on that fourteenth-century building."

When they reached the top, her head was whirling, and it wasn't because of the display of Tintoretto's flamboyant oils. To Marlowe, his very paint was alive: clouds swept across the sky by hidden forces; clothing moved with agitated energy; and crowd scenes revealed more than one story happening all at once. So many stories fixed in time yet they're available to discerning eyes. Her own story had been fixed, too, firmly tamped down and hidden away. But tonight in this magnificent place, she could not see Tintoretto's artistry because a familiar quiver of desire moved through her belly; a feeling Marlowe hadn't felt for a long while.

"Magnificent stuff isn't it," he whispered close to her ear.

People moved quietly around the room as if touched by a holiness. There were no carpets or draperies, and low voices, even whispers, seemed too loud. When someone dropped a book, the sound roared across the floor. The ceiling paintings were surrounded by elaborately carved frames, and all coated with gold. This was Venice after all. A pedestal in the middle of the room held a stack of mirrors to carry around to look at the ceiling. What a great idea she'd thought the first time she'd used one. They were about twenty-four inches by eighteen, nicely framed for ease of handling, but heavy. When all the mirrors were in use, people without one circle around the pedestal looking nonchalant always keeping a keen eye out for the next available mirror. She knew because she'd done the same. When a mirror is returned, there's always a polite scramble to snatch it. But Marc spotted one abandoned on a bench and handed it to her. He bent down, kissed her on the nose and said, "Wait for me after the concert," and hurried away.

Resist him. Don't let him sweep you along again. He can't help himself, he's a congenital-sweeper-off-the-feet kind of guy. Marc's fun and sexy but then what? He's a flirt and a temptation. She had resisted him as his secretary and she'd resist him now. She came to Venice to be alone. She had too much to sort out to be distracted by Mr. Marc Barove. But a part of her wondered if she *were* looking for a man to distract her, wouldn't she want one exactly like Marc?

She held the mirror but saw only her exhausted reflection. Her skin was grey with dark circles under her eyes from the long trip from Portland, Oregon. Maybe she should have gone straight to bed instead of coming out on her first night back in Venice. Marc looked fantastic as usual. Did he want to stir up old feelings? They'd both been attracted to each other until he'd disappeared without a word. She couldn't blame him—even though she wanted to. Marc and Fred Johnson were like oil and water. The truth was, Marlowe blamed herself for not getting out as soon as Marc was fired. She sighed, put the mirror on the pedestal and decided to wander.

Someone tapped her on the shoulder suggesting she return for the rest of the concert. She followed other stragglers down the stairs, but instead of taking her seat, she grabbed her jacket from the back of her chair and left feeling relieved that Marc was nowhere in sight. Vivaldi's bright notes soared upward and curled down into the dark shadows of the cold building. He'd assumed she'd hang around, but not this time. The rain had eased up and was spitting gently in her face. She looked up in time to see a hulking *vaporetto*, water bus, coming down the Grand Canal. Shivering from cold and fatigue, she barely noticed the moon's reflection on the water trying to remind her she was once again in Venice, *La Serenissima*.

* * *

After he'd left Marlowe holding one of those gilded mirrors, he went down the stairs thinking he'd learned she was in an apartment rather than a hotel. Probably meant she'd be here for a while. Would he have time to re-kindle that spark he'd *known* was between them back in L.A.? Time to nurture that attraction enough for her to accept the wretched facts of his past? As he reached the ground floor to gather his musicians for the second half, Marc's phone vibrated. The readout showed the Frankfurt number of Hochtief's *Baufirma*, construction company. Why at this hour? He stepped out a side door to return the call. Hans Mohr, the assistant to the director, apologized but thought Marc would like to know a personal problem had arisen. Did Marc want to meet with Herr Hochtief tomorrow morning since it wouldn't be possible two days hence? Of course Marc would be there. He couldn't let this deal slip away. He'd take a night train. He returned inside, explained to his group he had an emergency and left the building. *Damn, once again I'm running out on Marlowe!*

CHAPTER TWO

Marlowe awakened the next morning wondering if Marc was still married. When she'd seen him leaning his six and a-half foot frame against the wall and staring at her, she couldn't believe her eyes. Maybe he wasn't that tall, but for sure he was a good foot taller than her five four. Immediately, she'd looked down to the program to gather her thoughts. Elegantly dressed as usual, but his mustache and trim beard seemed darker. His hair looked as blond and thick as ever. More than once she'd wanted to run her fingers through it. And, of course, those exotic grey eyes with dark rings around the irises. She remembered how his eyes changed with what he wore. Last night they'd been silvery blue.

His dark slacks and soft jacket—cashmere no doubt—had draped his body in smooth lines, probably tailored in Italy. One ankle had been casually crossed over the other with the toe of a black leather loafer pointing to the floor. The man had to know what a fine figure he made. Classic slacks and jacket, sleek shoes and no tie—no tie in Italy? Typical Marc, flaunting tradition just a nudge. But when she'd looked up from pretending to study the program, he wasn't there. Had she dreamed him? Then from the front row she'd seen his blond head nod to the young concert-master, and the music began. It may have been Vivaldi but it was lost to her because memories flooded in. Exciting. Embarrassing. Disappointing. She thought she'd buried them all.

* * *

She wandered around her glitzy little apartment sipping from her first cup of coffee and realized just how 'frou frou' the place was. Except for the nothing kitchen, though, the furniture was good quality and the bathroom was a wonderland including a brand-new sink, toilet, bidet and large shower enclosure. The room held a chandelier of what seemed to be famous Murano glass with delicate, pink tulips. Two matching sconces were over the vanity plus three exquisite beveled mirrors: one over the sink; one on the opposite wall and another on the back of the door!

Her reflection was anything but exquisite. In the morning light, she looked all of her forty-three years and leaned in to inspect her puffy eyes. Mom always said she had brown eyes like Dad's, but she didn't. They were hazelly-green with dark brows and short eyelashes. Marc's lashes were long and thick, and as she recalled, he was a few years younger than she. Would she see him again? She had to admit she'd be disappointed if he didn't stop by now that he knew where she lived. She splashed cold water on her face hoping for a miracle. No luck. Rest, she needed rest. She'd pushed hard to get herself out of L.A. to stash her stuff with one of her best friends, Angie, in Portland before boarding the plane for a much-needed respite. Her things would wait until she returned to find a new job and a new life.

This first morning in Venice, Marlowe felt deflated but reassured herself it was only fatigue and the usual cold symptoms from bad air on long flights. She poured a glass of *succo di albicocca*, apricot nectar, her favorite juice in Italy. For ten years now since 1992, she'd come here alone and knew exactly what she had to do to recapture the mystical spirit of this city—the place she dreamed of living in forever. This spiritual bond with Venice always happened on the ugly steps of the train station. She strapped on her money belt, grabbed her backpack and headed out.

* * *

As a fifteen-year old on her first visit here with Aunt Belle, the morning had been overcast like this. They'd stepped off the train and walked through the stark-white, low-slung station from the 1950s which didn't fit in with the rest of the city. While Belle had negotiated assistance with their bags and arranged a water taxi to their lodgings, Marlowe had stepped onto the porch of the station. She saw domes that looked like over-turned tea cups, and tilted *campaniles*, bell towers, poking up here and there. Instinctively, she knew this was the back door of Venice and that she wasn't seeing the famous skyline, but heck, it was real. It looked better than the glossy pictures in library books.

That day the sun had begun to break through the clouds adding a luminescent glow over the whole scene. It had seemed she'd been holding her breath all the way across the causeway until finally drawing in her first taste of the moist, magical air of Venice. From the top of the broad steps and across the promenade was a silvery ribbon of water flowing past her feet. The ripples in the water had caught the sun's rays and it seemed as if that watery ribbon were studded with diamonds. A huge, stone bridge arched over the flowing water into the labyrinth of Venice, and she'd heard laughing voices of boatmen and gondoliers vying for customers. Gondolas! A whole year, she'd thought, to explore alone.

At age twelve, she'd gone alone into the streets near Belle's home in New York city with a map and Belle's phone number, and she could hardly wait to explore this watery city. Marlowe had grabbed Belle into a big hug. "Auntie Belle, thank you, thank you, thank you. What a glorious gift, a whole year, in this magical place. And you're right, no cars, no buses, no traffic lights. Only water everywhere. And gondolas. I can't wait to start!" Not caring what anyone thought, she'd thrown her hands wide and announced to the world that Venice was just as she'd wanted it to be, and some day she'd live here forever. Belle had smiled at her and said, "It's up to you, Marlowe."

* * *

This past year had held its share of sorrows. Earlier she'd lost a lover to an accident and then her mother succumbed to a long illness, still the city continued to call to Marlowe. Only in Venice could she suspend reality the way she'd done as a little girl back in Nebraska. She'd close her eyes and the tumult of the station would disappear. She'd wait. Then like smoke from heady incense, her spirit would merge into the soul of Venice. This time when she opened her eyes and took a deep breath, a gentle breeze carried a salty freshness reminding her how close Venice was to the sea—of the sea. Was Marc as bewitched by this voluptuous place as she was? Inhaling deeply once again, she felt the enchantment settle around her. Already she dreaded leaving after her two months were over.

But I'm here now, she wanted to shout, and felt the old magic working. She skipped down the steps with a sappy grin on her face. Time to celebrate, and she knew just how to do it. Taverna San Trovaso's *Spaghetti aglio, olio e pepperoncini* had been on her mind all morning. On foot, she made her way to the Academy Bridge passing glittering shops full of opulent objects—she'd stop and admire them another time. She patted a stone lion on its head, one of hundreds throughout the city—symbols of Saint Mark, patron saint of Venice. It would be a mighty project to count and catalogue every lion in Venice. She climbed the high wooden bridge in front of the *Accademia*, the museum crammed with Venetian paintings.

She stopped to take in the view of the most elegant part of the entire Grand Canal. It was a bridge broad enough to allow people to pass leaving space for some to lean on the railings and sort out landmarks—maybe sort out their own as well. Again Marc slipped into her thoughts as she hurried on to the Taverna.

The pasta in olive oil with crushed garlic and hot pepper flakes with a sprinkling of parsley and topped by shavings of Parmigiano Reggiano was as good as she remembered. With it she drank a glass of red wine, Valpolicella Classico, from the hills north of Venice. Mellow and soft. She raised her glass in a toast to her private celebration of being here again and finished with a crisp green salad tossed with spicy arugula.

By the time she reached the Zattere, the broadest quay in Venice bordering the immense Giudecca Canal, it was late afternoon. She relished her first frothy cappuccino back in town. For all the coffee shops in L.A. and Portland—even Seattle—none could make a cappuccino the way Italians could. She knew most Italians only drink cappuccinos in the morning but like Marc with no tie, she, too, enjoyed nudging tradition. With afternoon sun on her back, she watched vaporettos, barges, ferries, and a garbage scow glide by. All were followed by a grotesque cruise ship that towered over the fragile city. Sometimes Marlowe felt fragile too.

* * *

Bone weary she turned homeward hoping to sleep through the night, but when she finally crawled into the big bed, old memories crept in with her. Maybe it was jetlag weakening defenses she'd built over the years, but old feelings of shame and guilt seemed to drown her from time to time. No, it was never *her* shame and never *her* guilt.

From the start, Aunt Belle had assured her it was not her fault, but Marlowe hadn't been convinced. At fifteen, she'd been flattered by the handsome Italian teacher; she'd even flirted with him. She understood now—had for years—how he'd taken advantage of her. Giancarlo Corombo had been sympathetic when she'd mentioned her daddy never had time for her. Oh yes, so sympathetic. Until he got what he wanted. If she saw him again, she'd grab his testicles and twist them off. Anger helped. It had given her strength to move on.

He *was* gentle, I'll give him that, Marlowe thought, as she turned over and pounded her pillow once again. Gentle until he learned she was pregnant! Then it was all business. He just happened to know someone in Trieste to take care of things. He'd even help pay for the procedure. What a bastard! She and Aunt Belle had decided it'd be best if no one back home knew. Even her folks never knew about their grandson born two days before her sixteenth birthday. Where was he now, her little Tomaso? She'd named him in honor of the priest who'd sat with her every afternoon. On his birth certificate, baby Tomaso's last name was Cardinale, the convent's dorm where she'd stayed that year was Casa Cardinale.

It had all been such a fine lark they'd cooked up, she and Aunt Belle. A whole year in Venice. Belle wanted Marlowe to have a broader education than she'd ever get from that Nebraska village. She'd certainly gotten that! But everyone had been kind when she realized she was pregnant, except for Giancarlo.

Stop it. It's over. You've made a life. She sat up in bed to straighten the covers. But the shadowy torment of never knowing who raised her baby was with her. 'Life is now,' she reminded herself. Finally, shoving it all back into its separate compartment, she turned over again noticing the numbers on her travel clock, 3:20. Exhausted, she adjusted her pillow one more time and drifted off.

CHAPTER THREE

"It should be an excellent concert, a . . n . .d," Carla stretched out the word, "I want you to meet a good friend, Riccardo Tron. He's eager to meet you."

"Not you too, Carla," Marlowe whined.

"You'll like him. But if not," she said with her hands up palms out, "don't worry about my feelings... or his. He's a big boy."

Two years ago, Carla had been the English guide on a tour of the famous Marciana Library across from *San Marco*, Saint Mark's Cathedral. Marlowe had been her lone customer. Carla's command of English was fantastic, and by the end of the tour, they'd formed a bond, exchanged e-mails and stayed in touch. Married Italian women don't usually connect with foreigners except in a couples situation, but Carla was different. She didn't wear stilettos and tons of makeup. They'd agreed to meet this Sunday afternoon at St. George's Anglican Church to honor its 400th anniversary in Venice.

"Carla, I've been officially single for only three years and enjoy a freedom never experienced. You know I married at nineteen right out of my parents' house and—"

"You aren't marrying him. What can it hurt to meet someone nice for the time you're here?" she asked with a wicked little sparkle in her blue eyes.

"If he has the patience of Job, maybe I could practice my Italian on him. Is he an Italian Protestant like you?" she asked.

"I don't think he's anything... sort of like you. He comes for the music and to meet American or English women. Probably to annoy his cousins."

"He speaks English?"

"Oh yes, his mother is American. They have a wheat farm somewhere in Kansas."

"Wheat? Kansas?" and suddenly Marlowe's voice seemed too loud. The pastor had stepped up to the podium and sounded 'teddibly' British. It was restful to understand everything being said since her ear wasn't tuned into Italian yet, if it ever would be. Which one was Riccardo? She glanced around and wished she'd worn something more interesting but what could that be with her staid, dark travel wardrobe? At least she'd brought a few scarves for a touch of glamour. Glamour? There's no way she could compete with Italian women in that department. Besides, she didn't come here to find a man, she came to re-charge and indulge in her dream city. Carla tapped Marlowe on the arm and pointed. A folding door was opening across the far aisle.

"Come on," Carla said, "let's see what's on the tea table.

A tall, dark-haired man in the corner was talking to a willowy blond who held a cup and saucer aloft in the palm of her bejeweled hand. In this crowd of foreigners, he didn't tower over everyone but was taller than most, six feet or more. Marlowe was a sucker for tall men—like her grandpa—and wouldn't mind if he was Carla's friend. He wore jeans with a dress shirt open at the throat, her favorite male look. It had the close-fitting Euro cut that only comes with hand tailoring and was the color of old-gold which suited his olive skin and longish dark hair. Tall and dark, hmm. Carla pulled her toward the table, and the tall one eased away from the teacup blond and reached for Carla. They hugged and gave each other the standard two-Italian air kisses. Yipes, he *was* her friend. Marlowe felt like a teenager.

"Riccardo, this is Marlowe Osborne from Portland, Oregon."

"Nice place. I used to live in Seattle, but my home office is in Chicago now."

She nodded commenting that she had almost moved to Seattle but a close friend in Portland had lured her there. "Do you live in

Chicago? I thought you were from Kansas."

"Grew up there, my folks still live outside of Lawrence." He picked up a plate of small sandwiches and offered them to the women. They stood nibbling thin cucumber slices on buttered, crustless bread. Marlowe took a bite and chuckled.

"What's funny?" Carla asked.

"It's so British. They're good though," she said waving another one before popping it in her mouth.

"This is all the tea I can take, would you two join me for a coffee nearby?"

As they stepped into the small Campo San Vio near the Grand Canal, Riccardo said, "Have either of you been to the bar on Cate-cumeni?" Carla shook her head, but Marlowe said, "I think I've seen it. Is it behind Salute?" He nodded and they started off with one of his hands on each of their shoulders, then Carla stopped, looked at her watch and said, "Oh no, Pastor Stevens blathered on too long. Is that the right word, blathered?"

They both laughed and he said, "You nailed it."

"I must catch my train back to Pordenone. Sorry." She hurried away blowing kisses.

He looked at Marlowe and shrugged. "You still game?"

"Why not? Is that the bar where two ugly white posts almost support a decrepit shelter?"

"It is." And he grinned.

* * *

"Here we are," he said. Three small round tables were outside, maybe more were inside the dark cave-like establishment from which they could hear an espresso machine hissing.

"Is it too chilly out here?" he asked.

"It's perfect. When I arrived on October first, it was cold and pouring rain but this evening feels balmy." She hadn't brought a jacket to the concert but was comfortable in her standard long-sleeved, black silk turtleneck under a black cashmere pull-over. He indicated a chair at one of the tables and tossed his supple brown leather jacket over the other one.

"I'll see if I can rustle up a couple coffees. Anything else?"

She shook her head and admired him as he walked away. He had a nice tight butt and broad shoulders. While they waited for their coffees, he asked what she was doing in Portland. She told him she'd be looking for work and planned to be careful this time mentioning a job that had fallen through in L.A. "A story of broken promises," she said. "I tried to make it work for a while, but then it seemed time to move on. By then my divorce had finally come through, also a result of broken promises."

A shadow moved across his face and he nodded his head slowly.

"How does it happen that a Venetian is a wheat farmer in Kansas? Isn't there a huge tomb honoring a Doge named Tron in the Frari? Are you related to him?"

"Hold on, too many questions. One at a time."

"Sorry. The wheat farm?"

"Dad went to Kansas on a student exchange, fell in love and stayed there. He'd never wanted a banker's life even though his family has been in banking since the fourteen hundreds. And to answer your other two questions," Riccardo's dark eyes teased, "Old Nicolò Tron, *was* my ancient relative. He was doge in the 1470s and came away with a pile of filthy lucre from the Turkish wars."

"He put the Republic in debt for those wars didn't he? Then he came up with the idea of the Silver Lira and..." She stopped short and picked up her cup feeling embarrassed. "Excuse me," she said, "I was showing off. When Carla told me your name was Tron, I remembered the immense tomb and... Back to Kansas, please."

Riccardo's dark brown eyes were laughing. He reached across the table and put his hand on hers. "You're neat," he said holding her eyes a long moment.

Her stomach did that little wriggle when something might be happening elsewhere.

"Neat's a Mid-Western term, isn't it? Californians don't tend to use it," she said.

"I know," and he kept his hand on hers. She leaned back a little and withdrew her hand to take another sip of the smooth espresso, but they both knew not a drop was left.

"What about *you* and Kansas?" she asked.

"While growing up, I helped Dad on the farm. During haying season my buddies and I had contests to see who could toss the most hundred-pound bales onto flatbeds. Sometimes my back still feels as if I've been lifting those bales. It was fun driving heavy machinery, but most nights I wheezed with asthma attacks. Finally, Dad figured I might be allergic to farming as well as hay and shipped me over here to attend Scuola Superiore."

"You already spoke Italian?"

"Yeah. Dad spoke Italian to my sister Barb and me, and Mom spoke English. I don't remember ever noticing the switch."

"I envy that," she said with a sigh. "I grew up in Nebraska." He raised his eyebrows. "Everyone I knew spoke only *Amurican* always putting equal stress on every syllable. I can get by in Italian only because I've worked at it, but to learn by osmosis… that must be wonderful."

"I lived here with an uncle and aunt and two girl cousins. It was okay, but I missed my friends. And like you, I've been divorced a few years."

"I thought your nod was meaningful."

He left money on the table, got up and took her hand. They walked toward the Zattere. Marlowe felt comfortable with Riccardo, called Rich in the U.S. Night was coming on and the Giudecca Canal looked dark and foreboding, but a sliver of moon had risen toward the east. Its silvery path on the water kept pace with them. Their silence was easy.

"I don't know about you, but I haven't had much today except that cucumber sandwich which amused you. How about a bite of supper somewhere?" he asked.

She hesitated. She did like the idea but… but what? She'd been telling herself it was time to open up to something new.

"Have you eaten at Ai Gondolieri?" he asked. "They don't serve fish, none. One of the few in Venice who don't. Good food, though. You'll like it."

"Let's do it," she said.

The host led them past the bar near the door where a few men stood sipping grappa or wine. They followed him up a short flight of steps where about ten tables were set with white linens, a small vase of flowers and a tiny oil lamp on each one. At 7:30, only one other couple was there. First came a complimentary flute of Prosecco, the champagne-like drink of the Veneto, but Riccardo waved his away and asked for carbonated water. The server brought a plate of raw vegetables and a small bowl of olive oil with a dollup of dark mustard in it. She wasn't sure she'd like it, but decided it was good.

"Some wine with dinner?" Riccardo asked.

"I'd have a glass of red, but aren't you having any?"

"Never been able to acquire the taste for wine or any other alcohol. Wait, I'll take that back, I do like Bailey's Irish Cream."

"Bailey's is a bit like drinking dessert," she said grinning.

He looked sheepish, "Does that bother you? That I won't be drinking with you?"

"Not any more than my drinking wine while you drink Pellegrino."

"Good, that's out of the way, now what looks tempting?"

If she were honest she'd have to say *he* was, but instead, she said, "I've been considering the zucchini flowers. The only time I've had them was in a class in Perugia."

"Cooking school?"

"Not me, language school. A few of us decided to have a potluck once a week at our separate apartments with the rule to speak no English during the entire evening. One of the Australian women brought zucchini flowers, made a batter and deep-fried them. They were delicious, but when the group left, my tiny kitchen was a mess."

"How'd the Italian go?"

"We started out pretty rough but after a few glasses of red, we were absolutely fluent!"

He threw his head back and laughed in a short catch-in-the-throat way.

"The flowers sound good to me too," and Riccardo waved the waiter in. "What else?"

"Could you convince him to take orders as we go instead of all at once? I know they don't like to do it that way, but it doesn't look busy tonight."

"Sure, we can swing that."

"It can be tricky for a woman dining alone. For all the Italian classes I've taken, I should be more fluent, but I usually manage to get my wishes across and—"

"I'll bet you do." And he looked at her again, this time she sensed more than amusement in those dark eyes.

Riccardo had pasta with a thick bolognese sauce and offered her a taste. It was rich with intense flavors but she was glad she'd skipped the pasta. Crusty bubbles of bread had arrived with her wine and they provided plenty of carbs. They both enjoyed delectable, grilled pork chops and finished with a dark green salad.

"You were right, this is a nice place. Thanks for introducing me to it."

"Carla said you've been coming to Venice a lot through the years. What's your connection?"

Did she want to mention her year as a teenager? No, not now. Maybe never. "Haven't a drop of Italian blood, but ever since 1992 when I came with Ty—my ex—to a conference in Padua, I knew I had a connection to Italy, especially Venice. After that, no matter where else I visited in Italy, I started and ended at the Venetian airport. It's calmer. The whole place is."

Marlowe looked out the window of the restaurant where the water of a canal was lapping quietly. "I could be content here forever," she said.

"Where else have you been in Italy?"

"Places between here and Rome," she said. "I feel a strong connection to Orvieto."

"The Etruscan influence?" he asked.

She nodded. "A feeling of *deja vu* overwhelmed me the first time I walked through the tombs. I visit them each time I'm in Italy. Each time, the feeling is almost as strong."

"Had that feeling anywhere else?"

"Yes, here on the waters of the Lagoon. The first time I rode out to Torcello Island was a dreary day; hardly any one was on the vaporetto. I was sitting in one of those front seats outside. It was misting, and I felt mesmerized. When the vaporetto passed barren islands covered with salt grass, all of a sudden I saw myself in a flat-bottomed boat coming from the mainland with all my worldly belongings at my feet. For a moment, I thought I'd been hallucinating because the sense of fear and wonder had been so real."

"That is a powerful vision. Maybe it's the exotic that appeals," he said. "Sometimes when Dad and I walked in the Flint Hills of Kansas, I *knew* I'd walked there as an ancient Native American."

"Maybe," she said turning to look at him. "You do have nice high cheek bones."

He laughed. "We have a lot in common, don't we?" he said and signaled for the check. Riccardo pulled out his credit card and Marlowe had hers ready.

"Put that away, this one's on me," he said.

"Why don't we split it?" she asked.

"It isn't going to happen."

As they left the restaurant, Marlowe said, "Thank you, Riccardo. I've walked past here but never came in. For some reason, I felt sort of intimidated."

"Marlowe, you needn't feel intimidated anywhere."

As they drew near her apartment, he grabbed her shoulders and spun her around to face him. "Listen, day after tomorrow, I have to go away for a few days, how would you feel about seeing me two nights in a row?"

"I could handle that. How about I make a simple pasta and salad?"

"You're on. I'll bring a bottle of Montefalco Rosso. My cousins recommend it. Okay?"

She nodded. "And for you, *acqua minerale frizzante*?"

"*Perfetto*. About seven?"

"Seven's fine."

He bent down, pulled her to him and gave her a sweet kiss, not an air kiss. "*A domani*, until tomorrow, Marlowe."

"*A domani*, Riccardo," she whispered.

CHAPTER FOUR

As she made coffee the next morning, Marlowe thought about Riccardo Tron. What a beautiful man. She felt at ease with him, no sparring, but then, she had to admit she'd always enjoyed sparring with Marc. She would not think about Marc. Her mind was on the coming evening with Riccardo. The meal would be simple because her place was already sweltering. She grinned, thinking that Riccardo would be as happy to eat her as anything she could produce with two burners and a kitchen sink from hell.

It felt good to be free to dive into those dark eyes—eyes that seemed to smile from deep within. Certainly she was a free woman. Unmarried, no fears about pregnancy since her long-ago hysterectomy. Thank God Mandy was born before that trouble, but she was grown now and seldom needed Marlowe. All systems should be go yet her head kept putting on the brakes, and in Italy she'd always cautioned herself to look, but not touch. *Still, he is only half Italian.*

By late afternoon, the sun was still relentless. Sweat dripped down the sides of her face, trickled between her breasts and under her arms. After shampooing, she stood in a cool shower for a long time and decided not to dress until the last possible moment. Maybe a breeze would spring up when the sun went down. Olives and raw carrots were in the fridge along with a green salad. She started for the bathroom to tame her hair when she heard someone knocking on the door. It was only five, who could it be? Had Riccardo decided to come two hours early? She grabbed her white, waffle-weave robe and went down the six steps to the door that opened onto the *fondamenta,* the sidewalk beside a canal. This was the first apartment she'd rented in Venice that was arranged this way to keep water from the main part of the dwelling during *acqua alta*, high water times.

"*Chi è*, who's there?" she called.

"Marc Barove at your service."

What a time for him to show up. Too late now. When she opened the door and saw him holding a bright red begonia in a terra-cotta pot, she almost laughed. Here was this Viking-like giant holding one small flower in his hand.

"Why are you here?" she said.

"And hello to you too. I have a peace offering for not being around after the concert."

"Whew," she said swiping her brow, "I'm off the hook; I left before the second half."

"Shall I take the posy back?" he joked, but his face showed something else.

"No way," she said and grabbed it. "It's beautiful. I love red. Come on in, but only for a while, I'm expecting someone for dinner."

"You're a fast worker, aren't you?" he said following her up the steps.

"What?"

"You've been here all of a week and already cooking dinner for some guy?"

"What makes you think my guest is a guy?"

"Well?"

"You are a nosy Viking, I'll say that."

"Viking?"

"Aren't you from the Far North?"

"Marlowe, you know I don't have a clue where I'm from. I merely bumble through life pretending to be real."

"You bumble? Pretending?" She hooted. "I've always thought of you as mighty Thor, all powerful and persuasive. Around you, the skies could open and stars tumble down," and she threw her arms out wide.

"You give me too much credit because I'm oversized."

"Marc," she reached up and almost touched his chin knowing she'd like the feel of his beard but pulled back, "you are larger than life and not only in size."

He smiled, but like a flickering shadow on an old black and white home movie, for a moment Marlowe saw a frustrated little boy. Maybe being the biggest kid on the block wasn't all it was cracked up to be. People expected too much. But in a flash, he was the Marc she'd known five years ago.

"Say, I like your robe, The Heathman. I've stayed there. How'd you smuggle it out?"

She cinched the belt tighter and adjusted the lapels bringing them together and said, "The truth?"

"Always," he said.

"It's from a thrift shop."

"Not quite your size. You've got it wrapped around you almost twice and it comes to your ankles. Bet it would fit me. Here let's see," and he reached out as if to pull on the belt.

She jumped back. "Did you come here to critique my at-home wardrobe?"

"You're still a minx aren't you? Say, I don't know how long you're here for but we ought to catch up—compare notes. How does that sound?"

"Okay." A quick glance at the ornate clock on the bookshelf told her there was a little time to chat—unless Riccardo should arrive early. "But first can I get you a beer or some water?"

"Water'd be great," he said. "Hope this *scirocco* doesn't last long," then reaching to the fake archways designed to mimic the triple-lobed windows of the Doge's Palace, he said, "This place *is* over the top."

She nodded motioning him to the couch. When she brought the water, she chose a chair from the dining area not wanting to join him on the couch in a robe with nothing underneath. "Thanks to my landlord's mother, everything here is color coordinated, but the dark blue and gold couch is nice with the tans and pinks on the walls and marble floor. The real disappointment is that the only way I can see the rio flowing by is to go down the six steps or stand on the top of the toilet seat. All the windows are too high. Parduzzi fudged when I asked him if I could see the canal from the apartment."

Marc nodded in a knowing way.

"I love the location, though, and have stayed in a lot worse," she said. "Chandeliers in every room. I think they might be from Murano."

He stood up to finger the one over the tiny dining table. "Yeah. I'd say they are Murano glass. I told you once I'd been adopted by an Italian family, didn't I?"

"Yesss," and she recalled how surprised she'd been when he'd shared that back in L.A. She also remembered how uncomfortable he'd seemed when he told her—no matter how lightly he'd mentioned it. She thought of an adopted friend who still worried about who she really was.

"My Italian name is Marco Barovier. When Dad moved to California, he changed it to Barove. Here, his family runs a glass factory. When I was a kid—"

"Glass blowers! That's interesting. Sorry, you were saying…"

"Just that I hung out with the craftsmen and learned something about glass blowing. Later, I considered working in the family business but dealing with large construction equipment kept pulling at me."

"At San Rocco, you mentioned you'd helped Paolo Parduzzi with the re-do of this apartment. Is that what you mean?"

"No. My involvement in construction now is mostly in the procurement side of the business. I helped him locate a few materials. Not long after our… setback in L.A., I got involved with a friend of a friend here. It hasn't hurt that my family has contacts across Europe."

"That's why you disappeared in a… a thunderbolt?" and she

flipped her hands in the air pleased with her witticism. He got it but didn't grab on. "After you resigned from Johnson Development, I mean," she said.

"Resigned? Is that the line Fred gave out?"

She nodded. "Others believed otherwise. But I always thought he feared you'd suck all the power out of *him*."

"Hmm. I doubt that."

"Marc, when you were gone, I felt adrift. Should have left then and there. During my first week with you, the chairman of Thorson Company called to make sure I was going to stay, I might have been able to go there."

"I know why the man wanted you, your former employers seemed to think you walked on water."

"You called them?" She looked pleased at the good reports. "I always wondered if employers followed up on resume information."

"I did," he said grinning. Then his face fell and he pressed his lips into a tight line. "I'm guessing the expectations for promotion I'd built up for you at Johnson's disappeared when I was booted out. Truly, I thought I could make them happen. But Johnson hadn't played straight with me." He remembered how he'd been used by Johnson to hook up with Marc's father-in-law, a development mogul of Southern California. Once that happened, Marc wasn't needed, but he didn't want to mention that. Instead he said, "I *am* sorry, Marlowe."

She shook her head and flapped a hand as if it none of it mattered anymore. "Are you happy in Venice?" she asked.

He nodded. "I see it differently from when I was a kid and didn't want to leave my buddies in San Diego."

"I adore Venice," she said, "and come as often as I can. Mom died last year and I don't need to be there for her, so I'm indulging myself for a couple months before I join my daughter Mandy and find work in Portland."

"When did you move to Portland?"

"Minutes before I came here. After you left, I stayed on with Johnson for a while, but the wind had gone out of my sails."

"At least Fred sacked me quick and dirty."

"Yes." She looked down at her bare feet and took a swallow of cool water remembering the disappointment and betrayal she'd felt.

"Hey, Buttons, I wish it hadn't happened like that. I know I promised you the moon and the stars, and they all came crashing down."

She was quiet. "Other things happened too, but that *setback*, as you called it, gave me the kick in the pants I needed to go full-steam ahead in Law School."

"Law School? In L.A.?"

She nodded and explained that climbing the corporate ladder from a secretarial position was not going to work and law was something she'd always wanted.

"I'm speechless, and you surely know that doesn't happen often." He saw her glance at the clock for the second time. "Look, I'm taking too much of your time. I assume you want to get dressed before your guest arrives," and he bobbled his eyebrows in a fake leer. "How does dinner at Corte Sconta sound? I want to hear more about what happened when I took a powder. Does Wednesday suit?"

"I suppose," she said, thinking she ought to stay clear of him not knowing if he was still married.

"Good. Give me your number and I'll confirm the time." She followed him down the steps and stood one step from the bottom thinking she'd be on a level playing field with him.

"Thanks for the posy. When I first saw you there in San Rocco's, I couldn't believe it was you. It's good to see you again."

"Ditto, Wench. I like seeing you," he said as he lifted the lapel of her robe and peeked inside. "You better get yourself dressed—you're scary like that."

* * *

As he walked away, he sensed she wasn't sure she wanted more to do with him, but he wanted more of her. When he'd noticed Marlowe walking into San Rocco, his groin had tightened immediately. After not seeing her for five years, he'd forgotten the affect she had on him. She continued to dress soberly, but he'd always suspected her conservative style was an effort to hide her more playful self—a self often revealed by her sassy comebacks to his teasing. She'd wanted respect back then... seemed almost desperate for it. Who had treated her with disrespect, he wondered? He knew she'd been a recent divorcée when she'd applied for the job. Now he needed to know if she was still single. Hell, he wanted to know all about her.

CHAPTER FIVE

So much for a level playing field Marlowe smiled to herself. Always a jump ahead but…fun. Did she need another cool shower? She came here expecting quiet times and exposure to this beloved city, but with these two big dudes, she felt more than intellectually exposed.

With her glass of water in hand, she sat panting like a dog. What to wear in this heat? The long, cotton knit with tiny pink flowers all over its black background and a plain black Tee were the coolest things she had with her. She liked the lightweight loose-fitting skirt and knew she looked good in it. Birks without socks would work. She added small silver earrings and that was it. She was attracted to Riccardo, and eager to be with him. Eager for anything? Maybe. But before she could re-hash that again, he was at the door.

"*Chi è?*"

"*Sono* Riccardo."

She opened the door and there he stood, gorgeous in jeans and open-throated shirt. She wanted him for supper instead of plain old pasta but greeted him with a proper Italian air kiss which he side-swiped to meet her lips as he walked in. He held a bottle of wine in one hand and a bright red begonia in the other. What's with these guys and begonias? He handed her the red wine, which was the Montefalco Rosso as promised.

"Thank you. I'll open the wine later when it gets cooler. How about some ice water? Thanks for the plant too. I'm partial to red."

Riccardo chuckled, "The little florist guy said it was his last one and something about me being the second giant to buy a red begonia today."

She laughed. "As you can see the other giant brought me that one over there," and pointed to the one Marc had brought and chattered on about how, after her first time in Italy, she'd gone home and planted red geraniums in terra-cotta pots but didn't know a lot about begonias. She handed him a glass of sparkling water and continued talking. "Now that you're here, I'd like to leave the front door open. This place is like an oven."

"Do you have a fan?" he asked but was frowning at the red flower sitting on a high shelf. Then he turned away and stepped down to open the door.

"No, but tomorrow I'll ask my landlord for one. He agreed to bring a space heater in case warm air never reaches my feet come winter," and pointed to the vents in the high ceiling.

"How about a tour?" he asked. "I'm always curious what people do inside these ancient buildings."

"Sure but it'll be short; what you see is about it."

She led him across the living area to the space furnished as a bedroom although it had no separate door. She showed him the king-size bed with its shimmering gold curtain covering a brick wall behind it and the blue and gold damask bedspread that matched the couch in the living room. Mamma decorator must have found a good buy on that fabric.

"Except for the dramatic wall covering," she said, "the best thing about this room is its huge armoire with shelves built in the bottom." She opened the door to show him. When she turned to point out the drawers built into the dividing wall, he was so close behind her that his hands brushed the sides of her breasts. They continued to move around her waist and lightly caressed her hips as if looking for something.

"Even though there's no door separating these rooms, with that sofa bed out there, it ought to be okay when my friend Lucia comes from Florence," she said taking a breath as she slid sideways around him. She knew she was babbling and couldn't seem to stop.

"Mm-hmm," he said staying close.

She almost sprinted across the living room toward the only other separate space sweeping her arm toward the bath in a stagey gesture, "Ta da! The best room of all."

He back pedaled and followed at a safer distance. Why was she uneasy, she wondered? But, damn, he was moving fast. On the other hand, it was exciting.

"Who's your landlord?" he asked.

"Paolo Parduzzi. His mother and father helped him decorate." She moved toward the alcove kitchen. "But I can't think his mother spends much time in the kitchen with this artsy, flat marble trough masquerading as a sink The water splashes everywhere!"

"I've heard of him. He's in the process of buying and restoring a hotel on the Riva. I think he owns other rentals as well."

She turned back to the kitchen corner forgetting all about the olives and carrot sticks. "Hungry?" she said flipping the switch under the pot of pasta water waiting on a burner.

Riccardo came up behind and put his hand on her bottom, this time with more feeling, "I thought so, what are you up to, you little temptress?"

"What do you mean?" she said as he grasped her waist and turned her to face him His brown eyes examined hers and asked a question that she already had the answer for but couldn't speak because her throat was caught in a moment of panic and thrill. He reached over her shoulder, turned off the stove, bent down to pick her up and carried her to the bedroom.

"I thought you'd been having back trouble."

"It comes and goes. I hurled bales of wheat that were dead weight, but *Cara*, you're very much alive."

He eased her down beside the bed and held her. They kissed. His hands framed her face and his lips maneuvered hers apart. When his tongue entered, she opened for him. One hand spread across her rear pressing her against his groin. She felt his hardness, and a little moan slipped from her throat.

"You don't have a thing on underneath, do you?"

"Well, it was hot today and—"

"Shh. I don't mind. I want to know all of you anyway.

* * *

She woke to see Riccardo pulling on his jeans; the bedside clock showed 4:30. Feeling somewhat betrayed, she wondered if he was trying to get away before dawn. "What's happening?" she asked.

"Sorry, *mia piccola seerayna*, but I have an early flight."

"I'll get you coffee," she offered.

"Stay, you look too comfortable."

"I do feel rubbery."

He sat on the edge of the bed reaching under the sheet to lift her up for a kiss. "Mmm, you've gone all soft and cozy. Damn, don't want to leave."

Later when she woke, she caught the scent of him on the pillow and remembered his promise to call from Berlin. She stretched across the huge bed in a long cat stretch and felt more unwound than she had for years. Yum. And she curled back into more sleep.

Later as she held a cup of coffee, she realized she had truly let go of her head. When he'd discovered she wore no panties, he went crazy and then… so did she. For the first time in her life, an orgasm took her out of herself—a wild sensation. What was it he called her when he left? *Mia piccola seerayna*? She'd look it up. Then it hit her, *sirena*, my little siren. Was she? Did she intend all that? Thinking about it she felt horny again. She'd never felt so filled. He was large but was inside her almost before she knew what was happening and lasted. No performance anxiety with him and she came—more than once!

CHAPTER SIX

As soon as Carla and Marlowe settled at a table in Didovich's Bakery, Carla said, "I'm glad you called me yesterday because I got a recording that your number was not in service."

That must be why Riccardo hasn't called, Marlowe thought. "That's strange; my landlord called me last evening. I need the correct number for my daughter, Mandy, and others, too."

Carla shrugged as if phone mix-ups weren't unusual and asked, "Did you have trouble finding this bakery?"

"Not at all. I have a detailed map taped to a wall and scoped it out first. This Campo Santa Marina is unique with no anchor church. Was there ever a Santa Marina"

Carla nodded. "Ages ago, I think."

"You're right about the pastry here, Carla, it's scrumptious," and Marlowe finished off a buttery sugar cookie with tart-plum filling.

"Scoped? Does that mean figured out?"

"You're right."

"What did you do this morning?" Carla asked.

"I spent time in San Zaccaria. I love that dark old church with its walls covered with rich oil paintings by famous and not-so-famous-Venetian artists. Most museums would never hang theirs that close together, but in Zaccaria, all those glowing oils crammed together works. It has quite the reputation of having the most riotous nuns in all of Venice."

"And the richest," Carla said.

"From what I've read, they seldom observed vows of obedience or chastity," Marlowe said, thinking about her own lack of chastity lately. "I didn't get beyond the main sanctuary today, but I'll go back more than once while I'm here."

"How long will you be staying this time?"

"I'm booked for two months but already I hope to stay longer."

"You don't have to hurry back do you?"

She shook her head. "After settling Mom's estate, I was wiped out, but she left a little money and I'm taking some time here before finding work in Portland."

"Wiped out?" Carla asked.

"Sorry, it means worn out, stressed."

"Don't be sorry, I want to learn American sayings."

"So. Are you still belly dancing? Have you been on any job interviews in Pordenone? What's going on?"

"Wait, too many questions," she said holding a hand palm out. "I *am* taking lessons, but we're all disappointed because our wonderful teacher is pregnant and probably won't return after December."

"I know the feeling. In L.A., my folk-dance group lost an excellent teacher. We were almost demolished because of that," Marlowe said sipping her coffee.

Carla nodded with a serious look on her perfect oval-shaped face. She could have been the model for the Bellini painting Marlowe had admired in Zaccaria.

"What will happen to your group now?" Marlowe asked.

"Two friends and I want to start our own academy of belly dancing and—"

"That's exciting, tell me more."

"We've all studied about ten years and think we could make it work. Our skills are different, so we could split the teaching chores. Is that the correct use of chores?"

"Right again."

"A lot depends on the position in the state library back home. Spending an hour each way for this nothing job at the Marciana doesn't make sense. *Oddio*, Oh God," I must run to catch my train." On the way out she asked Marlowe about Riccardo.

"I forgot to thank you. I like him—a lot. After you dumped us…"

Carla had a mischievous twinkle in her eyes.

"We went to coffee and on to dinner."

"Will you see him again?"

"I think so." Marlowe wasn't ready to tell her about the sex they'd had almost the minute he walked in. She was surprised herself. "He went out of town and said he'd call me; now I know why he hasn't."

They hugged and Carla said, "Let me know the correct number, will you?" and she set off at a fast pace. She was lovely in a quiet way. Younger than Marlowe by about ten years, probably in her early thirties. She was thrilled to have an Italian girl friend. Marlowe's previous experiences had led her to believe it would be almost impossible to make friends with Italian women. Of course there was Lucia in Florence, but she was as American as Marlowe. After being in Italy seven years, Lucia had found only one Italian woman friend. That friend was a new widow when they met or she wouldn't have strayed from her married circle. Whenever Marlowe day dreamed of living here, she imagined herself trying to make Italian girl friends, but knowing she'd seek out American or English women, too. Lucia hadn't done that. She'd said she wanted to live here as a true Italian. Marlowe had kept silent knowing she would never limit herself that way. Close girlfriends were like life blood.

On her way home, she left a note at Paulo Parduzzi's office asking him to call her with the correct number and then noticed the time. Yikes, if she didn't hurry, Marc would be at her door before she was out of the shower. If he couldn't reach her, he'd just drop by. The phone was ringing as she walked in. Thinking it might be Parduzzi, she rushed up the stairs to grab it.

"Pronto," she gasped.

"Hey, Marlowe, training for the coming Marathon?"

"Marc, what number did you call?"

"Why yours, Buttons."

"Don't call me that. I wore that sweater all of two times. I'd bought it for the color but with all those tiny buttons, it was impossible to get in and out of."

"As I recall, I offered my services."

"And gave me that wacky name. You were a rascal." she said laughing. "Still are."

"Fire-engine red, wasn't it?

"Dark-cherry red."

"Whatever color, it had a nice shape."

"Seriously, Marc. This afternoon a friend told me she couldn't reach me on the number I gave her. How'd you get through?"

"Got it from Parduzzi."

"I've been trying to call him, even left a note at his office."

"When I called, he was on the way to his property in the mountains."

"Oh. What is the number? Tell me. He must have given me the wrong number from the start. I need to let others know," her voice was rising in pitch.

"Hold on, this is not life threatening."

"You're right. But, the number?"

"Okay. Let's start over. Take a big breath." He gave her the number, which she wrote on the five by three card beside her phone. "Will you be hungry about eight tonight?"

"I suppose," she said, still feeling cranky about the phone situation; she would certainly let Paulo Parduzzi know the problem.

"How about I drop by about seven?"

"Fine. And thanks, Marc, for setting my feet back on the ground."

"Sure, BU…See you soon." She could hear the laughter in his voice.

He has a marvelous sense of humor—at least at my expense. If the tables were turned…Maybe I could push some of *his* buttons and find out.

* * *

She chose her favorite black slacks made of a wonder fiber that held a crease, a black v-neck cashmere sweater, added a red, raw silk scarf and called it good. Thank God it had cooled down again. Shoes? she sighed. Her good walking shoes had to do. She wished she could have brought more interesting ones but needed to re-member her travel mantra "Go to see, not to be seen." She did add a touch of mascara and eyeliner. After five years, Marc had only seen her looking totally washed out. She shouldn't think beyond friendly fun with him, for all she knew he was still married. She would not ask. It did not matter. She would not become involved with Marco Barovier, but she did hope to wangle a tour of his family's glass factory.

Why hadn't Riccardo called? He could have called Parduzzi. Or Carla. Maybe he *had* been trying to slip away in the early morning after all.

CHAPTER SEVEN

"You look good in black," Marc said, "almost as good as in white."

"Thank you Signore but you'll not see me in white again. It doesn't make sense to travel in white."

He nodded in mock seriousness.

"You look great too, as usual," Marlowe said.

He looked at her as if surprised she'd compliment him, but he did look good. He was such a Viking. Tall, ah yes, with the shoulders of a linebacker who'd forgotten to take off his pads and those long, long legs. His thick, blond hair had a touch of red now that she looked closer, his beard too. Maybe he was related to Eric the Red. She did like bearded men, big bearded men. And those marvelous changeable eyes, green tonight. What color would they be if he were naked? *No. Don't go there.* Perfect-fitting navy slacks, probably custom made because of his size. No tie but carrying a soft navy jacket. Cashmere? Probably. His shoes were those same slipper soft, moccasins he'd worn at San Rocco's. Big for sure. But then, everything would be big wouldn't it? When she came out of her anatomical analysis of Marc, he was looking at her with such intensity, she wondered if he'd read her thoughts.

"Ready?" he asked.

She picked up the small purse lying on the end table and tossed its silver-chain strap over her shoulder.

"No jacket? It'll chill down later, and I'll have to be a gentleman and lend you mine."

"Just a sec." She came back wearing a short, black jacket of boiled wool. Light but warm.

He grinned, "Good girl."

She rolled her eyes and grabbed her purse again.

"Marc, do we have time to walk the long way instead of going by boat?"

"It's a long walk."

"I'd like to see how you maneuver through that complicated area between Dorsoduro and San Polo."

"Oh ho. That is the long way around." He checked his watch. "Our reservation's for eight, it's five after seven. Sure, we can go your way."

"I like living in Dorsoduro," she said. "I know it's kinda touristy but after staying way out on Sant'Elena once, I always try for this *sestiere*. What area do you live in?"

"I'm in a hotel at the moment. My family's place on Murano is being renovated and it's going too damned slowly even with me shepherding the supplies." They passed the Academy of Art. If they took the Academy Bridge, the route would be shorter, but now that it had turned cooler, she enjoyed walking.

"How is it you were playing shepherd to the string players the other night?"

"My dad used to play the viola in that group. The membership has changed, but one way or another he continues to support them. It means a lot to him. Since I'm here more than he is, I've been pulled into it. Like most artists, they need someone riding their tails in simple things like starting on time for God's sake."

"I saw you nod to the first violinist."

"They'd sit there shuffling and tuning up forever."

"You sound disgusted," she said, "but, Marc, you know very well most chamber groups manage to start on time all by themselves."

"You're right. Maybe I'm fed up being nursemaid to this group of spoiled 'artistes.'"

"Can't you get out of it?"

"I'm working on it. I've agreed to one more gig and then I'm done no matter how precious it is to Dad."

They passed Campo San Polo and moved into a cramped street leading to the Rialto Bridge. It was one of the oldest parts of Venice, and tonight it seemed the whole world was either going to or coming from the Rialto. Marc kept his hand on her shoulder guiding her around the cluster in front of the popular pizza- by-the-slice shop squeezed between two ancient pillars. They were pock marked and crumbling like much of Venice, but they held up the wall of that ancient building. The aroma was tantalizing, and she was tempted to suggest they stop and eat right there. They were almost to the Rialto, and she'd forgotten to notice what route he'd taken through the tricky tangle behind them. Marc pointed to a church entrance on the right and asked, "Have you ever been inside this one?"

"Never could find it, now I see why. During the day, all the vendors' stalls hide it. Do you recommend it?"

"Not for itself, it's been re-done too often for architectural interest, but there are a couple nice Pordenones in there and one lousy Titian."

She made a note to herself to go, if only for the lousy Titian. They climbed the high Rialto Bridge and from the top looked down at the Grand Canal to see five gondolas full of people approaching. They watched them glide along almost as one unit, and when they slipped under the bridge, Marc and Marlowe hurried to the other side to watch them emerge. They peeled off one by one to enter a narrow side canal. The last gondola carried a couple curled into each other's arms.

"That's the way to ride in a gondola," he said and slipped his arm around Marlowe.

"Yes," she murmured. She'd never ridden in one and resented Ty for being such a wimp on their first and only trip here. His former mentor had latched on to them and even though they were colleagues by then, Ty had remained under his thumb. She'd refused to go in a gondola with the old man.

"Have you ever been in a gondola?" Marc asked.

"Almost."

"What does that mean?"

"Don't want to talk about it."

"Okay," he said chuckling under his breath and maneuvered her into a narrow *calle*, Venetians' word for street. "Let's cut through here and get out of the crowd."

* * *

When they reached the trattoria, she felt disoriented. She'd been there before but never from this direction. "By the way, does the name Corte Sconta mean something about a hidden court-yard?" she asked.

"How'd you know that? Most people assume it has something to do with a discount—you know *sconto* means discount."

"I looked it up in the Veneziano-Italiano dictionary bought a few years ago in a dusty old bookstore."

"Filippi's?"

"Yes, that's the one."

Marc, pushed open the door. "There's a long, involved story about Corte Sconta; let's go in and I'll try to remember it."

"Buona sera, Signor Barovier" the host said and led them straight through the main dining room to the courtyard where Marlowe had never been. Maybe single women were never led there. A few paper lanterns had been threaded across the sky, and they cast a soft pumpkin-colored glow, but on this night they didn't have a chance against the peachy moon that moved in and out of the clouds drifting from the lagoon.

"It's wonderful out here," she said. "I've eaten here before but always inside."

"Too bad. I wanted to show you something new."

"But Marc, that doesn't take away from this treat. When you mentioned Corte Sconta, my mouth began to water. Their zaba-glione is to die for—they put a lot of Marsala in it. I was tempted to pick up the dish and drink it last time. Of course, the alcohol content was gone."

"Of course," he said grinning. "Let's ask if they have it tonight. If not, we'll go somewhere else and come back when they do."

"No. We'll stay here in this beautiful spot."

"Yes, ma'am."

"Red or white?" Marc asked.

"A glass of red for me, please."

"Red sounds good to me too," and at that moment, the waiter was there to take their order. It seemed that extra attention was being paid to Signor Barovier. He ordered a bottle of Zardini Valpolicella Classico Superiore. It was richer, sturdier and smoother than the Valpolicella she'd had at the Taverna, and she couldn't help but think of Marc in those terms. She had to be careful to not gulp the delicious wine and get herself in trouble. She still didn't know if he was married.

While the waiter left to place the wine order, she asked, "Do you think we could order as we go instead of everything all at once?"

"Eyes bigger than your stomach?"

"I do have that problem."

"We could, but tell you what. First we'll find out if they have plenty of zabaglione and then you'll have a better idea."

"Sounds good."

They did have the dessert and Marc requested an order held for her. She settled on gnocchi with a cheese sauce skipping an entrée and ordering a side dish of spinach sautéed in butter with slices of lemon. He ordered tagliatelle with fresh tomato sauce, *coda di rospo* for his entrée, the spinach and a mixed salad.

"I'm pretty sure I'll have room for zabaglione," she said after the waiter left, "but maybe not for all eight fancy cookies that come with it. We can stuff our pockets with them. They're super too."

The left side of Marc's mouth turned up at the corner; she wasn't sure if it was a smile or a grimace but instinct was telling her he enjoyed being with her.

When their first courses arrived, she tasted hers and said, "These gnocchi are heavenly and surely made in their kitchen as the sign out front claims. Want a taste?" she asked.

"No thanks."

"How's your tagliatelle? That tomato sauce smells divine."

"It is," he said taking a bite but not offering any. She could tell the tagliatelle was firm and chewy. The aroma from that sauce and the obvious texture of the pasta were driving her crazy; she was wishing she'd ordered what he had. They ate in silence. For Marc that seemed strange, but whatever was going on with him, she was indulging herself. The air was pleasant and the moon had parked right over their table.

His fish was served and grilled to a crisp brown, but she wouldn't dream of asking for a bite even if she were a fish eater.

"I've seen coda di rospo in the fish market," she said. "Fish aren't ever pretty, but those were freakish. What are they in English?"

"Angler fish and they are probably the ugliest critters on the planet. The males are much smaller than the females and all they do in life is search for a female."

"That sounds sorta normal," she said with a little grin.

"Are you squeamish?"

"Not at all, why?"

"Do you want to hear more about the coda di rospo?" he asked.

"I think so."

He lowered his voice, "The males latch onto the females with their teeth. They have lots of long, sharp translucent teeth and—"

"Translucent. Ick," she interrupted.

"They act like parasites and fuse to the female's skin then they move straight into her blood stream," he was grinning like a naughty boy hoping to upset her.

"That is devotion," she said aiming for flip.

He leaned in and whispered, "Then he loses his sight and all his internal organs and…just becomes a source of sperm."

"Yipes. I hope it tastes good."

Marc reared back and roared. The couple sitting across the courtyard turned to look but laughed too. His laugh was so genuine and infectious they couldn't help themselves. She loved it when she could spark his laughter. And this time, she'd turned the tables on him—a little.

He held out a forkful. "Wanna a bite? It tastes almost like lobster."

"Thanks, Marc, I'll pass." She broke off a piece of bread. Good bread and good wine were only some of her frailties.

"You sure lusted for my pasta, though, didn't you?"

"Did it show that much?"

"Babe, with you, every thing shows."

"Oops."

"No oops. It's what I like about you. You're... you're refreshing."

"I'll take that as a compliment."

"Meant that way."

With a silver-handled brush, the waiter leaned over the table and swept crumbs into a miniature dust pan; most of the crumbs were on her side. They ate their spinach in silence. She was savoring it but wanted to calm her thoughts. What was she doing with Marc? She didn't know yet whether he's married, and she had felt connected to Riccardo. She didn't want to hop from one man's bed to another, but Riccardo hadn't called, she didn't owe him fidelity, and that's no excuse for what she was thinking and... oh shit.

"Marlee? Marlee? Hey Venus to Earth?"

"What?"

"You've been traveling somewhere."

"No, no. I'm appreciating my food like all good Italians do. You've seen how they eat with full concentration, haven't you?"

"Liar."

"What the Italians do with spinach and grilled peppers and fava beans and—"

"Oh yes," he interrupted. "They do know veggies. And you're still a liar."

"You know what I like about you?"

"Tell me," he said leaning forward eagerly.

"You're a constant challenge, a gorgeous hunk, and lots of fun."

"Wow."

She *would* not ask if he was married but said, "So tell me your story."

"What do you want to know?" he said taking his last bite of spinach.

"I'm more interested in what you choose to tell."

"Hmm. Not only refreshing but dangerous as well."

Marc decided against the salad but mentioned the zabaglione to the waiter and ordered two espressos. He reminded her she already knew he was adopted but didn't know that when he was about fifteen he learned he'd been a replacement for a son who died shortly after birth. And that his mother couldn't have more children."

She nodded.

He looked a question at her with those changeable eyes that had darkened while telling his story. "What?" he said, "no poor baby, how you must have suffered?"

"I could unpack my pity violin, but it's a few years late, right?"

He nodded. "By then I loved my folks and knew they loved me, so I can honestly say I seldom anguished over being adopted."

"I'm glad. You were one of the lucky ones." *Was my Tomaso as lucky?*

"More?" he asked.

She tugged herself back from old thoughts. "What lured your parents to California?"

"Dad has three brothers. They're all gung-ho in the glass business, but he was never that interested."

"But why San Diego and why construction? That's a far leap," she said.

"This is where Mother came in. She was not Venetian and probably never felt quite at home here. Her family's from Lucca. You know Lucca?"

"Yes. An enchanting place with that beautiful park on top of the wall around the city."

"How's the zabaglione? Need I ask, the way you're devouring it."

"Am I embarrassing you?"

"Babe." He leaned over and kissed her on the nose then touched her lips with his tongue and smacked his.

"Tasty isn't it?"

Never taking his eyes from her, he said, "The Marsala or you?"

"Both."

"You little bitch," he said almost under his breath.

CHAPTER EIGHT

They left the restaurant and walked beside a quiet rio when two gondolas carrying passengers drifted by. He noticed how she watched them with what seemed to be a longing.

"Can you talk about your almost gondola ride now?"

"Why not?" and she told the story.

"Maybe we can remedy that missed opportunity while you're here, would you like that?"

"I would," and her voice sounded child-like to him.

They picked up speed to catch their vaporetto that was approaching. They crowded into the corner of the open-air space between the pilot's hut and the large enclosed passenger cabin of the ungainly craft. Marc stood behind her. When the boat pulled away, a surge jostled it back toward the *pontile*, the floating landing stage. The pilot managed to avoid striking the pontile, but Marc's arms came around to steady her. He left them there and she leaned back against him.

"So, your mother was the reason they moved to San Diego?" she asked.

Yeah, one of her sisters had married a San Diego man, and after we visited a few times, Dad saw his chance for work. Mom was willing since it was her favorite sister. I'm not applying for a job, am I?"

She laughed and felt him relax. "More another time?" she asked.

"Tell me about yourself," he said.

"I filled out an application when you hired me; you know everything, even my age."

"And I've always been attracted to older women."

"How much younger are you? I'm forty-three."

"Four years."

"So, you're a toy boy."

She could feel a low rumble in Marc's chest. His laugh was deep, and she loved the way the sound wound around her.

"Isn't that supposed to be boy toy?" he whispered.

"Is there a difference?" *What's wrong with me?* She'd been flirting shamelessly and still didn't know if he was married. What's wrong was that she was much too attracted to this man—married or single.

* * *

As they neared her apartment, Marc noticed she seemed more and more anxious with each step that brought them to her door. She pulled out her key and turned to him, "Here we are. It was a fantastic evening, Marc. Thank you so much."

"You're welcome," he said as he lifted the key out of her hand, opened the door, walked her inside and closed it behind him. "Don't worry, I'm not about to force myself on you, but I want to put you on eye level because I need to say something." With that he lifted her onto the second step leading to the main floor of her apartment.

"Yep, that's about right, eye to eye."

She appeared even more nervous.

"You think I'm betraying my wife."

She started to protest.

"Hear me out."

She nodded.

"Since I remember something you told me about being betrayed by your ex, I think I know how you feel."

"Wait a minute. I don't believe the 'other' woman or man breaks up a good marriage."

"But it bothers you that I'm married."

"I'm not bothered."

"You're such a lousy liar," and he laid two fingers on her lips. They lingered there a moment and the pad of one rubbed across her lower lip sending heat sing through his veins. He wanted to nip that full lower lip, but continued. "Elise and I are like a lot of Italian couples, separated but not divorced. The difference is that we have an agreement. After Daddykins dies, we *will* divorce. We both want it. Hell, she's practically living with a divorce lawyer. Ought to make it easier later," he groused.

"Marc, you probably know I'm attracted to you."

His grey eyes glistened, "*Cara*, I already said you show everything."

"It's a lot to absorb," she sighed. "You disappeared after Fred fired you and—"

"You made it clear you were involved with someone else back then. How'd that go?"

"It didn't. I'll tell you sometime."

He peered into her eyes, "Marlowe, I'm not going away this time. And I want to hear the rest of your story. All of it."

He put his arms around her, gave her a warm embrace and started to leave—then turned back. His voice was husky, "You feel too good." He took her face in both hands and his thumbs slid over her skin. Soft. What was going on with her, he wondered? He needed to know. He knew he should leave, but he touched her lips again and tugged with his teeth on that lower lip and feared he might lose it. God he wanted her. She might be a few years older, but he knew he was more experienced and could persuade her. But not this way. He wanted *her* to ask for him. Then she opened to his tongue.

* * *

Later, as Marlowe looked up at the heavy, dark rafters above her bed, she wondered if she were crazy to think about getting involved with these two men. When Marc thrust his hot tongue inside her mouth, she'd felt as if he were touching every sensitive nerve inside her body. She was about to tell him to stay when he handed her the key and left. Damn! She flopped over. But shoot. She didn't have either man's phone number and would not put her life on hold. Her time here was precious. She turned again and re-arranged her pillow one more time. But that was some kiss. She sensed a deep hunger there, and for a moment, she'd thought she would orgasm right on the spot. This trip was wildly different from all her expectations. And she was loving it.

CHAPTER NINE

"Auntie Belle, it's great to hear your voice," Marlowe said as she answered the phone the next afternoon. "What's going on?"

"Up to my neck in contracts—no complaints mind you, pays the bills—but I'm squeezing in a few social activities," and she snorted.

"What's he like?" Marlowe asked.

"Gorgeous and rich, Lovey, the only kind. Now, what's bothering my darling girl?"

Belle always knew when she needed a boost—usually it was when past losses crashed down, but this time Marlowe had something happier in mind. "How do you always know?"

"Magic, my girl, but now that I've got you, wait a sec and let me forward the phones."

She waited while Belle manipulated a complex phone system in her Manhattan home office for graphic arts the likes of which Marlowe hoped never to confront.

"Now my darling, tell me all."

She told her about Riccardo: his body, his charm, hints of his love-making and some of what she knew of his baggage. Then similar facts about Marc except she hadn't made love with him and didn't plan to. She also mentioned how comfortable she felt with Marc even though he, too, had problems.

"Wait right there, my darling," Belle interrupted. "What's your problem? You have two well-to-do, well endowed males after you. Go for both. Remember what Auntie Mame taught us about the banquet of life."

"I know, but Marc's married."

"Is he now? Just how married is he? Why don't you find out more about that? If he has the integrity you think he has, my guess is there's a lot more you need to know. Hmm. And he certainly seems to handle *his* baggage."

"He is tempting. They both are, but sometimes I—"

"Lovey, you've come through a lot. You're free of that no-good husband, and little Mandy Dandy's in college and… your mother's gone."

"Yesss, but—"

"But nothing, Sugar. Have you forgotten already the hard slog you had going to law school at night while working, studying for the bar exam—passing it—all while fretting over your sick mother? Then Paul dying on you. What a foolish man to fly with that idiot friend! Not easy things to deal with. Now, you're in Venice for well-deserved R&R. And, remember this, you're going into these two affairs with your eyes wide open. That's always the best line of defense… or offense," and she cackled. "Lovey, you've been careful too long. Have a fling. Two flings. You're in the city renowned for them. Relax. See what happens."

"Why am I not surprised by your advice? Any chance you could come while I'm here?"

"Maybe, Sugar, maybe. But keep me in the know," and with that she was gone.

Marlowe sat staring into space thinking that Belle hardly ever asks her about visiting the convent anymore. Maybe she wants her to forget what happened way back. And she keeps repeating, "life is now." She's right, of course, but can I ever let go?

* * *

"Riccardo, you're back." It was Saturday morning and Marlowe had just stepped out of the shower; her wet head was wrapped in a towel. "I missed you."

"Really," he said in a flat voice; his eyelids lowered. "I tried to reach you from Berlin but the number you gave me was no good."

"I know, I'll explain. Come in. Come in."

"Are you sure?"

"Of course, I'm sure."

"I see," but it was clear he didn't.

"I didn't know my number wasn't working until Carla told me on Wednesday. Didn't catch up with my landlord until last evening. He claims he was somewhere in the hills out of range. The number he'd given me was off by one digit and I've been calling people to correct it."

"I thought of calling Carla," he said.

But you didn't did you? "Why are you in a snit? You didn't give me your number or I could have called you."

"Are we having a fight?"

She laughed and so did he. "I haven't had coffee yet, would you like some?" she asked.

"How about I take you to Campo Santa Margherita for breakfast?"

"I better get dressed first."

"Yeah," he grinned, "that Heathman robe might not fly at the Campo. How'd you smuggle it out?"

Those were the exact words Marc had used. "Never stayed there. Found it at a thrift."

"Not quite your size but on you it looks good anyway."

"You know how to make a woman feel good, don't you?"

"I try," he said. His lips smiled and so did those deep-brown eyes.

"I'll only be a jiffy," she said and turned toward her bedroom. Then she heard a click at the front door. Now what had she done to hurt his fragile ego? But when she turned to see if he'd gone, she bumped into him.

"I couldn't get you out of my head," and with that he pulled the belt on her robe and moved it slowly off her shoulders. He nuzzled her neck right below the left ear finding the place that never failed to send shivers down her spine. He tossed her onto her unmade bed and began to undress. It was a better show than any male stripper she'd watched at Chippendales in Santa Monica. First his shirt revealed a broad chest and hard belly with a band of dark hair moving straight down its center. Then his long, muscular legs were stepping out of his slacks; and all that gorgeous olive brown skin took her breath away. By the time he removed his briefs, she felt herself gush. His cock was beautiful and ready. He moved onto the bed and hovered over her looking into her eyes. He bent to kiss her lightly, then slipped his tongue into her mouth as his cock brushed her mound. The smooth tip of his penis moved into her, but drew back out. She hung onto his tongue and pulled it deeper hoping he'd take the hint, but he continued his slow movement barely in and out until she was half crazy. When he finally entered her, she convulsed with wave after wave of pleasure. He waited. When her spasms subsided, he thrust again with an almost desperate force and she felt hot liquid pump into her. And she came again! She couldn't believe herself.

"What's happening here?" she asked him.

"Don't know, but it feels right… for now," he said.

"Yes, for now. No futuring."

"Futuring? I like that. But for the immediate future, I have a plan for breakfast. We're outta here in ten minutes."

"It'll take that long to tame my hair."

"Looks fine to me, up and out, milady," he said popping her lightly on the butt.

* * *

As they turned onto the walkway beside Rio di San Trovaso, Riccardo said, "I'm hungry for an American-style breakfast. How about you? I know a place much closer than Margherita."

"Bacon and eggs in Venice?"

He grabbed her hand and said, "Follow me."

They passed the grey San Trovaso church that sat across the canal beside the famous *squero* where an endless stream of tourists come to take photos of gondolas being made or repaired out in the open. Just before they reached the Giudecca Canal, he pulled a key from his pocket and opened a door she'd never noticed before. It was set into an old brick wall. They stepped into a courtyard with shrubs, lush grass, and ivy spreading across the back of the wall that took a right-angle turn to form a perfect nook for an armless statue of some sort of water sprite.

"What is this place?" she asked.

"My apartment for now. It's the family home. My cousin, Silvia and her husband, live above. The bank's up there, too, facing the Giudecca."

She was dazzled. She'd never expected to stand inside of a walled Venetian garden. Quiet and hidden. Intensely quiet.

"I've got some pancetta and eggs and a new loaf of Pugliese. Sound good?"

"Yes, I'm starving," she said following him in a daze.

"Giulia, my other cousin and her husband, live in San Polo. She rents this place when I'm not in town."

They walked up three, half-moon steps of red brick into the pink-stuccoed building and entered a large living and dining room with not one single ornate chandelier sprouting tulip bulbs of glass. A beautiful ruby-red vase, maybe from a Murano factory though, sat on the dining table. And the door they entered from the garden was all glass set within a heavy wrought iron frame painted white. The door itself was part of a glass wall entirely reinforced by white iron that looked onto the quiet greenery. She noticed a beige, full-length drape that could be pulled across the entire wall. This was a dream apartment. Restful in subdued shades of beige except for the dark-red leather chair in the living-room. The living room area was simple with two small couches, sensible end tables and a small tv. She presumed the bath and bedroom were to the left as she faced the couch, because the kitchen was to the right. It was an impressive kitchen with a real stove and oven. And she lusted for the sink deep enough to be useful.

"It must cost a fortune to rent this."

"Not too much. They could probably ask more, but they'd rather keep it occupied. Probably doesn't cost much more than what you're paying that trickster Parduzzi."

"Hmm. Giulia, you say? I met a Giulia in Parduzzi's office. In fact, a Giulia had recommended him when an apartment online was already booked. I bet that was your Giulia."

"That's her," he said.

"And you are the bookee," she said.

"That's me."

"Okay, what can I do to help?"

"Not much. Set the table and slice bread for toast."

"Consider it done. Tell me about Berlin. Friends say it's been beautifully restored."

"It's modern, of course, and has some experimental architecture. Many people are crazy for Berlin, I prefer Vienna."

"I was in Vienna once," she said. "Don't remember much except the swirling rococo architecture and whipped cream on everything."

"Yeah, *schlag*. Everything is *mit schlag*."

"And rich, melted chocolate poured over. I must be hungry."

"I heard the Vienna Boys Choir once and want to go back again. Say, would you like to go with me? I may have a few calls to make there next month."

"Maybe I would. I'm curious about how you sell hotels."

He laughed, "I don't sell hotels. I sell Hyatt services to corporations and such."

"You must have to spend a lot of time on phones arranging appointments. I tried selling life insurance once and the phone calls to set up appointments were the toughest part."

"I've never minded the phone calls, but a lot of my time is spent visiting individual hotels to find how their facilities and amenities work... or don't."

"I bet the hotel staffs treat you royally."

"They do, but I try to slip in unannounced to get a true picture. Want to be a spy for me?"

"Sure, I think I might be good at undercover work."

"Mmm, I've noticed," he said snaking out his arm to pull her to his side. He lifted strips of pancetta onto a paper towel with his other hand. "How do you like your eggs?"

* * *

They talked and walked the length of the Zattere and back. As with all new friends and lovers, it was fun to find out about each other. One thing was clear when she was with him, she liked herself again after the years of "put down" by Ty. A mild breeze had sprung up; it was a perfect afternoon, but it was painfully obvious Riccardo worried about commitment. A lot. He said "I'm not ready for commitment" at least three times that day. Who's asking for commitment? They'd only known each other a week. Was Riccardo the kind of man who could be a lover and best friend? At least this experience was showing her it might be possible to find true intimacy... somewhere. Maybe with Riccardo. Maybe not.

* * *

"We'll take this to your place in case another heat wave comes," Riccardo said pulling a fan from a storage closet.

"Parduzzi did bring a small fan, but this is much better. Won't you need it?"

He shook his head. "There's an air conditioner in my bedroom."

She noticed a red shopping cart. "Do you know where I might buy one of those? I've been using one of my carry-ons but it's awkward."

"Take this one, I don't use it and I've seen Silvia with another one."

"Maybe you should ask her first?"

"If she misses it, I'll get it back from you."

"Thanks. I'll take good care of it."

"Listen, every Saturday, I have a standing tennis date on Giudecca," and he looked at his watch. "I've got half an hour. Let's get you back with these, then I've got to run."

"You go ahead, I can put the fan in the cart and take it myself," she said.

"Are you sure you can manage?"

She laughed. "Of course, Riccardo. And thanks again, I've had a great time."

"How about calling me Rich? You called me that once." His dark, expressive eyes seemed to enter her inner self. "I liked how it sounded on your lips," and his eyes continued to reach for her central core.

"I will, Rich, I will." She turned to leave.

"Wait. Have you been down the Lido to Pellestrina?"

"No, but it's on my 'to do' list," she said.

"How about going on Wednesday? I've got family stuff tomorrow and have to go to Munich on Monday and Tuesday. I'll call you from there... now that I've got your number," he grinned and leaned down for a deep kiss. "Okay," he said with a rasp in his voice, "go before I forget where I'm supposed to be."

Nice. *But, I still don't have your number.*

CHAPTER TEN

Monday morning her phone rang. "Pronto."

"Pronto yourself," Rich replied.

"Ciao, Rich, what's going on in Munich?"

"I hate this part of my job having to spend time with drinkers. They never like it when I drink mineral water." A rep from one of the biggest breweries in Germany wants an exclusive contract in Munich's Hyatt and maybe all of Germany.

"Did you buy his proposal?"

"Nothing decided yet. It's the local manager's decision. He should have gone in the first place, but the beer rep insisted on me. You know, the prophet in his own land has no clout."

"Sounds Biblical."

"Yeah well."

She noticed that Rich said yeah well whenever he resisted talking about something.

"What have you been up to?" he asked.

She told him of a trip to Torcello the day before. "I adore riding out there dreaming about those first people who dared leave the mainland. The idea seems impossible. The old cathedral at Torcello was more beautiful than I remembered. I noticed a tear drop falling onto the mosaic cheek of the madonna. Imagine the skill of that ancient artist to create something so subtle with chips of stone," she said.

"Haven't been out there since a school trip," Rich said. "Are you still game to go the other direction into the Lagoon on Wednesday?"

"I am."

"Wear good walking shoes; I want to take you on the wall that holds back the sea. Do you have a rain jacket?"

"A full-length rain coat with a hood."

"That could be cumbersome, I'll see what Silvia has in her closet of wonders. In the meantime, I'll be thinking of you *mia sirena*."

* * *

Later that day, Marlowe answered the phone to find Marc on the line calling from Frankfurt. Construction was going well in Germany and Poland, and because of the falling dollar, his contacts were becoming more interested in dealing with U.S. products. He had high hopes for making sales for the U.S. companies he represented.

"Guess you're careful groundwork is beginning to pay off. Outside sales work is not easy; I tried it a time or two," Marlowe said.

"You?" he said. She could hear astonishment in his voice. "What sort of sales?"

"Mostly door-to-door like Fuller Brush, magazine subscriptions, life insurance and even doughnuts when I was a Camp Fire Girl."

"Well, Sprout, I'd buy doughnuts from you in a minute."

"They were the easiest to sell because people took pity on me as I timidly knocked on their door," she laughed.

"What was the hardest?" he asked.

"Life insurance, for sure. No one wants to think about dying. The best results came from pre-arranged appointments," she said.

"Did your company set up the appointments for you?"

"No. I needed to create my own leads and make my own appointments. I dreaded those calls far worse than knocking on doors. I wasn't much good. Thank goodness I finally realized it and went back to office work."

"You'd be good with the right training," he said.

"Several people thought so too." *They were always men on the make.* "But I didn't have the killer instinct. I don't mean that in a bad way, I have great respect for sales people. You can't dink around with too many details—which was my problem—there comes a time when you must ask for the order."

"You've got that right. I think everyone has to learn that the hard way," he said.

"The training and experiences I had, though, helped me understand something about the psychology of persuasion. And from what I've seen of you, Signor Barovier, you're a master!"

"Why do you say that? You've never been with me on a sales call."

"No, but when we first met, you were persuasion personified. I took the job!"

"There might have been other motives that day," he said chuckling. "What have you been doing lately?"

"Aside from resting up from the last months of Mom's life, my goal on this trip is to visit every venue that has a Tintoretto painting. There are at least thirty-five."

"Thirty-five, huh? Had no idea. Where are they all?"

"You know about those at the *Scuola di San Rocco,* of course, but most of the rest are in churches. I kept a brochure from 1994 that lists their locations. That was the year Venice celebrated his four-hundredth anniversary."

"How's your search going?"

"Not too bad for the usual places including the Doge's Palace and his own church, Madonna dell'Orto in Cannaregio, but it's a daunting job for others because many are in obscure churches that don't keep regular hours."

"Yeah. The times I've tried to get inside small churches, it's been almost impossible. Worse than cold calling on people who don't want to see you," he said.

"At least my livelihood doesn't depend on getting in Santa Maria Mater Domini over in San Polo," she said. "But I'll keep trying that door and sooner or later I'll break in!"

"Guess I need to get back to my livelihood, but I'm glad you're enjoying yourself in your favorite city."

"Thanks for calling Marc, and good luck with your clients."

"I have a feeling I will, after hearing your voice. Ciao, love."

Love, hmm. He listens. We had a two-way conversation.

* * *

On Wednesday morning she pulled on the black cargo pants worn for comfort on the plane, and shrugged into the same black Tee she'd worn when Rich came for dinner. It would serve double duty for at-home seduction and hiking-on-a-sea wall.

"Aren't you the rough and ready one," Rich said when she opened the door to him. "Where's your webbed belt and gun?"

"Couldn't get 'em through security," she said.

He dropped a jacket on the vestibule floor and gave her a hug.

"Have you had coffee yet?" she asked.

"I'm all set. Here's a jacket for you," and he helped her try on one of his own left in his cousin's closet. It engulfed her but if it rained, she'd be warm and dry.

"It's perfect," she said.

He barked his distinctive laugh that sounded as if someone had tickled him, and stuffed the jacket back into his large knapsack.

Later, as they drove down the long strand of the Lido, Marlowe looked at the barren beach with only beach grass between them and the Adriatic Sea. "I expected to be going by bus."

"We could, but it's slow. Hope you don't mind this little rental Fiat," Rich said with a worried look on his face.

"Not at all, we can stop wherever we want, can't we?"

"That's what I had in mind."

It's never made sense to me," she said.

"What?"

"That people would skip Venice and come to the Lido to gamble and lie on the beach. You can do that anywhere."

"Here's my plan for our day," Rich said.

"Okay," she said, but felt ignored and wasn't quite sure why. After all he *was* including her in his plan for the day, but...

"We'll park near this ferry point and walk along the outer wall re-built by locals after that huge flood in the sixties—the same one that swamped Florence. It's about six or seven kilometers to Pellestrina. Is that too far?"

She shook her head.

"When we're ready to go home, we can hop the bus to our car. We don't have to hurry."

"Great, but I'm thinking of those panini you mentioned. Could we have a bite soon?"

"Sure. We'll find a place to sit and look out at the sea."

She counted twenty steps to the top of the wall, which was about five feet wide. They walked south until they came to a rustic bench made by stacking bricks and shaping stucco material around them. The stucco had crumbled some and bricks were visible, but it felt good to have a backrest.

"This is wonderful. Thank you for bringing me here. She took a big bite of the crusty sandwich and hummed to herself. "Hmm, good."

"Everything's good out here in the sea air," he said.

"I've always been drawn to the Lagoon, but this is my first time to see beyond it. Look! There's a huge ship far out there. Something always happens near the sea, doesn't it," she said.

They sat eating in silence, the only way to eat such sandwiches. Rich pulled out two bottles of Pellegrino and screwed off the caps handing one to her.

"You've thought of everything," she said.

"Mostly I've been thinking about you."

She turned to look at him. His dark eyes searched hers.

"What?" she asked.

He took her panino from her hand and put it back in the pack.

"We'll finish eating. And we'll take our walk, but now I'm going to make love to you."

She looked along the wall. No one was in sight to the north or the south. Large, grassy bushes clumped toward the sea. He led her down steps to the beach, and under those bushes he spread their jackets. He worked her cargo pants down but had to stop and unlace her boots to get them off. She began to snicker as she worked on his belt and jeans, then he laughed since his boots had to come off, too. When he discovered she had two shirts on, he gave up and left her Tee in place which was just as well because they didn't manage to stay entirely on top of the jackets. Then under the Venetian sky with the sun dipping in and out of scudding clouds and with ships gliding far out to sea, they made love. He said he was selfish and couldn't wait, but that was such a turn on, she caught up fast. He came into her in a thrusting torrent. She wrapped her legs around him and grasped tightly with every plunge until she laughed and cried at the same time. She'd never felt so alive.

"Marlowe? Are you all right?"

"Yes, oh yes."

Side by side on their backs, they lay watching the clouds through the fronds of sea-grass bending over them.

"Are those clouds scudding?" she asked.

"Hmm?"

"Sorry, I didn't know you were sleeping."

"Just resting my eyes."

"Of course," she said thinking of her dad who used to say that. Dad with his melting-chocolate brown eyes. He was unable to relate to her, but at some level she knew he loved her. Didn't he? Rich's eyes were like her dad's, except Dad's were milk chocolate and Rich's were deep, dark chocolate.

After a while he said, "Never did know what scudding meant."

"Me either. They seem to move fast, though, don't they? Kinda like you."

"Sorry about that," he said. "Next time we'll go slower, I promise."

"Rich?"

"Yeah?"

"I'm not complaining."

He wrapped both arms around her and sighed.

After a while, he said, "Ready?" and stood up to pull on his jeans. She found her things and shook the sand out hoping it hadn't caught into her panties, but it probably had. She decided it had been worth a little sand.

"This sweatshirt feels good now," she said. The clouds had covered the sun and a breeze was coming from the sea.

"Do you want to go back?" he asked.

"Not at all."

When they got on the wall again, she turned around and looked at the place.

"Trying to see if someone could have seen us?"

"Mm-hmm. I'm not sure but the idea made it seem dangerous and—"

"More exciting?"

"A little."

"Me too," he said pulling her close.

CHAPTER ELEVEN

Rich and Marlowe continued walking south on top of the wall. "The old Venetians worked hard through the years to preserve their independence," she said. "They had to be totally committed didn't they?"

"I doubt modern people would have the guts to pull it off," he said.

"These lagoon waters kept them safe for a thousand years," she said softly.

"You're taken with Venetian history aren't you?"

"I spend lots of time reading about Venice when I'm not lucky enough to be here."

"You're a nervy one."

"Why do you say that?"

"You travel alone for one thing. I know of no Italian woman who would; don't know Americans either except for students with their reckless freedom. Why *do* you like to travel solo?"

"Let me count the ways…" she intoned. "Selfishness mainly."

"Selfishness?"

"When I first arrive and close the door on my place, whether it's a hotel for a night or an apartment for a month, I feel absolutely free. Not a single person knows where I am or can ask me why or tell me what to do. Is that selfish or what?"

Rich bent down and gave her a gentle hug. They walked on. The breeze from the seaward side of the wall was chilly but the sun warmed her back, and she felt a secret thrill to be way out here on a wall where most tourists never come.

"Other reasons?" he said.

"Well, if I'm alone, I notice more and get more practice speaking the language. And I like the challenge of figuring out practical things like the money or the bus and train systems. It's probably a way to pretend I belong here. How about you?"

"Haven't thought about it. My work requires a lot of alone travel, but I can relate to closing that door behind me. You didn't mention escape."

"Mmm. Travel's not escape for me. I haven't felt the need to escape since I wanted out of my parents' house, and then, when I knew I wanted a divorce. What are you escaping from?"

"Nothing now, but when I was married I needed it. Not from my kids, I got a kick out of being with them and often took them camping. Jean didn't usually join us."

They walked on in silence. "How about the rest of that panino?" she said.

"Sure, I see another place to sit up ahead. Can you go a little longer?"

She laughed.

As they sat eating again, she said, "This prosciutto tastes great and the view and the air—"

"You seem to enjoy whatever comes up, don't you?" he said.

"Maybe that's 'cause I'm choosy about what comes up for me," she said.

He was silent as they munched.

"Like you for example."

"What? You devil. For now, we'll continue our walk. We'll see what comes up later."

"I don't know where that came from?"

He laid his hand on her thigh. She couldn't believe how she was behaving. Sure, she'd been letting go of old constraints but had never been this forward in sexual matters—not so soon. But hot damn, it was fun to say whatever she was thinking. Maybe this is how it could be with someone like Rich. Someone who seemed to accept her—with no hidden agenda. On the other hand, she'd always felt accepted by Marc. His kiss at the door was certainly accepting. Ha. Lust probably had something to do with it, she reminded herself. Maybe Aunt Belle was right, Venice does inspire romance.

As Rich stuffed the remains of their picnic in his backpack, she said, "What are those poles and crosspieces out there?" She pointed toward the Lagoon side. "The ones with strings hanging down?"

"Mussel beds. Those 'strings' are *serragia* nets. They're coils of rope lying on the bottom waiting for crustaceans to wander in. An ancient fishing method in the Lagoon."

"I've read that shell fish aren't safe to eat here anymore, yet they're on all the menus in Venice."

"If I ate shell fish or any fish for that matter, I wouldn't eat it from the Lagoon," he said.

"Still, they create interesting silhouettes against the sky. They have a kind of beauty don't you think?"

"They do," he said smiling down at her. There was a softness in his eyes. "Hey, we're coming up to Pellestrina."

"Already?"

The strip of land was so narrow they could see the Adriatic on one side and the Lagoon on the other. It was the narrowest town she'd ever been in. Boats were docked a few yards from the doors of homes and shops.

"What a beautiful setting. If you lived in one of these buildings, you could listen to the creaking of the masts and clanking of the rigging every night while falling asleep."

Again Rich looked at her and smiled. It wasn't patronizing and not sexual either. She liked the feeling of acceptance—unconditional acceptance. Except with her grandpa, she'd never felt that. Certainly not with Ty who needed to find fault and correct her.

They found a small bar open onto the Lagoon side. But of course! The entire town faced the Lagoon and turned its solid back to the sea. The smell of fresh ground coffee drifted out with a come hither curl of its finger.

"Shall we?" Rich said with a regal swoop of his arm indicating the entrance.

The bar was like every other bar in Italy with a few small tables in front of its long counter and a polished mirror across the back. Here, though, the mirror reflected boats moored only thirty feet away. It was pleasant to sit not having to say anything. The door and windows were open to the breeze and they sipped their coffee listening to the rocking boats.

"How would you—" he started to ask

"How is it—" she started to ask.

"Go ahead," he said.

"No, you started first," she said.

They did the Alphonse/Gaston thing until she agreed to go first if he promised to not forget what he was going to say.

"How do you know Carla?" she asked.

"Through my mother. She often comes with Dad, and I signed her up for a tour at the Marciana Library. Carla was her guide."

"So they hit it off," she said.

"Mom thought she was marvelous and more so when she discovered Carla's a Protestant like herself."

"Let me guess. Your mom wanted you to meet Carla in the hopes that the two of you might link up?"

"Yes, but right away Carla let her know she was married— happily so." Rich heaved a huge sigh and said, "I love my mother dearly, but I cannot do the one thing she wants."

"What is that?"

"Until her dying breath, she'll want me to 'come to Jesus.'"

That's tough," she said. They were quiet. She lifted her cup for a sip and realized it was empty. Rich noticed and waved to the barista for two more.

"It helps that Dad's non-committal about religion. His philosophy is that each person has the right to decide. I'm guessing he made that clear to her from the beginning."

He moved the spoon in his coffee round and round. She waited.

"I had to get out of my marriage partly because of Jean's religious views but..." Rich looked out the window but wasn't seeing the boats. "Mostly it was her need to control. At first, I kind of accepted that because Mom seems to control Dad. He adores her and goes along most of the time," he snorted, "at least when it doesn't matter to him. It's the Italian way, and it works pretty well here. But I couldn't take it anymore. The more I gave in to Jean's demands, the more she expected."

"I'm sorry," Marlowe said. They sipped their coffees in silence. "Oh look," she said running to the open door, "it's raining—pouring!"

"Don't forget our car's at the other end of the island," he muttered.

"There is that," she said grinning over her shoulder, "but we can wait here for our bus, can't we? Squalls usually blow over."

"They say," he said coming behind to put his arms around her, and they watched the water stream down.

She inhaled deeply. "I love rain."

"I love it too—with you," and he snuggled into her neck looking for that ultra-sensitive spot he'd found once.

She wriggled away and turned to him, "What were you going to ask?"

"How would you like to come to a tennis match at Cipriani's on Giudecca Island? I could show you Hyatt's prized facility, and you could try the salt-water pool. Do you like to swim?"

"Swimming is one of my favorite things, but for the last couple of years, I had to give it up. First, I was too busy finishing up Law School and cramming for the Bar Exam, and second, most pools use too much chlorine. My eyes burned and my skin itched for hours afterward."

"It'd be neat if you were there... rooting for me, so to speak," he said. He seemed almost embarrassed. "There'll be a buffet after the tournament. Will you plan for that too? The tournament starts at three, but you could come earlier, say about one? The only problem is," he said with a small frown, "I'm going to be tied up until then. Hope you won't mind finding your way over there by yourself?"

She drew her head back and gave him a steely-eyed stare as if to say, you've got to be kidding. "Wouldn't mind at all; I've been wanting to explore more in that area anyway. Most people I've met treat Giudecca like a foreign country; all they do is sit on the Zattere and gaze at its pretty churches from a distance."

"Guess I'm remembering Jean never wanting to find her way in a strange place; she'd be in a tizzy if I didn't take her by the hand and show her exactly where to go each step of the way."

"I'm not Jean. I might even show *you* something new on Giudecca." she said.

"Of course you might."

"Where does that sarcasm come from?" she said. "Listen, I traveled alone in Italy long before I ever met you. There's no need to worry whether I could find your fancy hotel."

"Hey, I didn't mean to sound that way. Come here," and he held out his arms.

She stood her ground, not sure how she felt. He stepped closer and pulled her into his embrace. "I'm sorry I overreacted. Forgive me?"

She was surprised at her own overreaction and didn't push away. The driving rain began to ease, but the sky was still heavy with dark clouds.

"Wait here while I step over to the local "Seven-Eleven" and ask about the bus, okay?" When he returned, he said, "There's been a delay. What do you say we start out? From the wall, we can see the bus coming in time to flag it."

* * *

They got back to Venice around eight. He planned to go directly back to his place to finish up paperwork, but as they kissed goodbye, he pulled her into his arms and elbowed the door closed.

"I ought to go," he whispered.

"I need a shower and shampoo," she said.

"Your shower holds two, doesn't it?" and he slipped his hands under her sweatshirt and lifted it over her head. He began walking her toward the bathroom all the while removing her Tee shirt. With that she began to unbutton his shirt and soon their hands were lathering each other as they stood under the warm spray. His cock jutted out and she felt ready for him as he held her up against the tiles of the shower and slipped inside. Again, it was fast and exciting. She didn't come and he knew it, but when they stepped out and toweled off, Rich said, "And now, we'll go slower," and he half carried and half walked her to the bed.

Some time later, he got up and began to dress. She was disappointed he wasn't staying the night but grabbed an oversized Tee and pulled on her robe to follow him to the door.

"Will you be all right?" he asked.

"Yesss," she yawned. "I've been thoroughly entertained today," and reached for a hug.

"Me too," he said softly. "I'll call with details about the tournament."

And then he was gone. Fast. Sometimes, he runs away like a scared rabbit. Damn is he only interested in sex?

CHAPTER TWELVE

Saturday morning, Marlowe sat opposite the church of Santo Stefano and dawdled over a creamy cappuccino watching people move through the long, busy campo. Most campos in Venice had an anchor church sort of like a large department store anchors a mall back home. But this large, open space had two, Santo Stefano at this end and San Vidale at the end near the Academy Bridge.

She'd be meeting Rich in the afternoon, but her thoughts were lingering on Marc's call yesterday morning. She always felt uplifted and alive while talking with him. He'd been somewhere in Poland. Although he repped for several European companies, he hoped to sell a big-ticket package from a major player in the States. He wanted to know what she'd been doing and how she was coming in her quest for Tintoretto notches on her belt. She'd told him she was coming here to Santo Stefano to take another look at a small painting by Tintoretto that looked for all the world like a pink and white valentine. Of course, he wanted to know more—he always did. She liked that about him.

It was one of Tintoretto's versions of the traditional resurrection scene with Christ rising from the tomb holding his resurrection flag. What was curious was that Christ's legs were long and slender like a woman's and the border around him was made of cherubs' heads. From across the dimly lit room of the sacristy, he seemed to be framed by a lacy heart. Marc laughed and insisted she show it to him when he got back in town. He admitted that he was like many other residents, he knew less about the city's treasures than a lot of visitors.

* * *

What to wear to a tennis match in Venice? What else but black slacks and black Tee. She'd be the only non-bikini at the pool, but no way was she going to show her long, ugly scar at Hyatt's facility or anywhere else for that matter. There'd been no micro surgery for her, too much to explore the doctor had said.

As she walked across the glowing, dark marble floor of the Hyatt lobby, she noticed three huge crystal chandeliers above her. From Murano? Probably. With her backpack, she knew the desk clerks would soon be alerted to her obvious unworthiness to be there. For an instant, she was uncomfortable, but then began to enjoy the perverseness of it all. Rich had said he'd leave her name at the front desk. When Marlowe gave it to the young woman, who was dripping gold from her ears and neck, wrists and fingers, she fumbled with a stack of papers. When the girl turned to Marlowe shaking her head about to say she found no such name, very sweetly Marlowe said, "Riccardo Tron is expecting me."

She'd said the magic words. The transformation on the face of the elegant clerk went from indifference to a radiant smile in a nanosecond. Marlowe stifled a chuckle and followed the woman along a pathway of flowering shrubs to where Rich was sitting in tennis garb with other players. With tall drinks in their hands, they were chatting in the shade of a large white umbrella. Before she could be introduced, Rich was on his feet coming toward Marlowe with open arms. He was gorgeous in his whites. His long legs and arms were golden and only she knew how smooth his skin felt. *Maybe only I know.* Nevertheless, he did look edible. Marlowe thanked the young woman and sensed her adoration for him. In fact, she sensed other women noticing him and guessed they wondered who in the world this woman in flat shoes carrying a knapsack was.

Rich put his arm around her waist and drew her to his table. In her black Tee and black slacks, she felt like a scruffy crow squatting among graceful white egrets. But she savored each contrary moment and could hear Aunt Belle cheering her on.

"We've just finished a round of warm-up games. You're in time to see the beginning of the tournament," he said. "Before I leave, can I get you something to drink?"

Wine didn't seem the thing. Marlowe wracked her brain to think of a tall cool drink. "A Tom Collins, please."

"Done," he said and waved a waiter over.

A soft bell rang and players got up to go to the courts. It was fun to watch him play. Marlowe had tried tennis but hadn't pursued it. The only athletics she'd ever enjoyed was swimming. It was interesting to watch beautiful people in a beautiful setting. Rich moved well and focused intensely. He and his young partner were doing fine. It seemed that he scored the most points, but she was quick on her feet and missed few shots.

Rich and Lissy—his twenty-three-year-old partner—were holding their own and made it to the finals. The last game was close and ended with him lunging with an unbelievable stretch to smash the winning point. Then he went down with a thud and let out a loud groan. Lissy was to him in a flash with concern and kisses. Marlowe stood up starting toward him, but a couple of men helped him walk off the court. He'd probably pulled a muscle. She'd seen Ty and his friends suffer them before. He was holding his inner thigh and grimacing with pain. Someone called for ice packs as he sank onto a chair.

Marlowe leaned over and whispered, "Super shot, you won." He grinned and pinched *her* thigh. "Hey, be careful, I'll take your ice away from you," she teased.

He was congratulated for his winning shot and they all enjoyed the re-hashing aftermath. A staff doctor appeared to strap a real ice pack on his leg. He suggested the usual: ice for twenty minutes and then he could sit in a whirlpool of warm—not hot—water and then back to the ice. Not much else to do. "It'll take a few weeks," he said. "I've been there before. Damn."

"But you won. Isn't that the point?" Marlowe asked.

"Sure, but it's also a sign of creeping age," he said.

"That's true, old man. How old are you?

"Forty-five."

"You may have to take up checkers. I've only forty-three and already I've learned the game."

"Guess you have no sympathy for a older man injured on the battlefield have you?" he said pulling her close to him.

"None," she said laughing.

"Here's the plan. I'm going to the showers, by then my leg will be ready for the whirl pool. I'll ask someone to show you to the women's locker room where you can put on your swimsuit. You brought one didn't you?"

"I did, but that can wait for another time."

"You might as well see how you like salt-water. Lissy?" he called.

She came toward him with an expectant look. "Will you show Marlowe to the women's changing rooms and point out the pool?"

"*Certo*, Riccardo, *certo*," she said.

Marlowe had thought they'd swim together and wasn't in the mood but at this point, she went along with his plan.

Lissy did *not* want to help her. Marlowe wasn't bothered. More amused. She hadn't brought towels, Rich had said there'd be plenty at the hotel, but when she asked Lissy where they were, she asked, "Are you a member?"

"A member?" Marlowe smiled. "When Riccardo invited me, he said there'd be plenty of towels. If it's a problem, I'll forget about it. I'm sure he'll understand."

"No, no. Of course I can find you towels," she said. How many do you need?"

"Let's say three for good measure," Marlowe said.

"Measure?" she asked.

"Sorry, an American saying."

Lissy asked the attendant to bring her three towels and that was that. The little snot. Marlowe showered before putting on her suit and pulled on her old rubber cap. She didn't see Rich anywhere but dived in and stretched out to swim. It had been too long, but soon her legs and arms began to find their rhythm.

After only six laps, she had to stop; it was obvious she was out of shape. She turned over to do a few lazy back strokes and spied Rich in a whirlpool at the end of her lane. Beside him, Lissy was handing him a drink. My, oh my. She was darling in her tiny bikini. Wouldn't she be thrilled to see Marlowe step out in her old-fashioned one-piece. She probably thought ten points for her side. But Marlowe knew better. If she wanted Rich, Lissy didn't have a chance. How lovely to be a grown-up.

She lifted herself out of the pool and took off the horrid cap to shake out her hair. She knew she looked like a million bucks in her sleek, black suit. She walked slowly over to Rich letting him watch her every move. When she got there, she flicked water onto him and said, "How's the invalid?"

"Better now that you're here. Come join me. Lissy could you please find an attendant?"

She so wanted to ask him about his handmaiden but refrained. He had not a clue. "How are you feeling?"

"Numb since I took a pain pill. The doctor, if he is one, assured me it'd help the healing if I didn't let pain get started in the synapses or some such nonsense."

"The consensus seems to be that it's best to break a pain cycle early on."

He ignored her words and asked, "Are you hungry? The buffet still okay? With this bum leg, it appeals to me. It's usually quite good."

"Sounds fine. Will they provide you with a wheelchair?"

He seemed embarrassed but said, "Guess I'll submit to one."

"Makes sense. By the way, that pool is great. It's wonderful to be in soft water with no chlorine. I loved it."

"You looked as if you'd done some serious swimming before."

"Never competitively, although Mandy did as a child. When we were in Oak Ridge where the government had built a huge pool, I put her in a playpen while I took Water Safety Classes. She learned to swim almost before she could walk. Later, I taught swimming."

"Little kids mostly?"

"My first class was little ones, then a group of adult women wanted to learn. It was rewarding to work with their long-term fears. Once I got them to enjoy floating, the rest was easy." She realized she was bragging.

"Why am I not surprised?" he said. "By the way, you look fantastic in that suit."

"Thank you. You look fabulous in your little white shorts."

He chuckled. "As I sat in the whirlpool watching you, I over-heard some women behind me talking about you."

"Uh-oh."

"One was grousing about you trying to start an American trend for one-piece suits. The other one said she was jealous."

"If they only knew," I said.

"Knew what?"

"I'm not about to show my ugly scar to the world."

"You showed me," he grinned.

"That's different."

The attendant appeared and Rich requested a wheelchair. Lissy had disappeared.

"After we finish here, will you come to my place for a while?" he asked.

"You want me to tuck you in?"

"Something like that."

The wheelchair arrived. Refusing any help, Rich grunted himself into it.

"I'll meet you in the banquet room after we change. Anyone can tell you where it is.

"Don't worry, I'll find it," she said. *In spite of the handmaiden.*

He was right, the food was delicious. While others were away at the buffet table, Rich mentioned he'd be going to the States for a staff meeting in Chicago and then on to Lawrence, Kansas to his family. He'd be gone at least two weeks.

"Two weeks is a long time, I'm going to miss you," Marlowe said moving closer to him.

He was quiet for a moment and looked away saying, "You have all of Venice to explore, don't you?"

"Yes, of course, that's what I came for. Meeting you has been a bonus," and she laid her hand on his arm. "If I give you my e-mail address, would you drop me a line?"

She felt his arm stiffen, but he said finally, "Probably."

"Only if you have time," she said, and took her hand away busying herself with her food. She felt rejected; in fact, it seemed like a slap in the face. What was going on? She decided to back off and say no more. People came back to the table, and suddenly he was very interested in their conversation making it clear she was not a part of the group. A total switch from his undivided attention moments before.

They'd planned on splitting a hot chocolate mousse, but he said, "I don't feel like dessert; I'm thinking of going on to my place. You can go ahead and have some, if you want."

"No thank you," she said and gathered her things. Marlowe was puzzled yet knew she'd done nothing wrong. It was up to him to tell her what was going on. No more blaming herself for a man's mood swings, and she would *not* be tucking him in tonight or any other night until he did some explaining.

Rich borrowed the wheelchair and as they left the hotel heading toward the vaporetto stop, he said, "I've got loads of work to do when I get home."

"I can imagine," she said wishing she could run ahead to catch another vaporetto but decided to tough it out. In fact, she even helped push him until he said he could manage fine without her. When he said that, she lifted her hands from the back of the wheelchair as if it blistered her. At that moment, she had a devilish image of giving him a good, hard shove into the murky waters where garbage scows and barges went day after day leaving their filthy residue.

The evening was balmy, and as they waited for the vaporetto, she watched the silvery path of the moon and wondered how many silvery paths Venetians get to watch year in and year out. She stood behind him. He turned to look at her, "Are you okay?"

"Fine. Thank you again for the chance to swim in Hyatt's pool." Then she hurried ahead of him to get in line in order to start the process of moving away from him. As the water bus pulled up to the floating landing stage, people let him move ahead of them, and there he was beside her again.

"I'm not in such a hurry to work that we can't be together on the vaporetto. Do you want to stay out in the open or sit inside?"

"Sit where you want."

"Marlowe, I'm sorry if I was short with you," and as soon as they were on board, he grabbed her and pulled her onto his lap.

"What are you doing?" she said struggling to get off. He held on tight. Marlowe was not good at confrontation; she'd never made a public scene before and didn't have the will for one now. Two pre-teen boys were watching from their same corner. He took her chin in his hand and turned her face toward him. She frowned. He kissed her gently and tried to deepen the kiss. She didn't cooperate and held her body taut not opening to him. The boys moved farther into their corner and snickered.

"You're switching from cold to hot. What's going on here?" she said.

"Marlowe, please come back to my place and help me understand."

"What about all the work you *need* to do?" she snarled.

"I've been stupid. Please come. We'll wash all the muck away and I'll make love to you Venetian style."

He allowed her to slip off his lap when the boat docked. She helped push him onto the ramp leading to the broad fondamenta of the Zattere. Then standing to face him, she said, "Rich, it'll take more than hot sex to wash away all that 'muck.'" She turned and jogged away from him.

CHAPTER THIRTEEN

Marlowe answered the phone Monday morning with a tentative "Pronto," not ready to hear from Rich. When she heard Carla's voice, she let out a breath and said, "Carla! I'm glad you called. I need a heart-to-heart with a girlfriend."

"Would I do?" Carla asked.

"When and where?"

"That bad? How about lunch?"

"Today?" Marlowe said.

"Yes. My boss upset everyone by calling a meeting at three which means I'll have to take the last train home tonight, but have extra time in between."

"Sorry for you but glad for me. Name the place."

They agreed to meet at Remigio's, a small trattoria behind San Marco's.

* * *

Marlowe said, "I'm going to have some red wine, how about you?"

"Yes, it will help me through that boring meeting. *Allora.* What's troubling you or should I say who?"

"Yes, it's a who. Rich, to be exact."

"I see you're calling him Rich."

"Umm He liked the way I said it once and asked me to call him that."

"He's a sweet man, but?" Carla said.

The waiter brought their wine and took their orders. Marlowe sipped her wine and shared the whole tennis-day upset. They were both quiet until Marlowe said, "I don't believe sex can solve everything, do you?"

"Sex helps smooth *some* things over, but I agree, it never works in the long run. Franco tried sex a time or two when he wanted to avoid talking about something. I went along at first, but after that, I've always forced him to talk to me. Sometimes it takes a day or two," and she laughed, then added "Sex is always better after that!"

"Good for you, Carla."

"Riccardo, or Rich as you call him, probably needs more time."

"Lots!" Marlowe said taking a gulp of wine.

Their food was served, but Marlowe picked at hers.

"I heard his cousins have been playing matchmakers with their friends, even *married* ones," Carla said.

"Married ones? No wonder he's scared, but he's sure not scared when he feels horny."

"Horny?"

"It's a vulgar expression that means sexually aroused."

"I see."

"What would you call it? Do I embarrass you?"

"Not at all," and she leaned across the table. Marlowe did too. "The word we use is *arrapato*," she whispered, and they laughed softly.

"Now," Marlowe said, "tell me something good. What's happening with your job? And what about your dance situation?"

Carla told her the job at the library in Pordenone seemed to be hers, and Marlowe raised her glass saying, "*Congratulazioni!*"

"Maybe," Carla said bobbing her hands in prayer-like fashion. "But honestly, I'm more excited about the new dance school I'm forming with two others. The best part is that our teacher is already encouraging her students to switch to us when she quits."

"Super. What do you call yourselves?"

"Kismet. Do you know what that means?"

"Fate?"

"Yes. We decided after much coffee and many pastries," she laughed.

"By the way," Marlowe said, "do you know of any Balkan Folk Dancing in Venice?"

"Haven't heard of any, but I'll ask around," Carla said and raised her hand for the check.

As they neared the entrance to the Marciana Library, Marlowe said, "Maybe I need to accept that I'll never find a lover and friend all in one."

"I found one, Marlowe, don't give up yet."

This time they kissed each other's cheeks instead of the air and Carla hurried inside.

* * *

Thursday morning Marlowe was thinking about the pleasant call from Marc the day before when the phone rang. She felt apprehensive each time it rang and knew she was foolish to cower from confrontation with Rich. He should be the one cowering.

"Hey, Sprout. How are you?"

Her breath caught and she realized how excited she felt to hear from him again. "Ciao Marc, fine, and you?"

"Much better now that I hear your voice," he said. "Remember when you asked what the restaurant, Corte Sconta, meant?"

"I'm thinking you're going to tell me."

"Perceptive wench. How are you fixed for time today?"

"I'm guessing you're back in town."

"Yep."

It was 9:30 and she hadn't finished dressing. "My appointment book can probably be re-arranged," she said joshing.

"I could drop over say... in a half hour? I'll tell you the story, we'll find the secret place and maybe have lunch?"

"What a great idea. I was thinking about a second coffee, would you like one?"

"Sounds good, see you soon."

She put the water in the teakettle ready to turn on later and began measuring out the coffee. A reprieve from her planned visit to the convent. More and more she'd been thinking she should leave it all behind her. She straightened her shoulders, raised her chin and stepped into the bathroom to see what she could do with her hair. Frizzy, of course, but a drop of soy gel would settle her bob-cut back into shape—for a while.

What was the day like out there, she wondered? With Marc, she knew it'd be fun. She skipped down the steps flinging the door open and there he was in all his Viking glory. In the morning light, his hair shone like a handful of sunshine. She was tempted to tell him she saw sparks flying, but knew she'd worn out the Viking thing.

"Whoa there. What's going on?"

"Hi Marc. This dark little cave I live in gives me no clue about the weather. Come in."

"Sorry I didn't bring rain," he said. "I'm just back from Poland, and on the plane I thought of you and your question."

"Good. Want a biscotto or two with your coffee while you tell me the story?"

"I do."

In a few minutes, she carried two steaming mugs to the couch. After she brought a plate of biscotti, she settled herself cross-legged beside him. "I'm all ready for the story. Love stories with coffee and cookies."

He ruffled her hair and kissed her on the nose. "First off, Corte Sconta is a place name cooked up by a comic-strip writer named Pratt, and yes, he was born in Venice even with that name. His series starts in a mysterious place called Corte Sconta where the main character, Corto something, meets a sorcerer who's been living in Venice since 1300."

He drank some coffee and ate a cookie.

"Go on," she said picking up her mug.

"Corto complains that every time he's back in Venice, he becomes lazy because time is all stretched out. All he has to do is open a door in this hidden court and he can float in time. The sorcerer says it's the 34th of December and the new year hasn't begun yet. I like this part because I'm wishing October and November would stretch out so you'd be here longer," and he squeezed her shoulder.

"I *am* thinking of staying through December since Mandy will be with her dad in Greece for the holidays."

"Good, because I need more time."

She looked at him, puzzling what he meant. He didn't explain and before she could ask, he went on with his story. "Pratt wrote in the next issue more details about the magic place."

She reached for a biscotto and dipped it in her coffee, then sat back. Marc drank more coffee. "This is good, Sprout. What kind is it?"

"Illy, but I had to buy it already ground because I didn't bring a grinder."

He took another swallow. "Okay. Pratt dropped hints to his readers about this magic place and gave vague directions like going into the Ghetto, crossing three bridges, opening seven secret doors… you get the idea."

"No doubt his fans started searching for it," she said.

"They did. Next, he found an obscure place and wrote a fake place name on the regular street marker, took a picture and published it."

"And?" she said leaning back against the sofa.

"As fanatics do, Pratt's fans carried out their own investigations and identified the place. Just a non-descript corner of Venice."

"Did they turn against him?"

"Hardly. It's become so famous that Corte Sconta is used for other things too, not only our ristorante."

"Our" ristorante, she noted with a secret little pleasure.

"Who told you this story?"

"I've heard bits and pieces through the years but never put it all together until you asked. Then I checked it out."

"Awww, that's sweet. Thank you," and she rose up on her knees to lean over and kiss *him* on the nose.

But he wrapped his arms around her and pulled her close. At first she began to snuggle in but thought about the consequences and leaned back. "Shall we check out your research?"

"We shall," he said.

She reached behind the couch to get her black leather hiking boots.

"Babe we're not tromping through the wilds here."

"I know but when I wear these for long walks on the stone calles of Venice, my feet worship me later. They *are* nicely polished. See?"

He watched her lace her boots and his mouth twitched sensing a twitch in his cock, too. *Damn, why is it her goofy quirks turn me on?*

"This is a real treat, Marc."

"For me too, Marlee, " and he put his arm lightly across her shoulders as they started out.

"After the last two weeks' trip and the next few days of more travel, I can use a day of R&R with you." He pulled her closer to him as they walked. She reached part way around his waist hooking her thumb in his belt to support her arm. What was she doing? Hell, she knew exactly what she was doing.

After they found the secret place, he said, "Enough?"

"Yes. My feet are fine but my back feels as if I've been museum walking."

"Mine too. Let's loosen up by walking fast to Via Garibaldi where there's a place with good grub. Think you'll like it."

"Sounds like a plan.

* * *

On the restaurant's menu, she saw an entrée of *Sarde in Saor,* sardines marinated in sweet vinegar with chopped onions and raisins. Even though she usually avoided seafood, she'd been wanting to try this strange-sounding dish.

"I'm going to have it too, it's good here," Marc said. "Do you want pasta?"

"I might but——"

"I know, you'll wait and see."

She laughed. "I'm curious about something on the dessert menu called *Bruti ma boni,* Ugly but good. Sounds intriguing."

"It figures," he said with that tilted sideways grin she was beginning to appreciate.

"Do you know what they are?" she asked.

"Nope, but I will soon."

"What a great day, Marc. The minute you called, I knew it would be."

"Thank you."

She studied Marc across the table as he poured chilled Pinot Grigio into her glass. He was solid yet graceful and all his movements were precise and easy. *What else was he good at?* Ever since L.A., she'd been drawn to him on every level. She ate some of the crusty bread the server had brought with the wine. He ordered pasta with clams and she passed; she indulged in the bread.

After they'd eaten the sardine dish, she said, "The onions are sautéed. Guess I'd always thought they'd be raw. It's delicious." With coffee they shared *Bruti ma boni* which were misshapen cookies made with chopped almonds and marzipan. They were scrumptious and Marc had one, maybe two. She gobbled the rest.

"I have trouble holding back when something appeals to me," she said. "I keep telling myself to be more circumspect, but then——"

"Part of your charm, Marlee," he said, wondering if *he'd* ever appeal to her that way.

"I know you're making fun of me, but that's fine, I'll keep working on it."

He leaned back and chortled. "So, what have you been doing?"

"I've been re-visiting some favorite places. The doors of San Nicolò dei Mendicoli were finally open after two years of restoration. It's beautiful inside. The floors have that early -renaissance style of red Verona marble and a creamy marble—maybe travertine—laid in a checkered pattern. But the checkers are tipped to look like diamonds, beautiful marble diamonds. You've seen those floors in other Venetian churches, haven't you?"

"Oh yeah," he said. And for the first time, the subject of Venetian church floors was absolutely fascinating.

"The subtle greens and golds of the walls and art work in Nicolò are so elegant. Have you been there?"

"Not for ages. I'd like to go with you sometime, but at this moment, I'm curious about what happened after I disappeared. What happened to your relationship in L.A. that kept you at arms length from me?"

"It's not a pretty story."

"I've got broad shoulders."

That he did. She took a deep breath. "Paul, the man I was involved with back then, died in a plane crash over Catalina Island. The pilot had been flying without a current license."

"Jeezuz!" Marc said under his breath. "That must have been terrible for you."

She felt the old anguish and guilt and began drooping into herself.

"Marlowe?" he whispered and reached out to hold her hand.

She looked up from her slump. "The last time I saw him, we argued. Paul wanted me to go with him but I was taking my final bar exam that day, and he'd never been all that happy about the law-school thing anyway."

"Whoa, you mentioned law school earlier but I... Were you going to law school when you worked with me?"

She nodded. "Only one night class at a time."

"Why didn't you tell me? I thought we were pretty good friends back then."

"I... was trying out the waters and didn't want to mention something I wasn't sure of. I haven't even told my daughter, Mandy, because I preferred Ty not know. I hated to ask her *not* to tell her father."

"Why not let Ty know?"

She sighed. "He's like my mother was, any information might be used against me later."

Marc nodded as though he understood that.

"Enough heavy talk," she said. "Tell me about your glass-blower family in Murano."

"No one knew you were studying law at night except Paul?"

"My friend, Ellen, knew. In fact, she had introduced me to Paul and encouraged me to use the divorce proceeds to quit work and go full time. But I was too chicken and went part-time."

"Why didn't Paul like the idea of you studying law?"

"I never knew for sure. At times, he was overly protective. Maybe he feared I'd fail. He knew I was nervous about speaking in public and couldn't imagine me in a courtroom. I don't think fast on my feet."

"You hold your own with me just fine," he said.

"You make it easy, Marc. You're such a generous spirit." It was true, Marc did make it easy for her to be herself. And she found it exciting to have a man interested in *her* life not always needing to talk about his.

"Wow, thank you," he said.

"I bet you've never had stage fright." .

"Few Italians are afraid to stand up and speak their mind, particularly the males. Their mammas tell 'em they walk on water from the moment they take their first steps."

"I've heard that," she chuckled.

"Tell me more about your relationship with Paul."

"Marc, it's all in the past," she said squirming around on her chair.

"I know, but it's part of who you are isn't it?" he asked reaching to take her hand.

"Yesss, and that works both ways, Signore."

"I know," he said holding her eyes with his as well as both of her hands, "I know."

She inhaled and began, "Not long after he died, I realized it wouldn't have worked out anyway. Like Ty, he seemed embarrassed by me at times. You'd think I'd have seen those signs in Paul. Maybe I overlooked them because he didn't criticize me during sex as Ty did." She held up her hands and said, "Enough! What about your glass blowers?

"In a minute. What law school?"

"You are a bulldozer." He nodded wiggling his fingers in come-on signs with his left hand.

"Southern California Law School; not a famous one. They have two facilities: one in San Fernando Valley and one in West L.A."

"One last question," he said holding up a long forefinger. "Did you pass the Bar?"

"I did. By then, Ellen was the only one who knew anything about it so there wasn't much of a celebration."

"Well, I'll toast you now," and he raised his glass. They clinked and sipped.

"I knew you had smarts and guts, too, but… I'm impressed by your ability to work full time and go to law school too."

"Along with legal concepts, there's a massive amount of details to take in, but as a secretary, I'd learned to prioritize. And like many women, I knew how to juggle different parts of my life, running a house, raising children, the usual. Mostly, though, I was motivated."

He nodded, but she doubted he'd done all that much juggling. He was a man after all.

"Have you ever practiced law?"

"Not yet, but I will in Portland. After I pass the Oregon Bar and find a job, my goal is to work like a demon for a few years and somehow put enough away to come back to Venice forever. Crazy, huh?"

"Sounds like a decent plan, which reminds me, what is your daughter doing in Portland?"

"Another close friend, Angie, lives there and when Mandy visited with me a time or two, she checked out the Master's Program in Urban Planning at Portland State University and decided to go for it. As you can imagine, I'm proud of her."

"She must be a wise young woman to know what she wants."

"At twenty-one she's wiser than her mother ever was. She's also the apple of Ty's eye."

"But she has to know about your law degree sooner or later, right?"

"Yes and soon," Marlowe said finishing her wine. "The longer I don't tell her, the more it seems like a lie."

"Your turn," she said. "How did you decide to enter the construction field? Because of your father?"

"Counselor, that's two questions."

"The first will do," she grinned, "but you're still under oath."

"I know, but let's move a bit. Want to walk?"

"All fine and good, but…"

"I know, you won't let me off the hook," he said and called for the check.

CHAPTER FOURTEEN

They left the restaurant and walked along Via Garibaldi toward the island of San Pietro where a church could be seen in the distance. Marc said, "Did you know that San Marco was not the *duomo* until the nineteenth century? Before that, the cathedral of Venice was that one," and he pointed ahead.

"I did know that. And before you explain that a *duomo*, or cathedral, is not in every city because cathedral comes from the word seat, and there can't be a cathedral without a sitting bishop, I'm going to remind you that *you are avoiding* the topic at hand!"

A deep rumble burst out of his chest and he pulled her into his arms laughing. It was a loving laugh and intoxicating to her. Then, they stopped in front of a strange statue with live foliage surrounding a lazy lion sprawled at the feet of Garibaldi. Rough and ready Garibaldi marked this entrance to the Public Gardens of Venice.

"Shall we walk in the *Giardini*, for a while?" Marc said chuckling.

She nodded.

Marc began to point out various statuary when Marlowe stopped with her knuckles at her hips and cleared her throat.

"Yeah, yeah," he said. "But I better back up some before I talk about my vocational choice. Allowed, Madam inquisitor?"

"Allowed."

"When I was about ten, my parents sent me here to learn the Italian language and culture."

"I'm assuming you already spoke Italian."

"Right. As in other families like mine, my parents made sure I understood Italian knowing I'd learn English easily with kids at school. But they wanted me to be educated in more than the language."

She nodded.

"I moved in with my cousins, entered Scuola Elementaria, then Media and on to Superiore until I was fifteen. Went back to San Diego to enter high school. Those years here made a huge impression on me."

For a second she thought of her life in Venice at fifteen, but focused back on his story.

"And college?" she asked.

"I went to USC for God's sake. Even a frat boy, but never quite meshed with that crowd."

"Nevertheless, you were a Trojan of the crimson and gold."

He stopped to turn her to face him, "Cardinal and gold. One needs to be exact if one can distinguish between fire-engine red and cherry red in a certain sweater." His eyes glinted.

She smiled enjoying his memory of that inconsequential detail. "Back to USC," she said as they moved along the crushed-stone pathway passing other statues, shrubs and trees.

He graduated with a weird combo of ancient history and chemistry and "managed" to get into Pepperdine for an MBA, but not at the famous Malibu campus. In order to work for his dad in San Diego, he did his graduate studies at the Irvine campus. About the time he finished the business degree, his uncles in Murano wanted help. They had feared someone was embezzling and hoped he'd sort it out.

"Did you find a rat in the mix?" she asked.

"No, only a muddle with mixed signals. They needed one person to oversee the financial aspect. I stepped in as Chief Financial Officer, but only on an interim basis." He sighed. "They wanted to keep it all in the family and put the pressure on, but I held firm."

"Good for you," she said.

"Let's hop the next vaporetto heading toward the Arsenale. I could use a coffee and there's a nice bar in front of the Arsenale's grand entrance. Okay?"

"Sure, coffee sounds good."

As they waited on the pontile, Marlowe said, "Marc?"

"Yes."

"You can probably guess I'd love a tour through your family's factory."

"Sure, we can arrange that."

"I'm curious about how they create those brilliant colors in glass. I read that Vivarini was from a family of glass makers. You probably know about that."

"Vaguely remember something," he said as they stepped onto the vaporetto.

"Evidently his brilliant colors lasted because he knew some secret process for grinding colored glass, even gems, into his paint to create that famous dazzle." They found a place on the open deck.

"You're interested in everything aren't you, but you're not exactly a dilettante."

She turned to him, "You can't imagine what a compliment that is. My ex patronized me saying I was a dilettante and didn't know how to focus."

"He was a jerk to let you get away."

"Maybe I've learned a few things along the way," she said trying to waggle her eyebrows the way Marc often did.

"Could be, but you need more practice on your eyebrow acrobatics."

CHAPTER FIFTEEN

When they'd settled at a table under a large awning, he said, "Now, we can continue our catch up. Tell me more about what went wrong in your marriage. Something about betrayal?"

"Oh Marc, it's the old familiar story."

"Not yours. How about it?"

"Only if you'll let me know what went wrong in yours."

"I will. You go first."

"I'll try to condense it as much as I can."

"As far as I'm concerned, we've got plenty of time. Are you on a tight schedule?"

"No, but—"

"Now who's stalling," he interrupted with a gentle smile. "Some stories are difficult to re-open, Marlee, but if we're to know each other better... I hope you want to—"

"Yes, Marc, I do."

Marlowe and Ty had been high-school sweethearts and thought they were in love. She was eighteen, what did she know? They both went to the University of Nebraska, and except for a few rocky periods, she didn't date many others. She'd felt committed to him because they'd had sex.

"That's not the way it works for guys."

"I know. It doesn't for most girls now either what with the pill."

The waiter brought their coffees, and when he walked away, Marc asked, "How old were you when you married?"

"Nineteen."

"Wow."

"Yes, wow. Mandy was born when I was twenty-one."

"Then?" he asked.

"Surely you don't want to hear a heap of depressing tales."

"No one's life is all sunshine and daisies. If it's about you, I want to know."

"Well, after Mandy's birth, I had two miscarriages and then we had a son and…" she felt her throat begin to constrict. She'd thought by now she could breeze through this, but she heard her voice wobble and felt her insides start that awful trembling.

"And?" he asked putting his warm hand on hers as it lay on the table.

In a big rush, she said, "He didn't make it to his sixth-month birthday." She sucked in a gulp of air. Marc didn't say a word but moved his chair closer to her and held her. After a moment when she'd calmed down, he whispered, "What was his name?"

"Peter. He was the opposite of Mandy, my blue-eyed, blond beauty. Petey had dark eyes and hair and rosy cheeks. He seemed such a sturdy fellow; he'd just begun to sit up by himself."

"What happened? Could you tell me this once? I won't ask again."

"Some sort of infant pneumonia… he went so fast," then the tears came. Tears she'd thought had long dried up. Marc continued to hold her then pulled her up and began walking her slowly away from the bar. He signaled the proprietor who nodded to Marc. Gradually, her tears subsided. He had a clean handkerchief and gave it to her as they reached the row of stone lions lined up on one side of the Arsenale entrance. They stood before the gateway to the basin still enclosed from long ago by brick walls where the Venetian fleet had been built and sent out to conquer trade routes that made the city rich and famous.

They moved quietly toward four lions carved ages ago and brought—more likely stolen by Venetians—from the Greek island of Delos. Marlowe pointed to the second one. "She's always been my favorite. With that weary look, you just know she's carrying the weight of the world on that pock-marked swayback."

"She does seem to be telling us that, doesn't she?" Marc agreed. "I wonder how many lions are scattered all over Venice?"

"Who knows? They're everywhere," she said. "representing power ever since the Venetians adopted Saint Mark as their patron saint. When was it, the ninth century?"

"Around that time, I guess," he said.

"You ought to know, he's your namesake, " she said smiling up at him. "Anyway, I've conducted a mini survey—not a numerical one, more a personality one. Do you know that most Venetian lions are pussy cats? Have you noticed how some *seem* ferocious but up close, they're gentle… like you."

"Me?" he said with a little grin creeping across his face.

"Mm-Hmm. When I catch sight of a golden lion perched on a pole above San Marco gleaming there in the sunshine, I often think of you—a golden lion."

A flush crept up Marc's neck to his face. Marlowe had gone over the top with her romantic fantasy and blushed herself. Hurrying to the other side of the building, she said,. "This large one over here," she said turning to him, "has ancient runes carved on his side, probably by your ancestors."

Marc followed knowing exactly what she was doing. "Yep. They probably wrote something like 'Thor was here.'"

She laughed aloud.

That laugh made him feel good. Maybe she'd weathered the worst. "Let's get another coffee, okay?" he said.

"And maybe a cookie?"

"Or two?" he said smiling down at her as they walked back to the bar.

After they were seated again, Marc said, "Dare I ask what next?"

"More woeful revelations?" she asked.

He nodded.

Determined to finish this embarrassing stuff from her past, she told him of the creeping endometriosis that had spread fast shortly after Petey's death. She stopped. Then looked into Marc's eyes wondering if he could handle this female stuff. He didn't turn away—just waited—and she sensed that Marc could probably handle most anything she threw at him.

"It wasn't cancer," she said, "but the growth had advanced too far, and everything had to go, so—"

"How old were you then?"

"Thirty."

"Jeez, that's way too young, isn't it? Did it throw you into menopause?"

"Sure. But two months later, we moved to Ty's first faculty job at the University of Virginia where I found a knowledgeable doctor. I've been fine ever since," she said lifting her chin as if in defiance.

"Not much time to recuperate," he said. "After all that, *mia cara*, you've come through with an amazing outlook on life. I think I can guess what happened in your marriage with Ty as a new college professor."

She sighed losing her former bravado. "Our marriage was a mistake from the beginning, but it took a long time to figure it out."

"You're not alone," he muttered.

"It was classic, I suppose. He was already unhappy with me in bed and often blamed me when there was a problem."

"Why was it your—"

"Maybe he was right," she went on. "I tried to please him, but for years he didn't have a clue about pleasing me and…" She looked straight into Marc's silver eyes again, took a breath and rushed on, "I faked a lot. It's the worst thing a woman can do to herself and her partner, don't you think?"

What am I doing? She looked at her hands clenched in her lap and shook her head back and forth.

He stepped over to pay the bill and came back taking her hand. "Let's go home, love. I think our ride's coming." He guided her to a quiet corner of the vaporetto's open area. With his back to others, he created a sense of privacy. "I'm sorry. I shouldn't have pushed so hard."

"Glad you did. Next time, it'll be my turn to push," and a faint little smile curved her lips.

"How've you stayed this positive?" he asked.

"My Aunt Belle's influence, I think," she said standing up straighter. "And after the accident I finally got it."

"Accident?" he said. "What did you get?"

"Oh Lord, Marc, I thought I'd put that away for good."

"Marlee, what's that story?"

"How about switching to your story for a while?"

"We will, we will, but the accident?"

CHAPTER SIXTEEN

Marlowe knew he'd get the rest of her story, if not today another time for sure. He stood at her door but didn't lift her key out of her hand or move in as he had that night after dinner. She sighed thinking she might as well finish it. "Come in Marc. Would you like a glass of wine? I'm all coffee-d out."

He nodded. "I'd like that, but if you're—"

"It's good to be away from people. The barista must have thought you were with a hysterical woman back there."

"Don't think so. He seemed sympathetic. Barmen have seen it all, love."

She nodded. While he opened the bottle for her, she found some cheese. They carried things to the coffee table and settled around it. Marlowe took a gulp of wine, inhaled deeply and let out a ragged sigh, but said nothing.

"Marlee?"

"Marc, I can't talk about that accident today after all," and sank back against the couch.

"Sprout, I think you're due a good night's rest. He picked her up and carried her to her bedroom intending to lay her gently there and slip out quietly, but her scent lured him to hold her a little closer—a little longer. He dared not lay her down knowing he'd be there with her in a heartbeat. Instead, he sat beside her on the side of the bed. But, desire flared and was burning away all common sense. Even though he was sure she wanted him, he knew he shouldn't push her. Not tonight

"God, Marlee, I want you." Control. He needed control now as never before.

She gasped but didn't push him away. She swallowed hard and put her hand against his chest feeling his heart beat. Why was she resisting? She did want him. But he wasn't available. Not for sure, and she didn't want to be hurt again. This time it would be hurt by a man she desired but couldn't have. It was only sex, she could handle that, couldn't she?

He lifted her sweater and reached his hand beneath to feel her silk shirt. He pulled it out of her slacks and slipped his hand beneath to stroke the smooth satin of her skin. He leaned down to kiss her. He'd never stopped wanting her and was struggling to resist. She shivered as he traced the tip of her ear with his tongue and whispered, "I want to taste you, love. I want your breast in my mouth."

A little sound caught in the back of her throat.

"I want to be inside you, Marlee, all hot and slick around me."

Marlowe couldn't get those images out of her head and began to tremble. She felt fire rage through her veins. But then, words flew out of her mouth, "But you're not free! What happens when I have to leave Venice?"

He lifted his head and glared. "You won't fuck me until I make a promise I can't keep right now, is that it?"

Her face crumpled, "That's not what I said. Not what I meant!"

"Are you sure?" he said pulling away. "Has some other man in Venice already made you that promise, love?"

"What do you mean?"

"Never mind. I'd better leave. It's been interesting."

She followed him to the door. "Marc. You don't understand."

"What I understand is that you've been teasing me beyond what I can endure, Miz Marlowe Osborne," and his face had turned cold. For the first time, she noticed the aggressive Scandinavian angles of his face.

"It's you who teases," she said. "You who don't play fair! I thought we were getting to know each other. But in truth, it's only been me who's spilled her guts."

For a moment, his face sagged. He looked stricken. Then he drew back and said, "I can't do this."

"Can't do what?" her voice sounded petulant.

"I can't cram in a lifetime between now and when you leave. If you want to know more about me, you've got my number," and with that, he was gone.

She was stunned. As Marlowe walked back up the six steps feeling like the dejected lioness at the Arsenale, someone knocked on the door. Did he forget something? Did he want to talk it over? But when she opened the door, a delivery man stood holding a huge bouquet of red roses with a card that had one word, "Sorry."

CHAPTER SEVENTEEN

Sunday morning, Rich called about eight thirty.

"Hey, Marlowe, things aren't going so good."

She said nothing.

"I miss you like hell and want to say I'm sorry… sorry for last week. I think I need my head examined."

She should hang up.

"Guess you agree, eh?"

"I can't know what drives you."

"I've been thinking a lot about that. Did you get the roses?"

"Yes. They're beautiful, thank you."

"Listen, I'm in Hamburg but will be home about five on Tuesday, could—"

"I'm off to Florence to visit Lucia," she said.

"When will you be back?"

"Not sure yet, we may go to Arezzo for a special Etruscan exhibit."

"I see… Could we have a quiet meal maybe Wednesday or Thursday?"

"Call first."

"Marlowe don't push me away without another chance." She heard a door open and a man speaking. "Sorry, gotta go. I'll call you." And the line was dead.

Marlowe sighed and felt that everything had gone to hell. She pulled on her walking boots and grabbed her coat. She'd walk wherever her feet took her. She brooded and walked thinking she hadn't really learned a damned thing about relationships since her divorce. She felt empty when she replayed Marc's disgusted words.

It all came back on *her* for implying she wanted more than a fling. But... dammit, she did. How crazy was that? He was married. No matter it wasn't a real marriage, he wasn't free. She continued walking, avoiding open campos, sticking to dark, narrow alleys where shadows seemed to fit her mood. With Rich, she'd never thought of anything but a fling while in Venice, but something different was happening with Marc. At least something had happened to her. By four, she couldn't stand it any longer and went home to punch in Marc's number. It rang five times. She was about to hang up, when his answering service came on. She wasn't sure if she was devastated or relieved. She stammered, "Marc. I do want to know your story but I'm leaving for Florence tomorrow. Be back in a few days. Ciao."

* * *

When she returned the following Thursday afternoon, the stink of Rich's dead roses assaulted her. Before doing anything, she gathered them into a plastic bag and set it beside the door. At bedtime, she would put it out for the trash girl who came early each morning. This system of door-to-door collection happened all over Venice and seemed to work well. Marlowe asked someone once if the garbage scows dumped into the sea. The woman had seemed horrified at the idea and assured her they took it to a processing station on the mainland.

It felt good to unwind in solitude after her trip to Lucia's. A dear friend, but her intensity often left Marlowe exhausted.

* * *

Late Friday afternoon, someone knocked at her door. Before she could see who it was or call out, she heard, "Special Delivery for someone named Buttons."

"No Buttons here," Marlowe said frowning but opened the door to Marc.

"Lady, it's my last delivery of the day. You might as well see what's inside this package."

"Marc, you've got to stop dropping by bearing gifts."

"It's fun to surprise you. May I come in?"

"Of course, but... I wouldn't mind if you'd call me first."

"You're right, Sprout, I will from now on." He followed her up the steps and put the package on the small dining table as she turned to him. "Marlee, I'm so sorry. I took advantage of your emotional state. It won't happen again. Can we start over?" He held out his arms tentatively, but when she walked into his embrace, he groaned with relief.

"I'm sorry too," she said. "I do want to begin again... please forget that stupid remark I made. You need to know that whatever happens between us has no strings—none. We might even continue a long-distance friendship when I go back. I'm here only for R&R."

Oh shit. He had no doubt about wanting her for more than a vacation affair, but he'd fucked up royally when he'd accused her of withholding sex. Damn Elise for keeping his hands tied. He was not going to give up on Marlowe—not again. He knew there was something between them. Maybe something lasting. He released her from his embrace and handed her the package. "Well, Signora?"

She opened it to find a small bottle of Marsala Wine. "What a pretty bottle." Doing her best to keep things light, she said, "Is it happy hour yet?"

"Anytime with you, Marlee, is happy hour."

She groaned as if in pain, "What a line." But it was impossible to stay cross with him for long. "Come help me. I think I saw some aperitif glasses in one of these overhead cupboards."

He found them and opened the bottle. "Let's see if the wine's any good," he said carrying the glasses and the bottle to the couch. He sat on one end where his long legs could stretch out beside the coffee table. She scooted onto the other corner, kicked off her shoes, put one leg under the other and leaned back against a large cushion. He handed her a glass.

"Mmm, delicious. Thank you, Marc, but I do not plan to attempt zabaglione in this kitchen. What have you been up to?"

"I made a run to Paris to follow up on electrical switches and other modern fixtures that've been delayed for the Barovier palazzo. It hasn't been updated in my lifetime."

"Were you able to work out the problem?" she asked.

"Used the tried and true method. Parked myself on their doorstep until they handed the fixtures over. We'll all be settled in soon. And you?"

"Not as productive as your efforts for sure. Still pursuing Tintoretto's haunts and reviewing bar-review papers. But it's hard to get in the mood to study with all of Venice calling. More?" she asked holding the Marsala toward him.

"No thanks, but before we continue, I need to ask you something."

She tensed. Now what? After her stupid remark that last time, she wasn't sure how she felt about moving into a closer relationship with him.

"What's going on with your relationship with Tron?"

"What?" she jolted up hugging her knees tighter. "How do you know I have a relationship and with whom?"

"*Venezia è troppo piccola, tesoro, e le notizie si diffondono molto velocemente.*"

"I'm thinking you said that gossip spreads fast in little Venice."

"You've got it. And you, Cupcake, are a hot item in this burg. People are fascinated that a lone woman who noses around the city with a *zaino* (he pronounced it zyno) on her back, wearing clunky boots, no makeup and no jewelry except '*un paio di penosi orecchini placcati in argento*' seems to have snagged one of the most eligible bachelors in town."

"I do so wear makeup. And I've seen how Italian women view my footwear. Haven't they noticed the varicose veins and crippled feet on their grandmothers who hobble in house slippers after years on stilettos?"

"Guess they think it's worth it."

"Zyno? she asked.

"Knapsack."

" *Si, si, zaino.*" (She pronounced it zaheeno.) How could she forget that?

Marc had a puzzled look. "In Murano, we all pronounced it zyno."

"You ought to know, you grew up here," she quipped and hurried on not yet ready to tell of her time here as a teen. "Tell me again about my earrings. Evidently they think that well-dressed women wear only gold. Don't they know some people look better in silver?"

"Worse. You missed the silver-plated part—*placcati in argento.*"

"Hunh. Well, for their information—whoever *they* are—my earrings are white gold. Maybe white gold's worth less. Don't know. Don't care. The other word *penosi*. Penurious?"

"'Pathetic' in this case," he said enjoying himself.

"Who's saying such things? Glamorous Italian women, no doubt."

"Glamorous to their eyeballs."

"I'd like to see them take off alone with two carry-ons for a couple months and manage to look drop-dead gorgeous all the time."

Her eyes glittered and her hair seemed full of static. "You're something when you're riled. But you're right, it wouldn't happen in a thousand years. Back to the question."

"Repeat it please."

"Not necessary, counselor, you know the question."

Yes, she did. And what *was* going on between her and Rich Tron, she wondered? "Up and down," she replied.

"At this moment?" he asked with a slight frown on his forehead.

"Down."

"Well, then," he said, "how about we step out tonight? Have you eaten at Cipriani's on Torcello Island?"

"The truth?"

"Of course."

"Damn," she said. "I have."

"Okay, Marlee, it's okay. We'll go anyway. What dessert do they have that you lust for?"

"They're all good."

"How many have you had for God's sake?"

"Only two but I could tell they'd all be wonderful."

Again that twitchy grin. "Could we leave the Zattere around seven? That way we ought to get there in plenty of time for our 8:30 reservation."

That's why he looked so elegant when he'd just dropped by. "You've already made a reservation. You're so full of—"

"Maybe so, Marlee, but reservations can be cancelled," he said with his dynamite smile.

"You're the only person who calls me that. I like it. I've dragged this male-female name around a long time."

"Marlee it is. How soon can you be ready?"

"Let's see," she said, placing her index finger at the side of her mouth where a dimple would be if she had one, "I need at least an hour to apply several layers of makeup and—"

"Don't you dare," he said grabbing her shoulders for a quick hug, "no need for layers of any kind. It's 5:30. How about I run an errand and return around 6:30?"

"Fine."

They stood up, he gave her a light kiss and let himself out the door. She stepped down to turn the key and stood leaning against the door. Drawing in a deep breath, she wondered what she was getting herself into. Then she yelled. Whoeee! Auntie Belle, I'm going for it.

CHAPTER EIGHTEEN

While Marlowe dressed for dinner with Marc, butterflies jumped inside like they did when she got ready for the prom. Crazy, but damn, it was fun to be with him. And who else knew her fondness for zabaglione or Marsala? Or cared?

The phone rang and Rich said, "Where have you been all day?"

"Excuse me?" she said.

"I've been trying to reach you."

"I heard what you said. But wondered what difference it made?"

Silence... "I deserved that," he said. "Wish you had a cell phone. If you stay here much longer, I may surprise you with one. Would you like that?"

"Thanks, but I'm not sure. At home, I only carry one for emergencies. No one knows my number, and I like being unconnected."

"I see."

Marlowe said nothing.

"Guess I don't understand why you wouldn't want me to reach you?"

Oh really. "Rich, I was anti cells long before I met you. No one has alone time anymore."

She didn't want to lie, but she'd been glad he couldn't reach her. Even though she'd felt a kind of emptiness since their upset at the tournament, she couldn't say she'd missed him. At a safe distance when she can't *trap* him, he needs her, wants her. But let her get close, he turns and runs.

"Are you there?" he asked.

"Yes."

"I'm in Toulouse but will be back in Venice Monday afternoon. Would you have dinner with me? Some place quiet where we can talk?"

"I'm on my way out, Rich, call when you get in town?"

"It'll only take a moment for an answer, Marlowe." She heard a door open and a man's voice calling for Monsieur Tron.

"Damn," he said. "Gotta go. Are we on for Monday? We need to talk."

She hesitated. "Just call me."

"Marlowe, please. Six okay?"

"Okay," she sighed.

"Thanks. Ciao, Marlowe."

He did sound hassled. She tended to forget that he and Carla and Marc all had established lives, while she was on an extravagant R&R trip.

* * *

"Marc, tell me which scarf you like the best," Marlowe said holding up two.

His eyes roamed over her breasts, but it didn't feel creepy. Just the opposite.

"Do you need to cover the shape of that red sweater with anything?"

In a mock school-teacher voice, she said, "I'm wearing a scarf, Marc. Which one?"

"Okay, okay. The black with the red, stylized flowers, they're a perfect match for your sweater."

"Then I'm ready."

"Let's take this," he said and plucked her long, hooded raincoat from a hook near the top of the steps. "It could rain."

"You think a storm's brewing?"

"Might be. Does that bother you?"

"No, I adore thunder and lightning," she said, "reminds me of—"

"Don't say it," he said.

"I wouldn't dare!"

"You're a strange one to like storms," he said as they walked toward the Zattere.

"Hope you like strange," she quipped.

"The idea's growing on me," he said and laid his arm lightly across her shoulder. "You'll get plenty of rain in November. Is that why you come this time of year?"

"That and fewer pesky tourists."

"Oh yes, those pesky tourists of whom you are not one."

"That's right. Like Paul Theroux, I'm a traveler," she said lifting her chin.

* * *

She's an original, and damn if her quirky ways don't draw me straight into her circle like a moth to a flame. He remembered how her off-the-wall outlook laced with a kind of naiveté had sucked him in five years ago. Why in hell hadn't he kept track of her instead of slinking off with his tail between his legs when Johnson gave him the boot?

When they arrived at his launch with its glowing mahogany and gleaming hardware, he asked her to wait while he stepped down to open up. Then he lifted her into the rocking boat and shoved back the glass cover of a mini cabin.

"Sweet," she said running her hand on the smooth wood. "Is this a company boat?"

"Yeah. We all have use of this one; individual family members have their own. So far, I haven't invested in one, but seldom borrow because boat owners hate having someone else handle their boats even more than car owners do."

"I'm not surprised," she said. "From time immemorial, horses, carriages, cars and boats have all been symbols of status for men, don't you think?"

"Mm-Hmm," he said distracted while checking dials and gages before shoving off. She stayed quiet and watched.

It seemed to take a long time and Marlowe asked, "Is there a problem?"

"Don't think so, but I haven't used this since we've changed to LPG."

"LPG?"

"Liquid Petroleum Gas," he said tinkering. "The change is better for the Lagoon—it causes little or no pollution. But with an inboard motor, we have to use a conversion kit and… hot damn, I've got it!"

He was like a big boy with a favorite toy. But, didn't she feel like a princess going for an elegant ride? A freshness floated in the air. Was it ozone drifting in from the sea? Maybe a storm *was* brewing. She loved feeling those ephemeral vibrations in the air before a storm and sensed a stir in her stomach—that thrilling flip that comes sometimes in a carnival ride, but she suspected this flip had more to do with Marc than a possible storm.

With the motor purring, he guided them into the Giudecca Canal which seemed enormous compared to riding on a hulking vaporetto. They needed to dodge other traffic, all of which seemed larger—much larger—except for two hardy gondoliers maneuvering out there. Gondolas did have right-of-way, but still it looked treacherous for them. In spite of the inboard motor, it was too noisy for comfortable conversation, so she settled back to enjoy the ride as they slipped through the canals of Venice and glided under one small bridge after another. From water level, the buildings seemed immense, even ominous. It reminded her she *must* take a ride in a gondola before this trip was over. Old feelings of disgust for Ty rose up again. He'd known how much she wanted to go in a gondola that time but was too chicken to tell the professor he'd be taking his wife. The old man would have understood, but the trouble with Ty was he didn't have a romantic bone in his body. *Stop being such a jerk, you're letting the crummy past steal from this terrific present.*

They were into the open Lagoon and Marc sped up to roar past the walled cemetery. Even those pinkish-red brick walls that had always appeared fragile looked formidable from the vantage point of a small boat. As they passed Murano, she wondered which was the Barovier glass factory and hoped she'd get that tour. When Marc throttled down, she was ready to stop. Motor boats exhausted her with their constant throbbing and chopping against the waves. But what a vacation! For days she hadn't thought about all she needed to do when it was over or the dread of visiting the convent to hear another negative response about the whereabouts of her son.

"How're you doing?" Marc said cutting the engine to drift into Cipriani's dock.

Coming out of her reverie, she said," Great. Going through the canals was fabulous, and look at that beautiful sky. All those clouds rolling in. What a treat this is, a royal treat."

"It's nice to have a woman appreciate instead of demand."

He gave her a sweet hug as he lifted her from the boat onto the dock. She hugged back and brushed her lips along his neck which she was able to reach easily since he held her up for a longer than necessary moment.

"Go on in, I'll be there in a sec," he said with a look that made her feel adored.

It was barely misting and she turned her face to it. The little inn didn't look like much from outside. It was a squat two-story building of pale beige stucco. On the ground floor, geraniums in terra-cotta pots added some color. Two small balconies on the upper floor faced the canal they'd come in on. Otherwise its facade gave no hint of the elegance of food and decor inside. Marc caught up to her as she reached the open lattice-work canopy with the name painted in bright green over the front door. They walked into Locanda Cipriani together, and she wasn't one bit surprised when the same efficient head waiter—who didn't recognize her from her visit two weeks ago—recognized Signor Barovier. A lone woman tends to get stuck in a corner and forgotten, but they were seated near a window. Darkness had closed in, though, and they couldn't see the rose garden about which the inn's brochure boasted. The walls of the dining area were of burgundy-colored bricks. Pale pink tablecloths covered round tables set with scarlet napkins and a small bouquet of scarlet roses sat in the center of each. Old world charm and Marlowe loved it.

"What would you like?" he asked.

"You choose."

"Whoa, that's tricky," he said.

"I'll gobble up whatever you pick. No, wait," she said holding up her hand. "I shall enjoy everything in a sedate manner."

Marc's mouth turned up on the left side as he said, "What'd you have when you were here before?"

"Let's see. I had ravioli with porcini dusted with white truffles. Delicious but my palate is not sensitive enough to understand why white truffles are special. I didn't have a main course."

"Dessert I'll bet."

"Yesss, I had cremè brûlé made with Courvoisier. But I think I'll skip dessert tonight."

"Is that possible?" he asked.

"Is it possible to decide later?"

"Babe." Was he laughing at her again? No matter, she enjoyed watching him enjoy her.

Soon, they were served flutes of light, bubbly Prosecco and an array of crusty breads and canapes. What a lovely way to begin a meal, she thought, and forced herself to nibble. While Marc ordered, she made a trip to the ladies room, to check on the state of her hair but also because she wanted to be surprised by his order.

When she returned, he said, "Were you afraid you'd overhear my orders?"

"I was. This way, it'll be a surprise."

He raised his flute and said, "To surprises."

"To surprises," she said and they touched glasses. "Four people over there are looking at us. Do you know them?"

He looked over and waved. "I do."

"Will it be all over Venice that another eligible bachelor has been snared by the American slut?"

"Yep."

"Well then," she said, draining the last drop of her Prosecco and raising her glass on high, "To sluts."

He sputtered but raised his glass and mumbled, "Salute."

"Do you they know you're married?"

"Yes," and his eyes grew shadowy.

"Then that confirms my slutdom."

"Probably, but they don't know the whole story as you do."

Did she get the whole story, she wondered?

"Marlee, one thing you need to know, I don't lie—can't."

It was as if he'd read her mind. Was she that transparent? "I believe you, but I do want more of your story. Now, where were we?"

"Inquisition time, huh? You already know about college and my uncles calling me here for help, and... Looks like I have a reprieve," he said, "here comes our soup."

The server placed a large flat bowl in front of Marc and a smaller one for her.

After he left, she said, "What's with this dinky bowl?"

"You gave me carte blanche, didn't you? And knowing your eyes and your stomach—"

"Hunh. What if I *really* like something and want more?"

"Guess we'll have to come back," he said with that smile tucked in a corner of his mouth.

She leaned over the bowl and sniffed. "Smells divine." With great restraint, she waited until he picked up his spoon. He waited.

"Ladies first, Marlee, always—in all things. A lesson learned at my father's knee," he said looking directly into her eyes.

She took a large swallow of mineral water. She knew exactly what he meant and it had nothing to do with soup. They leaned over their steaming soup and enjoyed it in silence—lost in their own thoughts. She wondered what kind of lover he'd be, remembering the sexy images he'd planted earlier. Was he holding back this time, waiting for *her* to make the next move?

CHAPTER NINETEEN

"So," Marlowe said, "what led you into construction?"

"I haven't been avoiding your question, it's just not that interesting. Long before I finished the MBA, I knew I wanted something to do with construction. Either with Dad, or maybe with real-estate development. When we met at Johnson's, I was sticking my toes into development. Now, though…" and he gazed out the window at the dark sky and finished his Prosecco. "Sorry, I was dreaming. Guess I've become hooked on the European way of life."

I can understand that," she said, "it's certainly my long-range goal."

"For a long time?"

"Maybe since I read about Ancient Rome in the third grade," she laughed the response. "But for sure after actually coming to Italy."

"And here's our first course," Marc said. "Yours is saffron risotto with zucchini and mine is cannelloni with riccotta cheese and asparagus. What do you think?"

"I think I want both," she said, and he rumbled softly. She loved his rumbly laugh; it wrapped around her like a warm bathrobe.

"Tell you what. I don't care for saffron so your food's safe, but after you make space on your plate, I'll share some of my cannelloni with you."

"I'll let you know," she said.

"Don't wait too long, I'm hungry tonight." *Hungry for you.*

They ate awhile in contented silence. When a bottle of Montefalco Rosso appeared on the table, she recognized it as the same that Rich had brought the night they first...

"Is something wrong with the wine?" he asked.

She shook her head. "I've had this before. It's excellent." *Because I don't tell him the whole story doesn't mean I'm lying.* But something about Marc made her want to fess up.

He nodded. "How's the risotto?" He switched subjects, but she thought he'd sensed something. In truth, she relished his close scrutiny. Was she a narcissist? Certainly his genuine interest fed a life-long desire to have someone interested in her real self—not to catch her out the way Mom and Ty often did. At that moment, Marlowe added "genuine interest" to the list of what she wanted in a man along with being tall and strong—like Grandpa—having a sense of humor—also like Grandpa—and, of course, being gorgeous and great in bed and... she noticed Marc staring at her. She swallowed the bite she'd been holding in her mouth.

"This risotto is delicious," she said, "too bad you don't care for saffron, I *would* share you know," and grinned at him. "How did your parents react when you came back here instead of settling in San Diego?"

"They're on my side, Marlee. Something I'm thinking you never had."

She started to protest.

"Hey, I'm sure your parents wanted the best for you, but it sounds as if they couldn't see what *you* wanted. Hmm?"

"You're right. I envy you for the warmth and affection you seem to feel from all your family."

"Yeah, who knows where I would have ended if they hadn't stepped up for me," he said.

"Have you tried to find out more about your birth parents?"

He nodded and took a bite of his cannelloni. He chewed and swallowed, and said, "There's an agency on a retainer of sorts; they don't charge much until they find something definitive. I seldom think about it anymore."

"Do your folks know?" she asked.

"They're fine with it."

"What would you do if tomorrow the agent called and said, 'we've found your mother'?"

"You ask hard questions, Marlee. I have no earthly idea," and again he stared into space. "I suppose it'd depend on a thousand things. I've read lots of documented stories that show why a reunion could be devastating. It's probably crazy to keep on looking."

It was Marlowe's turn to stare into space. Her chair felt as uncomfortable as the ones at the convent. She shifted. She felt overly warm—almost queasy.

Marc looked at her obvious discomfort. "Are you all right?" he asked.

She nodded taking a swallow of the smooth red wine and reaching for a piece of crusty bread. The waiter came by to pour more wine. Feeling more composed, she said, "Life is a mix, isn't it? By the time we're our age, oh excuse me, I should say 'my august age,' you being much younger. Anyway, it's good to know oneself."

"Four years older doesn't make you very august, besides, you know I prefer older women." He tweaked her nose lightly, "But I agree, it is good to know oneself. Do you?"

She sighed and slouched back in her chair. "Now you're asking a hard one. Guess I'm still learning. But I've quit worrying about what I cannot do—almost. Instead, I try to keep Auntie Mame's philosophy in mind."

"And that is?"

"'The world is a banquet and most poor suckers are starving!'"

"Marlee," he said through a mini-rumble, "you are *not* starving. From what I've seen, you seem to partake of that banquet with gusto," and his bottomless grey eyes glistened.

"Thanks. I'm taking that as acceptance," she said.

"Oh yes. You are accepted. Here's another one for you, Hemingway I think. Hang on, see if I can get it right, 'The world breaks everyone, then some become strong at the broken places.'"

"I'm guessing that fits you, Marc," she said and then wanted to take back her words.

"How's that? Not knowing my birth parents? Given the luck with my adoptive ones, I can't see how that's broken me."

Should she go on? He was too good at reading her. "I was thinking more of your married situation."

The waiter's assistant approached in a flourish to clear their plates and bring their entrées proclaiming each dish with elaborate ceremony as he placed them before them.

When he swanned away, she said, "Mine is beautiful and the aroma is heavenly. What is *faraona*?"

"You're having breast of guinea hen glazed with a white-grape reduction. Dig in."

"And you're having squid. If nothing else I can tell by the color. What else is in there?"

"Radicchio in a cognac sauce. Wanna bite?" he asked.

"No thank you. I'll concentrate on mine."

* * *

The group of four got up to leave and the woman Marlowe had been admiring broke away and came toward them. She was one of those striking Italian women with large features: a strong graceful nose, large dark eyes, nicely arched brows and long lashes. Her Mediterranean complexion glowed and her sleek dark hair was swept back from her forehead. She wore large gold hoops in her ears, and a necklace of gold links lay on a full bosom. She'd been a lively conversationalist and laughed a lot with her friends. Dressed in a form-fitting, long-sleeved black dress, she was stunning. But as she stood and walked toward them, Marlowe couldn't help noting with a little evil glee in her heart that she had thick legs and ankles.

She spoke rapidly in Italian, "*Marco, non ci vediamo da così tanto tempo che,* it's been a long time since we've seen each other."

He stood up and gave her the double air kiss then turned to Marlowe saying in English, "Marlowe Osborne, I'd like to introduce you to a long-time friend, Donatella Brunetti."

"*Piacere*," Marlowe responded smiling and was glad she wasn't fluent enough to blurt out something stupid about Donatella being related to Marlowe's favorite fictional Venetian detective, Commissario Brunetti.

"*Piacere*," Donatella said reaching her be-ringed hand to Marlowe and they shook. Her hand was warm, her handshake firm, and Marlowe liked her right away. In careful English, Donatella said, all the while smiling at Marlowe, "Marco you must bring Marlowe sometime." He smiled. She pursed her shapely, scarlet lips into an exaggerated "kiss, kiss" and turned to join her group. And Marlowe watched Donatella's surprisingly large ass move away.

Marc sat down. "That's over," he sighed.

"Is she one?"

"One what?"

"One that called my earrings pathetic."

He turned to her stifling a laugh, "Lord, I don't want her to think I'm laughing at her."

"Don't worry, both women went into the ladies room. Well?"

"She is somewhat of a gossip, but I didn't hear it from her. I knew she'd come over to check you out, though. She's a good egg at heart. We were in school together and she's been trying to hook me up with some of her friends. Is your food cold?"

She took a bite. "No. Yours?"

"Nope. She was wise to not interfere long while we were eating. A good Italian trait."

"Particularly at Cipriani's," Marlowe said. "Marc?"

"Yeah."

"May I call you Marco?"

"No."

The lights blinked. The wind had picked up.

"Be right back, I want to check the boat."

That was a definite no, she thought. She continued to nibble at her food and thought of her summers working in Nebraska cornfields, and now sitting here at this beautiful table on the ancient island where Venice began. Even better was this gorgeous, witty, considerate man beside her. It was too much like a dream and she feared it might slip away. *Well, Mame, while it lasts I'm going to sample all of him*, and then she wondered… did she mean all?

"So far everything's in order," Marc said. "I tied it down even more than I already had and one of the guys will make sure there's plenty of fuel; we might need extra to get home tonight."

"That's a good idea," she said.

"Worried?"

Marlowe shook her head, "I feel safe in your hands, Marc."

"Carte blanche again?"

"Absolutely."

"Power, absolute power, it could go to my head."

The waiters were placing large candles in hurricane holders on the tables. Their server poured the last of the wine asking if Marc wanted more. He looked at her; she shook her head, but Marc asked him to wait a moment. "I didn't order dessert. Thought you'd like to choose."

"Believe it or not, I'll pass, but a small green salad might be nice."

The waiter understood and asked if Marc wanted one too. He nodded.

Marlowe took a last bite of the guinea hen and scraped the remaining sauce with a spoon.

"I believe you enjoyed that dish," he said as she dabbed her mouth with the napkin.

"A perfect choice," she said. "*Grazie, grazie.*"

"*Prego prego*," he said leaning back obviously pleased.

As their plates were cleared, there was a huge crash of thunder. The long window panes rattled. Outside, men were going from window to window wrestling to close large shutters.

"Maybe we should have left sooner," he said. "I'll ask if they have any rooms available."

Now I'm going to have to fish or cut bait. She took a gulp of water and counted ten diners left. Were they all staying? She remembered reading they had only six rooms. But Marc wouldn't force himself, not again. He had too much self respect. With him, it would be up to her. And that was the problem. The salads were delivered but she felt too nervous to eat.

CHAPTER TWENTY

"There's no room at the inn," Marc said as he sat down, "but I will not start out in this. The surf's all over the place. We'll ride out the storm in the boat. I've got a full tank of gas and we can fire the heater if need be. Signor Tassi, the manager, has offered pillows and blankets. We can be fairly comfortable."

"Whatever you think."

"Thanks, love, appreciate your confidence. The boat is snug, tied down from all angles, and we can come in any time during the night to use the facilities."

The sky was tarry black as they stood at the open door of the inn ready to go out. Signor Tassi thrust a flashlight into Marc's hand, but at that moment a flash of lightning showed the way. A young waiter held blankets and pillows ready to follow, but Marc told him to wait until he called him. Marc took Marlowe's hand and started ahead of her, then stepped into the boat, shoved open the cabin door, and turned to deposit her inside all in one smooth motion before signaling the guy. He came running, and they were in the bobbing boat and the boy back to the inn within minutes.

"Whew," Marlowe said. "Can we relax now?"

"I guess," but he continued fussing with pillows and blankets.

"What should we worry about? Can I help you?"

"Help me worry?"

"Yeah," she said laughing as she plopped on the curved bench.

"Let's see. You can worry about the moorings tearing loose and us floating out into the Adriatic." And he sat beside her.

"Great, I'll worry about that." She turned toward him. "What will you worry about?"

"You."

"Ah."

"Are you warm enough? I can turn—"

"Only my feet; they're a little cold."

"Your shoes are probably wet. Take them off, and I'll wrap your feet in one of these extra blankets." Before she could do so, he swung her feet onto his lap and took her shoes and socks off. His gaze at her was almost hypnotic as he slowly rubbed her feet with a towel. She felt her heart beating a wild pulse in her throat as his long fingers gently massaged her feet and ankles, then chafed them until they were toasty. His warm hands on her feet were seductive—erotic even—and her heart kicked into high gear.

"Hang on. I'll look in these cupboards for extra socks and sweats. Your slacks are damp too. Here's a bunch of things to choose from." He turned the lights up and they sorted through a box of pants, socks, jackets and hats.

"I'm going to get into other clothes too; they may not fit, but at least we'll be dry. It's going to be a long night, no need to be miserable," he said.

She found a pair of dark-green sweats and thick grey socks and began looking around for a place to change. There was none.

"Look, no I mean, don't look," he said. "What I mean is, I'll turn my back and change and you can do the same. Okay?"

"Sure."

In a few moments, he said, "All clear?"

"All clear," she said. "That does feel better."

"Come sit," he said. "Want some coffee or whatever else is in this package from Tassi?"

"Hardly. Our meal was fabulous. I'm satisfied but not miserable thanks to someone who ordered perfectly-sized portions."

He smiled.

"I want to serve *you* dinner some time. It'll be simple. You've seen my kitchen and cooking isn't my best talent anyway, but—"

"I'll take you up on that if we ever get back to Dorsoduro."

"Have you had bad times on the Lagoon?" she asked facing him on the curved bench.

"Mm-hmm. Once Giovanni, my oldest cousin, and I were messing around on the sea side of Pellestrina when a big one came up fast. We were blown up to a wall the locals built. We thought we'd be safe there but could not climb onto the wall and the storm kept knocking us about. At first we tried to maneuver south toward Chioggia, but the winds and water fooled us and pushed us farther north. After rehashing it many times, we realized we were lucky because the tide and winds took us to the slot that opens near Alberoni. Are you familiar with that part of the Lido?" he asked.

"I've pored over maps and read Donna Leon's book about Commissario Brunetti solving a crime in Pellestrina." Knowing it'd be a big lie if she didn't tell the rest, she forged ahead, "Riccardo Tron and I drove down to Pellestrina a couple weeks ago. It was magical to look back at Venice from that village with boats parked at their front doors. I'd like that part but wouldn't like the claustrophobia of such a tiny place." She grabbed a breath and said, "When we walked on that wall, I finally understood how important the whole Lido is to Venice. That long, spit of land has protected the city for centuries."

"Okay," he said. But he didn't feel okay. The moment she had said Tron's name, his thoughts had gone dark and veered close to turning deadly toward the man. He'd never had such primitive thoughts before. He felt more possessive of Marlee than he'd ever imagined he would of any woman. He wanted Tron out of the picture. *Damn, what's happening to me?*

"Okay," he says. What did okay mean? At least she got through it. "So what happened when you got to the inlet at Alberoni?" she asked. "I bet the water was crazy wild in that slot."

"Oh yeah." She could see him shifting gears from... jealousy maybe? Was she secretly thrilled about that? She'd never liked jealous vibes from men before.

"To this day, I don't know how we managed to get that little craft around to the lee side. I thought it'd break into pieces and I'd never see land again."

"How old were you?"

"Fourteen. Giovanni was eighteen and tough as nails. He knew every move of that boat and steered it with one hand like holding the mane of a bronco while his other hand was swinging wildly for balance. I idolized him before, but after that, I was his slave. He took advantage of it too," he snorted. "We've never told the whole story to anyone."

"How many other cousins in that family?

"Two more brothers now and one sister, four in all."

Lightning flashed through the glass cover. Marc put his arm around Marlowe in anticipation of the thunder to follow. When it came, she jumped anyway and he tightened his hold on her. "Sounds worse than it is. Nothing on the boat will draw it to us."

"That's good." After a bit, she asked what Giovanni did at the glass works.

"He's the brightest star in the galaxy, a true artist, not only in our *fabbrica* but in all of Murano. You could say I'm biased, but he is a genius with glass. I'll make sure he's on when I take you through and you can see for yourself. Plan on a full day."

"It would be exciting, Marc, but only when it's convenient for you all."

"Sure. Are you sleepy?" he asked.

"No, are you?"

"Nope. We can continue our catch up," he said. "I want to know about the enlightening accident you had."

"You won't forget your promise to tell what went wrong in your marriage?"

"Marlee, I will tell you," and he took both of her hands and kissed the palms, "that's a promise I *can* keep tonight."

"I'll try to shorten this accident thing as much as I can," she said.

"We've got all night the way that wind is howling." He held onto her hands.

She explained how her marriage had unraveled publicly on a camping trip to Cape Hatteras. They were with foreign graduate students at the U of Virginia. Ostensibly, Ty and Marlowe were the advisors for the group, but in truth it had become a hunting ground for him. When he didn't come back to their tent the first night of their three-day weekend, she had to face the signs she'd been denying for too long.

Marc nodded, remained quiet but continued to envelop her hands in his.

The following night she couldn't face that tent again and headed back to Charlottesville, but as she reached an overpass near Williamsburg, she nodded off. "I remember hitting something. I wasn't afraid. My life didn't pass before me—I was more in awe of the suspended moment." And she was back there in that strange interlude waiting for the end.

"Marlee?" he squeezed her hands.

"What? Oh yes," and she focused on his eyes. "Turns out the bridge was being repaired and the car had struck a large scaffolding mounted on wheels. Every time the auto hit it, the scaffold moved and then again and again until—"

"Until?" Marc prompted as lightning flashed and he pulled her closer.

"A six by eight plank broke through the shatter-proof glass of the windshield."

Marc crushed her to him. "Jeezus," he gasped.

She explained that the seat-belt system in Ty's souped-up Pontiac GTO had a shoulder strap separate from the one around her lower body. She hadn't fastened the shoulder part. If she had, her head would have been torn off by that plank.

"Guess my head was thrown forward at that exact moment," and she held her fingers curled as if holding the wheel putting her head down to demonstrate. "The only injuries were splinters in the tops of my fingers and a bruise on my right hip where it dropped onto the center console."

Marc sucked in a breath. "And you just climbed out?"

She nodded. "It took me a few days and a trip back to look at the car in the State's impound lot to recognize the full meaning of what had happened. It sounds trite, but when I saw that hole in the windshield where my head should have been, I experienced a blaze of insight. I didn't hear a choir of angels, but I *knew* I'd been given another chance. That's when I felt freed up to live for me. That's when I finally grabbed onto my Auntie Belle's favorite mantra about the banquet of life."

"An excellent mantra," he said, giving her another hug, more gently this time. "Who's this wonderful Aunt Belle? I think I want to meet her."

"My dad's youngest sister. She's always been the black sheep of the family, but we connected when I was twelve." Marlowe smiled up at Marc, and said, "She'd like you; the two of you would click."

All of a sudden, Marlowe's energy was depleted and she collapsed against him. The rain drummed on the roof soothing and lulling her. When she woke, they were lying together spoon fashion. His back was to the curved bench. He seemed to be asleep yet his arms held her securely against him. Blankets covered them. She felt warm and secure—almost too warm—his body was like a furnace. The boat seemed to rock less but the rain continued to pound on the glass dome. She felt stiff and wanted to stretch but didn't want to disturb him; she liked being surrounded by this gentle man. To take her mind off wanting to wiggle, she tried to match her breathing with the rhythm of his. Soon images appeared of her little Venetian apartment. Would it stay dry? Were those six steps up from the canal enough? She grew drowsy imagining the water moving under the door and rising up the steps one by one by one...

Later Marc stirred and she moved too. "What time is it?" she asked.

The glowing numbers on his watch showed 3:10. "I need to use the bathroom," he said.

"Me too."

They waited for a slight lull and dashed for the door. In the dim light of the lobby, she saw Marc and burst out laughing. Beneath his dark blue rain jacket and hood, the royal-blue sweat pants he'd scrounged, came to just below his knees like old-fashioned knickers.

"At least you're color coordinated," she said.

"He executed a soft-shoe routine doffing an imaginary top hat."

"Bravo," she said clapping. "Where'd you pick that up?"

"Mom insisted on dancing lessons when I was feeling big and awkward."

"It worked. You are grace personified." She was still chuckling as she went through the door marked *Donne*. But when she looked in the mirror, she wasn't little miss perfect. She stuffed her mangled scarf in her coat pocket, splashed cool water on her face, finger-combed her hair and called it good. When she stepped out, he was talking to the manager, who had heard them enter. A door marked *ufficio*, office, was ajar and she saw the end of a cot with a blanket spilling over the edge. She went over to thank Signor Tassi for everything.

Marc said, "The inn's short-wave radio reports the storm is abating but there's no 'all clear' yet for the Lagoon. Signor Tassi insists we come into a staff dining area for fresh coffee."

"That is tempting but he's going way beyond the call of duty isn't he?"

Marc shrugged, "I've already agreed as long as you can put up with my costume."

"For fresh coffee? *No problema, Signore.*"

They were led into a room that held four, plastic tables and chairs. A couple minutes later, Signor Tassi came carrying a dressing gown and helped Marc into it. It was his size and full-length to his ankles.

"That looks made for you," she said.

"It was."

"There's got to be a story here."

"Not much of one. A couple weeks ago, when my quarters were uninhabitable, I stayed here a few days and left it on the bathroom door. Haven't been back for it until now."

She looked at him.

"What?"

"Surely, with the kind of service they offer, they would have delivered it to you."

"You don't miss much do you?" he said giving her shoulder a light squeeze. "They did offer, but I was hoping to bring you here and thought I'd get it then."

"Even more interesting. Were you planning we'd stay overnight?"

"They say hope springs eternal," he said wagging his hands in prayer position. "But we were going back to Venice after dinner. Otherwise I would have reserved a room ahead."

"Someone said once that reservations can always be cancelled."

"That's not what happened. With the storm, I forgot the stupid robe!"

"*Calma, calma,*" she said putting her hand on his arm. He lay his hand on hers and seemed embarrassed. He *can* be riled. Fun.

A sleepy-looking waiter staggered in with a large silver tray holding a pot of coffee and cups and cream and sugar and brioches and butter and jam and more mandarini.

"Saved again," Marc said.

CHAPTER TWENTY-ONE

"Oh no you don't. I was promised *your* marriage story. Why not here?"

"You're right, Sprout. Where to start?"

"Wherever you think it began."

"I think it began with a prologue. Okay?"

"Of course," and she started to peel a *mandarino*.

"I have an eleven-year old daughter from a previous marriage. She's my starry-eyed wonder. Her name is Katy."

"Tell me about her," and Marlowe put her hand on his arm. *Geez. Two marriages.*

"She's a live wire and can wrap me around her finger. And knows it. The thing is, she doesn't abuse that special charm; I'm proud of her for that. She has dark hair and olive skin like her mom and big grey eyes."

"A brunette with eyes like yours, a lovely combination."

"She'll be a beauty. Julie, her mother, is attractive."

Marlowe thought his "attractive" probably meant beautiful.

"We met at Pepperdine. She was a history major. We thought we were in love and then we got pregnant."

Marlowe liked "we got pregnant."

"She'd been told she couldn't conceive and wasn't on the pill. She and her folks were delighted she could have a child, and Julie coerced her dad into footing the bill for a huge wedding. He wasn't too happy, but didn't have much say against his wife and daughter."

"Did she stay in school?" Marlowe asked but really wanted to know if he was still in love with Julie.

"Not after the wedding. I think she'd been biding her time until something better came along. At the time, she thought I was it," he said, and his eyes darkened. After Katy was born, I was working with Dad and finishing up my dissertation. She got bored. She said I was never there and worked too much. But she shopped way over my budget and..."

Marlowe detected exasperation and frustration in his voice triggered from long-ago emotions; she understood well that sudden surge of left-over feelings.

"She took a job as a night waitress in an upscale restaurant but spent everything she made on clothes, jewelry and cute things for Katy."

"Then?"

"Another familiar tale," he sighed. "She met an older, richer man."

So while Julie was going out, Marc was working during the day, studying and babysitting at night *assuming* she was working late at the restaurant.

"Always the last to know, aren't we?" she said, thinking he *had* learned how to juggle parts of his life after all. Did he still feel the pain of betrayal?

"I'm sorry, Marc."

"It's long over."

"And Katy's with her mom and step father. Did he adopt her?"

"No, it hasn't come up. I wouldn't agree anyway. But Phil's good to Katy and I think she's happy—as happy as any kid with divorced parents."

"Any other siblings?"

"A brother now. He's about three so she can play little mother."

"Has Katy been to Italy?" Marlowe asked reaching for another juicy mandarino.

His face fell. "Not yet, but now that Katy's interested, it won't be long. She'll make it happen. When I'm there, though, there's no trouble any more about taking Katy with me."

"What about bringing her into your life with Elise?"

Marc stared at his empty plate and sighed.

"I'm sorry, Marc, maybe I shouldn't be asking that."

"It's a natural question." He heaved a huge sigh and said. "Now Elise."

The waiter came in. It was a good time for a break. Marc was visibly agitated about the next part of his story. She *would* hear it but didn't need to be brutal and went to the ladies room. When she returned, it was to a magnificent Nordic lord standing in his robe of grey-blue damask with eyes to match. Why would any woman walk away from him?

Then, the lord spoke. "The storm is easing but Tassi won't hear of us heading out before the all clear. I wouldn't try anyway; the channels have probably shifted. Until full light, they'll be hard to see."

"Whatever you say, milord," Marlowe said trying for a curtsy.

"I'm impressed."

"No, **I** am. You're magnificent in that lordly robe."

"You're something," and he gave her a quick hug. "We'll wait it out, but I'd rather wait in the boat. Then we can head home at first light. Sound good?"

She nodded.

CHAPTER TWENTY-TWO

As soon as they were inside the boat, Marc began shedding the sweat pants without asking her to turn aside.

"Nice legs," she said. "Not a bad tush either."

"Watch it, Wench. Nowhere to run in here."

She wanted to say, who wants to run? From the first day they'd met years ago, every sensation she'd felt with him had been sexual. The constant sassy bantering. The hormonal rush. The fluttering in her groin. And her desire to lose herself in him. Then she whispered, "Who says I want to run?"

Marc turned to look at her. "Did I hear right? Because I can't take much more of these close quarters with your sweet ass within reach."

"So?" she said stepping as close as she could and still see his face when she looked up.

His voice was low and rough, "Marlee, you know I want you. But here?"

She looked around. "Hmm. Seclusion. Wind. Rain. Seems about perfect to me."

In a heartbeat, he swept her up. His lips were on hers pressing and urgent. His mouth dragged her lips apart with an aching hunger he'd never thought possible. He caught his breath and then pulled back to rein in his passion. He wanted their first time together to be special for her, but he also needed to claim her. *And where did that come from?*

They locked eyes for a moment, then he covered her mouth again probing inside with his tongue. Their tongues flirted back and forth until his dominated but slowly. He explored more only to pull back again. With a more delicate touch, he moved inside her mouth as if tasting her. He hummed a deep tone and withdrew to sip at her lips before entering again. His kiss was so symbolically sexual that she felt hot wetness begin to pool between her legs. She threaded her fingers into his thick, silky hair and held on as he kissed her eyes, her cheeks and down her throat all the while holding her up against him face to face. Then she was slipping slowly down his hard chest, past his hard abdomen until she felt his erection hard and full. As her toes touched the floor, strong hands settled on her lower back pulling her closer as if to make sure she understood how much he wanted her.

His hands moved cautiously, almost tentatively, under her sweater to touch her breasts through the silk shirt. As he felt her nipples respond to his touch, he sighed. Her arms were already raised up with her hands at his neck and he slipped the sweater over her head. The sleeves got entangled, and laughing, she disengaged her arms.

"Still too many clothes," he murmured. Again he ran his fingers lightly across her breasts and felt her nipples harden even more. Abruptly, he slipped the silk turtleneck up and over tossing it into the enclosed space of the boat that was rocking wildly again. Bracing his legs apart, he ignored the boat's motion and leaned back to look down at her as he tenderly—incredibly tenderly—ran his fingers over the swell rising above her lacy, red bra. She caught her breath. He caught his as he breathed in her scent. Oranges? Clove? He hadn't expected such sexy lingerie. He loved that about her—one more surprise. He kissed her gently pulling her against him to probe deeper with his tongue.

She felt on fire as he slid the straps down. His large hands were warm as he slowly lifted her breasts from her bra feeling their weight in his palms. Only one light on the dash of the console revealed their eager bodies. It was enough. Ordinarily she would have been embarrassed but was surprised how calm and adored she felt as she stood half naked before him. His deft hands reached behind to unfasten the bra giving it a toss. The ragged sound he made when he stared at her bare breasts took her breath away and more hot liquid pooled. She'd never had a man look at her like that.

"So soft," he groaned deepening his kiss and pulling her against him as he explored her mouth again. Marc was completely male and for the first time in her life, she felt uninhibited and fully female—fully feline—as she curved her body against him. She slid her hands under his shirt tracing the hair coursing down the center of his chest. Her fingers followed the path as it led down his torso, but hesitating to go lower, she moved them back up across his flat, male nipples causing them to harden. When she unbuttoned his shirt, he sucked in his breath again. She needed to feel his skin touch hers and began to shove the shirt away. He shrugged out of it and tossed it. They clung to each other chest to chest, tongue to tongue. His rock-solid flesh seemed to scorch hers.

"I want your breast in my mouth, *amore mio*, my love. Want to taste you." His voice was hoarse and rough. "I want to feel your nipple between my lips."

A soft mewling sound escaped her throat.

"I want to be inside you. I want to feel you around me tight and hot… and slick for me."

Marlowe's thoughts had already been spinning with those same seductive images he'd left in her mind a week ago.

Then he pressed his face into her breasts taking a nipple into his mouth and began to suck. She trembled and moved against his erection as he continued to nuzzle and suckle. Before she realized it, he had pulled the drawstring of her sweat pants and slid them down dragging her bright red, bikini panties with them.

"Oh, God, Marlee, I've thought about this moment since you first walked into Johnson's office." He rested his hands on her hip-bones and caressed her waist. He palmed the cheeks of her bottom pulling her closer into his groin where she sensed his cock growing fuller and harder. The sound from his chest was low—animalistic, and she responded with a shudder.

"Wait," he said and bent to smooth the blankets and pillows already spread on the bench. Then he lay her down reverently as if she were a fragile glass flower all the while looking at her with adoration. She had never felt so desirable and something more. A passionate fever raced like hot lava in her blood. She'd never thought she was a sexual being, but in the dim light when she saw his eyes liquid with wanting, she felt more heat rage through her veins. He slid his briefs down and leaned over her, she looked at his flat belly and strong thighs but more important to her at that moment was his magnificent penis. It looked aggressive as it jutted out from his groin full and heavy... and huge. Could she take it all?

She couldn't wait to try. Crouching over her with one knee on the bench and one foot on the floor of the rocking boat, he kissed her forehead, the corner of each eye, her nose, her cheeks, and nipped at her earlobe. He was moving at an agonizingly slow pace as he caressed her neck and then on to stroke one of her breasts with his tongue. He licked a nipple and feather-kissed it until she felt it harden all over again. She whimpered. He turned to the other one and took more than the nipple into his mouth sucking it greedily. She gasped. He suckled until it almost hurt—a good hurt. She'd never felt so loved. So adored. Her breath came in short spurts as he moved his mouth down her belly, over the long, ugly scar kissing it all the way as he continued his downward journey. She couldn't bear any more delay. Her insides were pulsing. She couldn't have stopped that throbbing if she'd wanted to.

"Easy, easy," he whispered. "Easy does it, Marlee."

She didn't want easy. She wanted him now. Now! But he teased and tantalized and continued to kiss and nip and sip. For a moment, she knew she must taste salty after all this time. She felt grungy and worried... and then, it wasn't important anymore. She arched her back upward toward him in a female motion born in the lost ages of time. He waited.

"Easy, Marlee. Let's take it easy. We have time. Just... let... go."

Yes, let go, she thought. Yes. And then he put his face into the dark triangle of her mons and found the entrance of her cleft with his tongue. He flicked his tongue and lightly played all around her entrance until his finger slipped inside. She drew in a raspy breath and tried to grasp his cock, but her arms weren't long enough. She wanted to touch and hold him. But he moved back up her body and her mouth was near his chest again. She ran her tongue across one of his nipples until it hardened. He hissed. She continued to tease it again. This time, her hands did follow the stream of hair coursing down his abdomen. But he raised up and his cock moved against her. At last he began pushing into her vagina.

"Yes. Yes, there," she said and reached to guide him but his cock knew exactly where to go. He pushed inside then eased out again. Slowly he thrust inward again, but waited to let her body adjust, then—even more slowly—slipped back out. She felt herself gush. He felt it too, and this time he pressed farther. Inch by inch he made more forays. She opened her legs and wrapped them around his waist which drew him deeper. Her hands on his back felt his slick sweat; it thrilled her, and aroused her even more. His sweat smelled clean, almost peppery. He lifted her up to slide a pillow beneath her hips and lengthened his thrust. But still eased out again.

"Stay, stay."

He chuckled softly and entered again. Hesitant at first, then he probed deeper, carefully. "You're small," he murmured. "Are you okay?"

"I want you inside me," she panted, "I... can... take... you."

"Yes," he whispered, "you can, love. You will. All of me."

His finger made circles around her clitoris, never touching, but circling, circling, closer and closer driving her insane. Then, oh Oh OH. He brushed that eager nub as he thrust his swollen shaft farther into her core and she exploded in wave after wave of ecstasy. The pulsing inside her rocked with the movement of the boat as if in synchrony with it. He stayed quiet but her waves of pleasure went on and on. Then he began moving again, this time faster. "Oh sweet heaven! Mar-leeee," he groaned as he gained release to pulse inside her.

"All of you," she sighed. At the last possible moment before he would have collapsed onto her, he slid his body sideways lifting her on top of him. For a long time, they lay there sated listening to the wind and rain blend with their own moans and pulsings.

"Marc?"

"Hmm?"

"I did too."

"What?"

"Wanted this since that first day."

"I know," he said tightening his arms around her.

They dozed, still connected. When he reached for the blankets, he slipped out of her, and she reached for his cock. "You'll have to wait a while, Wench."

"Mm-hmm. Just want it nearby." His chest rumbled. She smiled to herself. Ah, that deep rumble. A sound of pleasure and maybe contentment. He drifted off. She lay there content herself. She'd never experienced such tenderness in love making and was glad for Aunt Belle's encouragement. She must have slept but later in the breaking dawn, she woke to feel Marc's cock stiffening against her. He nuzzled and kissed her neck. She turned to open her lips to his tongue which moved slowly into her mouth. She drew it in. He sucked hers back into his mouth. His hand reached her entrance and found her wet again. His fingers moved inside. She was hungry for him again. She couldn't believe herself, but then, his erection was full too! He lifted her. She found a place on the bench for her knees and with his help raised herself up to the tip of his upright, quivering cock. He supported her above him as she slid slowly, ever so slowly downward impaling herself until she took more of him. He held her. She was filled—again. He lifted his body to her and she began to ride. With her hands on his shoulders, she supported herself. He cupped her breasts kneading and shaping them. When he squeezed her nipples, she burst again and prayed her orgasm would never stop. He moved slightly. She trembled. His finger or was it his thumb? No matter. It did that circling thing again. She lifted herself and with the help of his other hand raised higher until the tip of his cock was almost outside, then once again she began another slow descent and her inner walls contracted.

"Oh Babe. Oh… my… God." His thumb brushed her clit, and once again: pulsing, vibrating, shuddering, boat rocking, wind sighing, rain pelting, they reached paradise together.

* * *

A grey dawn had finally arrived and Marlowe was wrapped as if in a cocoon. Marc was up and dressed.

"How did you get out from under me? Where's my toy?"

"Next time it comes out to play, we'll be in a real bed. My aching back!"

"Are you all right?"

"I will be," and he began to stretch but the cabin was too low for anything meaningful. "You want to put something on? Maybe we can get out of here before Tassi tries to be helpful."

And in that moment, she felt shy. She found her things at the end of the bench where he must have gathered them and began to dress under the blanket.

"What are you doing? I've been inside you and now you're going all modest?"

"But," she stammered, "you're dressed and—"

"Get over it." Then he stopped in his tracks and leaned over to kiss her lightly, "Aw, Sprout, I'm sorry. I'll get things organized outside."

"Thanks."

She heard some clunks and thumps, but he was back within minutes.

"Everything seems intact—you included," he said kissing her nose. "Ready, love?"

She nodded. "It's been an eventful evening," she said finding her shoes.

"Yes, it has," he said and came over to plant a soft kiss on her bruised lips and nuzzle her neck. She loved the rough feel of his beard against her skin.

The grey sky was heavy with water, but the sea was calm. Birds wheeled near the islands finding delicious goodies stirred up for their breakfast. She felt stirred up herself. She moved to stand beside him at the helm, and he pulled her into the curve of his free arm. She stayed close to him the rest of the way feeling the mist on her face as she watched the fairytale skyline appear. Then the sun broke through; the domes of San Marco gleamed and one golden-winged lion atop a flagpole showed itself before the sun ran for cover again. Venice looked more real to Marlowe than it ever had, and it was still magical and pulsing with life. Yes, pulsing and satisfied with life.

* * *

Later at her door she stepped onto the second step and turned to face him.

"Marc?"

"I'll get back to you about that tour. Probably be Thursday."

She put one hand on each side of his face and looked straight into his big grey eyes, "I loved being with you—every minute and was glad to learn more of your story."

His eyes darkened.

"I believe every word. But, I'm a curious female and want the rest of your story."

He pulled her to him in obvious relief rumbling with laughter.

"And you shall have it, Wench, you shall have it."

She stood and watched him walk to the bridge; he turned and waved. She liked that about him. To her, his wave meant she wasn't out of his mind.

CHAPTER TWENTY-THREE

Marlowe was barely out of the shower after Marc had left still feeling deliciously satisfied, when the phone rang. Rich again.

"I'm glad I caught you at home. You're not there much, are you?"

Had he been trying to reach her last night? Did she care?

"Anyway, I'm looking forward to seeing you Monday evening. Okay?"

"It'd be good if you'd call me when you arrive," she said hearing coolness in her voice.

"I will be there at six," he enunciated carefully. "Oh damn, gotta go, sorry."

What a downer! She'd been basking in a glow from the night with Marc and didn't want to think about Rich but had to deal with him—soon.

* * *

Sunday morning had turned cold. She hurried back to bed with her first cup of coffee and realized her journal was more about these two men than the glories of *La Serenissima*. Her plan today was to attend mass at San Marco, for her, always an adventure into another world. As she dressed another call came from Rich.

"I know I'll see you tomorrow, but I wanted to hear your voice."

Jeesh! leave me alone.

"Sometimes I'm wondering why I'm in this job. These endless meetings! It's too long to be with these people."

"Are they being difficult?"

"It's not them. Guess I'm feeling down on myself."

Was he asking for reassurance? Advice? Or was this manipulation?

"My problem is I can't get you out of my mind. I miss you."

"That's strange because I've been telling myself I should not miss you," she said.

"Oh? Why?"

Was he that clueless?

"Sweetie, we're going to talk about a lot of things on Monday evening. Okay?"

"Sure."

"You sound doubtful. We need some face-to-face time. It'll be good to see you and your beloved Venice. Because of you, I'm beginning to appreciate it again."

Marlowe wondered if she'd ever take Venice for granted—if she'd ever have that chance.

"I need to sign off. I'll be knocking on your door about six tomorrow." He was gone.

Damn, what's wrong with me? Why didn't I say no, no, no! It's strange that he always calls on the run. If I'm so important… but that didn't matter now that she'd been drawn into Marc's vortex where everything mattered.

* * *

She was in San Marco for the ten-thirty *Messa,* Mass. For a moment, she felt like an intruder overwhelmed by the vibrations of millions of prayers offered here over hundreds of years. Incense. Bells. Organ. Choir. All beautifully pagan. One priest in green was swinging incense in a brass censer. She caught that aromatic fragrance. Sage maybe? Another priest in black carried a golden icon. As if in some neolithic ritual, they moved slowly down from the high altar to the strains of the booming organ disappearing into the shadows during a long prayer. When the music began again, they paced back up to the sacred area. *Neri secoli dei secoli,* centuries after centuries, the priest droned and the choir's voices filled the golden space again. These powerful rites have held people in thrall year after year. In spite of all the stolen treasures from Byzantium, Marlowe sensed the spirits of hungry souls who had come here for peace through the ages. Maybe it was the afterglow of her sensual time with Marc, but she, too, felt calm and a sense of peace.

Outside the duomo, she pulled up her hood against the heavy mist. Before heading home, she walked toward the Piazzetta to see what the Lagoon was doing. The breeze felt stronger than when she had entered the church. Would the waves rise up again as they did two nights ago? What a night. Then she noticed a silhouette of a tall man leaning toward a small woman. When she realized it was Marc, she felt a stabbing pain of jealousy. Her first reaction was to slip away, but it was too late, he beckoned to her. He seemed protective of the woman as he held a large umbrella over her otherwise he would have moved toward Marlowe. *Wouldn't he?*

"Ciao, Marlowe," he said. "Come meet Luisa. Luisa Petrelli, Marlowe Osborne."

He's such a gentleman. His mamma taught him well, or maybe it was papá since papá had certainly taught him other good things.

"*Piacere,*" Marlowe said holding out her hand. Luisa responded. Such a pretty young woman, yet so haunted.

"Did you attend Messa?" he asked.

"I did. My first time inside that incredible place since I've been back. I'd almost forgotten how glorious it can be in that golden lair with the bells and candles and the thundering organ. Were you there too?"

"No. We've been window-shopping along the Merceria, something we do once in a while to check out the latest wares for rich tourists. Right, Luisa?" he said turning to give her shoulder a little squeeze. "We're on our way to the Zaccaria stop, come walk with us."

"I don't want to intrude."

"Not at all. I've been trying to convince Luisa to come to Caffè Chioggia for a hot chocolate, but she turned me down. Could I entice you?"

Marlowe hesitated. Of course she wanted to go and realized she was behaving like a school girl. Aunt Belle would say, "Woman, what the hell do you want to do?"

"Hot chocolate sounds great after shivering in San Marco," Marlowe said.

By the time they got to the stop, the rain was pounding down hard and they ducked into the shelter of the pontile to wait for Luisa's vaporetto. Marlowe could feel Luisa's need to be gone and not have to make nice, but Marc insisted they stay.

As the vaporetto pulled away, Marlowe said, "She seemed distraught."

"She's struggling with grief. Maybe I didn't tell you that one of my brothers—I mean cousins—died a few months ago on the Autostrada. Venetians don't have enough auto savvy for that crazy highway. I'd never say this to my family, but I suspect Marco had gotten himself in the fast lane and when someone crowded him, he lost control. He could handle a boat on the Lagoon in any situation, but..." his voice trailed off. "We all love her and want to help, but maybe there's no way anyone could understand unless—"

"Does she live in the family complex?" Marlowe interrupted hoping to change the subject before he remembered her own loss.

"She and Marco did when he was alive. She was taking classes at the University and family members pitched in to care for little Gianni. But now that he's gone, she and Gianni are in a small apartment near the Arsenale. *I nonni*, grandparents, are upset about it, but the rest of us say she needs to be away from where they'd been happy together."

"Living in one building with family members next door sounds overwhelming."

"It's a way of life here," he said.

"Surely kids benefit from relatives all around, but I'm not sure I could handle it."

"Most glass families buy or build next to their factory to share the furnace chores because they often need to keep the ovens going twenty-four-seven. In our case, we've added on from time to time to a massive building already in the family. We each have an apartment with a separate outside entrance and work hard at guarding our privacy."

"To be where people could drop in without warning, I don't—"

"I know," he said grinning, "you like to be forewarned. As a kid, though, the advantage was built-in buddies." And Marlowe remembered the fun she'd had visiting her cousins.

They rounded the corner of the Doge's Palazzo and the wind whipped at them. Up close, the fanciful, frothy building that looked like gothic lace from across the basin, was sturdy and had withstood stronger gales than this one.

"Here we are. Can't sit outside and listen to jazz today. Let's go in and get something hot." He led her to a table in a corner away from the door.

"I like this place," she said. "I wonder why I never came inside before, it has a much nicer ambiance than those two pompous cafés on the Piazza proper. And the outside area has a fantastic view. I've always enjoyed walking through the multiple arches that lead straight to the tethered gondolas doing their funny lop-sided jig."

"Lop-sided jig," he said, "that's a perfect description of how they bob when they're tied along the quay. Are you hungry?"

"No thanks, but hot chocolate sounds perfect. I noticed when you introduced Luisa, her last name was not Barovier."

"Italian women don't give up their maiden names, although if Marco had been with her, I'd have introduced them as the Baroviers. Otherwise, she's Luisa Petrelli."

"So that's how it works. More American women are doing the same. When I left Ty, I went back to my maiden name. I hope Mandy keeps hers when she marries, if she marries."

"Speaking of marriage, is this a good time for me to tell you the rest of my tangled story?"

"If you're ready."

"I'm ready. At least I can begin, but here comes the chocolate."

"It's a good thing they serve this with a spoon," she said, "it's almost as thick as the spoon fudge my cousins and I used to make when Grandpa was at his office."

"Spoon fudge?"

"Yeah, we purposely undercooked it."

"Mm-hmm, yes," he said spooning some into his mouth with obvious pleasure. "Okay, here goes. As I said, Elise and I haven't lived together in any sense of the word for a few years."

"How did you meet?"

He sipped more chocolate and watched the rain stream down the windows.

"How did we meet?" He sighed, "I'd just come back from another trip over here with that accounting problem and was working with Dad in San Diego. We went to an opening of one of the big, regional malls built by Andy Midas, her father. He's made a fortune in California and across the country with those malls. Dad thought I might be interested in the possibilities. She was there, a tall, elegant ice maiden, and I set out to melt her. At first she looked through me, but by the end of the weekend, she turned off her aloof button."

"She was no dummy," Marlowe said.

"I don't know what she saw in me. I had no job and more important to her—as I later found out—no connections. I'd come from Venice, had an Italian name and spoke Italian, maybe that was exotic enough to spark her interest."

"Maybe she was tired of the slick playboys in her own circle," Marlowe suggested.

"I never did know what was going on with her, but we dated. She intrigued me. So different from more accessible women."

"With your looks and style, I'm sure women have always been accessible."

He just looked at her. *Does he really not know how attractive he is?*

"Do your cousins set you up with women here?"

"Yes, but I've been playing wounded hound. If I do go out, I stay vaguely polite.

"Gosh, I bet you've broken many a Venetian maiden's heart."

"Don't tease."

"I'm not. You're…you're the archetype of the ideal male women dream about. You must know it."

He flushed. "I know one thing, my female cousins have grown disgusted with me and are learning to back off. Anyway, at that big event, thanks to Dad, I made some connections and landed a job with a reputable construction company that was looking for a business type. That damned MBA was leading me away from the hands-on work I'd *thought* I wanted."

He scraped the remains of chocolate from his cup and took a drink of water. "I pursued Elise and after a time, we became an item. An item in the society pages too, which I thought was cool at first, but it didn't take me long to make a bunch of major faux pas that sometimes amused her, but more often, embarrassed her. It was like she'd found a rough-cut diamond she could polish. One thing led to another until we were walking down the aisle with a cast of thousands."

He turned to face her and said, "Marlowe, I've never told anyone something like this about a woman, but Elise was not a giving lover. She took and seemed mildly content, but by the time we got back from our honeymoon, she made it clear it was over. Hell it was over before it happened," and he stared out the window again.

"What made her change?"

He shrugged. "Maybe I wasn't worth polishing. I was disenchanted too, but her dad, Andy, took to me, and I liked him. I learned a helluva lot from him, too. Elise didn't want children but Andy talked grandchildren non stop. Finally she told him we couldn't have children which was true because unknown to Andy—and me—she'd had her tubes tied. Even though I reminded Andy I'd had a child, he put me through a bunch of tests.

"Did he ever find out about her?"

"Of course not. With Andy's money and power, she knew he'd manage to see her records as well as mine. She found a doctor who falsified her medical records. Maybe bribed him or, more likely... found something to hold over his head. Then she began the charade of pretending to adopt. Andy was relentless. Of course that trait was why he became a huge success."

"When did *you* find out about her tubes?" Marlowe asked.

"Not until much later when she was more sure of control over me. You see, I was her third marriage, and when Andy grew suspicious that all wasn't well with us, he threatened to give a big part of her inheritance to charity if she divorced again. She managed to convince him everything was fine. About that time Andy found a new bimbo to keep him distracted, and the pressure was off for a while. Unless he's hired a detective, he doesn't know what she's up to."

"Did you know?" she asked.

"She didn't care because she knew I'd never tell Andy about our separate lives."

"How could she be so sure?"

Marc leaned back against the wall and sighed, "Marlee, there's more. I'll keep my promise, but could we continue in your quiet place?"

"Sure, it *is* noisy here, but thanks for bringing me."

"Good, I'll finish the story there or die trying," he said and began helping her into her raincoat. "The hardest part is yet to come."

"What you've told me already sounds bad enough," she said zipping up her long coat.

"Well, you know I'm big and supposed to take it."

"Being big isn't always that easy, is it?"

"It has its pros and cons. But one thing it's good for is sweeping certain little people off their feet." And with that, he shocked everyone in the place, her included, by picking her up, striding past several tables of people straight out the front door and down the steps into the drenching rain. When she realized what he was doing, she leaned back to turn her face into it; they both laughed and then ran around the corner to the vaporetto stop.

"Elise would never—could never—abide such craziness."

"Look what she's missing!" Marlowe said wiping the rain from her glowing face.

CHAPTER TWENTY-FOUR

Are you soaked?" she asked as they hurried into her apartment.

My pants are damp but this jacket works well. You?"

"Not in this long monk's cloak. It's all your doing, you know. If we had walked out in a dignified manner and—"

"Yeah, yeah yeah," he said laughing.

"I see Parduzzi left a heater, he's not all that bad as a landlord. You could take your pants off and I'll hang them near it."

"I'm fine," he said.

"Let's see if it works," and she plugged the heater in putting it as near the couch as the cord would reach.

He stood beside it for a while but said, "What the hell," and stepped out of his trousers.

Marlowe watched and wanted every bit of what she saw. She had not gotten enough of him. He looked up to see her face.

"It's not polite to stare," he said with a huge grin on his face.

Was I drooling? "I'll get a blanket for you and a hangar for your pants," she said going to the bedroom thinking about his legs and that bulge in his briefs. *Oh lord.*

When she came back, she said, "Come sit and tell me the rest of your story."

"Marlee, when I finish you may want to kick me out into the rain without my pants."

"I might toss your pants out but I'd keep you," she said and patted the sofa again.

"Should I be afraid?"

"You'll have to be brave and find out." She drew up her knees as she had once before and waited for the rest of the story.

He heaved a big sigh. She waited. Until now, she'd never noticed the ticking of the clock on the bookshelf. Obviously this was difficult for him.

"I have to back up again to my first marriage." His gaze was not in the small room where they sat; he was re-living something painful. Marlowe tried not to move.

"One night when Katy was about three, I was home studying; and Julie was working—at least I thought so. Katie fell in the bathroom. She'd pulled her little stool to the sink and was trying to climb up. I wasn't aware she'd gone in there; we usually kept the door closed. I raced with her to the emergency room. She was examined and even x-rayed. Only bruises but she was frightened. I was too. I'd been negligent and admitted it, but out of the blue..." Marc got up and walked to grab his pants that were hanging near the small heater. "You don't want to hear the rest of this story. I better put these pants on and walk away."

"Marc, I can't believe you're reneging. Come back here! Whatever happened, it's in the past. Please."

"Jeez," he said. "This is harder than I thought," but he sat beside her again facing her. He inhaled and then spit it out. "Julie accused me of sexually molesting Katy. She claimed there'd been other signs and started proceedings to prevent me from being alone with my little girl."

"Unbelievable!" Marlowe said.

He got up again. This time he jammed his legs in his trousers and moved toward the door.

Marc was one of the most gentle men she'd known, she refused to believe this cruel accusation. She followed him as he reached for his coat hanging at the top of the stairs. She grabbed his sleeve and pulled hard. "What are you doing? Why are you going?"

"The look of horror on your face said it all, Marlowe."

"Yes, horror that someone—anyone—who knows the least thing about you could accuse you of such a thing. The idea is insane!" She put her arms around his waist and hung on tight tugging him back into the room. Then she patted his pant legs and said, "Besides, you can't go yet, you're still wet!"

He laughed and responded by holding her against him for a long time. "You believe me?" he said, holding her away to look in her eyes.

"Of course I believe you. And Julie knew better too. What was her real reason?"

They sat down together again. After Julie dragged him into court, he lost almost two years with Katy except for monitored calls. He fought it and spent money he didn't have. He shook his head still dumbfounded that anyone would think he'd harm his precious baby girl.

"Then?" Marlowe continued to badger him.

"Thank goodness for that young intern at the E.R. Totally thorough. Not only had she X-rayed Katy, she'd taken photos and wrote a detailed report. I was exonerated, and eventually, Julie was forced to admit she'd lied. "Over reacted," she called it. She's never admitted she was out to get rid of me, but it was clear that she wanted to throw attention away from her because by the time it was resolved, she was living with Phil and Katy was ensconced with them."

"How horrible for you… and Katy." A strange calm came over Marlowe. She felt certain he had no yearnings for his ex-wife.

He nodded slowly looking at the bookcase across the room but not really seeing it. "Julie and I try to keep up a good front for Katy's sake. But, kids often think it's their fault when parents split don't they?"

"Sometimes," Marlowe said. They were quiet for a while. "Would you like some water or tea?" and she went to the kitchen corner. "That chocolate's sticking in my throat," she said.

"Water please."

* * *

"Okay. Back to Elise," he said, "the woman I'm legally chained to. That old term ball and chain fits in this case," and he sighed.

"The other day when you asked if Elise was blackmailing me, I couldn't believe how close you were to the truth. I won't file for divorce until her father dies, not because I'm an honorable Viking, as you called me once, but because I don't want Katy to find out."

She handed him a glass of water and took a sip of hers. He drank most of his in one gulp.

"Elise threatened you with that?"

He nodded. "She's all about power, and to her money is power."

Marlowe raised up on her knees and scooted closer to Marc. She ran her hands into his hair and cradled his head against her chest. "I'm so sorry."

After a while she sat back and asked, "How many here know?"

"Only Giovanni. We've had no secrets from each other since I was ten and he was fourteen. I roomed with him from the start because the family figured he wouldn't feel jealous of me and the younger boys might have. He showed me how to be an Italian boy. There was no competition between us, only admiration on my part. Together, we decided no one else need know. Of course, the rest of the family knows that Elise and I are going our separate ways for now. They see a lot of that here in Italy."

"I'm eager to meet this idol of yours."

"You will."

"Your mom and dad know of course."

"Yes. They gave me their total support and avoid Julie whenever possible." He was quiet for a moment. "They avoid Elise too," he said. "I haven't done well with women... until now," and he pulled her into his arms.

"I appreciate that you trust me with this."

"I promised, didn't I?"

What about not trusting Marc with her own past? The gale seemed to be screaming down her narrow rio. And rain blew against her front windows usually protected from the wind. "Do your folks in San Diego know about Elise's blackmail?"

"They know."

"Life does throw punches doesn't it, but you've grown stronger, right?" she said burying her face in his neck kissing him gently and inhaling his scent. A fresh soap smell with an under layer of something musky—male, yes very male.

She raised up and looked straight at him, "Maybe it's time for you to forget all that and take on Auntie Mame's philosophy."

"Yeah, life *is* a banquet isn't it? And the *pièce de résistance* is right here beside me. I've been wanting to make love to you properly. Would this be a good time?... It's raining."

"Rain's always good," she whispered.

He wrapped her in his arms. They sat quietly but he made no move, wondering if she wanted him as much as he wanted her. As if in answer to his longing, she turned his face to her and kissed him on his eyes and nose and cheeks and ran her tongue lightly across his lips, tugging on his mustache. She edged her tongue into his mouth. Finally, he drew it inside then released it to touch her lips with his. Then his tongue dipped slowly into her mouth. Meanwhile, his hands went around her waist and under her sweater moving to caress the swell of her breasts.

"Mmm," he said. She shivered with pleasure. He hummed a low, hungry tone. She reached under his shirt and brushed his nipples hearing him suck in a quick breath. She loved that he was sensitive there too. He leaned over and kissed her neck. She squiggled; he rumbled. Then he stood up raising her with him. He turned the light out as they went to her bed. A nightlight glowed beside the bed as they stood holding each other.

Someone knocked on the door.

"Shhh," she whispered. "Don't want to answer."

Whoever it was tried to insert a key, she froze. Marc started toward the door.

"No," she rasped.

The key didn't work for whomever it was. He left. That's happened a couple of times," she said still whispering. "It's kinda scary."

"It appears Parduzzi's changed the lock but better check with him. Do it tomorrow."

"When I asked him about renting next month, he said there's a doctor from Rome who usually comes in December. He's waiting to hear from him. Maybe that doctor had an extra key made last year, but I thought he told me—"

"Shhh, he's gone. Now where were we? Oh yes, I saved a place right about here," and he slipped her bra straps down. "Hmm, lacy black this time," he said reaching behind to unfasten it and going straight for her matching panties. He was grateful for the light. He wanted to see every feminine curve. And this time, he'd make it better for her—much better—no rocking boat and time to explore every inch of her soft, creamy skin.

She pushed and tugged his shirt off his shoulders and he stepped out of his pants and briefs. She took his penis, already firm, in her hands and wrapped her fingers around him feeling its girth and hardness. She drew in a breath and sat on the bed moving her hands all along his hot, hard shaft from the velvety tip to the solid root that grew from a thicket of rust-colored curls. He stood before her, unabashed, allowing her to examine him as it hardened even more into her hands. Then gently he pushed her down onto the bed and lay beside her.

"This is luxurious after the cramped quarters on the boat," he said forcing himself to tamp down his passions a little longer.

"Mmm, but it was special with that storm raging outside while we—"

"And here we are with another storm raging."

Then they didn't talk. They kissed and once again he began a slow, tantalizing voyage sipping her from head to toe and moving back to her breasts. Her soft mewling responses each time he sipped or touched her made him hotter and harder when his intent had been to drive *her* so wild she'd never want anyone else. His fingers found the mat of black curls at the vee between her legs. He slid a finger inside to check her readiness. She sucked in a breath. She was slick and hot and getting wetter. Her spicy scent rose up driving him wild. He didn't know how much longer he could hold off. He slid his mouth past her belly and spread her thighs to have full access to all of her. He needed to taste her; lick and suckle her until she burned for him—only him. She arched upward against his mouth obviously seeking release.

She felt the scratchiness of his mustache when his tongue began circling to find that special nub. She would go up in smoke if he didn't… But he dipped his tongue inside and sucked and licked until she cried out and orgasmed almost bucking off the bed. The fierceness of the climax was more than she could stand, but he was relentless and found her clit again and moved his tongue across that swollen nub again and again.

"Marc, it's too much, I can't stand it."

"Yes," he said raising his eyes to look at her, "yes, you can. You can take much more." Then he raised up on his knees lifting her legs onto his chest with her feet touching his shoulders. Slowly, ever so slowly, he began to slide his full cock into her hot, wet channel. She watched and wanted it—all of it and sucked in a breath.

"Relax, love. Easy does it."

"Yes," and she exhaled slowly.

"You're tight," his voice rasped.

"But I can—"

"Yes, you can."

She panted, "Take me, Marc. Now."

He growled softly and began a long, slow slide downward but withdrew never quite losing contact. Each time he moved inward, she opened more. At last she was filled and held her breath. He stopped. Moved again. "More, Babe, more." She felt herself pulsing around him. Panting. Pushing. Arching.

"Easy, easy."

His hands brushed her breasts, pinched her nipples. Once again she felt that good, little pain. Then he took a mouthful and suckled hard. She gasped in pleasure. He caressed her belly and continued on to her mons. His full erection had stretched her until that sensitive nub was exposed. His thumb circled and circled.

As it drew closer, she thought she couldn't wait another second. He surged forward, withdrew and thrust again picking up speed, more insistent but still feathering her clit. Again he withdrew, then with a another passionate thrust went deeper yet. Driven by his fervor, she was touched off and convulsed with a hoarse cry. He drove once more and erupted too. They hung there suspended pulsing with each other.

He fell onto the bed next to her. They lay catching their breath. Her heart was like a fist pounding against her chest. In time, it slowed and she said, "That's one way to get me to hush."

"Yep," he said and then began to laugh from deep in his chest. She crawled on top to feel every vibration.

* * *

Marc had gone for a family dinner and company meeting. It was a good time to be alone. She didn't know where this lusty woman was coming from, but she liked the results. After leaving Ty, she'd had a few sexual adventures, but sex with Marc was beyond what she'd ever expected. Marc was the first man who had taken time to arouse her, to arouse her beyond what she'd thought she could endure. And he was willing and able to wait until he brought her to sexual heights never before reached. To think she'd begun to accept that she was not a sexual creature. Acknowledging her own sexual pleasure as something right and good was… liberating. Yes. She was feeling freer, more powerful as a woman than ever before. Maybe Aunt Belle was right, maybe she was coming into her rightful lust.

CHAPTER TWENTY-FIVE

Monday morning the sun on the canals was blinding. Each time the breeze ruffled the water or a gondolier broke the surface with his oar, arrows of light burst in all directions like shards from a glass chandelier. Yesterday, drenching rain and today, this. Pity the poor weather people. *And pity my poor psyche flip flopping between Rich and Marc.* But no! Not true. It was over with Rich even if he wasn't accepting it. That was his problem. *And my problem?* Her thoughts about Marc had been slipping into a future with him even though it wasn't possible. Where did she stand with him? Laughs and good sex and then what? Maybe she should stop taking herself and him so seriously. Venice had been her constant lover through the years. Today, she'd focus on the city. It was time she re-visited the Frari which held tons of beautiful art by famous artists especially Titian's *L'Assunta,* the Assumption of Mary.

Marlowe took the vaporetto to the San Tomà stop. For her it was easier to find the Frari from there rather than work her way on foot even though the distance from her place wasn't far. She got off the vaporetto and made her way past the Scuola di San Rocco to the *Frari,* or more formally, *Santa Maria Glorioso dei Frari*, Glorious Saint Mary of the San Franciscan Brothers.

Titian's masterpiece of Mary ascending into heaven was stupendous, and Marlowe never tired of looking at her. A pale blue sky shimmers at her feet and a peachy-gold sky awaits her irresistible drive upward. It's a breath-taking sight in the dark church with one strong beam of light focused on her. That vibrant crimson gown and blue mantle swirling around her proves that Titian knew drama. As Marlowe stood in awe again, the organ boomed its majestic call to worship and her stomach trembled.

When she finally left the church, she moaned for the thousandth time that she needed to live here. A glimpse every year or two was not enough! She wanted to stamp her foot in frustration like a child. To console herself, she went around the corner to her favorite gelato shop in all of Venice, *Mille Voglie*, A Thousand Desires, and bought a cone with a scoop of dark chocolate on the bottom and one of tart lemon on top. As she walked and indulged in the delicious stuff, she decided she had plenty of time before Rich arrived that evening. She would take a round-trip to the Lido, not to be there, but to feast her eyes on the sight coming back.

The water was smooth, smooth as dark Karo syrup, and the lumbering water bus pushed through it leaving little wake behind. She wanted to ride and not think, but, of course, she started to worry about Rich's arrival. Did she think she could make a difference in his life? Was it up to her to rescue him? No! and No! As the boat plowed on, her anxiety began to dissolve, and soon she slipped into her old habit of dreamy speculation. In her mind's eye, she saw ancient sailors coming home to this same sight—truly a skyline designed by lovers of the impossible.

* * *

Later as Marlowe sat dozing over a book, the phone rang.

"Ciao, Marlowe," Rich said before she could answer.

"Um… Rich? You caught me napping."

"Glad to catch you home because I'm about to leave for Berlin and won't make it to Venice tonight."

"A problem?"

"They think so in Berlin, but I'm aiming for Wednesday. Can we postpone 'til then?"

"Hold on a moment." She thought Marc's tour was set for Thursday, but went to her calendar. She would break it off with Rich for sure, but not over the phone. "Wednesday's fine," she said.

"Your social calendar picking up?"

"In the social whirl," she said hoping he was catching on.

"I see," he said. She heard a dark quality in his voice and could almost see his eyelids get that hooded look.

"They're boarding my plane, gotta go. See you soon. Take care," he said.

"You too."

For a moment she'd felt uncomfortable for not explaining— over explaining—and hoped he didn't think she was playing games. To hell with what he thinks, after all what had he been doing? She noticed the relief she felt that he wouldn't make it back. That said it all.

* * *

Tuesday morning, Paulo Parduzzi, her landlord, was in his office, and she told him about the person trying to get in. He was shocked. Last August, he'd changed the lock his father had installed, and the only people who rented after that were from Canada just the month before she had arrived. He couldn't believe Doctor Carocci, the doctor from Rome, would sneak around like that or, as Marlowe had suggested, would have loaned his key to someone.

"Why would anyone try to get in when it is already occupied?" he asked.

"I think someone left something and wants it back," Marlowe said.

"Surely not. Besides, there's no need to worry, that new lock is safe; it's from one of the best lock companies in Germany."

She asked him again about the apartment's availability for December. He said he'd let her know as soon as he heard back from Doctor Carocci. He offered the one she'd stayed in once before in Sant'Elena beyond the Giardini.

"No, Signor Parduzzi, it was nice but isolated. I want to wake up in the heart of the city."

"My wife and I agree; we live near San Vidale at the foot of the Academy Bridge."

She reached down at her feet to pet little Napoleone and gathered things to leave. "What a quiet fellow Napoleone is. Poodles usually bark a lot don't they?"

"Napoleone is not the least nervous. He's quite comfortable as long as I'm here, but when I'm gone, I'm told he guards the office with much barking," and he laughed.

"Maybe I need a pooch like him for the apartment."

"Yesss," he said in a concerned way for the first time since she'd arrived. "Do keep me informed if that person comes back."

"What could you do?" *Shove it under a rug, no doubt.*

"I could alert the polizia; they could keep a watch. Tell me again, when did this begin?"

"About a week ago, and as I said," trying hard to not let sarcasm color her voice, "it's happened three times."

"Marlowe, I'll contact the polizia today."

"Thanks, Signor Parduzzi and—"

"Do call me Paolo, " he said. "We agreed on that when you moved in, remember?"

"*Va bene,* Paolo, and you will let me know about December?"

"*Si, si,*" he said walking with her to the top of the stairs leading to the street.

"Ciao, Marlowe."

Hunh! she grunted as she left his office and turned onto Calle dei Fabbri which took her to the Rialto. From there she was soon in Cannaregio. Even though she wasn't ready to visit the convent, she liked walking in that familiar quiet region where the wide-bottom, working boats were moored along the canals. Sometimes they were loaded with large, heavy machinery and tools reminding her that everything—absolutely everything—had to be done from boats. By the time she reached the heart of Cannaregio, she was starving. There weren't many restaurants away from the station area and those few were well hidden, but she struck it rich at *Trattoria all'Antica Mola,* Trattoria of the Ancient Millstone.

She sat at the canal's edge and enjoyed a sumptuous lunch. Maybe everything seemed special because she was dining at a table covered with white linen and napkins right beside a rough work boat. The air was crisp and the sun warmed her back. For a moment, she didn't want to be anywhere else in the whole universe. And then, for the first time in Venice, she felt lonely and wished Marc were with her. He'd enjoy the whimsy of white linens and work boat. Rich might too, but with Marc... In that moment, she thought she might know Marc better than any other man, maybe better than Ty with whom she'd lived for twenty-one years. She had no doubt that Marc already knew *her* better than Ty ever did. Marc always seemed in tune. He got the same pleasure she did in figuring out what makes people tick. She remembered their time together at Torcello Island in the close quarters of his boat talking and talking, and making beautiful love. Never has anyone expressed such an intense interest in her, except maybe to get laid. But Marc was interested in who she was and wanted to be. What a turn on.

* * *

"Hey, Marlee, I'm glad to find you home," Marc said.

"Can't sit by the phone all day," she teased.

"Wouldn't expect it of a wench like you. What have you been up to?"

"I wandered in Cannaregio and had lunch at Antica Mola and thought of you. I think you'd enjoy it, in fact, I plan to take you there as my guest. When are you free?"

"Let's try next Monday, but why was it so special? What did you have?"

"First, p*asta e fagioli* and then *tipico fegato alla Veneziana*. The bean soup was thick and reeked of garlic. It was wonderful. Liver's not usually a choice I'd make, but since it was billed as typical of Venice, I tried it. It was a far cry from the kind I used to bury under catsup. But Marc, the best part was to sit at a table covered with white linens right beside a work boat tied to the fondamenta. And to top it off, the espresso was served with a hollow-handled silver spoon."

"That must have tickled your juxtaposition bone."

"How'd you know?"

"You told me."

"When?"

"Every time you describe something that catches your fancy, it has to do with odd combinations."

"Ah. Must be why I find you fascinating."

"Me? An odd combination? Hmm. I want to know more about that. Your tour of our fabbrica is definitely set for Thursday. Giovanni plans to create something brand new. Can you be there?"

"Oh yes, yes. I'll be there, just say the time and give me directions."

"Love it when you say 'yes, yes.' I'll pick you up. Need to be in Venice early that morning. Say 8:30?"

"Perfect. If the time changes, give me a call; I'll stay in that morning," she said.

"Where would you be at that hour?"

"Sometimes I wake early and go for a walk before the city wakes up."

"Not in the dark, I hope. What about that creep trying to get into your place?"

"That reminds me. I saw Paolo Parduzzi today," and she told him of their conversation.

"A police presence might scare someone off—if he wasn't too determined," he said. "By the way are you free tomorrow evening?"

"No, I'm not. Tonight though?" and she wished she could be with him tonight.

"Can't tonight. Guess it'll have to be Thursday."

"Have you been busy?" she asked.

"Catching up on paperwork and coordinating with Julie, my ex, about my time with Katy while I'm in the States. I want to bring her here for the holidays, but so far, I'm not hopeful."

"She is pretty young to be interested for more than a day or two."

"You might be right, but she's been reading up on Venice and mentions certain artworks she wants to see. It'd be nice if you could share your favorites with her."

"Sure, that'd be fun for me."

"Sorry, gotta go, but plan on spending all day over here and… the evening too?"

"Like pack a bag?"

"Babe."

"Okay. Ciao."

"Ciao, love."

CHAPTER TWENTY-SIX

At Campo San Giocomo dell'Orio, in the heart of sestiere San Polo—the most confusing section of Venice—Marlowe found a bench in the sun facing the back of the stumpy old church for which the campo is named. She had walked through here two days ago, but for a while today, she thought it had "disappeared." Then miraculously it reappeared again. That's Venice. A couple of grandmas sat across the way watching their charges ride bright pink and yellow plastic tricycles round and round the large open space. Marlowe could be happy in this general area where most tourists don't come. Something would turn up for December with or without Parduzzi's help.

And what about these two men? Her efforts to live in the moment with both was not working. Only to herself did she admit that she had wanted more than a fling with Marc. But he was not free and Rich was afraid of commitment. What did more mean to her? Marriage? Children? If they wanted more kids, they were out of luck with her. At least she'd been up front about that. Hadn't she? Marc certainly knew, but did she ever tell Rich? Did he ever ask? He didn't ask many personal questions. Maybe he was afraid such questions would set him up for entrapment. From time to time Marc made noises like he wanted more, but was it only lust talking? Oh yes, he was a lusty one. Since he wasn't free, though, maybe he had made those noises feeling a comfortable impunity. That sounded cynical, but after Ty and all his lies, her natural trust in people—men—had been eroded. Still, she didn't want to believe that about Marc.

She sat up, inhaled and threw her shoulders back. Here's how it had to be. She'd enjoy the heck out of Marc and come January, walk away. Men do that sort of thing all the time. She began to tick off on her fingers: 1) stay with Angie until she finds her own place; 2) find a law-clerk job 'til she passes the Oregon Bar; and 3) find a real job in law. With her own place and a job, she'd feel grounded again and could make a good life. This would be her last fling in Venice. Last? Yes. It'd be years before she could come back for more than a week or two. Deflated, she sagged back against the bench fearing she'd have to give up her dream of living here.

* * *

Back in her apartment, her phone rang.

"Angie! What's going on in Portland?" Marlowe asked.

"What's going on with your two hunks?" Angie asked.

"They are not my hunks, and I'll have you know they're decent men, a little bossy sometimes, but—"

"They may be decent, but Gumdrop, keep an eye on *your* main path, don't let some gorgeous guy lead you onto his."

"Never again. Now, Miss Angelina, what's going on with your love life?"

"That's why I called. You'll be happy to know there are plenty of hunks here in Portland and I've been sampling a few!"

"Hey, hey! You dumped Gary for good?"

"I did."

"Yea oh yea!" Marlowe hollered, jabbing her fist in the air. "Has he called you?"

"Mm-hmm. And you know something? I had no desire to engage in the scathing harangue I'd rehearsed for months. It all felt like a waste of energy."

"I know that feeling; I rehearsed a lot of those in my day with Ty."

"Would you believe, the very next week I met someone who asked me out?" Angie said.

"Well sure. Your pheromones are flowing."

"I'm thinking, Sugar Plum, yours are permeating all the rios and calles of Venice."

"Could be," Marlowe laughed, "because I feel horny most of the time."

"When are you coming back?" Angie asked.

"I'm thinking first of the year."

"You've always wanted to be in Venice over the holidays. I'm going to spend time with little bro in Connecticut."

"By the way, Miz Angeester, are these new guys tall enough for you?" Marlowe asked.

"Yep, I can even wear heels with them."

"Angie, I'm thrilled for you."

"I know you are. Meanwhile soak up your beloved Venice and enjoy those two hounds sniffing your tail."

"You're wicked!"

"We'll talk about your travel plans after the Christmas frenzy. Love you," Angie said.

"Love you, too."

She was right, Marlowe thought. She'd stay focused on her own goals and felt rejuvenated and unafraid for her future as she got ready to face Rich.

* * *

"Will you forgive me, Marlowe?"

"That's a loaded word, but I'll accept your apology for putting me down when all I said was I'd miss you."

"Marlowe, I'm sorry. You didn't deserve that. But now I want to make it up to you," he said pulling her into his arms and sliding his hands toward her breasts.

She stiffened.

"What's wrong?" he asked leaning back, moving his hands back to her waist and looking into her eyes.

What to say, she wondered? You hurt my feelings. You shut me out right after you'd invited me into your bed? It all sounded petty.

"Marlowe talk to me. I dropped everything and got here as soon as I could. The plane left Berlin late, even the Germans had to wait for the weather." And he tried chuckling.

Ignoring his attempt at humor to smooth everything away, she began, "Maybe I'm not as good at going from hot to cold as you seem to be."

"I said I was sorry. Can't we start over? Work pulls me between clients here and the company in Chicago. My ex blames me for problems she has with my children when I'm not even there. My mother pulls me to come back to the church. You're the only bright light in my life."

"I'm not a happy pill, Rich. Not something to take for a quick fix and then shove back into the medicine—"

"That's not fair, Marlowe."

"Isn't it?"

"You were a hot bitch when you invited me into your bedroom.".

"As I remember you carried me there."

"And I can do that again," he said as he bent his knees to pick her up.

She backed away.

"Who's cold now?"

"Riccardo - Rich - sex with you was wonderful, I don't deny that."

Now he backed away.

"But it isn't only about sex... or is it?" He looked hurt. Insulted? "I cannot," she took a big breath, "I *will* not walk on eggs worrying about what I can or cannot say."

"Maybe I need a cold shower to go with the cold shoulder here, and he started for the door. Then turned, "Marlowe, can we have that quiet dinner we talked about and sort this out. I'll be back in an hour, how's that sound?"

She hesitated not sure she could eat a bite. Not sure she wanted to listen to him vow it wouldn't happen again.

"Please," he said.

Damn, she was falling into his dark eyes and wanted to forget all about words.

"I'll be here," she sighed.

CHAPTER TWENTY-SEVEN

At the restaurant, Rich asked, "How's your pasta?"

"Excellent. *Aglio e olio* looks simple. I keep trying, it's only garlic and oil, but can't ever get it right."

"Are you going to give me another chance to get it right?" Rich asked putting his hand on hers lying beside her wine glass.

"Everyone deserves another chance," she said. "But—"

"But, what?"

"What I wanted to say earlier… what I mean is… great sex is powerful. But it can become a bondage.

"Bondage? No. I don't want that. Surely you know I wouldn't—"

"I don't mean *you* would force any kind of bondage. I mean that because our lovemaking was good, I could slip into tiptoeing around every other issue that comes along."

He was quiet.

She took a deep breath and said, "Rich, sex can't always make up for being rejected or put down."

He said nothing.

They walked back to her apartment in silence holding hands. When they reached her door, she opened it and turned to say goodnight. As he'd done on their first evening, he grabbed a kiss, deepened it and held her as if he was afraid to let go.

"I'm sorry, Rich, but I need to be alone tonight."

He dropped his arms and backed away. "I see," he said. Of course, he didn't. He'd been away and probably planned to rush in and make it all up with wild, wonderful sex. Now she was holding him off. "Tomorrow evening?" he asked. "We could drop into

Venice's famous Casino and see how the filthy rich throw their money away."

"A friend has arranged a tour through a glass factory on Murano and said it would be an all-day thing with dinner after."

"Are you playing some sort of game with me?"

"No! I'm trying to express how I feel. It is *not* a game."

"Okay... okay. Saturday?" he asked grasping her shoulders. She was quiet.

"Saturday evening?" he repeated. "We could go to dinner either at the Casino or somewhere else and drop in and watch the high rollers."

"Call me that morning," she said.

He pulled her into an embrace, but she remained unresponsive.

"Rich. I hope we're coming to a better understanding."

But when she locked the door after he left, she knew they hadn't. She'd been too weak. She adjusted the gauzy curtains to cover the windows and door and dragged herself to her bedroom. She fell into bed exhausted but glad for saying what needed to be said. Damn, for a moment she'd been tempted. Her emotions had never run amok like this before, but those dark eyes were pleading, loving, wanting. Still, Rich could *not* be here when Marc appeared in the morning. *Lord, I'm not cut out for this.*

* * *

She lay in the dark hoping for sleep, but then heard the familiar scratching at the lock. She'd been leaving the key in it because Marc had said it'd be harder for anyone to get it open even if they had the right key. Still she felt helpless. She should have taken that Karate class last summer. Then refusing to lie there like a victim, she grabbed her robe at the foot of the bed and got up. She remembered the heavy flashlight she'd found in the furnace closet and crept barefoot into the living room. Her eyes were already adjusted to the dark, and with the light coming through the curtains, she saw its dark shape lying on the table. She reached for it but in her agitation nudged it off instead. It made a horrendous noise on the marble floor. She froze. Whoever was out there froze too. She held her breath trying to listen but her heart was pounding so much she couldn't hear a thing.

Slow down. Breathe, she told herself. She should call the police but couldn't remember the number written on her card of numbers beside the phone. Slowly she picked up the torch, found the card and moved to a corner in the bedroom behind the dividing wall and tried the light. It still worked. She memorized the number and slipped back into the living room. He was still out there, she could feel him. Now he was trying a key again. She punched in the numbers for the police and waited. Then whispered into the phone. Would the police person hear her? She gave her information as best she could, and the operator said they'd come soon.

What if they didn't get her address right? Oh lord. In the meantime, she needed to find out who this miserable creep was and crept toward the top of the steps. At least she could shine the light in his face, then if he was ever caught, she'd be able to identify him. And, if he *should* get the door open, she'd smash his head with the heavy light. She made out a shape at the door. He looked small but how could she tell for sure when he was crouched over? He had a lot guts standing there under the light mounted over her doorway. She could see him, but he could not see her. Like a mantra she repeated *he cannot see me, he cannot see me.*

His keys jangled and he tried again. What does he want? Who could he be? Inch by inch hugging her back along the wall, she crept down the stairs. Her feet were freezing but at least he couldn't hear her move. She felt the rough edges of the bricks snagging the back of her robe. She heard him snarling in frustration. He was close. Only a thin wall of bricks between them. Only a glass-paned door between them. She was sweating and could smell the fear coming from her pores. At street level, she planned her next move. With her left hand, she'd yank the curtain away from the glass. With her right, she'd point the light straight at him. One, two, three! The man looked up. His eyes went wide, startled, and then she heard the whee-whaw of the European siren and saw blue lights blinking as a boat came up the canal. The man was gone.

A dark cap had been low on his brow and he had a scraggly, Fu-Manchu-type beard on his chin. That's all she could remember. It seemed that he ran toward the Zattere. The police boat came in from the Grand Canal. She was breathing hard and shaking all over when someone knocked on her door calling out Polizia! She pulled the curtain aside and saw two policemen standing there. She opened the door with the flashlight in her hand. She flipped the light switch at the bottom of the steps and invited them in.

Two men in uniform followed her up the stairs. She spoke a mix of Italian and English and told her story. They seemed to understand. They asked her name and wanted to see her passport. When she got to the drawer in her bedroom where her money belt held her passport, she realized the big torch was still in her hand. She dropped it on the bed and went back to the officers waiting in the living room. When she asked them if they'd seen a man run away from her door, they nodded and said two men had gone after him. They took notes and told her someone who spoke better English would call later. Then they left. She felt some better but decided to leave the television on. She muted it hoping for some sleep. She reasoned that Fu Manchu always seemed to come when it was dark, and if he did come back, maybe he'd see the light from the tv and go away. She made a cup of camomile tea and took it to bed not expecting to get a wink of sleep.

CHAPTER TWENTY-EIGHT

Marlowe struggled to climb out of her dream—the old dream where the latch slipped and the cellar door had slammed shut. She was eight again in the pitch black of Grandpa's cellar and wasn't supposed to be there. She had to find a way out. The thin light of day showed around the edges of the slanted door over the steps leading upward to the outside. She kept that line to freedom in sight. But the first step was huge; she had to stretch and scramble onto it. The next one, even bigger. Her heart was pounding, but she knew she had to pound on the door to get out. Then something grabbed her ankle and tried to drag her back into the darkness. She strained and lunged upward swinging her leg onto the next step just before "it" reached for her foot again.

She couldn't get her breath. Then sat up in bed drenched in sweat. The same old dream, but this time, the pounding came from the outside. She listened remembering how she'd strained to listen for the key man last night Was that creep back? No, it wasn't pounding after all, more like knocking. Someone was knocking at her door. She sat on the side of the bed rubbing her hands over her face as if washing it. Grabbing her robe, she shoved her feet into her slippers and saw the flashlight on the floor by the bed. She picked it up and held it high—ready—as she went down the steps to the door.

Easing the curtain aside she saw Marc. She let out a breath she'd been holding and almost sank to the floor in relief. Thank heaven for Marc. He wore a pale blue chambray shirt and faded jeans with a wide leather belt. He'd never looked so good. He'd know what to do.

"Oh Marc, thank God," she cried as she threw open the door and pulled him in. She threw her arms around his waist and held on.

"Good morning to you too," he said dropping a heavy bag on the floor and drew her into his arms. "What's wrong, Sprout? You're all sweaty."

"What time is it? I must have overslept. So glad you're here. I thought someone was after me, but the pounding was on the outside."

"Shhh," he said as he moved the damp hair away from her face.

"I guess it was a dream," she sighed collapsing against him.

"Some dream. It's only me. You're safe, Bambina, you're safe. Come up and sit. Take a breath. Coffee? Tea?"

"But the pounding wouldn't stop," she said still clinging to him.

"Shh, shh," he whispered. "Look at me. Marlowe. Look! Take a long, deep breath—easy does it."

She sucked in a breath.

"Would you like coffee?" he asked again.

"Yes. Coffee please."

"You *are* agitated," he said smoothing down her wild bed hair chuckling in his rumbly way. And at that instant, she understood why his rumble was always a comfort. It was Grandpa's deep laugh. She heaved a huge sigh, settled back against the couch finally feeling safe.

"What'd you mean the pounding was on the outside?" he asked.

"I'm a mess. I need a shower," and she ran to the bathroom. When she came out, she smelled coffee. She'd heard a grinder through the bathroom wall. He must have brought one with him. *This man's a keeper.* Then she remembered he wasn't available. She'd think about that later and followed her nose toward the heady aroma. Her traveling coffee press and a cup were waiting on the coffee table.

"Marc, you're a life saver."

"Why'd you have the tv on? And muted? Did that jerk come back?"

"Last night." She told him what happened, and that she'd left the tv on because the light would show toward the street.

Marc watched her and listened in that quiet focused way he'd done before.

"I think the guy tries to get in when the lights are out. Remember when he came that night after you turned out all the lights?"

"Yes, I remember," he said giving her a gentle squeeze.

"Last night, I lay in bed frozen with fear. Then I got mad and picked up the big flashlight."

"Babe."

"I wasn't going to open the door, but I needed something if he got in." She looked around, "Where's my flashlight. It's the only weapon I have!"

"You had it in your hand at the door. I laid it on the ledge."

"Good. Perfect place for it," she said.

"What were you planning with that big torch?"

"Mainly I wanted to startle him. I could hear him shaking a bunch of keys and growling to himself. Do you think he has a set of skeleton keys? He must be desperate."

"Did you see him?"

"Sort of," and she told what she remembered.

"Do you know how big he was? What color was his hair?"

"When I saw him, he had a watch cap pulled down low—he might be bald."

"Was he big or small?" Marc asked.

She stopped, and shook her head. "I only saw him for a moment then the cops scared him away, but... don't think he was much taller than me."

Marc pushed the plunger down and poured her some coffee. She sat back against the sofa, and sipped. "Ah. It's Illy brand isn't it? You brought a grinder and beans too?"

"How can a coffee afficionado manage without?" he said.

She put her cup down and hugged him again. She buried her face into his chest inhaling the scent of him, his soap—amber maybe? And his maleness. Ah yes, his maleness.

Then she got up and said, "We better hurry."

"You're not late, I'm early. I came to install a heavy duty latch bolt with double cylinders on your door. It's stronger than any chain would be. Once you're inside, no one can break in even if they have the right key—even if they break the glass panes. And my little wench, that's all that matters," he said encircling her. She pressed into him again burrowing closer wishing she could crawl under his skin. So warm and strong.

She raised her head to him and asked, "Did you check with Parduzzi?"

"Phoof! He'd futz around making noises and do nothing. I'd think he'd be grateful. I'll handle him, don't worry yourself."

She smiled. She treasured her independence, but in truth she wasn't brave—not brave at all—and didn't mind one bit when a man like Marc took charge.

"Tell me about that dream. I'm thinking this creep is the reason for it.

"Maybe," she said, and told him a little and admitted she hadn't had it for ages.

"You want to get ready to leave while I do my thing with the lock?"

She went back to tame her hair and pull on black slacks and black sweater, what else? But she did add a scarf of cobalt blue with geometric shapes of energetic yellows, reds and even greens that reminded her of colors in glass paper weights from Murano. She put her pathetic earrings on, chuckling as she stuck one through an ear lobe.

"What are you chuckling about?" he called from down the steps at the door.

"Putting on my pathetic earrings."

"Glad you see that as funny now."

"Me too," and she stepped down to take a look. "That *is* heavy duty. Marc, I feel safer already. Now, how does this latchbolt thing work?"

He demonstrated it and promised to find a solid, deadbolt to make sure no one could get in when she was away.

* * *

They took the same launch they'd used on their stormy night. He pulled her in out of sight of anyone to kiss and hold her close. "Good memories here," he said with a hoarse voice. She nodded and laid her head against his chest.

It was an easy ride to Murano. The waterways seemed different in the early-morning brightness. Not as mystical. She could see cracks in the old buildings and moss and crud that had built up on the sides of the canals. Not that she wasn't still enchanted; reality's good too, and a big part of that reality was beside her. Minutes after they passed the cemetery isle, they were slowing into a canal in Murano. He pulled up to tie along Fondamenta Vetrai.

"This is it," he said. "Barovier & Toso now, but Barovier has been in Murano since 1295."

"That long?"

"Would I kid you?" He seemed lighter even more at ease than his usual relaxed manner. This was his home territory and it showed. "The name Jacobellus Barovier is on an official Venetian document dated 1292, the year a law forced all furnaces to move from Venice to Murano because of frequent fires. That means old Jake was probably working glass before then. The family considers him their founder. Let's go meet some people."

CHAPTER TWENTY-NINE

His uncles weren't in. Marc had said once they were happy to
let their sons do much of the day-to-day work, so she was meeting
the cousins he'd grown up with: Matteo and Luca, and of course
the master artist, Giovanni, who wasn't there yet. Sounded Biblical. But where was Marco to round out the four gospel writers?
Then it struck her why Marc had refused to let her call him Marco. Their Marco was the one killed on the Autostrada.

In spite of being built like tanks, Matteo and Luca were trim.
Luca did have a developing paunch, but what beautiful eyes. They
were a sea-green color like waves curling over on themselves when
sunlight shines through. She wandered around the gallery that
displayed samples of their products while the cousins conferred.
Exquisite old-style glass objects were displayed alongside ultra
modern ones. She was drawn to the older goblets but knew it was
necessary to offer fresh ideas or the fickle public would pass on by.

"Ready to go in the back?"

"Yes. These samples are stunning."

"Thanks," he said and put his hand on the small of her back
and guided her to the inner workings of Barovier & Toso. She
could barely contain her excitement to be there.

"Where are the others on tour?" she whispered to Marc.

"You're it."

"Honest? I'm thrilled."

"I know," he said. "Relax, it's only you and me. I'll give you
the spiel."

"Good."

"You've probably seen Lampworking before," he said.

"Is that when a welding-like torch is used to shape glass into small objects?" she said.

"Pretty much."

"My favorite, though," she said, "is what they do in a hot shop like the one at the glass museum in Tacoma, Washington. Dale Chihuly's inspiration. You know about him, no doubt."

He nodded.

"They make larger objects in the furnaces, right?"

"Which would you like to see today?" he said.

"Both, you know I'm greedy. But truth to tell, I prefer the big stuff… like you."

He broke into a soft rumbly laugh.

"Giovanni may do both today, but I know he'll be working with the furnace. He won't have much time now, but afterward you can ask questions."

"Great. May I see the supplies of colored glass and stuff like that?" she said.

"Yes, but let me find out his schedule, we can see the supplies any time."

She couldn't believe she was in one of the most famous glass factories in the world. She would be quiet and calm—not pushy. After all, she knew only a few things about this ancient company and she planned to keep her show-off mouth shut.

"Giovanni, here she is, the curious one who wants to steal your secrets," Marc said to the man approaching them. From across the room, the first thing she saw was the man's acquamarine eyes. He was taller than his brothers, at least six feet. Lithe and loose limbed. His hair was a much darker blond than theirs, almost brown. He was grinning and had the whitest teeth she'd seen in Venice. Did standing at white-hot flames have something to do with that? What foolishness. She was feeling as giddy as a school girl.

"*Piacere, Signora Osborne,*" Giovanni said holding out his hand.

Up close she noticed deep dimples on each side of his mouth. What a gorgeous man.

"*Piacere, Signor Barovier,*" she said. "*Grazie per permettermi di osservarla mentre crea un capolavoro.*"

A quick silent exchange went between Marc and Giovanni, then they both burst into laughter. She was mortified assuming she'd made a horrible blunder with the phrase she'd been working on.

"*Lei è carina, eh? E forse furba?*" Giovanni said to Marc.

She remained silent pretending she didn't understand but she'd caught *carina*, cute. Was she being patronized? *Furba?* Didn't that mean sneaky or maybe street smart?

"Please forgive me, Marlowe," Giovanni said in perfect English. "I'm flattered that you expect me to create a masterpiece, but each time I begin something new, I have fears of messing up. Maybe like your fear of saying the wrong thing a moment ago. Believe me, you did not, but it was so unexpected, and... very nice." His smile would melt all the glass in Murano.

"I can't begin to express the thrill I feel to be here. I won't try...and certainly not in Italiano! But thank you for letting me come."

He smiled. His blue-green eyes smiled, too.

"My team's waiting. We'll re-hash everything later."

"That sounds wonderful," she said. And he was gone.

"Okay, Marc, what was so funny?"

"Exactly what he said. Your remark was unexpected and particularly so because it was in Italian. You don't speak Italian often, it caught me off guard too."

"But I saw you two exchange thoughts before you broke out laughing."

"I told you how close we've always been. We just have this rapport," and he twisted his hand in the air. "I guess we were asking each other, or rather he was asking me, if it was okay to laugh and not hurt your feelings. I took the chance."

"Sure, after he reassured me. He must have read my face."

"You did show yourself, Marlee. Don't ever try to play poker."

"Good advice."

"Let's get a bottle of water to drink while we're in the hot-shop. We don't have that nifty cone to draw hot air up and away as they do in Tacoma."

"You've been there?"

"Yeah. Giovanni too. He gave demonstrations there at Chihuly's request."

"I bet Giovanni flustered female hearts in Tacoma, he's an attractive man."

Marc nodded. It was very warm and noisy from the roar of two furnaces, "the glory holes." Adding to the noise, fans were blowing from somewhere behind in the huge space. A few chairs were in the back of the room. Marc brought a couple closer to the action. She took off her jacket and draped it over the chair wishing she'd not worn the silk turtleneck under her sweater.

"Are you too warm?" he asked.

"Of course but I ain't about to leave!" she said as she took the bottle of water he handed her. "But, is there a place nearby where I could shed this turtleneck?"

"The toilettes are out in the gallery, but you could go behind the *tempera* and have some privacy."

"*Tempera?*"

"Sorry, the annealing oven, that green cabinet-like thing."

"Oh yes. They called it 'the garage' in Tacoma," Marlowe said. "For now it's my dressing room. Save my place," she said and walked behind the tempera

* * *

He smiled to himself thinking what fun it was to be around her and her whimsical surprises. If he knew her for forty years, he'd probably never figure out her quirky mind. She wasn't polished and smooth and didn't walk the finishing-school path like some women who *always* knew the politic thing to say or do. They grew tiresome after a while. Marlowe was anything but tiresome.

When she came back to Marc, he was talking to a dark beauty with lovely olive skin. She was small and slender, and Marlowe felt twinges of jealousy.

"Marlowe," he said. "This is Sandra, Giovanni's wife. She works in shipping."

"Piacere," Marlowe said holding out her hand.

Sandra's lustrous, dark hair was piled on top of her head with a large comb clip. She was elegant in a simple, white Tee-shirt and dark slacks. *"Piacere,"* she said. "I came to invite you for lunch when Giovanni's finished. Can you come?"

"Oh yes. I'd be delighted. Thank you for inviting me," Marlowe said. "I hope you haven't gone to a lot of trouble. After all, you work here and have children, don't you?"

"It's no problem, the children are at Nonna and Nonno's today."

"They're lucky to have grandparents nearby," Marlowe said.

"And there's a wonderful deli that helps me more than anyone knows," Sandra said.

"Even so, it's good of you to invite me," Marlowe said.

"Until later. Ciao," she said and slipped out.

"This day is turning into a total treat," Marlowe said.

"Nice to see you relaxed and having a good time."

"All thanks to you. First of all, I have a strong lock on my door and will sleep well tonight, and now I get to see behind the scenes of the most famous glass fabbrica in the world and—"

"Calma, calma, Marlee."

"I did read that Barovier & Toso is one of 100 oldest companies in the world. That's true isn't it?"

"Yes, but of those 100, we're the youngest."

"So? You made the cut didn't you?"

There was that lift of his mouth again. She knew he was trying not to laugh at her, and at the same time she sensed he found her endearing in some way.

"What is that large, green glass goblet with three spouts on it?" She pointed to a bench close to the oven.

"That's Giovanni's *Goto* In Venetian dialect, a Goto is any oversized drinking cup, but in the Muranese tradition, each maestro creates his own unique Goto to use while he works."

"Goto. I like that idea."

"Thought you would," he said and looked at her with such tenderness, she felt like melting into a puddle at his feet. "Look," he said, "the furnace must be ready; Giovanni's taking out the first gathering."

CHAPTER THIRTY

Giovanni and his team worked with the molten glass turning it, shaping it, cutting off a piece and attaching another. Then his *servente,* chief assistant, brought another gob from the second oven to add to the side of the first that Giovanni was holding. With the heavy molten glob at the end of the *canna da soffio,* the blowpipe, he blew into it. Soon a large globe took shape. All the while, Marc kept up a running commentary. Giovanni thrust it all back into the furnace for more heat and quickly drew it back out twirling the rod as he carried it to the table called a *marver.* He laid it on the marver and rolled the molten glass again pinching it with a tool that looked like long-handled pliers called *borselle.*

"But aren't *borselle* handbags?" she asked.

"Many terms in glass blowing come from Italian but they've evolved into the glass-blowers' special forms—a mixture of Venetian dialect and Italian."

She nodded. "What are those flat, wooden things they're using to shape the glass?"

"Those paddles? They're probably graphite. Sometimes paddles are wood, but graphite has a lower density and absorbs heat, so when it touches the molten glass, there's minimal temperature contrast. Less chance for shock to the glass. You may even see Giovanni use bunches of wet newspaper for hand shaping."

"There's much to think about while handling such dangerous material," she said musing aloud. "Oh look! Look at the color. It's beautiful."

"You do like red don't you," he said.

Giovanni and his assistant continued to work in complete harmony. "It looks as if the red glass has bits of gold running through it," she said.

"It does, doesn't it."

Giovanni left his helper to deal with the red object and moved to the far oven where two more men were preparing a much larger gob of molten glass for another project, a commission for a large, complicated chandelier, Marc told her. They all seemed to move as if in a graceful, choreographed dance.

At some point, Giovanni had removed his outer shirt and was working in one with the sleeves torn off at the shoulder seams revealing the sculpted strength in his beautiful biceps. They'd have to be strong to lift heavy, molten lumps of glass and control them on the end of a long, wobbly pipe. Marc said the ovens ran at 2100 degrees Fahrenheit. Giovanni must have been burning up. Here she was feeling too hot to live, and he was next to that scorching furnace. But the big difference was that he was "in the zone" unaware of anything except his art.

He came back to their oven, and with the long pliers, began shaping the lips of the red goblet. Back it went into the oven briefly, then Giovanni let a drop of water fall just below the base of the goblet, and as the *servente* turned the steel tube, Giovanni held his pincher-tool onto that area. After that, he jammed his hands in large, asbestos gloves and when his assistant gave the pipe a sharp tap with a short metal rod, the goblet fell into Giovanni's hands. He turned to Marlowe and Marc and held it up. It was a blood-red, over-sized goblet. A Goto. And this time she was sure she saw gold sparkles inside the stem. She stood up and clapped as if applauding the primo aria of a performance. To her, he'd performed a perfect aria in glass. He laughed and took a bow. Then he handed it off to his assistant, who took it to the *tempera* to "heat-soak."

Marc explained, "The piece must cool slowly in the annealing oven until its temperature goes below a certain point, usually about 900 degrees Fahrenheit. Then it can safely be dropped to room temperature."

"May I come back tomorrow and have a look at it? Maybe touch it?"

"We'll ask Giovanni about that," Marc said. His grey eyes were alive with silvery glints. She grabbed Marc around the waist and gave him a big hug not caring who saw her. "Thank you so much for making this happen."

"You're welcome, Marlee, but let's get the hell out of here."

"It's one o'clock! We were here almost three hours. It seemed like one," she said.

"It doesn't seem that long to me now, but when I worked with Benvenuto, my uncle Bennie, it seemed much longer. The heat was intense. I never could adjust."

"Must be the Norse in you," she said waiting for his reaction.

"Could be," he said squeezing her shoulder. "Let's go out for a walk. We have time."

"Great idea. Do you think Giovanni would mind if I asked him some questions?"

"He expects it. He's heard all about you, you know."

"How much has he heard?" she said stopping to put her hands on her hips and narrow her eyes in mock suspicion.

"Enough," he said with a devil-grin. "Don't worry, I don't kiss and tell if that's what you're thinking."

"Sort of."

They went to the end of the sidewalk, turned back to the Barovier & Toso facility and walked around the entire complex. The fabbrica and palazzo took up most of that piece of Murano real estate that faced Venice. Neither structure was an architectural wonder but each had served the family's purposes for years.

The weather was perfect. Cool but not cold. Misting but not drenching. She was in her personal heaven, weather-wise, and having Marc beside her made it even more ideal.

"I'm starved," Marc said." Let's check in with Sandra; she'll let me have a bite or two even if Giovanni isn't ready."

CHAPTER THIRTY-ONE

With his hair damp from the shower, Giovanni offered Marlowe his hand to shake, but she took it in both hands and kissed it lightly.

"He's not the Pope, Cara," Marc said laughing.

"Maybe he should be with the miracle he performed today. Giovanni, what an honor to see you work."

He grinned and looked over at Sandra who rolled her eyes. "Did you get warm in there?" he said.

"Yes, but after a while I didn't notice. The time flew. If I ever live in Venice, would it be possible to take lessons in glass making? Are there classes like Thom Price offers for gondola making?"

"I don't know of any. But if you lived here, something could be worked out, I'm sure," and he gave Marc a knowing look.

She laughed, "I know I'm making a fool of myself. Anyway, you're safe because I can't afford to live here unless I find a job. Say, maybe I could sweep the floor at the end of your day."

"What would you like, white or red wine?" Sandra asked.

"Red please," Marlowe said and wondered if Sandra was miffed about all the attention on Giovanni. "Sandra, how do you bring Giovanni's head out of the clouds when someone like me comes along praising him to the heavens?"

"I have a few ways," she said with a sparkle in her eyes that lit up her face.

"This is a charming apartment. One would never guess from the outside. That's something I like about Europeans; you keep all the best inside."

"What do Americans do?"

"Most make the outside look as showy and big as possible. It seems they want to let the world know how successful they are."

"What about the old Venetians who did just that?" Marc said. "If they hadn't, we wouldn't have those magnificent palaces along the Grand Canal."

"That's true," she said, but when the Americans show off, the results are often tacky instead of magnificent." Turning back to Sandra, she said,. "Sandra, these antipasti look fantastic."

While they'd talked, Sandra had brought to the coffee table an antipasto tray of salamis, olives, cheeses, raw veggies, pickles and tiny, fried fish. A basket of crunchy bread had already appeared as Giovanni poured their wine. "This is a feast right here," Marlowe said wishing it were the main course, but knowing it wouldn't be restrained herself as best she could.

"Marlowe, have you seen glass making before? "Sandra asked.

"Not until I went to the Glass Museum in Tacoma. Before that I'd watched people create little figures at state fairs or carnivals. After seeing that hot shop at Tacoma, though, I was hooked and never dreamed I'd get to watch a master in Murano."

"What appeals to you most?" Giovanni asked side stepping the compliment.

"You mean what kinds of objects appeal or what activity at the furnaces?"

"At the furnaces."

"I guess I'd say what fascinates me the most is the skill it takes to know the exact moment when you can cut that gob of molten glass and get it to stick to another piece of molten glass. The timing must be precise—and dangerous—to make it all work."

Giovanni looked at Marc and something passed between them, but he merely said, "That can be a troublesome time."

"I have many questions but I suppose you're tired of hearing them."

He shook his head. "I don't talk to many non-glass makers. I'm curious about your questions, Marlowe."

"Okaaay. This one is none of my business, and I don't mind if you tell me it's privileged information, but why did your family add the Toso name?"

"Marriage."

"Ah."

"But in the 1850s, the Toso Brothers played a big part in the revival of Murano glass. I think it made good sense to merge. Right, Marc?" Giovanni asked.

"Probably, although I've always wondered if it was necessary aside from the marriage."

"In the long run," Giovanni said, "I think it strengthened both."

"*Vengano, vengano,*" Sandra said calling them to her table.

Marlowe had been so engrossed, she hadn't noticed that Sandra had slipped away again. I should have helped her, she thought, and vowed to help with the rest of the meal.

Giovanni jumped up to carry in a big pot of steaming pasta with the delectable aroma of porcini mushrooms rising from it.

Marc took Marlowe's hand and almost lifted her from the couch. She needed his hand to steady her, the wine had gone to her head. Her cheeks felt hot and were probably flushed, but she didn't care, it was all too exciting. He looked down at her and softly said, "Babe."

After they were seated and served, she held her hand over her glass when Giovanni tried to add more wine. He grinned and those dimples emerged. No doubt he could tell by looking that she was almost wasted. She didn't realize she'd drunk too much. Maybe it was higher alcohol content than usual. She'd ask Marc.

"This is delicious," she said to Sandra and didn't talk for a while knowing her brain needed food to slow down and make sense of itself.

Marc put his hand on her shoulder and neck and massaged. It was uncanny the way he sensed what was going on with her and cared. He also poured water for her and she took the hint.

The three of them talked about family matters, their uncles, their children, and whether Marc would be able to bring Katy over this year. Marlowe heard it all in a kind of fog and kept quiet. Sandra stood up to clear the table, Marlowe started to get up, but Marc took her forearm and tugged. She sat, feeling embarrassed but grateful. Giovanni helped Sandra carry in salad. By the end of the salad, Marlowe's head had cleared a little.

"Giovanni?" she asked. "Is Carlo Tosi as good as everyone claims? Is he part of the Toso family? Did you study with him?"

"There she goes not two but three questions this time," Marc said with an adoring smile.

"Oops, shall I rephrase that?"

"No need, Giovanni said. "Yes, yes, and yes."

"Tell me more, please."

"I'm not exactly sure why Carlo calls himself Tosi. Probably some family dispute among the Toso Brothers years ago. They created exceptional objects, particularly goblets. In fact, Carlo has been called the goblet maestro. Did you know his nickname is Caramea, Venetian dialect for *caramelo*, candy?" Giovanni asked.

She nodded.

Marc turned to her and said, "You've been busy."

She smiled. "I was curious about your family's fabbrica and one thing led to another."

"I'm not surprised," he said squeezing her thigh under the table.

"Because Tosi made light, fragile goblets, someone thought they were like spun sugar. He *was* amazing, and yes I was fortunate to be his *servente* for a few years. He came to work with old Ercole Barovier when he was sixteen. By age twenty, Ercole offered him the position of first master glassblower. A maestro at twenty. Unheard of... then."

Marlowe looked at Marc with a question on her face, but he shook his head almost imperceptibly and she let it go. He knew she was guessing that Giovanni was made first master at a young age too.

Giovanni went on, "Tosi stayed with Barovier for more than thirty years."

"Are there samples of his work in your gallery?"

"One or two, but most have been donated to the civic museum."

This time when Sandra stood to clear the table, Marlowe did too. She also helped her bring biscotti and coffee into the living room.

"Surely other companies tried to lure Tosi away?" she asked hoping to revive the conversation once they'd all settled around the coffee table again.

He nodded. "He had many offers even in other countries, but he was content to work here. Of course, he was treated like royalty and could create whatever came to mind."

"That reminds me," Marlowe said, "what about young Gianni Tosi taking off to the U.S.? What did the Murano community think about that?"

"A few old timers saw him as a traitor, but most realized what a young maverick he was. Another one of those child geniuses with glass."

Marc chimed in, "In the late 70s, Marvin Lipofsky, a big shot in the glass world of California, invited Gianni to be his star in a glass-blowing U.S. tour." Marc took a bite of biscotto. "Tosi fell in love with the freedom over there. He sold his studio and moved to New Jersey."

"I think he works alone somewhere near Baltimore now," Giovanni said.

Marlowe was digesting this information and delighted they were willing to talk about the industry with her.

Giovanni continued, "Times have changed, Marlowe. People exchange secrets without being threatened with death as in the old days. Most everyone here agrees it's a good thing. Many glass makers belong to international groups and even attend conferences concerned with environmental issues."

"I heard recently that fish from the waters around Murano

are loaded with heavy metals," she said and immediately worried about offending Giovanni and Sandra.

"God yes," Giovanni said. "What has been dumped in the water for centuries will take more centuries to clear out—if ever. Only recently factories have added bag filters—the inexpensive kind. They hang inside the chimneys, but their pores clog up fast and have to be replaced often. The best filters send waste gases through a flue on to an electrostatic precipitator for treatment before being sent back out the chimney. But the cost of the electrostatic kind is very expensive. Most fabbricas in Murano use the simple bag system."

"Whew, maybe that's more than I want to know," Marlowe said.

They all laughed, but she was dying to know which kind Barovier had installed.

"And to answer your unspoken question," Giovanni said dimples showing, "we've also gone with the cheaper method. Only for now, I hope," and he looked at Marc who understood a lot about the company finances.

She felt her face grow hot. Yikes, he's a mind reader too, it must run in the family. "Thank you for allowing me in for a private viewing, Giovanni. And Sandra, for this sumptuous lunch. *Grazie, grazie tante.*"

"Marlowe, it's been a pleasure to have somebody genuinely interested."

"Could I ask one more question?" she said, and looked over at Marc.

"*Certo,*" Giovanni said.

"I've always wondered how the Venetians were able to stay ahead of other glass makers around the world for such a long time."

"A good question. They had a huge advantage for a while because it happens that the local quartz pebbles are almost pure silica—excellent back then for making clear glass. They ground them into a fine, clear sand and combined it with soda ash imported from the Levant. Since Venetians were masters of the sea, they had a monopoly on the soda ash."

"Fascinating," she said sitting back quietly to sip the last drop of her coffee.

Marc stood up to go and so did she.

"Thanks again, both of you," Marlowe said. "Do you think you'll come to the Northwest any time? I'm in Portland, Oregon, down the road from Chihuly's territory. You're invited to come for a visit anytime."

"Giovanni and Sandra, you're privileged, believe me, I haven't had such an open invitation," Marc said.

"Maybe you need to play your cards differently, Marc," Giovanni said punching him in the belly. "Thanks, Marlowe. We have no plans, but who knows what our universe will bring."

"Changes do keep coming, don't they?" Marlowe said gathering her jacket and bag.

"By the way," Giovanni said. "Marc did play his cards right in bringing us into the twenty-first century, in several ways. Ask him about the Henokiens."

They said goodbye and slipped out.

"They looked tired, particularly Giovanni. You should have nudged me out sooner."

"Don't worry, Sprout, I would have if I thought we were overstaying our welcome. Giovanni seemed to bask in your interest."

"Hope so. What an experience. It is good to be out in the mist, though."

"For a while there, I thought I'd be carrying you out. What happened?"

"I don't know. The wine hit me fast. I didn't think I drank more than usual. Did it have a higher alcohol content?"

"I doubt it. I bet you were dehydrated from the hot shop."

They walked on aimlessly as the street lamps came on. People were out for their stroll before dinner, the usual *passeggiata* happening all over Italy at this hour. The mist was almost gone and the western sky was turning rosy. People nodded but no one stopped to chat or press him to introduce her. Good, she thought, because she was talked out and had no desire to talk to anyone... except Marc. Soon they were at a door with a mailbox slot marked number four.

"Here we are. My apartment's up these steps."

"Do you receive your own mail here?"

"Of course. But some families do receive all their mail in one box. Crazy idea. After you, Signora," and they started up a narrow staircase.

"This brings back fond memories of following you up the stairs at Johnson's," he said.

"I remember you always insisted I go first. I didn't think that was pure chivalry then and *know* it isn't now."

"It's still fun to watch."

"Glad to hear it after that remark you made at San Rocco's."

"You heard after all," he laughed and put his hands on her behind and didn't let go until they reached the top.

CHAPTER THIRTY-TWO

They stepped onto the golden flooring of his living/dining room area. Straight on through she saw a kitchen with numerous cupboards and plenty of counter space. A fridge, full stove with an oven, and best of all, a spacious sink. The window over the sink looked toward buildings of Murano with a church dome in the distance. The dining table and chairs were in the center of the open area and to the far right, two large leather chairs and couch formed a comfortable group around a fireplace.

"The floor, Marc, is it bamboo?"

He nodded.

"It's exquisite. And the sink is wonderful," she said and hurried toward it. "May I have a glass of water? I bet glass-blowers drink a lot of water."

"Sure, help yourself, glasses are on the left. I'll have one too." He was picking up a few things but the apartment was already tidy. The grey-blue walls and the tans and dark teaks of the sleek Scandinavian furniture gave a nice minimalist touch, not too spare but calm and restful. No drapes were at the windows, instead, narrow-slatted wooden shutters stained in a dark chocolate brown that blended with the caramel-colored leather. Near the fireplace, a round coffee table of dark teak sat on a gorgeous, round rug of bright oranges and yellows.

" This is beautiful. The wooden shutters are elegant with the other colors," and she took a turn in the middle of the room holding her arms out. "It's serene, and that rug is perfect. Is it a Rya?"

"Yeah, when I found that, I snapped it up. Until then, it all seemed too subdued. Now I think it works."

"It does. You have hidden talents yet to be discovered."

"And you're the very one to discover all of them, SuzieQ," he said. "Let me show you the rest. I want you to know this place in case Parduzzi kicks you out in December. You could stay here while I'm in the States. I'll probably leave on Sunday, the first, be gone about two weeks. In fact... you could stay on here the whole month."

She stared at him.

He raised his hands and said. "I know, I know. You need your own space. So do I. If you were here when I came back, I could move down the hall into the studio apartment. It's comfortable. Then I could visit you from time to time," he said waggling his eyebrows.

"Marc, I'm overwhelmed. You're so generous... in many ways." She was thinking of his love-making.

"You needn't make a decision; I know it's a hassle to move, but I'd help. I could bring a couple boxes for items that don't need careful packing. Your clothes could go in your suitcases and we'd have you settled in no time."

"You've done some thinking about this haven't you?"

"Yes. I don't like you there with that creep coming round. And I never want to see you that frightened again," he said and drew her into his arms. She inhaled a hint of musky amber again. Then he broke away and said, "Here's the bathroom, a little different from yours."

It had a sleek, blue-grey pedestal sink with toilet and bidet to match. The mirror over the sink was of a crystalline, beveled glass. The simple lines were soothing after all the curlicues in her apartment.

"You have a shower *and* a tub." she said. "Most places I've rented don't offer tubs."

"You're welcome to come take a long soak anytime," he said. Opening a door into a room with a pair of twin beds, he said, "This is the guest bedroom." It had the same color theme as the rest of the apartment with a smaller Rya rug in electric blues and yellows.

"Niiice." Katy'd love this room."

"I'm hoping to have her here for the holidays, but for sure I'll spend special time with her while there since I won't stay for Christmas. My family knows how I hate Christmas U.S. style."

"Amen, to that," she said. "I'd rather be here through December too since Mandy isn't in the States. But I'm hoping she'll stop by on her way home from Greece. Are your folks coming over?"

"Around the twenty-third or fourth. I want you to meet them. They'll stay in Murano until after January sixth, Epiphany, in order to enjoy the family celebration of Festa della Befana. A long-time family friend comes dressed as the old Befana who brings children presents or lumps of coal. We all enjoy her antics. Before returning to the States, Mom and Dad will probably go to Lucca for a few days."

"Where will your parents stay?" Marlowe asked feeling nervous about them.

"Their one-bedroom apartment is on the ground floor around the corner from mine. This used to be theirs but they passed it on to me since I'm here now—maybe permanently. I can point to theirs from my room, come," he said taking her hand.

They entered a huge room dominated by an immense floor-to-ceiling bay window facing north and west. To their right as they stood in the doorway, sat a king-sized bed.

"That window's fantastic," she said. "You must have a marvelous view from your bed. How do you ever leave this room?"

"And here's the master bath." It also had blue-grey fixtures, the color of his eyes when he wore blue, but the tub was longer and wider and had a jacuzzi.

"Just changed my mind," she said. "I'll take my soak here."

"It figures."

The floor-to-ceiling window was the only one in the apartment with drapes. They were heavy and dark brown matching the rugs lying on both sides of the bed like dark rafts floating in melted butter. A small caramel-colored leather loveseat and an immense recliner chair in dark-brown leather formed an enticing arrangement around a gas-log fireplace built into a corner. Bookcases filled the rest of the walls except for louvered doors leading to a walk-in closet which held a massive chest of drawers and a full-length mirror.

"Definitely a man's room," she said. "Nothing small or dainty here, but handsome, like you," she said smiling up at him.

"I'm speechless, but thank you."

She went to the big window and looked out. Toward the west, silhouettes of Venice were backlit by the setting sun. To the north, she could make out white-capped mountains in the distance. "Are those the Dolomites?"

"Mm-hmm," he said coming behind to put his arms around her. "You smell nice. Feel nice too," he said. "Would you stay with me tonight?"

She turned in his arms and reached up putting her hands on his chest. "I thought you'd never ask."

"It makes sense if you want to see the Goto Giovanni made, and I never did show you the supply of colored glass and powders, and—"

"Hush, I want to stay," she said in a husky voice.

CHAPTER THIRTY-THREE

One large hand cupped the back of her head while a finger from the other tipped her chin toward his mouth. He was gentle. Do all big men worry about being too forceful? She trembled a little at the rough feel of his mustache as it scraped across her mouth. It triggered a pulsing response between her legs that set her on fire. Never had her body felt this sensually responsive with a man before. His kiss was slow but demanding. He caressed her lips with his tongue and slipped inside. She drew it in. He moved farther inside to touch and taste. She caught it and began sucking on it. He groaned and pulled her to him. She felt him harden against her and angled her pelvis in order to feel his erection even more. She was whimpering with a desire that had been building since they'd entered the fabbrica that morning. He lifted her toward his big bed and lay her down on a crisp, pale-blue sheet with a matching duvet which he shoved back. He wedged her hips between his knees. "Marlee," he breathed while his hands slid underneath her sweater as if making sure everything was there. He traced his fingers across the swell of her breasts and sighed. With her help, he raised her sweater up and tossed it aside.

"These might be two of the softest places in the world," he said slowly sliding the straps down her shoulders to lift her breasts from a cobalt-blue polka-dot bra. He pressed his face into them. "I could spend a lifetime here." He went on to circle a nipple with his tongue as he reached underneath to unfasten the bra and toss it. "Polka dots today. Red was nice too," he said chuckling softly. Slowly, he circled the other breast until he'd raised both nipples into hard peaks. "These brown buttons hold the secret code," he growled softly, "to a beguiling place where I intend to be very soon." He looked up at her and said, "I'm thinking these are exactly what I had in mind when I first called you Buttons way back when."

She didn't mind the nickname anymore. He could call her anything; she was intent on unbuttoning his shirt. She needed to feel his solid chest and ran her fingers through the sandy hair that spread across his chest curling around *his* nipples. When she tickled one, he sucked in a breath. Ooh what a sensitive giant. She was pleased with herself. He came back to her mouth and began sipping her lips slowly all the while looking into her eyes willing her to look into his grey, silvery ones. As he made love to her mouth with his tongue and teeth nipping and nibbling, she wondered if she would drown in those eyes. His sensual kisses took her breath away. He'd surely known they would after that first one at her door a few weeks ago. Soon he had the rest of her clothes off, but she wanted *his* clothes gone too. Following the drift of hair from his chest down the middle of his flat abdomen, she slipped her hand underneath his belt trying to move on downward.

"Help me unfasten my fly, Babe, I'm dying inside these damned jeans."

She got the belt buckle unfastened, and he opened the top button. Then she managed the zipper down to reach carefully inside to free his stiff cock. He sighed. She held him for a moment then slid her hand slowly to its root and gently back toward the tip feeling it quiver and grow. She thrilled to feel that marvelous shaft grow right into her hand. His hand moved down her belly and a long finger reached into hot folds of pulsing flesh.

"Marlee, you've got a molten flood waiting for me."

She couldn't speak, she felt drunk on sex.

* * *

Later waking from heavy sleep, she heard a thud and felt a tremor move up through the building. Lazily, she recognized what

14635380R00222

Made in the USA
Charleston, SC
22 September 2012